THE

MASTER OF ST. BENEDICT'S

BY

ALAN St. AUBYN

COMPLETE

as much for them as lay in his power. He had educated the younger branches, and provided for the declining years of the elders. He had kept his two maiden sisters, one an invalid, in comfort and affluence. He had paid the mortgage off the farm and passed it over unembarrassed by debt to his elder brother. He had taken that brother's grandson and given him an education at his own University, and in due time had arranged for him to be presented with a college living. It was not a rich living: it was the only one that fell vacant when Richard Rae most wanted it, and he had accepted it gladly. He had married upon it, and brought up a family, six children, of whom one only was now living, a girl child, with whom this story has to do.

The old Master of St. Benedict's had aged perceptibly within the last few years. He was already in his second childhood. His strength had become enfeebled and his memory impaired. He could not walk down the long gallery of the lodge now or across the grass in the Fellows' garden without assistance; he could not remember the things of yesterday or of last week, but the crabbed characters of his old Semitic manuscripts were still as familiar to him as ever. He had lost a great deal since that stroke of paralysis five years ago, but he had not lost all. He remembered his old friends, and he could pore over his old books, but he was dependent upon his womankind for many things—for most things.

Mary Rae opened his letters and conducted his correspondence. She had conducted it so long that she knew more about the college than the Master. She transacted all the college business that had to be transacted in the lodge, and when any public function required the Master's presence in the Senate House Mary Rae took him up to the door on her arm and brought him back. It was also rumoured that she instructed him how to vote.

She was assisted in her responsible duties by the Senior Tutor of St. Benedict's, who would in the natural course of things succeed to the office of Master when it should fall vacant.

Mary Rae was a handsome woman well on in the thirties. She was a woman who could not help looking handsome at any age, and the few gray hairs that had put in an appearance in the smooth brown bands drawn back from her broad forehead only added a new dignity to her mature beauty. Perhaps the Senior Tutor thought that they supplied the only touch lacking to make Mary Rae a perfect and ideal mistress of a college lodge.

It was whispered in the combination room, where the old Fellows met after their Hall dinner, and discussed the affairs of the college over their walnuts and their wine, that when the Master received his last preferment she would not have to pack up her small belongings and leave the lodge.

It was one morning early in the Lent term that Mary Rae sat at breakfast in the cheerful bow-windowed room of the lodge. The Doctor's wife still presided over the breakfast table. She was younger than the Doctor, and had worn better. She was still active and cheerful—a bright, gentle, patient old soul, ever watchful and considerate for his comfort, and anticipating his every want.

While Mrs. Rae poured out the Master's tea, Mary Rae buttered the Master's toast and read his letters. There were not many letters this morning, but there was one with a black seal that lay uppermost. The writing was unfamiliar, and before opening it Mary glanced at the postmark.

'A letter from Dick, uncle,' she said across the table. She had to speak in rather a high key, as the Doctor was a little deaf, and some days he was deafer than usual.

'What does Dick say, my dear?' he said, smiling at her across the toast she had buttered for him. His voice was not very strong, but there was no North-country burr in it now—a kind, mellow old voice, courteous and gentle in tone, with a quaver in it now and then. 'I have not heard from your uncle Dick for a long time. I am very glad he has written now. I cannot remember when I last heard from him.'

'It is not from Uncle Dick,' said Mary, opening the letter; 'it is from his son—at least, his grandson—Cousin Dick, of Thorpe Regis. Don't you remember, uncle?'

'Ye—es, my dear; and what does Dick say?'

Mary read the letter in silence, and looked across the table with a shade of anxiety on her face.

'It is not Cousin Dick who writes; the letter is from his daughter; he had only one daughter—Lucy, little Lucy. You remember her, uncle?'

Mary Rae was evidently speaking to gain time, and the shade of anxiety deepened on her face as she spoke.

'Ye—es, I remember, my dear. Lucy was her mother's name; she was called after her mother. What has Lucy got to say about Dick?'

'She has not much to say, uncle; she is writing in great distress. Her father has died, almost suddenly. He was preaching a week ago, and now he is dead. The poor child is writing in great trouble.'

'Dick dead!' the old man repeated with a bewildered air, and putting down his cup with a shaking hand. 'Dick dead, did you say? He was not so many years older than I, and always hale and strong. I ought to have gone first. There were only three of us, and Dick was the eldest.'

'It isn't your brother, Anthony, that is dead; he died long ago, dear. It is his grandson, little Dick—Dickie you used to call him. You had him up here, and he took his degree, and you gave him a college living. You remember little Dickie, Anthony?'

His wife's voice recalled his wandering thoughts.

'Yes, yes, my dear; certainly, I remember little Dick very well. He took a second class; he ought to have done better. He disappointed me. I had no son of my own to come after me, and I should have liked my brother Dick's son—grandson, to be sure—to have done well. He did his best, no doubt; but he disappointed me. If he had done better, he might have got a Fellowship. So Dickie is dead, you say, my dear?'

'Yes, uncle; and he has left poor little Lucy unprovided for. She has written to ask you what she ought to do. She wants to go out as a governess—a nursery governess.'

'A nursery governess? Dick's little girl a nursery governess! No, my dear, that will never do. Tell her to come here; there's plenty of room in the lodge for Dick's little girl. Write to her at once, Mary, and tell her as soon—as soon as the funeral is over—her father's funeral—poor little girl!—to come to the lodge. What do you say, Rachel?'

'I wish we could spare Mary to go to her,' the Master's wife said, wiping her eyes. 'Someone ought to fetch her away at once, as soon—as soon as it is all over. I think Mary ought to go to her.'

The Senior Tutor met the Master's niece in the court as he was coming away from a lecture during the morning, and she told him all about the letter her uncle had received and the death of his nephew, or, rather, his grand-nephew.

'You remember my cousin Dick?' she said; 'he was my second cousin. I am a generation older than he,' and she smiled at the admission. She was not the least ashamed of her age

The Senior Tutor smiled too; he was thinking how well she wore her years, how her age, or the signs of it, her gray hairs and the lines on her face, became her. She would grow handsomer with the years, he told himself as he stood talking to her in the spring sunshine, and her face would grow finer as time went by: it was a fine face already; it could never by any chance grow plain. He had watched a great many faces grow old in his time—old, and lined, and soured—but he had never seen any face grow finer with the years like this woman's face had grown.

'Yes,' he said, 'I remember your cousin, Richard Rae, very well; he was one of my pupils. He disappointed me, and he disappointed your uncle; he ought to have taken a first class. He went into the Church, and we gave him a college living, I remember—a very small living—and he married, I believe, directly after.'

'He married, and he had a large family and a sickly wife, and very small means. It must have been a hard struggle for him, poor Dick! He lost his wife, and his children died one after the other; there is only one left. And now he is dead, and the girl is left quite alone.'

'Oh, it is a girl,' said the Tutor in a tone of disappointment; 'if it had been a boy we could have done something with him here.'

'Yes,' said Mary, with a sigh; 'pity it's a girl; it would have been so much easier if it had been a boy. She must come here, of course; there is nowhere else for her to go.'

'What will you do with her when she comes?'

The Senior Tutor looked grave; the question had come into his head as he stood speaking to Mary, what should he do with this girl of Cousin Dick's when he occupied the Master's place? Of course Mary would stay, and Mrs. Rae—he could not separate the old woman from her niece during her few declining years; she would certainly remain an inmate of the lodge; but this girl? he could not make the college lodge an asylum for all the female members of the Rae family.

It was an idiotic question to arise; he was ashamed of it the next moment.

'I think you ought to go to Thorpe Regis,' he said, 'and be with your poor young cousin at this trying time. I will look after the Master while you are away, if that will make the going easier.'

'Ye—es,' said Mary slowly, 'it will make it easier. You really think I ought to go?'

There was a hesitation in her tone he could not but note; he put it down at once to her reluctance to leave the old Master.

'Most certainly you ought to go,' he said promptly. 'I will come over to the lodge every day. I will fill your place as far as I can. You are not afraid to leave the Master with me?'

'Oh, no, no! I am sure you will do all, more than all, that I do for him. I was not thinking about him. You are quite sure it is right to bring this girl back here? She is very young, not twenty, and—and she may be——'

'She may be attractive,' said the Senior Tutor with a laugh, 'and turn all our heads. I think, in spite of her attractions, her place is here with you and under her uncle's roof. We must protect ourselves against the wiles of this siren. We must not wear our hearts on our sleeves for Cousin Dick's little daughter to peck at.'

CHAPTER II.

DICK'S LITTLE DAUGHTER.

The Senior Tutor need have been under no apprehension for the men of St. Benedict's. They had no occasion to cover up their sleeves with their academical gowns. Cousin Dick's little daughter showed no inclination to peck at their too susceptible hearts, whether they wore them skewered on to their sleeves or out of sight in their accustomed places.

Lucy Rae was too full of her recent loss, the great sorrow that had fallen upon her and swept away all her household gods, to have a thought to spare for the undergraduates of St. Benedict's.

It had almost swept away all her moorings, too, but not quite; she still clung tenaciously to one idea—it was all she had left of the old life to cling to: she still desired to be a governess.

It was not a very ambitious idea. She wanted to be independent, and earn her own living in the only way that was open to her. She accepted the shelter of the Master's lodge thankfully, but she had no idea of settling down in the dependent position of a poor relation. When she had recovered from this shock, and the horizon cleared, she would find something to do, she told herself, and go away.

She was a soft, shy little thing to be so independent. She only looked like a girl to be kissed and petted and comforted; she didn't look at all fit to stand in the front of the battle.

She talked over her prospects—her little, humble prospects—with her cousin Mary a few days after her arrival at the lodge. Mary was sitting at the Master's writing-table in the library of the lodge—she was writing some letters on college business—and Lucy was sewing in the window.

It was a big gloomy room, and it was not at all a cheerful place for girls to sit in on a chilly spring afternoon. There was a fire burning in the old-fashioned grate behind the brass fire-guard—there were wire guards to all the fires at the lodge since that last seizure of the Master's—but it had burnt low; Mary, who was sitting near it, had been too occupied to notice it, and Lucy's mind was full of her prospects.

There had been no sound in the room for some time but the scratching of Mary's pen as it travelled over the paper, and Lucy sewed on in silence. She didn't like sewing, and she put down her work two or three times and yawned or looked out of the window. The window looked out into the Fellows' garden. The sun was shining on the lawn beneath, which was already green with the new green of the year, and the crocuses were aflame in the borders, and the primroses were in bloom.

An old Fellow was hobbling slowly and painfully round the garden—a bent, drooping figure in a particularly shabby coat and a tall silk hat of a bygone date. He was lame, Lucy remarked, and dragged one leg behind him. He had a long, lean, sallow face with deep eye-sockets, and his hair was long and gray—it didn't look as if it had been cut for years. Lucy wondered vaguely at seeing this shabby old cripple in the grounds of the lodge; if she had seen him anywhere else she would have taken him for a tramp. He had been a Senior Wrangler in his day, and had taken a double-first; perhaps he was paying the penalty.

'I am very dull company, child,' Mary said, as she blotted her last letter and pushed the writing materials aside. 'I have left you to your thoughts for a whole hour, and we have sat the fire out. What have you been thinking about, Lucy, all this time?'

'Oh, the old thing,' said Lucy, looking up from her work. 'I have been thinking what I can do.'

'Well, and what conclusion have you come to?'

"There is but one conclusion—that—that I can do nothing!'

The work dropped from the girl's fingers, and her eyes overflowed. She had wanted an excuse for weeping for the last hour, and now she had got it.

'Oh yes, you can,' Mary said cheerfully; 'the case is not quite so bad as that. You can sew, for one thing. See how nicely you are sewing that frill!'

'I hate sewing! And I shall never wear that frill when I have hemmed it! I can only do useless trumpery things!'

Lucy let the poor little bit of white frilling she had been hemming fall to the ground, and she got up and began to walk up and down the room.

Mary watched her in silence. It was not the first time her young cousin had shown impatience, but it was the first time she had shown temper—just a little bit of temper.

Mary had praised her in the wrong place: she was hurt and angry at this learned, superior cousin implying, with her misplaced praise, that she was only fit to do work—mere woman's work!

It was an unusual sound, that rapid pacing to and fro of impatient feet, in that scholarly room. The Master tottered feebly across the floor; the Master's wife moved with slow dignity; Mary walked quietly, with soft, firm footsteps that awoke no echoes. The floor creaked audibly beneath Lucy's rapid, impatient steps; the old boards that had echoed to the slow tread of scholars for so many, many years, shook and trembled—actually trembled—beneath the light impatient footsteps of Cousin Dick's little daughter.

The colour that that useless sewing had taken out of Lucy's cheek had come back, and her gray eyes were eager and shining beneath her tears.

Mary watched her pacing the room with a smile half of pity, half amused, as she sat at the Master's table. Perhaps she understood the mood. She may have been impatient herself years ago; she had nothing to be impatient for now. Everything was happening as it should do; and when a change came—well, her position would not be materially altered.

'I am sure you can do a great many useful things, dear,' she said presently, when Lucy's little bit of temper had had time to cool. 'You could not have kept your father's house so long, and done the work of the parish, without being able to do more useful things than most girls.'

'I don't mean that kind of usefulness; anyone can do housekeeping and potter about a parish. I hated parish work! I never took the least interest in it; no one could have done it worse than I did. I hated—oh, no one knows how I hated—those Bands of Hope, and Sunday-schools, and mothers' meetings, and visiting dreadful old men and women who would insist upon telling me all about their unpleasant complaints!'

Mary looked grave. She was accustomed to hear a great deal about old people's complaints, though she did not do any district visiting.

'Really,' she said gravely, 'most girls like these things! They are over now, and done with, and you will begin afresh. Tell me what you would like to do.'

'Like!' Lucy held her breath as she spoke, and her cheeks grew crimson. 'Oh, I should like to be a scholar, Cousin Mary!'

Mary looked at the girl with a kind of pity in her eyes. She had seen a good many scholars in her time, men and women; some of them were as eager once as this girl—eager and impatient with feverish haste to climb the hill of learning; they were hollow-eyed now, and narrow-chested, and their cheeks were sunken and sallow, and some limped like the old scholar in the Fellows' garden—that is, those who had lasted to the end; but some had turned back in time and regained their youth: most likely this girl would turn back.

'You would like to go to a woman's college?'

'I should love to go! I shouldn't mind whether it were Newnham or Girton, whichever uncle thought best. If I could only have three years at a woman's college, I should be provided for for life. I should want nothing further. I should be able to make my own way. Oh, Mary, do you think he will let me go?'

She was very much in earnest. She had stopped running up and down the room in that ridiculous manner. She was standing beside the table with both her hands pressed down upon it and her little lithe figure bending eagerly forward. Her eyes were shining, and her cheeks glowing, and her lips parted. She looked exactly as if she were making a speech.

The door opened as she was standing there, and the Senior Tutor came in. He shook hands with Mary, and he nodded across the table to Lucy. He thought he had interrupted a scene.

'I saw the Master as I came up,' he said, speaking to Mary; 'he had just finished his nap. He asked me to tell you that he was quite ready to take a turn in the garden, if you would put on your hat. I think you should go at once to catch the sunshine. You'll get it on the broad walk if you go now.'

Mary rose at once.

'It is lucky I have finished my work,' she said, glancing down at the little pile of letters, sealed and stamped ready for the post, that lay on the table. 'Poor little Lucy here was telling me about her plans. If you can spare time, Mr. Colville, sit down and talk them over with her, and advise her what she ought to do, while I am in the garden.'

The Senior Tutor could spare time; and after he had opened the door for Mary, he came back to the window that overlooked the garden and sat down.

He did not belong to the old school of Cambridge Dons. He belonged to that newer school that came in a quarter of a century ago with athletics. He was not lean and hollow-eyed, and wrinkled and yellow, like a musty old parchment, and he hadn't a stoop in his shoulders, and he didn't drag one of his legs behind him. He had rowed 'five' in his college boat, and his shoulders were as square now as ever. His shoulders were square, and his forehead was square, and his iron-gray hair was closely cut—it was only iron-gray still—and he had tremendous bushy eyebrows that, Lucy thought, made him look like an ogre, and that frightened the undergraduates dreadfully, and close-cut iron-gray whiskers, and a big red throat like a bull. His throat had not always been red; he had been mild-looking enough in his youth; but he was now a portly, pompous Don of middle age, with a florid countenance and fierce aspect.

'Well,' he said in his easy, patronizing way, as if he were speaking to a freshman who had just come up, 'and what do you propose to do, Miss Lucy?'

The colour went out of the girl's cheeks, and the long eyelashes drooped over her eager eyes, and her pretty little slender figure grew limp, and she didn't look the least like making a speech now.

'I am sure I don't know,' she said meekly, and she went back and sat on her old seat in the window on the opposite side to the Senior Tutor. It was a big bay-window, and there was a table between them littered with pamphlets and manuscripts in Semitic languages. The girl tossed them over as she sat there with a gesture of impatience. They were sealed books to her.

'What were you discussing with your cousin Ma—ry when I came in?'

He lingered over the name, and prolonged the last syllable. He seemed loath to let it go.

'I was telling her that I should like to go to a woman's college—to Newnham or Girton.'

'Exactly.'

The Tutor nodded his head. He was listening to the girl, but he was looking out of the window.

'No one is educated now—no woman—who does not go to Newnham, or Girton, or Oxford. No one has any chance of success in teaching who has not taken a place in a Tripos or done something in a University examination.'

The Senior Tutor was smiling, but he was only giving her half his attention.

'And what Tripos do you propose to take?' he asked in his bland, superior, lecture-room manner.

'I? Oh, I don't think I shall ever be clever enough to take a Tripos; but I might learn something—a little. I might learn enough to pass the—the—Little——'

'The Little-go?' suggested the Tutor; 'or, more properly speaking, the "Previous."'

'Yes; papa used to talk about the Little-go. He had dreadful difficulty in passing it. I should be quite satisfied if I could pass the Little-go.'

'I don't think you will find any difficulty in passing it,' he said. 'I do not remember that your father had any special difficulty; I was his tutor. He disappointed me in the Tripos. With his great gifts he ought to have done better.'

It was Lucy's turn to smile now, and to sigh.

'Poor papa!' she said; 'there was a reason for his failure. Perhaps you did not know.'

'No; I knew of no reason.'

'He had just met my mother, and—and he was in love. She got between him and his mathematics; he could think of nothing but my mother. Oh, if you had known her, you would not have wondered.'

The Senior Tutor looked across the table with a new interest in his eyes at the sweet downcast face. If her mother had been like her, he didn't wonder at poor Richard Rae getting only a second class in his Tripos.

'Are you quite sure that you will not fail from the same cause? are you sure that at the momentous time you will not do like your father—that you will not fall in love?'

'No—o,' said Lucy gravely; 'I don't think I shall fall in love. I don't think Girton girls do very often.'

'They do sometimes. They generally end by marrying their coaches.'

Lucy looked shocked.

'They can't all marry their coaches.'

'No, not all—only the weak ones. The superior minds never sink to the low level of matrimony.'

Lucy was quite sure he was laughing at her.

'I am not likely to need a coach,' she said stiffly; 'I shall never be clever enough to take a Tripos. I shall be content to pass the—the—the "Previous."'

She was going to say 'Little-go,' but she remembered he had called it the 'Previous,' and she checked herself in time.

'We shall see. You will have to begin with the "Previous" in any case. You need not take it all at once: there are three parts; you can take them at different times.'

'I should prefer to take them all at once.'

'But if you are going no farther, if you are going to stop at the "Previous," why should you be in such a hurry to get it over?'

'I don't know. It might be as well to get it over; but I have to get into Girton or Newnham first; I don't know that they will have me; and I have to get my uncle's consent.'

She hadn't fallen naturally into the custom of the lodge of calling Dr. Rae 'the Master' yet. It came easier to say 'uncle.'

'There will be an entrance examination,' the Tutor said, looking out of window and watching the Master walking in the garden below leaning on Mary's arm. 'I believe it is nearly as stiff as the "Previous" and takes in the same subjects. You will have to pass an examination before you can become a student at either college.'

'Do you know what the subjects are?' she asked eagerly; 'could you—could you get me the papers?'

He hardly heard her; his heart was out in that wet garden with Mary. How very indiscreet of the Master at his age to walk over the damp grass! He was actually sitting down on the bench under the walnut-tree. Lucy followed the direction of the Tutor's eyes, but she only saw the Master sitting in the sunshine. A tall, lean figure bent with age, with white, silvery hair falling over the velvet collar of his coat, and his rugged, worn old face turned up to the sun. The figure of the old scholar sitting on the old bench in the sunshine beneath the branches of the old, old tree, where he had sat in sunshine and in shade, oh, so many, many years, had no poetry for her. She only wondered, as she saw him sitting there, lifting his dim eyes to the sinking sun, whether he would let her go to Newnham.

The Senior Tutor didn't see any poetry in the situation, either. He was sure the old Master was catching a dreadful cold; and he was wondering whether Mary had changed her slippers.

'Could you get me a copy of the papers set at the last examination?' Lucy asked meekly.

'Yes, oh yes,' he said absently; 'I'll try to remember; but I think I must go down now and bring the Master in: I am sure he is taking cold.'

CHAPTER III.

ONLY A FRESHER.

It was rather hard work to persuade the old Master of St. Benedict's that Lucy ought to go to Newnham. He belonged to the old school—he was almost the last left of that school—that did not believe very much in women. He believed in a girl learning to sew, and to spell, and play a little air on the piano—he was very fond of 'Annie Laurie,' he could listen to it by the hour; he went so far, indeed, as the three R's in a woman's education—and he stopped there.

He had no sympathy whatever in the movement for the higher education of Women—spelt with a big W. He had voted consistently all his life against women being admitted to any of the privileges of the University, against their being allowed to take degrees; he had even voted against their being 'placed.' He regarded every concession made to the weaker sex as a step towards that dreadful time when a female Vice-Chancellor will confer degrees in the Senate House, and a lady D.D. will occupy the University pulpit.

With these views, and with his prejudices growing stronger rather than weaker with the years, it was no wonder that Mary Rae had great difficulty in reconciling the Master to the idea of Lucy becoming a student of Newnham.

He had to look at the question all round, from every point of view, and he had to talk it over a great many times. Sometimes he talked it over with himself after dinner, when he woke up from his nap, or didn't quite wake up; and sometimes he talked it over with his nieces.

'I don't think your father would approve of it, my dear,' he said one day when he was talking 'it' over with Lucy. 'He was a plain man, he hadn't the advantages of education that I had; but he had what served him just as well, he had common-sense. He knew what was wanted in a woman. A woman, he used to say, ought to be able to milk, and make butter, and bring up a family. Dick's wife could do all these, and her poultry was noted in all the country round.'

Lucy sighed. She had no ambition to make butter and bring up a family, and she had a distinct aversion to poultry. She hated cocks and hens and broods of yellow downy chickens. She remembered how they used always to be getting into the Vicarage garden and digging up her flower-seeds.

'I am afraid I couldn't get my living by making butter, uncle,' she said meekly, 'or milking cows.'

She never could remember to say 'Master,' like everybody else.

'No, my dear, no; I suppose not. Some girls have the knack of it, and some women, I've heard my mother say, may churn for hours and the butter will refuse to come. Dick's wife, your mother, my dear——'

'Great-grandmother,' murmured Lucy almost inaudibly. The Master hated to be contradicted, and he was always telling her that these far-off ancestors were her father and mother, this humble ploughman and his homely wife. There had been two generations of culture between, and Lucy had quite forgotten, until her uncle reminded her, that her great-grandmother used to carry her eggs and her butter to market. The worst of it was he used to tell everybody it was her mother.

'Yes, yes,' the Master repeated testily; 'my memory is not what it was. But it does not much matter which. She was a good woman; she did her duty here; she brought up a long family—nine children—and she has gone to her reward. She did not know a word of Greek or Latin, and she only knew enough mathematics to reckon up the price of eggs; but if she had gone to Girton or Newnham she could not have done more. She did her duty here; after all, that is the great thing, my dear. There is nothing else that will bring comfort at the last.'

It was a delightful reflection. It comforted the old scholar who had done his duty in this place for over sixty years, who had done it so well that by common consent men called him Master; but it didn't comfort Lucy at all. She was quite prepared to do her duty, only she wanted to do it in her own way.

There were other difficulties in the way of Lucy going to Newnham beside the Master's prejudices. There was a dreadful ordeal to be gone through before those sacred portals would be opened to admit her.

There was the entrance examination. The Senior Tutor was as good as his word; he brought Lucy over the very next day, not only the papers set at the last 'Previous' examination, but a copy of the last Newnham entrance papers. The next examination was to take place in March, and it was now the middle of February, and there were only a few weeks to prepare for it.

Lucy looked hurriedly through the papers while the Tutor stood by, and he saw her face fall and the pretty April colour, which was Lucy's especial charm, go out of her cheeks.

'They are stiffer than you thought,' he said.

He couldn't help putting a little feeling into his voice; he couldn't help being sorry for the girl. He could see she was dreadfully disappointed.

'I did not think they would be so hard,' she said, with something like a sob, and striving to keep back the tears; 'I had no idea that so much was required.'

Her voice was scarcely steady, and she finished up with a little wail—she couldn't keep it out of her voice—and she laid the papers down.

'You don't think you can do them?'

'No, I am sure I can't.'

'Not if you work hard—very hard?—you have three weeks before you—not if I help you?'

'You! Oh, Mr. Colville!'

The colour leaped back into her face, and her eyes brightened. She was quite trembling with eagerness.

'If you think with three weeks' hard work you can get through, I will help you,' he said.

It was something new to the Senior Tutor to have a pupil so eager and willing. The eyes of the undergraduates of St. Benedict's were not accustomed to brighten or their cheeks to flush when he proposed to give them a few hours' extra coaching.

'I am sure I can!' she said eagerly; 'and—and you are sure, Mr. Colville, you will not mind the trouble? I am a very slow learner, but I will do my best, my very best.'

'I am sure you will,' he said; and then he noticed that little helpless quivering about her lips that touched him with quite a new sensation. He had never seen Mary's lips quiver. 'It will be no trouble,' the Tutor said softly in quite a different voice; he even noticed the difference himself, with a strange sense of wonder. 'I shall be very glad to be of use to you.'

He had often been of use to Mary. She always consulted him about the college business; she made use of him every day; but his voice had never faltered nor his cheek grown warm when he had offered to help her with the Master's correspondence.

Lucy began her work the next day. She turned out from the little shabby box she had brought with her to the lodge some well-thumbed old school-books. Small as the box was, it contained all her personal belongings, and the books were at the bottom of the box.

Like Jacob, she had come into a strange land with very little personal impedimenta. It could all, everything, be stuffed into one small box, and the books were at the bottom. The books were shabby, like the box. They had belonged to her father, and she had read them with him.

There were his old Virgil and Xenophon, and a dilapidated Euclid with all the riders missing, and an old-fashioned Algebra. There had been newer editions since Richard Rae had used these in his college days more than twenty years ago. There had been delightful editions full of notes, and directing-posts along the royal road to a classical education; but Lucy had been plodding along the old, rough, dusty way.

The Senior Tutor smiled as he turned over these old books. They brought back to him the old days twenty years ago, the hopes and dreams of those early days, and the familiar faces. The dreams had been realized—at least, some of them—but the familiar faces had faded with the years, and the hopes—what could a man hope for beyond being Master of his college? Nevertheless, the Senior Tutor sighed. The sight of these old books had carried him a long way back.

'I think we can find some newer editions than these,' he said, smiling.

He not only found some newer, but he found the very newest. He found delightful books that smoothed away all the difficulties and made stony places plain. There will be a royal road to learning by-and-by. The road is getting smoother every day, and the way is getting shorter—a short, straight, macadamized road that one can travel over without any jolting or sudden pulls-up.

Old scholars who remember the dear old rough road, and the stony ways, and the hills of difficulty they had to climb, sigh when they look back. There is no time now, in these hurrying days, to toil over stones and climb unnecessary heights. The new ways are so much better than the old; but the old men, if they were to begin again, would go the old way, the dear old way, with all its difficulties. They will still tell you the old ways are best.

Lucy Rae was not a scholar yet, though the desire of her heart was to be one—a perfect Hypatia—and the new royal road was exactly what she wanted.

She made such rapid progress by means of these short-cuts and easy paths the Senior Tutor led her through that she was quite ready for that dreaded entrance examination when it came. She did as well in it as the girls who had been working for it for years.

There was nothing now to prevent her becoming a student of Newnham. Cousin Mary had talked the old Master over and smoothed away all the difficulties. She had wrung from him an unwilling consent. The Senior Tutor had done his part, too, in overcoming the Master's prejudices. He had backed Mary up in the most loyal manner; no girl could have had better advocates. When the Doctor had urged that there had been no precedent in his family of girls construing Latin and Greek when they ought to be making butter and carrying their eggs to market, the Tutor had reminded him that neither had there been a precedent in all the generations of the Raes of one of their number being the Master of a college.

He, on his part, had set up a precedent, and Dick's little daughter was going to set up another—perhaps a more astonishing precedent.

Lucy Rae went up to Newnham the next term. She ought to have waited until October, when the academical year commences, but she was much too anxious to begin at once. She couldn't wait till October.

She had taken a little draught of the divine nectar, and she was thirsting to drink deeply, ever so deeply—deeper than any woman had ever drunk yet. She was going to do very big things, and she couldn't afford to lose a minute. She would gain a whole term's work if she went up now, she would get in ten terms' work instead of nine, like the men, for her Tripos. She would get a whole term's start of them.

With this thirst upon her, and this emulation stirring in her heart, Lucy packed her little box and carried it up to Newnham. She did not exactly carry it in her arms like a housemaid going to a new place. It was not far to carry it, and for the weight of it she might have carried it easily, but girls do not generally go to Newnham carrying a bandbox, or a bundle tied up in a coloured pocket-handkerchief, and with two out-at-elbow little brothers lagging behind carrying a shabby box between them. Lucy, alas! had not two out-at-elbow little brothers, and she had respect for the feelings of Newnham, so she drove up to the door of Newe Hall in a hansom, with her modest little box on the roof.

She thought it was the happiest, the proudest day of her life, this first day at Newnham. She had been looking forward to it for weeks. She had lain awake all the night before picturing what it would be like, and it was not the least like anything she had pictured.

She had pictured sunshine and a blue sky, and the lilacs in the hedge budding, and the daffodils blowing beneath the windows. It was the middle of April, and she had a right to expect these things; it was very little to expect.

It had been raining cheerfully all the morning, and it was raining still when the hansom drew up at the gate of St. Benedict's; it couldn't draw up at the door of the lodge, because college lodges are cut off from the outside world by cloistered courts, and even royalty, when it visits the master of a college, has to leave its carriage at the gate and perform the rest of the journey on foot.

Lucy met Mr. Colville in the cloisters as she was hurrying through, and he put her into the hansom, and he told the man where to drive, and quite a crowd of undergraduates, who had come up early in the term, stood round the gate watching her drive away.

It was quite a new thing, a girl going from St. Benedict's to Newnham. It was the newest thing under the sun. No daughter, niece or granddaughter of any Master of St. Benedict's had ever driven from those gates before to Newnham.

Perhaps when there is a mixed University, and a female president at the lodge, they will not have to go so far; they may find rooms beneath the same roof.

Who shall say?

Lucy couldn't have driven away with more depressing surroundings. The sky couldn't have been grayer, and the trees were shivering overhead, and the hedges were dripping, and there was a nasty mist settling down over everything. She forgot all about the lilacs and the daffodils she had been picturing as she stood, a forlorn little black figure, in the big, cheerless vestibule of Newe Hall, paying the driver of the hansom. There was no one at Newnham to receive her, no one to show her to her room, only a housemaid, who went away directly she reached the door. She didn't even open the door of the room; she only pointed to it and went away in another direction.

It was a little bare room, it couldn't have been barer. There was a couch that served for a bed, a bureau with some drawers beneath, a table, a couple of chairs, and a thinly disguised washstand with imperfect crockery; and that was all. Unless, indeed, a chintz curtain drawn across a corner of the room for hanging gowns behind could be called a wardrobe.

There was no fire, and the barred windows were steaming and blurred with the mist outside, and the raw spring afternoon was closing in.

Lucy shivered and looked round the desolate room. She didn't know what she was expected to do next, or how she was to begin this new life. She was a member of the University now, she told herself with bated breath; she was really a female undergraduate, and she had got to begin as undergraduates began.

Should she begin with lighting the fire? While she was debating this point, and drawing off her gloves, a girl came in. She had left the door open so that anyone passing could look in and see her standing there, and the girl passing by looked in and saw her, and something in her attitude touched her, and she came in. Perhaps it was her black frock and her white face.

'Can I do anything for you?' she said. She didn't throw any sympathy into her voice; they never do at Newnham. 'I've got a kettle boiling if you'd like some water, or'—looking round the bare room and seeing that Lucy's things were not unpacked—'perhaps you'd rather have some tea.'

'Ye—es,' Lucy said quite thankfully; 'I would rather have some tea, please.'

'Then come into my room.'

Lucy followed the girl, a solid-looking girl with no profile to speak of, and a turned-up nose and violent red hair. She had not to follow her far, only across the passage.

There was a card slipped into a frame in the door of the room, and the name of the occupant was written on it—'Stubbs.'

'That's my name,' said the girl, pointing to it; 'Maria Stubbs—Capability Stubbs they call me. I suppose you are a fresher?'

'Yes,' said Lucy, 'I'm a fresher; I've only just come up. My name is Rae—Lucy Rae.'

'Not a bad name; but you won't have any use for it here. They'll call you Lucifer most likely; they don't call anybody by their right name here.'

Maria Stubbs' room was unlike most Newnham rooms. It was distinctly utilitarian. There was nothing æsthetic about it. The most prominent thing in it was a bookshelf full of books, and there was a cabinet in one corner with a lot of narrow drawers, which Lucy found out after were crammed with specimens. A bright fire was burning in the little tiled grate, and a cloth was spread, and some tea-things were laid on the flap of the bureau, which was let down for the purpose, and there were some cakes in one of the pigeon-holes.

'Take off your hat and sit down,' said Maria, drawing a low chair to the fire; 'there's nothing to hurry for, they won't bring in your things for a long time; they never hurry themselves at Newnham.'

'I don't think I ought to take off my things until I've seen someone,' said Lucy. 'There's Miss Wrayburne I certainly ought to see. Perhaps she doesn't know I'm here.'

The girl laughed—or cackled, rather; there wasn't the least fun in her laugh.

'Perhaps not,' she said, as she busied herself about making the tea; 'and I don't think it would make any difference if she did. You don't think the Dons are running about the college all day long shaking hands with the girls? You'll see Miss Wrayburne at the "High" at dinner, and she'll say "How d'ye do?" and smile—she always smiles—and that's all.'

'I didn't know,' Lucy said humbly. 'I'm only a fresher, you see; I shall know better soon. But it struck me as a very chilling reception.'

Miss Stubbs cackled in her unfeeling way.

'Chilling! that's lovely! You've come to the wrong place if you expect any warmth at Newnham, or sympathy either. It would be nothing better than a big girls' school if we were always "How-d'ye-doing" and shaking hands with each other—we should get to kissing soon! Thank goodness there is no spooning here! We are barely civil to each other; and we make a point of ignoring everybody if we meet 'em out-of-doors. I hope you won't, on the strength of this tea, nod to me if you happen to run against me in the street, because I shan't notice you.'

'No,' said Lucy, 'I certainly won't nod to you.' She didn't say it at all humbly, but she drank Miss Stubbs' tea. It was very good tea for Newnham.

CHAPTER IV.

PAMELA GWATKIN.

Lucy saw the Principal, as Miss Stubbs had said, at dinner. She came into the hall rather late, and took her seat at the High table.

It is necessary to spell it with a capital H, as it is distinctly a proper noun, and in Newnham parlance, like the tables in men's colleges where the Dons eat their dinners, it is known as the 'High.'

Miss Wrayburne came in rather late, after the rest were seated, and took her place at the head of the 'High,' and then followed a moment's interval for grace, and then the murmur of tongues began—a low, distinctly female murmur, and occasionally a laugh—a little low laugh. There was a good deal of talk to-day, as everybody had come up fresh, and the atmosphere of the vacation was still about them, and nobody had begun work yet. They would unpack their books by-and-by, and then everything would be changed.

Lucy did not know a soul in the place, except Maria Stubbs, and she sat at another table. She sat quite at the other end of the room, and never once looked Lucy's way, and brushed by her in the corridor as if she had never seen her before.

'She needn't be afraid I shall notice her, the horrid red-haired thing!' Lucy said to herself with quite unnecessary warmth, when Maria looked the other way. 'I wouldn't notice her for the world!'

There were quite half a dozen tables between her and Maria, long narrow tables, with some half-dozen girls at each—girls who ignored everybody else except their own set, and talked across a stranger as if she were a dummy.

They talked across Lucy, and she listened to their talk with a red spot burning on her cheeks and her heart beating. She had not much appetite for the dinner, and she got up from the table with a strange choking sensation that brought the tears smarting to her eyes. She took some comfort in the thought that some day she would talk across a fresher. Her turn would come some day; and while her mind was occupied with this agreeable reflection Miss Wrayburne smiled at her, and said:

'How do you do?'

'How do you do?' may mean a great deal, or it may mean nothing. It didn't mean very much from Miss Wrayburne's lips, and the smile that accompanied it meant less. If it had been a whole smile, or a smile meant entirely for Lucy, there might have been something in it; but it was only the fag-end of a smile that had already been distributed over half a dozen girls.

Lucy accepted it meekly; and with those red spots burning on her cheeks and a choky feeling in her throat she went back to her room—her little desolate, bare room. She felt so utterly miserable and lonely on this wretched first night that she sat down on the side of her bed and had a little weep. Everything was so different to what she had expected; all her castles had been so rudely thrown down.

And then, while she was weeping these foolish tears, she remembered a little curate—a weak-minded young man with red hair; perhaps Miss Stubbs had recalled him—who had once asked her to be his wife. She had refused him indignantly. What girl in her senses would accept a curate with red hair and one hundred and fifty pounds a year? She was not sure, if he had come to her now as she sat in that dismal room, feeling so utterly lonely and miserable, that she would have given him the same answer. She wanted a little love so much; and he loved her in spite of his red hair. She was not so certain, after all, that the higher education of women is quite the best thing—the thing most to be desired in the world. There are other things—she had not thought of them till now, as she sat weeping at the edge of the bed—that make up a woman's life: love, religion, duty, ministering to the wants of others; but love chiefly. She was not sure, after all, if this was not the summum bonum of a woman's life.

Lucy was so utterly miserable as she sat there weeping that, if the red-haired curate had come to her at that weak moment, she would have thrown over all her ambitions, she would have given up the higher education altogether, and she would have gone away with him to that poor little moorland cottage, and pinched, and pared, and slaved for him, as dear women before her have pinched and slaved for those they love ever since the world began.

While she was still thinking of the curate, and the tears were dropping into her lap, there was a knock at the door, and someone came in. Lucy started guiltily, and hurriedly wiped her eyes. It was not the red-headed curate. It was a girl—to be more correct, a woman. Everybody is a woman at Newnham. A second-year girl, who had called to see if she could help her to unpack her things and get her room in order.

It wasn't a formal 'call.' Calls at Newnham are usually made after ten p.m., when work is supposed to be over and one is yearning for bed. The second-year girl was a little bit of a thing—smaller than Lucy. A girl who looked as if she had shrunk—as if she had once been round, and plump, and bright-eyed, and soft-cheeked, and red-lipped as a girl ought to be at twenty. She was none of these things now. She was lean and angular; her eyes were dull, her lips were pale, and her cheeks had lost all their youthful roundness and rosiness, if they had ever had any. The roundness had gone into her figure, her back was quite round, her shoulders were bent and stooping, and her chest was narrow and flat like a board.

She had been at Newnham two years, and she was twenty now, and wore glasses, but, alas! not 'sweet and twenty.' She looked exactly like a girl who had used up all her brains.

'I think you have made a mistake,' she said, as she knelt upon the ground unpacking Lucy's books, 'in taking Classics. You should take the Natural Science Tripos. Classics are a thing of the past. They are quite worn out. They will be superseded altogether shortly. Soon—very soon—Latin and Greek will not be compulsory in the examinations; we shall have more useful subjects. Life is so short—so very short' (she was just twenty)—'that we have no time for learning things that will not help us in the rush. Life is getting more of a rush every day, and Science is the only thing that can help us forward. There is no knowing where Science will lead us!'

She clasped her hands, and gasped at the bare thought of it.

'No,' said Lucy, in a low-spirited way.

She hadn't the least interest where Science was going to lead the girl on the floor—it wasn't likely to lead her very far—but she did object to see her pet Classics turned out of the box in that scornful way.

'You will learn all this trash,' the girl continued, opening the pages of Lucy's Euripides and letting the leaves drop through her fingers as if they were not of very much account, 'and you will pore over these rubbishy stories of a quite barbarous age—stories and fables and metamorphoses that, if they were written at the present time, would lay the writer open to a prosecution for perverting the public morals. You will soak your mind with all this nonsense and impurity, and you will think that you have attained culture. Oh, to think how girls waste their lives!'

'I'm sure Classics are ever so much nicer than Natural Science,' Lucy said with some spirit. 'Look at the dreadful subjects you have to study! and to sit side by side with men in lecture-rooms, and listen to lectures on things most women would blush to speak of! Oh, I wouldn't be a Natural Science student for the world!'

The atmosphere of Newnham was beginning to tell. A few hours ago Lucy was as meek as a mouse, and if anyone had slapped her on one cheek she would have been quite ready to offer the other. Now she had plucked up sufficient spirit to defend her choice of a Tripos.

If Newnham doesn't do anything else for a girl, it teaches her to take her own part.

Lucy didn't learn the lesson all at once. It takes a long time to learn, when one has been brought up in the old-fashioned way, to consider other people first and to think of self last. It would never do to practise such a foolish doctrine at a college for women. There is only one person to consider—self, self, self!

Lucy had a great deal to unlearn when she came to Newnham, and a great deal to learn; and she did not learn it all at once. She had always had somebody else to consider first, and now it was ever Number One. Oh, that horrid Number One!

Everybody called upon her in Newe Hall the first week, and some of the girls from the other Halls called later on. The girls at Newe called generally after ten o'clock at night, when she was too sleepy to talk to them, and they went away and voted her 'stupid,' and took no further trouble about her.

Among the girls who called upon Lucy when she was nearly asleep, and went away and voted her stupid, was Pamela Gwatkin, a girl who was much looked up to and worshipped at Newnham. It was no wonder Pamela thought her stupid. She was the leader of the most advanced set in the college, and held opinions that would make one's hair stand on end.

There will be a good many Pamela Gwatkins by-and-by, when there are more Newnhams and the world is ripe for them. They will quite revolutionize society.

They will not be misunderstood like the Greek women of old. Nobody will question their morals because they seek to lead and teach men. Men will be quite willing to be taught by them. It will no longer be a shame for a woman to speak or preach in public. There will be nothing to debar them from taking orders.

Women have proved long ago that they can reach beyond such heights of scholarship as are demanded from a candidate for ordination. But women of Pamela Gwatkin's order will not go into the pulpit—their demands will be even more audacious.

Lucy hadn't any opinions in particular, she was only a fresher; but she was such a poor-spirited creature that she went with the herd and worshipped the very ground that Pamela Gwatkin walked upon.

She hadn't even the excuse of a nodding acquaintance with her after that unlucky call—she only caught glimpses of her at a distant table at Hall, or met her by chance in the library, or ran against her in the streets, coming and going from lectures, when Pamela looked over her head in her superior way and ignored her completely.

She could very well look over Lucy's head, for she stood six feet in her shoes—they had rather high heels. A tall, fair girl, not plump or round by any means, nor rosy-cheeked—she was not a milkmaid; she was an advanced thinker—but lithe, and elastic, and dignified—very dignified.

Lucy thought she had never seen anyone so dignified in her life as Pamela on the night of the first debate of the term at Newnham.

She opened the debate on this particular evening—it happened to be some question of woman's rights which she was always advocating—and she spoke for half an hour without a single pause or hitch.

Some people confess that they cannot bear to hear a woman speak; that when a woman stands up to speak in public it always gives them the sensation of cold water running down their backs. No one who listened to Pamela Gwatkin would have this uncomfortable sensation for a moment. It seemed as if she had been made to stand up in public; as if Nature had intended her for a female orator, and had given her the voice—the clear, penetrating, resonant voice—the quiet, assured manner, the full, free flow of words, without which no woman may attempt to stand on a public platform.

Pamela Gwatkin had all these rare gifts, and she had opinions—very advanced opinions—on every subject under the sun—religion, morals, science, philosophy—nothing came amiss to her. When women are admitted into Parliament she will probably represent an important constituency, perhaps the University.

Lucy, looking down from the gallery above, listened breathlessly, and when the debate was over watched her sailing down the hall in her pale violet gown, with the soft folds of her train gliding noiselessly after her. They didn't rustle and sweep like the frills and furbelows of the other girl, who came frou-frouing down the room, pencil in hand, counting the votes. She might have spared her pains; of course, every girl in her senses voted with Pamela.

There was a dance as usual after the debate, and the unique spectacle of fifty female couples spinning round untainted by the arm of man. Pamela Gwatkin danced as well as she spoke, but she didn't put any enthusiasm into it. She took it as the least troublesome way of taking exercise, but she didn't put any spirit into it. She didn't smile once all the evening, except in a weary, disdainful way when her partner broke down or fell out of the ring. She never broke down or fell out herself, and when she had tired out one girl she took up another. Lucy remarked that she always chose small girls—the smallest girls she could find—and that they were invariably 'gentlemen.' Lucy was wondering how ever they could drag her round, when, to her consternation, Pamela stopped in front of her.

She had worn out all the other small girls in the room, and she had to fall back upon Lucy. The silly little thing stood up in quite a flutter. If a Royal Highness had asked her to dance she could not have been more flattered. Of course, she would take 'gentleman'! She told the most outrageous fibs, and said she preferred being 'gentleman;' she always chose it when she had the chance.

After she had dragged Pamela round until she was fit to faint, and had ascertained how hard her whalebones were, and how regular her breathing, and that her favourite perfume was heliotrope, and that dancing with a goddess whose chin was on a level with the top of her head was not all pure bliss, she had her reward.

Annabel Crewe, the Natural Science girl, asked her to 'cocoa' after the dancing was over, and here she met Pamela. It was Lucy's first experience of a Newnham 'cocoa.' There was quite a spread on Annabel Crewe's little writing-table—sweets and cakes and fruit, and cups brimming over with the nectar of Newnham.

Pamela Gwatkin came in last; there was a crowd of girls in the room when she came in, filling it quite up, and occupying all the chairs and the ottoman and both sides of the bed. There was an art covering thrown over the bed embroidered with dragons, and a cushion with an impossible monster with a flaming tail; nobody but a Newnham girl would have dreamed it was a bed.

Lucy was occupying a low cushiony-chair—the nicest chair in the room—and she got up directly Pamela came in and gave it up to her. She accepted it in her superior way, and flopped down into it as if it were in the order of things for everyone to make place for her. Then that wretched little sycophant, Lucy, waited upon her in her servile way, as if she were nothing short of a Royal Princess. She brought her her cocoa, and sweets, and cakes, and fruit. She positively snatched them from the other girls to offer them to Pamela, and be snubbed for her pains. She hadn't the spirit of a mouse.

Everybody was talking at once, and there was such a clatter of tongues that Lucy couldn't have heard the goddess speak if she had deigned to speak to her. She did deign just before the party broke up.

Lucy hadn't anywhere to sit, and she was tired out with dragging Pamela round, and she had found an idiotic three-legged milking-stool, and she was trying to sit upon it. It was an objectionable stool; in the first place, it had been painted with yellow buttercups, and varnished before the paint was dry. It was not dry yet, and it stuck to Lucy's black gown and left a proof impression of the buttercups on the back. In the second place, the legs hadn't been stuck in firmly, and it wobbled under her weight and threatened to collapse every moment. Lucy sat in fear and trembling, trying to look as if she were quite comfortable and used to wobbling, and while she sat the goddess spoke:

'I have a brother at St. Benedict's,' she said; 'I dare say you know him; he is in his third year.'

Lucy murmured that she hadn't that pleasure; she didn't know any undergraduates.

'No, I suppose not,' Pamela said wearily—she generally spoke wearily, as if commonplace subjects were beneath her. 'They are an uninteresting class; only Eric is so quixotic; he does such absurd things that I should not have thought he could have been anywhere long without being known and laughed at.'

'Really!' said Lucy, in rather a shocked voice; she didn't know what else to say.

'It was one of his absurdities to come up here as an undergraduate. He had qualified—fully qualified—for another profession. He was a doctor, and when he had passed all his examinations, after seven years' work, he threw it all up. He found out that he had missed his right vocation. He had some absurd notion that he was specially called for the Church—that the Church couldn't do without him—and so he has come up here.'

Pamela spoke scornfully, with her thin upper lip curling, and just a suspicion of pink in her face—her beautiful worn, weary face.

'Perhaps he has done right,' said Lucy. 'A man ought never to go into the Church unless he feels that he is called. Papa might have been Senior Wrangler, but he felt his vocation was the Church. He gave up everything for it, and——' 'And mamma' she was going to say, but she looked at Pamela and stopped short.

'It would be all very well if the Church were going to last,' she said wearily; 'but it isn't. Everybody knows that it isn't. Nobody but women and children believe in it now. Its methods are all exploded; its teaching is preposterous; it has had its day, like other beliefs, and now a new day is dawning. Oh, it was ridiculous of Eric to go into the Church just as it was falling to pieces!'

Lucy was past expressing an opinion. The milking-stool had collapsed. The three idiotic legs had all gone different ways; it had fallen quite to pieces, like the Church was going to, and Lucy was seated on the floor.

CHAPTER V.

AFTER CHAPEL.

The day succeeding the debate was Sunday, and Lucy went over to St. Benedict's to morning chapel.

She was so glad to go. It was quite a relief to get outside Newnham and shake from her skirts the atmosphere of so much learning. It was a distinct relief to take her place in the stalls of St. Benedict's and look down upon the men who took life so much more easily.

She was only just in time for the college chapel. The bell was going as she crossed the court, and the men were hurrying in in their white surplices. They were all smiling and debonair. There wasn't a single cloud on the brow of one of them, except the cloud of last night's tobacco. They were lusty and strong and fresh-coloured, and some of them had frames like giants; and they came across the court with a swinging stride, and health and life and vigour in every movement. Men take things so much more easily than women.

The choir and the Master came in directly after Lucy had taken her seat. The Master looked across his wife and Mary, who sat between them, and nodded to Lucy.

'Very glad to see you, my dear,' he said in quite an audible voice.

It was a longer service than usual at St. Benedict's on Sunday mornings. The Master read the Litany, and he took a long time in reading it, and Lucy had plenty of opportunity of looking among the men for Pamela Gwatkin's brother.

He was a twin brother, she had learned from Annabel Crewe, who knew all about Pamela, and therefore he ought to be exactly like her. Tall and fair and thin-lipped, with clear, steady eyes—blue ought to be the colour, or gray, she was not sure which; but she could not mistake the profile. There could be no doubt about that clear-cut face, without an ounce of superfluous flesh upon it.

Lucy looked at the men eagerly one after the other; she looked at every man in the chapel. The Senior Tutor from his stall on the other side saw her looking down at the men. She didn't look at him, and he wondered at the change in her. Her eyes were not wont to rove over the faces of the men sitting below in that eager way; they might have all been sticks and stones for the notice Lucy had hitherto vouchsafed them.

Was this the outcome of a week at Newnham? Had she seen so much—so very, very much—of women in her new developments that she was thirsting for the sight of man?

Cousin Mary saw her looking down at the undergraduates in the seat below, too, and sighed. She remembered the time when she used to look across the benches. She had seen so many generations of undergraduates come and go in fifteen years. She may have looked more than once in all that time to see if among them there was that one face that was to be her beacon through life; she had ceased to look for it now.

Lucy had decided before she left the chapel that the man in the third row near the top was Pamela's brother. A tall man with a thin, fair, fresh-coloured face and firm lips—a capable face, a face quite worthy of the brother of Pamela Gwatkin.

Lucy watched the men file out of chapel, and the man in the last seat of the last row naturally came out last. She refused to go into the lodge with Mary. She let the old Master and his wife toddle off down the cloisters together, and she stood holding Mary back and begging her to wait 'just a minute.'

The man in the back seat came out at last and took off his cap to the Master's nieces as he passed.

'There!' said Lucy breathlessly, 'this is the man I waited for. Is he Eric Gwatkin?'

'Eric Gwatkin!' Mary repeated impatiently; she objected to being kept standing in the court watching the men come out of chapel; she could see them every day—twice a day if she liked—and she had seen them for fifteen years. 'Eric Gwatkin?' she repeated. 'The man who has just come out is Wyatt Edgell, the best man of the year. He will take a very high place in the Tripos—perhaps the highest—and Eric Gwatkin is only a Poll man. He is taking the theological Special, I believe, and I dare say he will be plucked.'

'Oh, I am sure there is some mistake!' Lucy said hotly; 'Pamela's brother never could be plucked. She is awfully clever, and—and he is a twin.'

Cousin Mary didn't take the least interest in Pamela's brother; even the fact of his being a twin didn't move her. She went into the lodge and looked after the table that was spread for lunch. She altered the arrangement of the flowers, and put some finishing touches to it, and Lucy stood beside the window that overlooked the court watching her.

She couldn't help pitying Mary for being interested in such small things, for being taken up with such petty cares. She had lived in the midst of culture for fifteen years, and yet she could potter about that dinner-table and be absorbed in the arrangement of the flowers.

'I am very glad to see you, my dear,' the old Master said to Lucy when she had dutifully kissed him and whispered to her aunt how well he was looking—the sure key to that dear, kind, simple heart was to tell her how well the Master was looking. It would be a sad day when those welcome words could no longer be said.

'And how is the Greek getting on, my dear? Who would have thought of my brother Dick's daughter learning Greek? She didn't get the taste for it from her father, for he was no scholar. He was good only for his own work, none better. There was not a man in the parish who could drive a straighter furrow than my brother Dick, and his wife was famous for her poultry. I remember her carrying her butter and eggs to market. She had the corner stall in the old butter market, my dear. I mind the very spot.'

'It was my grandmother, or great-grandmother, rather,' said Lucy, feebly trying to set him right. 'Mamma never kept a stall in the butter market.'

'Never mind which it was,' said the Senior Tutor, who had just come in, and was shaking hands with Lucy; 'a generation or two doesn't matter.'

It didn't matter to him, who knew all the homely details of the Master's humble history; but suppose he were to go maundering about that stall in the butter market to Pamela Gwatkin, it would be all over Newnham that it was Lucy's mother, and that Lucy herself used to milk the cows. With such a pedigree there was no excuse for her tumbling off a milking-stool.

If Lucy hadn't been so full of her own concerns that she had no eyes for others, she would have seen the reason for Cousin Mary's anxiety about the dinner-table. The Senior Tutor was coming to dinner.

The lunch, or rather the dinner—for it was a real dinner; except on state occasions, the old Master dined in the middle of the day—was spread in the dining-room of the lodge—an old, old room panelled up to the ceiling with dark oak, with a delightful carved frieze running round the top, and a big oriel window with diamond panes and stained glass coats-of-arms of the old Masters who had occupied the lodge since it was first built, centuries ago.

There were portraits of some of them in their scarlet gowns on the walls, looking down upon them as they sat at meat. It was a ghostly company, so many old Masters, and soon there would be another to hang among them. He was painted already, and hanging in the gallery outside; he would come in here soon, and take his place, not at the table, but on the walls with the rest.

Perhaps the Senior Tutor was thinking of that not far-off time as he lay back in his chair glancing up at the dingy old walls that wanted beeswaxing dreadfully. There would be plenty for him to do when his time came. There had been nothing done here for years. He would have to go right through the house; he hardly knew where he should begin.

And then Lucy broke in upon his pleasant reverie, and asked him about Eric Gwatkin.

'Gwatkin?' said the Tutor absently. He was just considering whether he should have the oak varnished or beeswaxed. 'Ye—e—s; he's going in for his Special, but I don't think he'll get through.'

'Only his Special!' Lucy hadn't got through her Little-go yet, but she regarded the Special from the Newnham standpoint. No woman has ever yet descended so low as a Special. 'His sister is one of the cleverest girls at Newnham. She has already taken a first in one Tripos, and now she is working for another. She is sure to take a double-first. He is her twin brother, and I'm sure she expects great things of him.'

'Then I'm very sorry for Miss Gwatkin,' the Tutor said with a laugh. 'If he gets through it's as much as he will do.'

He declined to have anything more to say about Pamela's unpromising brother; and he talked to Lucy until the ladies left the table about her life at Newnham, and the progress she was making with her work.

The old Master did not sit long over his wine; it had come to one glass now after dinner—one glass of that old, old wine that had already lain a dozen years in the darkness of the college cellar when he had come up a raw scholar to St. Benedict's. It did him quite as much good as a dozen glasses of a less generous vintage. It brought a warm flush into his wrinkled cheeks, and a light into his dim eyes, and stirred the slow blood circling round his heart, and it sent him to sleep to dream again of the old time, and to win afresh the laurels of his youth. While the Master sat nodding in his big chair on one side of the wide fireplace, where a fire was still burning, and his faithful partner sat nodding on the other side, Lucy slipped out of the room.

She was only going to the old study to find some books, but she had to pass through the picture-gallery to reach it. The gallery of the lodge of St. Benedict's was very much like the galleries of most college lodges, only it was narrower—a long, low, narrow old room extending the length of one side of the cloistered court. It had been built when the cloisters beneath had been built, and it had suffered few changes since. The walls were panelled to the ceiling with oak, and it was lighted with deep, old-fashioned bay-windows; not particularly well lighted, as the diamond panes were darkened with painted arms of founders and benefactors, and old, dead and forgotten Fellows. The walls of the long gallery were hung with portraits from end to end. They began in the right-hand corner by the door in the fourteenth century—flat, angular, awful presentments of men and women whose names are household words in Cambridge, and they went on and on until it seemed that they would never cease. The walls were so full that it would be difficult to find room for another Fellow.

Lucy paused on her way to the study, and looked round with quite a new feeling on these old painted faces. They represented something to her to-day that they had not represented before.

She began dimly to understand what had made Cambridge the power it is in the land. It was these still faces looking down from the walls who had built up this great Cambridge. It was the men, after all, the patient men of old, whose toil had accomplished so much; and now the women were entering into their labours.

There were not many portraits at Newnham; it was only in its infancy. There would be plenty by-and-by. Lucy ran over in her mind the women whose portraits would hang upon those white walls between the windows. She could not in that brief retrospect think of any who were doing such great work that they would earn that distinction, only Pamela Gwatkin. She was sure Pamela would one day hang on the walls. She would be an old woman then, most likely, a lean, wrinkled, hard-visaged old woman, with gray hair and spectacles, and she would have a big book beside her—a book she had written or explained—and she would wear—what would she wear?

She would have gone quite bald by that time, like the old Fellows on the walls; her head would be bald and shining. She would wear it covered, of course, with—with a scholar's cap, with a long tassel depending over her nose, or a velvet Doctor's cap, which would be more becoming, and she would wear a scarlet Doctor's gown and hood. The picture would look lovely on the white walls of Newnham.

Lucy had just settled to her satisfaction how Pamela Gwatkin was to be handed down by a future Herkomer to another generation, when the Senior Tutor entered the gallery.

He, too, had been thinking. He hadn't been paying any attention to what Mary Rae had been talking about while the Master took his after-dinner nap; his thoughts were with Lucy in the gallery. He had watched her narrowly at dinner, and he had detected a change in her. He was used to watching men, and now he had begun to watch women. He remarked that her eyes were no longer soft; they were hard and eager, and had a hunted look in them. He knew the look; he had seen it in boys come up fresh from school—not brilliant boys from the sixth form of big public schools, but frank, fresh-faced fellows who had come up from country parsonages. He had seen the look on their faces when the work was new to them and the strain had begun to tell upon them. They lost it after a term or two when they bossed their lectures, and drifted away with the stream, or broke down, and went back to the country parsonages, and never came up again.

He had seen this hunted look on boys' faces, but he had never seen it on a girl's face before. He wasn't sure if it wouldn't be well to take Lucy away before she broke down. She would never want the mathematics she was getting up with such labour for the Little-go; she would be able to add up the butcher's book quite as well without. As the future mistress of the lodge—it had really come to that; he had ceased to think about Mary, and he had almost unconsciously put Lucy in her place—he would have liked her to have the prestige of Newnham, and, considering her humble antecedents, it was quite as well that she should win her spurs. She had pluck enough, if her strength would only hold out. She was a brave little thing; he had never seen a girl so brave. The Little-go examinations would soon be over, and then, if the result was satisfactory, he would speak. She would have quite culture enough after the Little-go—quite enough to condone even the stall in the butter market.

'I think you had better let me coach you for the exam.,' he said, as they talked about her mathematics; 'for the Additionals, at any rate, you'll find the dynamics and the statics rather stiff.'

'Ye—es,' Lucy said with a sigh; 'they are dreadfully stiff.'

'When will you come to me? Will you come here, or shall I come up to Newnham?'

'Oh no, no! It would never do to come to Newnham!'

Lucy turned quite pale at the suggestion.

'You have male lecturers,' said the college Don with a laugh. 'The difference would be that I should only be lecturing one girl instead of six.'

'I'm sure it wouldn't do; I'm sure Miss Wrayburne would object. I would rather, if you don't mind, come to you,' Lucy said meekly.

'Come, by all means. You had better come to my rooms; there will be less interruption than at the lodge. I can give you four hours a week, but it must be in the afternoon. When will you begin?'

Lucy was quite ready to begin at once. She settled to go to the Tutor's rooms the very next day. She didn't even think of consulting Cousin Mary about the arrangement, or the Master, or the Master's wife. She had already made a distinct advance; she had decided for herself; she had engaged a University coach, and arranged to spend four hours a week alone with him in his college rooms. The woman of the future could not do more.

CHAPTER VI.

BEHIND THE SCREEN.

Lucy went to her coach the next day. She ought to have known her way about a college staircase by this time, but she had never yet penetrated beyond the outer courts. She had never ventured up those mysterious stairways sacred to gyps, bed-makers and gownsmen.

A great many gownsmen must have climbed the stairs that led to Mr. Colville's rooms before her; they had left their marks here, if they had left them nowhere else in the annals of the University. Mr. Colville's rooms were in the oldest part of the college, and his staircase was as narrow and steep and dark as any lover of mediæval architecture could desire.

It was so dark that when Lucy reached the first landing she didn't see where to go; there was a passage in front of her and doors on either side. Instead of looking at the names painted over the doors, she went down the passage and knocked at the door at the end.

There are several ways of knocking at a door, but there is only one way of knocking at a college door if one expects to be heard. A timid rap with the knuckles is wasted effort; the knob of an umbrella, or the handle of a walking-stick, or any other form of bludgeon one happens to have at hand, is more effective; or a succession of well-delivered blows with a fist, or the body falling heavily against the door, have been known to attract the attention of persons within the room; but Lucy had recourse to none of these devices. She knocked feebly with her gloved hand on the door and waited. She was sure it was the right landing. She had read the directions painted on the door-post at the foot of the staircase:

First Floor—Mr. Colville.

She knocked again presently; and then, as nobody answered, she went in. The Senior Tutor was expecting her; it was surely right to go in. She thought she heard voices as she opened the door—at least a voice, a voice that had a familiar ring in it; she heard it clearer when she opened the first door; there was an outer oak, as usual to a college room. Lucy opened both doors and went in. She went quite into the room, and closed the door—there was a screen before the door—before she saw the occupants of the room.

What she saw didn't exactly make her hair stand on end, but she gave a little cry. She couldn't help crying out. On the couch behind the screen a man was lying, with the blood flowing from a wound in his throat, and on his knees beside him was a man praying.

The man who was praying stopped and looked up at the sound of that startled cry, and saw Lucy standing in the middle of the floor. He got up from his knees, and with a gesture of silence went behind the screen and fastened the two doors.

'I am glad you are come,' he said, going back to Lucy. 'I did not know the doors were open. You must be sure to keep them fastened. We don't want the authorities to know of this, and the Senior Tutor has the next rooms. You must be sure not to let him suspect anything. If you can do what is necessary for Edgell by day, I will sit up with him at night. It is not a bad wound; I don't think it is at all serious.'

Lucy stood frightened and speechless. What did the man mean? Did he take her for a nurse?

'I am afraid there is some mistake,' she said in a low voice; she couldn't keep from shaking. 'I—I thought this was Mr. Colville's room.'

Then a light seemed to break in upon the man, and he looked at Lucy with a quick, startled glance.

'Oh!' he said, 'I thought you were the nurse. I beg your pardon. There—there has been an accident here; our friend has not been quite himself—he has been over-working—and—and this has happened. Thank God it is no worse! It might have been fatal; a mere hair's breadth and it would have been fatal. We are anxious to keep it from the authorities. It would be very serious for him if it were known. It would ruin him for life. May we ask you to keep the chance knowledge of this most deplorable occurrence secret?'

What could Lucy say? Clearly it was her duty as the Master's niece to go straight to the lodge and acquaint him with the state of affairs. It was her duty to summon Mr. Colville without a moment's loss of time; he was only separated from the scene of this tragedy by a narrow passage.

Of course, the man lying bleeding there ought to have a doctor and a nurse, and his friends should be telegraphed for, and the whole college ought to be thrown into a commotion. Suppose the man were to die, what would her feelings be if she were particeps criminis in this dreadful secret?

All these things flashed through Lucy's mind as she stood there looking at the man on the couch. She knew him now; it was the man who had taken his hat off to her as he came out of chapel.

It was the man that Cousin Mary said was going to take a very high place in the Tripos, perhaps the highest. It was Wyatt Edgell.

She made up her mind in a moment.

'Yes,' she said, 'I will keep your secret. But I cannot go away from here and leave you like this. There is something I can do. I am used to nursing and sickness; tell me what I can do.'

She had torn off her gloves and thrown down her books, and was kneeling beside the couch where the man lay, wiping away the blood that was trickling beneath the bandage, and dropping down over his chest.

There was so much she could do that a woman could best do, and the man with his hand on the wrist of the patient stood by and watched her while she did it.

'You know something about medicine?' she said.

'I have been a doctor. I have spent seven years in acquiring a knowledge of surgery—seven years out of my life—but it has not been wasted if I have been the means of saving him;' and he nodded towards the bed.

'And you think you have saved him?'

Where had she heard this man's voice before, and where had she seen his eyes? She was asking herself this question as she was speaking to him.

'Yes, I think he is saved. He will do very well with careful nursing. One of the men has a sister at Addenbroke's, and he has gone to fetch her. I thought she had come when I saw you standing there. She will certainly be here presently. I don't think we need detain you.'

'I shall not go till she comes,' Lucy said with such decision that she quite frightened herself. 'I shall certainly stay here as long as I can be of any use.'

She had been of a good deal of use already. She had removed all traces of the dreadful deed; she had washed up every stain that could be washed away, and she had covered up the rest. She had fetched a pillow and some coverings from the adjoining room, and straightened the couch, and anyone coming into the room and seeing the man lying there with a white handkerchief over his throat, and the quilt drawn up over his chest, would not have dreamed of the ghastly sight beneath.

He looked as he lay there as if he had broken down in the middle of his work, and had thrown himself down there in a sudden attack of faintness. His face was dreadfully white, as white as the coverlet, and he was breathing hard, and there was a strange faint odour Lucy noticed as she bent over him. He was not sensible, but once he opened his eyes and looked at her with a strange, far-away look in them that haunted her for days.

They were beautiful eyes, tender and dreamy as a woman's, with a depth in them Lucy had never seen in any eyes before. But then she had not been accustomed to look into young men's eyes. She could not remember bending over a man before and seeing herself reflected in his eyes.

Perhaps it was the novelty of the situation that moved her. Having done all, everything she could do, she settled herself down in a chair by the head of the bed and began to weep.

The man was nothing to her, she had never heard his name till yesterday, and here she was sitting by his side weeping for him as if she had known him all her life.

The man who stood by let her tears fall unchecked.

'I don't think you will disturb him,' he said with a smile; 'I have given him an anodyne. Nobody could tell what he would do if he were left to himself, so I have made things sure by quieting him for a time. Pray have your cry out if it does you any good.'

He evidently knew something of girls. There is nothing like a little weep for soothing the nerves.

While Lucy was availing herself of her woman's privilege, he turned down the coverlet and examined the bandages; the blood was trickling down beneath them, thick and black where it had congealed, and a paler streak behind.

'It's broken out again,' he said quietly. 'I think there must be a stitch. Can you help me?'

If Lucy had been told an hour ago that she could have stood by and assisted as the man sewed up that gaping wound, and never by word or look betrayed faintness or alarm, she would not have believed it.

It was the little weep that did it.

'I think it will do now,' said the man, drawing up the coverlet over his work. 'There is only one thing we can do more for the poor fellow, and that is commit him to God. Will you kneel down beside him while we ask His blessing on the means that we have used? Remember, when two or three are gathered together—we are two, and—and I am sure his mother is here with us.'

Lucy knelt down beside the couch while the man prayed aloud.

He talked to God as he knelt there as one who knew Him as a Friend of old. He made no preamble in entering this solemn Presence Chamber, but went straight up to the throne with his petition, and laid the poor, blind, suffering soul at the foot of the Cross.

Lucy had been brought up in the bosom of the Church; she had heard prayers read every morning and evening of her life, and she had never missed being in her place on Sundays. She had heard her father read the prayers hundreds of times, and she had heard, oh, so many sermons, but she had never heard a man pray like this.

It was heart speaking to heart; it was the spirit of man speaking to the Spirit of God.

While he was still speaking the door, or doors, rather, opened, and someone came in. He did not stop or get up from his knees, but went on wrestling for the blessing that he sought.

Lucy felt dreadfully guilty kneeling there. She heard the door open, and people—distinctly people—come in; and she had an awful overwhelming sense of guiltiness, as if she had been consenting to a murder. She was afraid to get up; she expected to see the Senior Tutor standing there and her cousin Mary. She didn't at all know why she expected Mary.

She was almost afraid to look up when she rose from her knees, and she felt herself shaking all over. But it was not Mary, and it was not the Tutor. It was a man that Lucy had often seen in the courts below, and he had a girl in a nurse's dress with him.

He looked over to Lucy in some alarm, and took off his cap.

'It's all right,' said the other. 'You didn't lock the door after you, old man, when you went out, and this lady found her way in—at least, God showed her the way in. If she hadn't come at the right moment it would have gone hard with our friend here. I am glad you have brought your sister. And now,' he said, turning to Lucy, 'we need not detain you any longer. This lady will stay with us, I hope, till late; and I shall sit up with him to-night. To-morrow, I hope, the worst will be over.'

'I hope so,' Lucy said with a sob she couldn't choke down—she hadn't the heart to say any more.

'I am sure you will respect our secret,' the man said, as Lucy was drawing on her gloves.

She didn't answer him; she only looked at him, and she saw the blood flush up under his skin. She remembered somebody else's cheeks she had seen flush in the same way—not a man's.

'I beg your pardon,' he said humbly.

Lucy was so angry with him for doubting her that she did not see his proffered hand; she drew her gloves on hurriedly, and picked up her books and went out into the passage, but she beckoned the nurse to follow her.

'I don't think the man's going to get better,' she said in a hurried whisper. 'It's like consenting to a murder to let him lie there and die; but I am not going to tell. I think his mother ought to know. I think someone ought to write and tell her that he is ill—dying!'

The nurse shook her head.

'It would kill her!' she said. 'She has such faith in her son—her beautiful son! He is such a noble, splendid fellow! Oh, it is a dreadful pity!'

'Why did he do it?'

'Why? Oh, don't you know?'

'No——'

The door of the room opened as they were speaking, and the nurse's brother beckoned her to come in.

'Come to me to-morrow morning at Addenbroke's,' she said. 'Ask for Nurse Brannan;' and then she went into the room and shut the door.

Lucy crept guiltily down the stairs. She quite shivered as she passed the Tutor's door: she would not have encountered him for the world. She didn't feel safe until she had got outside the college gate, and then she ran all the way back to Newnham.

CHAPTER VII.

LUCY'S SECRET.

Lucy felt dreadfully guilty all through that wretched evening. If she had assisted in a murder she couldn't have felt worse.

She had no appetite for dinner, and when she went back to her room, what was still more unusual, she had no appetite for her work. A Newnham girl is a gourmand where work is concerned; she may leave her meals untasted, but that terrible craving within creates an appetite that is akin to ravenous where work is concerned. When that craving ceases she goes down—or breaks down.

It had ceased quite suddenly with Lucy; she hated the very thought of work; she loathed with an unutterable loathing the sight of those mathematical books she had brought back from St. Benedict's. She shrank from them with a dreadful sense of faintness and sickness when she attempted to open them. They smelt of blood, or else she fancied they did.

The air was full of fancies. It was a stormy night, and the wind was wailing round her corner of the building, and every now and then a sharp blast of driving rain would strike upon her window. She heard the rain distinctly dropping down the pane like tears, and she fancied—oh, it was a dreadful fancy!—that it was drops of blood.

She bore it in that lonely room as long as she could, and then she got up and went out into the passage. The lights were out, and the place was quite still; everybody had gone to bed. Dark and deserted as the corridor was, it was not so lonely as her own room. There were girls sleeping behind every one of those closed doors. She heard them—for the ventilators of most were open—breathing audibly, and some were moaning in their sleep.

Lucy walked up and down the long corridor; her feet were bare, and she had thrown nothing over her shoulders. Cousin Mary would have scolded her dreadfully if she had seen her, with her white garments trailing on the stone floor.

She never thought of the draughts or the cold stones; she only thought of getting away from that everlasting drip, drip of the window-pane, that brought the scene of the afternoon so vividly before her. She was nervous and overwrought, and she was burdened with a secret she ought never to have bound herself to keep.

Wild horses shouldn't tear it from her, she told herself, as she paced up and down that draughty passage. Whatever happened, she would be true to her word. It would be hard if a girl couldn't be trusted as well as a man. What was the use of coming to Newnham if gossip and emptiness—the habits of the slave—still had dominion over her?

It was all very fine and high-sounding; but she would have given the world to have told somebody, to have eased her overburdened mind and poured out the dreadful story on some soft feminine, sympathetic bosom.

And then, while she was telling herself all these fine things, and repeating Lord Tennyson's nice verses about that open fountain that was to wash away all those silly human things and make woman perfect—quite perfect—a strange thing happened.

She heard the voice of the man praying. He was praying now; she heard him quite distinctly, but she could not catch the words. She was quite sure it was the voice; it had sunk down so deep into her ears that she could never forget it. Lucy paused in the darkness and listened. The voice came from a room at the door of which she was standing. She had no idea, in the darkness, whose room it was; she was only sure—quite sure—of the voice.

An overpowering desire to see the speaker—perhaps to get her release—seized her, and she opened the door of the room.

There was no man there praying; there was only a girl sitting reading by the light of a shaded lamp, and she was reading aloud. It was Pamela Gwatkin, and she was reading a Greek play.

Lucy went a few paces into the room and stood there as if spellbound, listening to the girlish voice, in low solemn accents, mouthing the rhythmic Greek. She didn't read it as if it were Wordsworth, or Cowper, or Keats, or even Tennyson; she mouthed it; and the noble words, falling in noble cadence, brought back the voice of the man wrestling with God for his friend.

Pamela heard the door open, and she looked up. She didn't divide the shuddering night with a shrill-edged shriek, and bring all Newnham about her, as she might have done at the sight of the white-robed figure standing in the doorway. She thought it was a girl walking in her sleep, and she got up softly and went towards her.

For a moment, as she came forward, she saw the figure swaying in the doorway, and as she came nearer Lucy tottered forward with her arms out-stretched like one walking in a dream, and fell upon her bosom—literally fell, with her clinging arms around her, and her head pillowed on Pamela's bosom.

'Oh, it is Eric Gwatkin!' she sobbed, 'it is Eric Gwatkin!'

Pamela got her over to the couch—it was a bed now, not a couch; the serge rug had been removed, and a snowy coverlet was in its place, and a real pillow, not a sham roundabout bolster covered with an embroidered dragon.

Pamela Gwatkin laid the girl down on her own bed and covered her up. She was shaking dreadfully, and her hands and feet were like ice, and she was sobbing hysterically.

When Pamela had covered her up, she shut the door of the room; it was no good making a scene and arousing everybody, because a girl—a little weak-minded fresher—had broken down under the strain and got hysterical. All girls get hysterical at times, only the stronger ones lock the door and wrestle with the enemy in secret.

'Oh, Eric Gwatkin!' moaned the girl on the bed. 'I can't keep it any longer; I must tell!'

'What have you got to do with Eric Gwatkin?' Pamela asked severely. 'I am sure he is nothing to you; he is never likely to be anything to anybody.'

'Oh yes, he is! He is everything to—to Wyatt Edgell. He has saved his life. Oh, you don't know what he is to him!'

'Saved his life? What are you talking about? What has Wyatt Edgell got to do with you, and with Eric?'

'He sewed it up—the wound—the dreadful gaping wound!'

Lucy covered her eyes with her hands to shut out the dreadful sight, and she was trembling so dreadfully that the bed shook with her. Clearly the girl was in a fever, and her mind was wandering. The name of Wyatt Edgell was familiar to Pamela; it was familiar to everybody in Cambridge. He was the coming Senior Wrangler. What could Eric have to do with him—poor Eric, who was grinding for his 'Special'?

'What wound?' said Pamela impatiently; 'and who sewed it up?'

'Eric sewed it up, and I helped him. I drew the edges together, while he put the needle in the quivering flesh. Oh, it was horrible!'

Lucy sank back on the couch, and her lips grew pale, and her cheeks gray, and Pamela thought she was going to faint. She hadn't got anything but eau-de-Cologne to give her—not a nip of brandy for the world; not even a pocket flask is allowed at Newnham. She went to the water-jug and poured out some water in a basin, and dabbed it over the girl's face and hands, and made her own bed streaming. Perhaps there was something in the girl's story, after all! She couldn't have dreamed these hideous details.

'Where was the wound? how had he hurt himself?' she asked presently.

'He had cut his throat.'

Pamela let the basin of water she was holding fall on the floor. She didn't scream as any less well-regulated mind would have done, but she let the basin slip out of her hands, and the water made a dreadful mess on the floor.

'Cut his throat?' she repeated faintly—she was nearly as white as Lucy—'and Eric——'

'Eric sewed it up.'

'Is—is he dead?'

She asked the question hoarsely, in a voice Lucy couldn't have recognised for Pamela's, but she was past noticing voices.

'No—o; Eric has asked God to give him back his life, that he may begin it afresh.'

'What use is that?' said Pamela bitterly.

'I am sure God heard him—we were praying for him when the nurse came in. He was asking that the nurse might be sent quickly, and she came while the words were on his lips.'

'Of course the nurse would be sent; you can get a nurse at any moment from Addenbroke's without praying for one.'

'Oh, you don't understand!' Lucy moaned; 'you don't know the worst. It had to be done secretly: no one must know. It would ruin him for life if it were known.'

'You don't mean that they haven't told anyone? that they are trying to hush it up, and not let the tutors know?'

Lucy moaned.

'Oh, what folly is this! I am sure Eric is at the bottom of it.'

'Yes; it was Eric made me promise I wouldn't tell, and I have told you,' Lucy murmured helplessly.

'Of course you have told me. Having told me so much, you must tell me all—you must keep nothing back.'

And so Lucy sat up in the bed with her arms round Pamela—she couldn't have told her without having something to cling to—and told her her wretched little story, and how she had pledged herself to keep this young man's secret.

'What do you think I ought to do?' she asked weakly, when the recital was finished.

'Do?' said Pamela, but she didn't answer the girl's question. She disengaged herself from her clinging arms, and she paced up and down the room, her feet dabbling in the water on the floor. She stopped presently in her walk, her chin up, and her face set with the light of a high resolve upon it towards the light that was breaking in at the east window; she might have been reciting that Greek play. 'Do?' she repeated, and her face was hard and cold and tired. The old weary look had come back to it—no wonder; it was three o'clock in the morning. 'Do? Why, go to bed, of course!'

She refused to say another word about Lucy's secret. She helped her back to her room, and put her to bed, and tucked her in, and drew back the curtains, that the light of the new day might drive away the ghosts of the night.

Pamela did all this without speaking a word; but when she got to the door of Lucy's room she stopped and looked back. She could see from the tremulous motion of the clothes that the girl was weeping, and she went over to the bed and put her cool lips to Lucy's forehead.

'Good-night, dear!' she said softly. 'I think you have behaved beautifully!'

CHAPTER VIII.

WATTLES.

As soon as she could get away from Newnham the next morning, Lucy went to Addenbroke's to see Nurse Brannan. She couldn't get away very early; there was a mathematical lecture at nine o'clock that wasn't over till eleven, and she had to plod, plod through those weary diagrams while her mind was far away. Oh, how she hated those problems and riders, and all the dreary, dreary round! She made one or two futile little diagrams on her paper, and then she rubbed them out again, and sat staring at the blackboard, and watching the perplexing white lines come and go while her mind was far away. She was calculating what would happen if the man had died in the night.

'What would they do with the body? Would Eric Gwatkin expect her to keep the secret, and assist, perhaps, at some mysterious obsequies?' It was with a distinct feeling of relief she saw the duster sweep over the blackboard and wipe all those cabalistic characters away. It was like wiping out the record of her guilt.

Lucy shook off the dust and gloom of the lecture-room and ran off to Addenbroke's. She really could run a good part of the way. She went across the Fens, as less frequented, and giving her space to breathe and think. It was such a blue day, and the fresh green of the year was over the low-lying fields, and the chestnut-tree by the bridge was budding, and the pollard willows that marked the winding course of the river were sallow-gray in the sunshine, and the daisies were in bloom. Lucy walked over quite a carpet of flowers; she crushed the little tender pink buds remorselessly under her feet in her hurry to get to Addenbroke's.

She had never been to the hospital before, and she was rather afraid to go in when she got there. There were a lot of people coming out with newly-bandaged limbs and white faces, and some children were carried in in their mothers' arms. There were people of all ages, men and women, and little children all with that sad patience on their faces which is born of suffering. Lucy was so sorry for the people. She had no idea her heart was still tender; she had rather prided herself on its growing cold and hard like Maria Stubbs and the rest of the Stoics of Newnham. There was a tired-looking woman coming up the path with a puny little creature in her arms, with, oh! such a white, white face. Its eyes were open, and it was smiling a wan little smile up into the mother's face, and she was crooning over it; she was a poor, weakly thing, and she carried it as if even its light weight were too much for her. Lucy turned to look after the sickly mother and the sickly child, and she noticed the child's arm—a lean, puny little arm—had escaped from the shawl in which it was wrapped, and was feebly embracing the mother's waist.

The sight of that small clinging hand brought a rush of tears to her eyes. There was compensation even here; there was something here between that sickly mother and child—there wasn't much to show for it, only a crooning voice and a wan smile and a little wasted clinging hand—that would last longer than the Stoics, that would last 'to and through the Doomsday fire.'

Strangely softened by this every-day sight, Lucy crept up the wide stone staircase to find Nurse Brannan. She looked so lost that a man going up, a medical student, asked her where she was going, and took her to the ward where Miss Brannan was nurse.

'I am afraid the doctors are going their rounds,' he said, as he looked in at the door, 'but I will take you into Miss Brannan's room, and you can wait there.'

He led Lucy through the ward—a large, delightful chamber, well lighted and cheerful, and with quite a bank of tall palms and ferns on a table near the door, an oasis of verdure for tired eyes to feast upon.

Lucy saw all this at a glance, and she saw also a group of men round a bed, and the nurses standing near, and she crept softly into Nurse Brannan's room.

She had time before the nurse came to her to see what a nurse's room was like. It was a tiny bit of a room partitioned off the ward, and it seemed all walls and ceiling. There was a little floor room, however, and a big window that went nearly up to the ceiling.

It was not unlike a room in a woman's college, only that there were texts on the walls, and there are no texts on the walls of the Stoics.

The occupant of the room must have understood Latin and Greek, for there were texts in both these languages. There was one text only in our common tongue, and that was over the mantelpiece. It was not an illuminated text, and it had no lovely floral border. It was written in plain, bold characters in black and white: 'Inasmuch as ye do it unto the least of these My brethren, ye do it unto Me.'

Lucy couldn't keep her eyes off those familiar words which she read now in a new light. There wasn't much else in the room to look at. There was a bed that was a couch by day; it was a bed still, though it was past eleven o'clock; Nurse Brannan had evidently not long risen from it. The room was in the disorder of the early morning, and the day arrangements did not yet prevail. It was as untidy as a nurse's room well could be: the breakfast things were still on the table, and the demure little bonnet and cloak looked as if they had hastily been taken off and thrown on the bed, and a pair of outdoor shoes were lying in the middle of the floor.

While Lucy was still noticing these details Nurse Brannan came in.

She was a little bit of a nurse, with pink cheeks and steady blue eyes and fluffy hair. She was not at all a formidable person.

Lucy ran up to her when she came in, and took both her hands. She couldn't ask the question that was on her lips, she was moved out of all sense and reason. The anxieties of the night and the mathematics of the morning, and the lean little encircling arm had moved her strangely, and now she was hardly master of herself.

Nurse Brannan shook her head.

'He is no better,' she said.

She didn't say it at all sadly. She was so used to such things—to sickness and suffering and death—it didn't move her in the least.

'I have just come back from St. Benedict's, and there is no improvement. He has had a dreadful night. They thought at one time of calling up the Tutor.'

'And they have not told him yet?' Lucy asked, pale to the lips. 'Are they going to let him die?'

'They have not told him; they have not told anyone in the college; but I don't know about letting him die.'

'You think he'll get over it? Oh, do you really think it possible with that—that dreadful wound he can get better?'

Only talking about the wound made Lucy sick and faint. She was made of very poor stuff. She would have been no good at Addenbroke's.

Nurse Brannan smiled.

'The wound is nothing,' she said: 'it is not at all serious. He will get better if he is well watched, and they protect him from himself. When the attack passes off he will not be much the worse—only it may occur again at any time.'

'The attack?' Lucy said feebly; she was quite at sea as to Nurse Brannan's meaning.

'Oh, you didn't know he did it in a fit of delirium tremens. This is the second time he has had an attack, and he has attempted his life both times. His friends ought to take him away and put him under restraint.'

Lucy didn't know what delirium tremens meant; happily she had been spared all her life from such miserable knowledge. She vaguely knew it was a 'possession' of some kind, an awful 'possession' like that which used to seize the men of old.

'You think the fit will pass?' she said.

'Oh yes; there is no reason why it shouldn't pass, and then the less they say to him about it the better. It would be well if he never knew; but the scar will remain, they cannot cover up that. There is no reason why he shouldn't be well enough to take his Tripos and go "down." The best thing that can happen to him will be to "go down."'

'Go down'—he looked very much more like going 'up,' Lucy thought, as she recalled the white face on the pillow; but she was immensely relieved by the nurse's assurance.

'And you have seen him this morning?' she said.

'Yes; I ran over for a minute directly I got up. I was not up till late. A woman was dying in the ward, and I stayed with her till she died. She did not die till daylight, and then I lay down for a few hours; and I had just time to snatch some breakfast and run over to St. Benedict's before the doctors came their rounds. I was only just back in time. I had to throw my things down and put on my slippers—I hadn't even time to put my cap straight. They were waiting for me in the ward when I came back. Oh dear! what a mess I left my room in!'

Her pretty plaited nurse's cap, that ought to be worn in the most demure fashion, that ought to be as straight as those lines of that detestable blackboard, was all awry, was positively jaunty, and her fluffy hair was quite outrageous. She didn't look the least like a real, staid nurse who is called upon to face death at any moment, and is always doing dreadful disagreeable things. She might have been playing at nursing, only her eyes were steady, and her lips had a great calm about them; they didn't quiver, and tremble, and curl, and ripple with laughter, like other girls.

Lucy was almost angry with her for the cool, not to say unfeeling, way in which she spoke of these dread realities—death and suffering. 'She has no heart!' she said to herself as she went back over the Fens to Newnham. 'Nurses are so used to pain that they have no sympathy. I wouldn't be a nurse for the world!' Then she remembered the words over the mantelpiece: 'Inasmuch——.' Was this the secret of that little fluffy, girlish nurse's hardness and endurance?

They don't do very much for other people at Newnham; and they do nothing for each other. They positively ignore each other. Perhaps this is owing to culture—the higher culture—and it hadn't reached Addenbroke's yet.

Lucy had written to the Tutor of St. Benedict's when she got back the previous day, excusing herself, in an incoherent fashion, for not keeping her appointment, and promising to come to his rooms at the same hour the next day.

She knew her way quite well this time, and she was five minutes before the hour she had appointed. The Senior Tutor's door was closed, and the way was quite clear. There was not a soul on the staircase; there was not a soul in the passage. Lucy could not resist the desire to knock at that closed door at the end of the passage, and find out for herself how the man was. She hadn't much faith in that thick-skinned little nurse; she would see for herself.

She knocked at the door at the end of the passage in her futile way, but of course nobody answered. If she had wasted all her strength upon it, it would have been the same thing, as the inmates of that mysterious room only gave admittance to privileged individuals upon preconcerted signals.

Lucy hadn't got the secret of that 'Open sesame,' and she was turning away. She hadn't got to the end of the passage, when the door really did open and someone came out. It was the bed-maker with a tray. Somebody had been having a meal, and she was carrying the débris away. Lucy stopped her at the end of the passage, and the two women stood looking at each other—the bed-maker suspiciously, and Lucy eagerly. There was no mistaking the anxious eagerness in Lucy's eyes.

'How is he?' she asked, more with her eyes than her lips, and she laid her detaining hand on the woman's arm. There must have been some Freemasonry in the touch, for the bed-maker softened, and the look of suspicion gave place to one of pity.

'He's quieter,' she said in a whisper, drawing Lucy back into the passage, out of sight of the Tutor's door; 'but he's been orful bad all the morning. As much as two of 'em could do to keep him in bed. It's a sad pity, miss, and such a nice gentleman—there isn't his fellow in the college!'

The bed-maker sniffed; she would have wept, no doubt, but she held a tray, and it would have been inconvenient, so she sniffed instead, and regarded Lucy with a watery eye. She evidently thought Lucy was his sweetheart.

Lucy took a coin from her slender purse and laid it on the tray. She didn't give it to anybody in particular, she only laid it on the tray, and the bed-maker curtsied.

'Will you ask Mr. Gwatkin if I may come in?' she said—'the lady who was with him yesterday.'

She didn't give her name, but the woman knew her quite well—every bed-maker in St. Benedict's knew her. She wasn't the least surprised at the Master's niece taking an interest in one of her gentlemen—the nicest gentleman in the college. She had a tender spot in her withered bosom, under that rusty old shawl, and she was quite flustered at an affaire de cœur on her staircase.

She toddled back, tray and all, and by a preconcerted signal the door was opened, and she said a few words to someone inside, and then Eric Gwatkin came out into the passage and led Lucy in and closed the doors behind her.

He was looking dreadfully tired, she thought, and there were quite deep lines on his face; he seemed to have aged since yesterday. Perhaps it was with want of sleep, but Lucy put it down at once to his guilty conscience. She was feeling old herself, years older than yesterday.

'He has had a very bad night,' Eric Gwatkin said, speaking in a low voice and with his lips twitching, 'such a night as I pray God I may never witness again. You were not praying for us last night. You did not pray for him—for me—when you went away.'

Lucy bowed her head; she remembered she had not prayed for these men. What were they to her that she should pray for them?

She had been walking about the passages and frightening Pamela out of her wits instead, when she ought to have been on her knees.

The screen had been moved since yesterday; it had been drawn nearer the bed, so that the middle of the room where they were standing was left clear.

'He does not like to see anyone whispering,' Eric explained; 'he is very suspicious, and the least thing excites him.'

'You were alone with him all night?' Lucy asked, with a perceptible quiver in her voice; 'you have been up two nights.'

'That doesn't matter,' he said, 'I shall have all the strength I need; but last night he was very violent, and—and I thought I should have to call Mr. Colville. It was a great temptation—I could hardly resist it.'

'Oh, why didn't you?' said Lucy. 'Why do you take all this responsibility upon yourself?'

Eric Gwatkin smiled. His smile was not the least like Pamela's. Lucy couldn't help thinking, as she stood there, how it would change Pamela's face and take the weariness out of it if she had that smile.

'I don't mind the responsibility,' he said, 'or the anxiety, if I can save him. It would be worse than death to him to have it known. Oh, I think you must go home and pray that he may be brought through this, and may be kept for the future. He will need all our prayers.'

'What on earth are you whispering about, Wattles? I wish you would speak so that a fellow can hear what you are saying.'

The voice came from behind the screen—an impatient voice, not weak by any means.

'All right, old man; Miss Rae has come to ask how you are. He saw you yesterday,' he said, turning to Lucy and speaking in a lower voice; 'he remembered you quite well.'

'It's awfully good of you,' Wyatt Edgell said as Lucy came from behind the screen; 'I'm afraid we don't look like receiving visitors. Old Wattles here insists upon making a mess.'

He was lying back on the pillow with a wet bandage round his head, and a basin of lotion and some rags on a chair beside the bed. His shirt was torn open as if in a struggle, and his chest was bare. There was a scarf round his throat, a large silk scarf striped with the colours of his college that concealed whatever was beneath. Lying there with his head thrown back and those wet bandages, and his chest open—his splendid manly chest with all the muscles exposed—he looked like a man stricken down with fever, or some head trouble; no one would have guessed what the scarf thrown so loosely around his neck concealed.

'I am so glad you are better,' said Lucy softly, coming over to the bed and bending over him; 'you ought to get well soon, you have got such a good nurse.'

'Old Wattles, yes; he's very well, only he persists in keeping me in such a mess.'

He took the bandages off his head as he spoke, and rolled them up into a ball, and flung them to the other end of the room, where they rolled under a heavy piece of furniture, and Wattles, or Gwatkin rather, had to go on his knees and fish them out.

'There!' he said, 'that will give Wattles an excuse for going on his knees. He has been going on his knees all night. He would be a good fellow if he weren't always preaching and praying.'

He rolled his head impatiently on one side, and flung the pillow after the bandages, and Lucy, looking down upon him, saw a dark light in his eyes she had never seen in any eyes before. It wasn't exactly terror, but it was disgust and loathing and impatience.

'I beg your pardon,' he said, 'but there was a creature on that—a toad. I hate toads!' He shuddered as he spoke, and his eyes followed the direction of the pillow. 'It's there now! I wish Wattles would put it outside. It's been here all night.'

Gwatkin took up the pillow and shook it, and appeared to take something off it, and opened the window and made a gesture as if he had thrown the thing into the court below.

'There, old man,' he said reassuringly, 'it's gone now. It can't trouble you any more.'

And then he brought back the pillow, and Lucy put it under the poor fellow's head while he supported it, and she arranged it and smoothed it as only a woman's hand can arrange a pillow.

When she had done this, she put on the wet bandages afresh and bathed his head, and as she bathed it the dark light seemed to fade out of his eyes.

'You are very good,' he said with a sigh; 'you have exorcised that hideous little beast. It is gone now'—and he looked round the room fearfully—'quite gone.'

'Thank God!' said Gwatkin. 'Your visit has done some good, Miss Rae, if it has dispelled that hideous nightmare that has been pursuing him all night. I think he will sleep now.'

'I'm sure you ought to sleep yourself,' Lucy said, as she suddenly remembered the time and began dragging on her gloves. 'It is quite gone,' she said to Edgell, bending down over the bed; 'I am going to pick it up as I go out and carry it away.'

Having told this little fib, she went out, and Gwatkin closed the two doors after her.

She had to tell another fib or two when she went into the Tutor's room. He had been waiting for her exactly fifteen minutes, and he had waited an hour the day before.

She was absent and distrait all through the lesson; she was thinking about the man in the next room, and the creature she had promised to pick up in the court.

The Senior Tutor had never coached such an unpromising pupil. She would never get through her Little-go, he told himself—never, never. She would get plucked to a certainty.

Oh, it would never do for the future Mistress of St. Benedict's to be plucked!

He debated with himself while he was bending over her, and remarking what a dainty little profile it was, and how the little rings of chestnut hair clustered on her forehead, and how clear, how deliciously transparent, was the carnation tint of her cheek, and the shapely curve of her throat—such a little throat he could clasp it with his hand—he debated with himself, as he remarked these quite every-day things that no man in his senses except an old bachelor Fellow of a college would have noticed, whether it would not be better to settle the thing at once, and stop all this unprofitable work.

If Lucy knew what was before her, she would have other opportunities of fitting herself for her high position besides poring over mathematics, for which she clearly had no vocation.

'I'm afraid you find the work rather hard,' he said with a preliminary 'H'm' and 'Ah' to clear his throat. He didn't know exactly how to begin. What comes by nature at thirty is uncommonly hard at sixty. It is like going in again for a hurdle-race, or taking the high jump. He could have done it easily years ago, but he couldn't do it now. He stopped with that preliminary 'Ah.'

'Yes,' said Lucy, 'it is not very easy, but I am going to work eight hours a day. It is more than a month to the exam.; if I work very hard eight hours every day, I think I may manage it.'

Eight hours a day for a whole month! She was so much in earnest; and when she lifted her little pale drooping face to his, with just a suspicion of a tear on her eyelashes, he was really sorry for her. He was very near taking her in his arms and kissing away that fugitive tear and settling the matter—he was never nearer in his life.

Perhaps it was the best thing he could have done, but he missed the chance, and Lucy picked up her books and began to talk about the work she was to prepare for the next lesson.

'I wouldn't work eight hours a day,' he said; 'you will get through easier than that. I would give an extra two hours to tennis.'

He had never given a man this advice—perhaps it was not needed. He watched her, out of his window, cross the court. She did not happen to pick up the thing by the way as she had promised. Her step was less elastic, he noticed, than it used to be, and her face was paler—paler and thinner. She would never, never be young again, and life would never open afresh. There is only one young life, one time of roses, one sweet blossoming time, and it was just a question in the Tutor's mind, as he watched Lucy cross the court, whether the loss of this were worth all the mathematics in the world.

CHAPTER IX.

A WOMAN'S PARLIAMENT.

Lucy saw Pamela Gwatkin once only during the day, and that was at dinner. She only caught a far-off glimpse of her at the High table. Pamela very often sat at the 'High' among the Dons. The younger Dons were very fond of her: her opinions kept pace with theirs—they were very advanced opinions—and sometimes they outran them. She would be a Don herself some day, and she would be a pioneer in quite a new school of thought.

Lucy watched her with a feeling of awe as she sat among those great minds eating gooseberry pie—Lucy wouldn't have sat there for the world. The presence of so much learning would have taken away her appetite. The presence of the Master of St. Benedict's at the dinner-table never took away her appetite, but the dear old thing never talked above her head. He was very fond of recalling those old days, as he sat at meat, when Dick—not Lucy's father, but her great-grandfather—used to drive a team afield, and his good wife kept the stall in the butter market.

But the President and the Dons of 'Newe' never discussed such commonplace topics. They talked of literature, philosophy, science, with a fine breadth of handling which is peculiar to a woman's college. Pamela Gwatkin was in her right place among them.

There was the weekly political meeting held after Hall—a little miniature House of Commons—where the affairs of the nation were discussed, a foretaste of what will be by-and-by, when things are rearranged.

When the House took its seat at nine o'clock, Lucy found herself in the Opposition, and a long way off from the benches occupied by the Government of the country.

Lucy only represented an insignificant little borough that nobody else would stoop to represent. She had a little freehold in it—her only freehold—six feet of earth beneath the east window of her father's church at Thorpe Regis. Most people have a freehold of this sort, but it does not always give them a voice in the affairs of the nation. Lucy was returned unopposed on the strength of her little freehold, and as her views, if she had any, were not at all advanced, she found herself in the minority.

Pamela Gwatkin, or, as the girls called her, Newnham Assurance, was the Leader of the House, and Annabel Crewe Secretary for the Colonies, and Capability Stubbs had been unanimously elected Chancellor of the Exchequer; every girl that was worth anything had a place in the Cabinet.

Lucy hadn't much interest in the business that was going on, and she took out her knitting and turned the heel of a sock while the great affairs of the State were being discussed.

It was quite clear from what she did gather from the speeches on the Ministerial side that the country had been misgoverned long enough by the feeble race of men. It was quite time there was a change. A great deal of time had been lost; ages had been lost in the history of the world. Men had been first in the field; women took a longer time to ripen. They had ripened now; they were quite, quite ripe; they were ready for the change.

Oh, it was beautiful to hear the girls speak! There is an idea among narrow-minded people that debating societies encourage volubility of speech. Perhaps they do among men, and the practice of public speaking is apt to make them too loquacious, too apt to air their elementary knowledge and crude information in senseless verbiage. But garrulity is not the sin of the students of colleges for women. They not only know a great deal more than men know, but they have the delightful gift of ready and accurate language. They do not haggle and hesitate, and 'H'm' and 'Ah,' and have that dreadful difficulty in finding words that even prevails in a real House of Commons.

It was remarkable to see with what ease the Newnham girls handled those topics which old-fashioned legislators have been puzzling over Session after Session. There was a certain fine breadth in their way of handling them that would have taken a Conservative Leader's (the Leader of a real House of Commons) breath away.

It didn't take anybody's breath away in the Ladies' Parliament. Everybody knitted and listened unmoved, and when eleven o'clock came two very important Bills that had been brought forward from last Session were advanced a stage.

There was an exciting division before the House separated, that resulted in an overwhelming majority for the motion, 'That the Legal Profession and the Church be thrown open to women.'

That foolish little Lucy voted in the minority; there were not a dozen girls in Newnham who showed such a poor spirit, and of these five, it was rumoured, were engaged to curates.

The girls ran off to their rooms when the sitting of the House was ended in the highest possible spirits. Some of them sang snatches of songs, and some caught each other round the waist and waltzed madly down corridors. The thing was practically settled. The Bar and the Church opened vistas, immense vistas, for every sort of talent, and especially for the kind of talent that Newnham produced.

There would have to be more colleges for women—Newnham and Girton could not turn out nearly enough—there would have to be a great many Newnhams. Some girls, no doubt, sat down at once and began to prepare a sermon, and others took down Blackstone and began seriously to study law.

Lucy went back to her room alone. The Chancellor of the Exchequer, though she 'kept' next door, wouldn't take the slightest notice of her. She had lighted her lamp, and was just thinking what she would give for a cup of tea, when someone knocked at her door. It wasn't a girl with a cup of tea, as she hoped it might be—the Chancellor of the Exchequer, with all her fine airs, generally brought her in a cup of tea before she went to bed, and sometimes she condescended to sit down for five minutes and discuss the burning questions of the day. It was not the Chancellor of the Exchequer—it was a far greater person—it was the Leader of the House.

'Well?' she said, when she came in and had shut the door after her—'well?'

She had come in so suddenly, and Lucy's mind was so full of the motion of the evening—this Parliamentary business was quite a new thing to her, and she had taken it au serieux—that she could not collect herself sufficiently to think what Pamela meant. Her mind was so full of the lady curates and the female barristers that she looked up at the Leader of the House in bewilderment.

'Well,' said Pamela impatiently, 'how is he? I saw by your face at Hall that he was not dead. Is he going to get well?'

Then Lucy remembered all about it.

'Oh dear!' she said, 'how could I have forgotten! Yes, he is going to get well, I think. He will owe his life if he does to Eric. Oh, Eric has been lovely!'

'Eric has done no more than anyone else would have done,' Pamela said coldly; 'no more than a woman would have done if a woman had been in his place.'

'I don't think a woman could have done what Eric has done,' Lucy said.

She was thinking of those stitches he had put in, and how he had struggled with the poor fellow all night, and how he had been watching and praying beside him for two whole nights and days.

Nurse Brannan would have done as much as most women, but she would not have done all this.

'Oh, you don't know what women can do!' Pamela said, with a little curl of her lip. Her lips were so thin and so hard—such crisp lips that they couldn't help curling. 'You are only a fresher; when you have been here three years you will have found out what a woman can do. He would never have cut his throat if a woman had been near him.'

'No,' said Lucy eagerly, 'I am sure he wouldn't—not if a woman he loved had been near. Oh dear! you should have seen the wistfulness in his poor eyes when I put the wet bandage on his head! It was enough to melt one's heart. Eric says he will be sure to do it again—at least, that we must never leave off praying for him. I am sure that there is only one thing that can save him from doing it again.'

'Only one thing?' Pamela repeated, with just an inflection of scorn in her voice. 'And what is this panacea for his wickedness and folly? What is this fine thing that is to save him from himself?'

'Don't speak of it so lightly; it is not a little thing!'

There were tears in Lucy's voice as she spoke, and in her eyes. She had the picture before her of the strong man, with his beautiful bare chest, and his splendid frame, and those wistful eyes, and the loathing and the dread with which he shrank from the creature on his pillow. The pity of it was strong upon her, and she was deeply moved.

'A great love would save him—the love of a good woman. He would do a great thing for a woman he loved; he would make any sacrifice. I don't think anything else would save him.'

The Leader of the House of Commons turned from white to pink. Lucy might have been talking about her. She wore a very pretty white gown of some soft silky stuff, and it was folded across the bosom, and the folds heaved up and down as Lucy spoke, as if she were breathing heavily.

'Perhaps he has done this for a woman's sake,' she said bitterly. 'Men are such fools! they will do anything for a woman's sake—not always a worthy woman.'

'I am sure he has not!' said Lucy hotly. 'He has been working too hard, and he has broken down. I heard at the lodge that he was working ten hours a day; that he was certain to come out first. Oh, you don't know how they are building upon him at St. Benedict's! It isn't a woman—it's overwork.'

Pamela smiled.

'You are a capital champion, my dear, only don't suffer yourself to get too much interested in this foolish young man; it will interfere with your work. You must not make a mistake and let pity drift into—love.'

She made a little pause before the word, and the colour came again into her cheeks. She looked ever so much prettier talking about pity—and love—than she did speaking on those troublesome Bills that had already occupied the time of two Sessions.

'Oh, he is never likely to love me!' said Lucy. 'He could only love his equal; no one else would have any influence over him. He would only love a queen among women.'

'Perhaps he has found his queen already. Most men have before they are twenty-three.'

The colour went out of the girl's face, and the cold light came back into her eyes, and her lips, that a moment before were tremulous and tender, were hard and firm.

'I wouldn't go too often to Mr. Edgell's rooms, if I were you, dear,' she said when she went away. 'The authorities would make a fuss if they heard of it. We are not supposed, you know, to visit a man's room without a chaperon. I don't think it would do to take a chaperon there. If you have any more interest in him, I will find out for you how he is going on from Eric.'

'Thank you,' said Lucy warmly; 'I can find out for myself. I can hear all about the St. Benedict's men at the lodge.'

She was quite frightened at herself for speaking in that way to the Prime Minister. She had got into the way now, since she had been at Newnham, of taking her own part; she was beginning to have no respect for dignities.

CHAPTER X.

'THAT CONFOUNDED CUCUMBER!'

Lucy didn't go to Wyatt Edgell's room again. She caught sight of the friendly bed-maker once or twice on the staircase when she went to Mr. Colville's room to be coached in mathematics, and she held a little whispered conference with her on the stairs.

Edgell was better: he was up again and at work—working very hard, the woman said (and bed-makers know something about work). He was 'going on as quiet and as steady as any gentleman on the staircase.' This verdict from such a quarter was as good as a college testimonial.

When there is a mixed University, and a lady President at the lodge, and a female Vice-Chancellor, and the affairs of the Senate are conducted by dowagers, bed-makers will no doubt be required to sign college testimonials.

The first time Lucy saw Wyatt Edgell after that day when she put the wet bandage round his head, and promised to pick up the dreadful thing Eric had thrown out of window, and carry it away with her, was at the college chapel.

It was a fortnight after the day when she had picked him out from among all the men of St. Benedict's as Pamela Gwatkin's brother. He was sitting in the same place, and he was very little changed; he was paler, Lucy thought, and he was muffled up round the throat for that warm May day. She couldn't help looking at him. Her eyes would wander over to the bench where he sat, do what she would to keep them fixed in quite an opposite direction.

The Master took such a long time over the Litany that morning. He had read it for so many years in that college chapel, Sunday after Sunday, but he had never read it so slowly as he was reading it to-day. The men yawned and fidgeted as he read, and the old fellows in the stalls opposite looked across with grave, questioning eyes—they would have to elect another Master shortly—and the women-folk kneeling by his side looked up anxiously; but Lucy's eyes had wandered again to the end seat on the last bench, while her lips were murmuring:

"'That it may please Thee to raise up them that fall, and finally to beat down Satan under our feet.'"

Wyatt Edgell looked up while she was praying for him—she was distinctly praying for him, she had prayed this very prayer for him every night and morning since Eric had told her how he needed her prayers—and their eyes met.

Lucy was covered with confusion. She was quite sure in that swift momentary glance that he had read her inmost thoughts. She was ashamed that he should know that she had been praying all this time that he should be strengthened and comforted and helped and picked up again when he fell, and that the enemy should be beaten down under his feet. She never looked at that end of the chapel again all the rest of the service.

It was over at last—the long, long Litany and the slow, faltering prayers: the men need not have been so restless, they would not hear them much longer. The old walls would echo another voice soon, and the feeble lips would be repeating another Litany elsewhere.

The old college chapel was full of echoes and shadows; there would be another shadow shortly, and the echo of a tremulous, quavering voice would join those other ancient echoes in the roof. It was a dark, gloomy old chapel; it had been built for hundreds of years, and it was full of old memories. Every bench and stall and desk had a memory of its own, stretching back, far back, into quite early ages—memories of old Masters and Fellows and scholars and undergraduates who had worshipped there through, oh! so many generations.

There was a musty smell of old Masters rising up from the vaults beneath and pervading the chapel, and in the ante-chapel beyond there were monuments on the walls, and brasses—quite lovely old brasses—on the pavement, and great hideous tombs of long dead and gone Masters and Fellows. It was touching to see how they were forgotten after a generation or two; how even their very tomb-stones were hidden away in a corner, and covered up with organ pipes. There was the marble effigy of an old, old Master, whose learning and virtues were recited in a long Latin epitaph on an elaborate tablet hidden away behind the organ.

Everyone had forgotten him years ago, and his old monument was in the way, and so they had covered it up. Music is so much more delightful than old memories. They will all be swept away soon, and a new chapel will be built. There will be no old memories and old ghosts and old storied windows, no decaying woodwork or musty odour of old Masters. It will all be fresh and bright and sweet-smelling and shiny as new paint and varnish can make it, and there will be a new organ with electric stops. It will be dark and shadowy no longer; the old echoes and the old ghosts will all be scared away—they will vanish quite away in the blaze of the new electric lamps with which the chapel will be lighted.

Lucy vanished out of the college chapel almost as rapidly as the ghosts will by-and-by. She did not linger in the cloisters to-day. She hurried back to the lodge, and left Cousin Mary and the Master's wife to toddle back beside the Master.

'How do you think your uncle looks to-day, my dear?' the old lady asked Lucy when they had got him safely back to the lodge, and had put him in his great armchair, and given him some wine.

There was a shade of anxiety in her voice as she asked the question. Lucy hadn't seen the Master for a week, so she might have been expected to notice any change in him.

'Oh, I think he looks lovely, aunt! He walked back from chapel quite strong.'

Mrs. Rae shook her head; she was not quite convinced.

'There were two of us supporting him, my dear, one on either side, and I thought he leant rather heavily.'

He had nearly crushed the poor little soul into the ground; she could not have supported his weight a dozen steps more.

'Perhaps you are not so strong yourself to-day, auntie dear; you are looking pale. Most likely the weakness is yours, and you are not so well able to bear his weight. He always leans heavily; I often wonder how you and Mary can keep him up!'

'Perhaps so, my dear. I hope it may be so!' But still the cloud on the dear old face did not quite vanish. 'I fancied that his reading in chapel was slower to-day than usual—that his voice was weak. Did you notice it?'

'Oh yes; I noticed that he read lovely! I never heard him read so well as he read to-day.'

'You really think so? I am very glad! The fault must be in me. I don't think I am quite so strong to-day—I can't expect to be at my age; but I am very glad there is nothing unusual the matter with the Master. You would have been quite sure to have noticed it, my dear, if there had been, as you haven't seen him for a week.'

She kissed that mendacious little Lucy and tottered out of the room. She was very feeble to-day—perhaps the Master's weight had been too much for her; but there was quite a glad smile on her patient face. She was so happy, the brave old soul, to feel that the weakness was hers, not his.

Wyatt Edgell went back straight from chapel to his own rooms. He met Eric coming out of chapel, and they went back together.

'Where have I seen that girl before?' he asked Eric when they got back to the room.

'Oh, you've often seen her in chapel. She's the Master's niece, or grand-niece, or something of the kind,' said Eric evasively.

But the other was not so easily put off.

'I have seen her somewhere else, besides in chapel,' he said thoughtfully. 'I've seen her in this room. I've seen her beside my bed. Good heavens! Wattles, you didn't let that girl in—when—when——'

'When you weren't quite yourself, old man,' said Eric cheerfully, filling up the gap. 'What on earth should the Master's niece come in here for? Be reasonable, and don't ask such foolish things!'

'Foolish or not, I'll be hanged if I didn't see her in this room, standing where you stand now! You may as well tell the truth, Wattles. You may as well say you called her in and showed her the spectacle!'

He was a very determined-looking young man, and he didn't look like one to be trifled with, as he stood with his back to the empty fireplace, leaning against the mantelpiece, and his great hands stuck down well in his pockets.

'Dear old man, you may take my word for it: I did not call her in; I should as soon have thought of calling the Master in!'

'I wish to Heaven you had called the Master in—I should have known the worst then; but for this girl to see me—in—in that state!'

He paused and groaned, and two upright lines came out on his forehead.

'You take too much for granted, old man,' said the other; but he couldn't put any heartiness into his voice. 'Haven't I told you that not a soul in the college but Brannan and myself came into the room—while—while you were ill?'

'Yes,' said the other moodily—'not a soul in the college; but this girl from Newnham came in. I'll swear it! I saw it in her eyes.'

It was no use Eric pretending. Edgell was not in a mood to be trifled with. He was a great big, determined fellow. He could have taken Eric up and flung him to the other end of the room with the same ease with which he had flung the pillow.

'Go on,' he said moodily; 'go on, and tell me all about it. Tell me why this girl came in, and the spectacle she saw. Let me know exactly the degradation to which I have sunk!'

There was no help for it. Eric had to tell him all about Lucy's visit—Lucy's second visit; he didn't say anything about the first. How could he tell the poor fellow that she had come in at that dreadful time; that it was her hands that had wiped up all the traces of his crime; that it was she who had helped him when he had put those stitches in that gaping wound in his throat!

Eric told him quite enough. His head had fallen forward on his breast, and he looked a picture of despondency. A despondent giant of six feet, with a great broad chest, and big muscular limbs, and a splendid head splendidly set on a splendid full white throat—it was muffled up now, but it was as white and shapely as a woman's beneath the crisp, close-cut whisker curling down below the cheek. His chin and his great square jaw were close-shaven, but there was a thin, slight, crisp moustache on his upper lip, and his short hair curled crisply at the edges. He wore it parted in the middle, not very neatly parted, and tossed back off his forehead. Everything about him denoted strength and courage—such a man could not be despondent long.

'Then she knows the worst,' he said—'the very worst. There is nothing else she has got to learn about me. There is only one thing to be done, Wattles, with a girl who knows so much about me: I must marry her. You must introduce me again, old man, and I shall make her an offer, and—and she will marry me.'

His gloom and depression had quite gone, and he was smiling again. He was a delightful fellow when he smiled. Not a man in the college could resist that delightful smile; it disarmed the wrath of all the Dons, and it won the hearts of bed-makers.

'Marry her!' said Eric, turning quite pale. 'Dear old man, don't be in such a hurry. Think it over. She isn't the sort of woman for you, Edgell.'

Wyatt Edgell laughed. His laugh was a full-blown edition of his smile; but Gwatkin looked serious.

'Perhaps you'll tell me, Wattles, what is the sort of woman for me.'

'Oh, I wouldn't pretend to say; only, old man, don't trifle with this poor little thing. She's the sort of girl to break her heart for a man. I wouldn't break her heart if I were you.'

'Perhaps she'll break mine,' said Edgell dryly; and then he sat down and ate his lunch which the bed-maker had already spread out on the table.

It was a very nice college lunch. It was not tinned beef, or brawn, or tongue, or any questionable dainty that had been soldered up a year or two in a metal case. It was a lovely head and shoulders of salmon, and it had been judiciously pickled, and there was cucumber cut up in a dish—little delicate flakes of cucumber which Edgell ate with the healthy returning appetite of a man who had long been denied this delicacy.

The salmon was followed by a chicken and a ham, to which he also applied himself with the same zest. The edge was quite taken off his appetite, when Eric pushed these things aside and set a jelly just freshly turned out of a mould before him.

'I don't want any of that stuff,' he said, and he pushed over his glass in the direction of the claret.

'I don't think I'd take any more, old man,' said Eric; 'you've already had four glasses. I wouldn't have any more. Have a soda?'

'I'll be hanged if I do!' said the other doggedly, 'unless you put some brandy in it. I must have a nip of brandy, Wattles. I'm sure that cucumber has disagreed with me. I haven't had any cucumber for an age, and it never did agree with me.'

Eric got up and unlocked a cupboard, and took out a liqueur-bottle more than half full of brandy, and poured a small—a very small—quantity into a glass, and filled it up with seltzer-water.

He had put the bottle back into the cupboard and the key into his pocket, and was putting on his gown to go out. He always took a service somewhere in the country, or did some open-air preaching on Sunday afternoons, and he was in a hurry to get away.

'I wish you'd leave that key behind you, Wattles,' Edgell called out when he got to the door. 'That confounded cucumber or the pickled salmon has disagreed with me. I may want the key before you come back.'

Eric took the key out of his pocket reluctantly and laid it on the mantelpiece.

'You'll be careful, old man,' he said; 'you'll be sure to be careful. Remember——'

'Shut up!' said the other angrily. 'Do you think I'm such a fool?'

Eric went out and shut the door. When he came back two hours later the liqueur-bottle was on the table empty, and Edgell was breathing heavily on the floor.

It was all that confounded pickled salmon and cucumber!

CHAPTER XI.

IN THE FELLOWS' GARDEN.

That mendacious little Lucy, in spite of all her assurances to the Master's wife, was a little anxious about the Master. He had not taken his dinner with his usual appetite; he had scarcely eaten a morsel, and he had not had his usual nap after.

He had left half the wine in his glass, and he had got up from the table earlier than usual; but he had not fallen asleep in his chair after, as was his wont. He had sat talking to Lucy all the afternoon about the old time. His memory was wonderfully clear about the things that had happened, oh! so long ago—more than half a century before she was born—and he talked to her about them as if they had happened yesterday.

He was always so glad to see Cousin Dick's little daughter; she brought back the past to him, and seemed a link between the old far-off time and the present. He recalled to-day his very earliest years, his first remembrances. He recalled the time when his brother Dick carried him on his shoulders to the fair.

'It was Midsummer Fair, my dear,' he explained, 'and your father left off work early; he was very fond of fairs, and junketings, and wrestling matches. He liked bull-baiting, too. I mind the bull-ring at the end of the village on a piece of waste ground; I dare say it is there now. I've seen many a bull baited there in my day. There was never a fair within ten miles but your father was there in his best, with a flower in his button-hole—he always wore a flower in the button-hole of his plum-coloured coat. I remember that coat well; it had gilt buttons, and he wore a waistcoat to match, with two rows of buttons on either side—it was the fashion then, my dear. He carried me on his shoulder all the way to the fair; it was held on the green; there was a large green in the middle of the village in those days, but it is built over now; things have altered since then.'

The old Master shook his head and sighed. He hated changes of any kind; he would have liked the world to go on in the same old grooves for ever. He was silent for some time, and his watchful women-folk thought he was going to sleep—that he would have his after-dinner nap, after all; but he was only thinking. Those old chambers of memory were unlocked, and the old faces of his youth were crowding around him.

'Yes,' he said presently, brightening up, 'your mother was there, too, my dear. Dick met her in a dancing-booth. She wouldn't look at Dick at first, she had so many sweethearts. She was a proud little thing, with a spirit of her own; she nearly broke Dick's heart before he married her, but she made him a good wife—a good wife and a good mother, and always in her place in church, and bringing her children up to work and to fear God. I don't know that women do more in these days when they learn so many things.'

Lucy couldn't help thinking of that motion in the House of Commons, which was carried with such an overwhelming majority, that was to admit women to practise at the Bar and in the Church, to say nothing of those other learned professions that were already practically open.

The old Master's views were very, very old-fashioned; the world had made rapid strides while he had been sitting in his armchair and reading his Sunday Litanies in that musty old college chapel.

'Your father had a spirit of his own, too, my dear,' the old man babbled on with quite surprising vigour—these old memories made him quite young again; 'he wouldn't stay there to be slighted, with all the neighbours looking on. He left your mother going round with a young spark who had come down from London, and with me on his shoulder he went through the fair. I mind the booths quite well, with the gilt gingerbread, and the toys, and the trumpets, and the drums, and the merry-go-rounds. There was a show with a fat woman—I have never forgotten that fat woman. I have never seen anything like her since. There was a dwarf there, too—the smallest dwarf that was ever seen. I remember him strutting about the stage with his little sword; he wore a sword, and a gold-laced coat, and a cocked hat. The fat lady took his arm when the performance was over—she had to stoop down to do it, and he had to stretch up. I shall never forget seeing them go off the stage, arm-in-arm—the funniest sight I have ever seen—or how the people in the show laughed and clapped their hands when the showman made a ridiculous speech as they went out. "That's the way they go to church every Sunday of their lives!" he said, pointing after them. I believed him, if the crowd didn't, and for years after I used to watch the church door to see them coming in; but I have never seen them since.'

Lucy was so anxious about the old Master that when she went for her lesson to the Tutor's rooms the next day she could do nothing but talk about him.

The Tutor was anxious too, perhaps, in another way. He had noticed a change in the Master, and he went over to the lodge with her as soon as the lesson was over.

The Master was very feeble to-day, but he was up, and downstairs, and he was talking about going out into the garden. He was very fond of the old Fellows' Garden, and the seat beneath the walnut-tree—a sunny seat in the winter, a shady seat in the summer. It was shady now, but the garden was full of sunshine; the lilacs were in bloom, and the laburnums were a blaze of gold, and the thorn-tree was white with may. It was the blossoming time of the year, and everything was at its prime.

The Tutor took him out on his arm and sat him down on his old seat. He noticed how heavily he leant upon him as he tottered feebly across the grass. He would have crushed a woman with his weight. The Master's wife came out too, and sat by his side, with his hand in hers, and Lucy walked with the Tutor in the shady, winding paths beneath the trees. The trees were all old and gnarled, and some had broken down with age, and were propped up. The borders were full of old-fashioned flowers—perennials that went down into the earth every winter, and came up again every spring. There was nothing new here.

The Senior Tutor, as he walked by Lucy's side, was thinking how he should change all this by-and-by. He would cut down those useless old trees, and he would have the turf rolled and laid out for tennis. Nothing could be better for Lucy than tennis, and she could invite her Newnham friends. Those old flower borders should be all dug up, and some standard rose-trees planted. He would have nothing but first-rate sorts, the very latest. He would do away with that vulgar cabbage rose in the corner, and that poor, shabby little pale blush that hung in clusters on the wall. It had hung there for so many years; it was quite time it should be cleared away. It seemed a pity to lose time. There were so many improvements to be made; it seemed a pity not to begin now.

Looking across the grass and the sunshine at the old stooping figure under the walnut-tree—it was bent more than usual to-day—he could not but feel that the time was not far off when it would be there no longer. There was nothing pathetic in the sight to him. He had waited for the place—the Master's place—so long. If he waited much longer he would be feeble and old and white-haired, too.

There is little pathos in the young. The sad realities of life touch only those who know something about them. One must have suffered one's self to have any sympathy with suffering.

Lucy, looking across the sunshine, was touched, in spite of herself, at the group under the walnut-tree. It didn't affect her as it affected the Tutor. It would be no gain to her if the old Master were to die; it would mean loss and change and being driven out again homeless into the wide world.

But it was not this consideration that moved her. She was touched by the tender picture of the two brave, patient old souls sitting hand-in-hand in that calm closing evening of their life.

Here was a love that Lucy knew nothing about—a love that had weathered all the storms of life, and was burning brightly at its close. Riches and honour and learning were nothing to it. They were the Master's still, but they were nothing beside love. He would leave these behind him, but love would cling to him out of time. He wouldn't shake that off when he shook off everything else.

Lucy didn't put the idea into words, but it touched her; and then, strangely enough, rose up before her the face of the man who had sat on the last seat in the chapel and had caught her looking at him. It was quite ridiculous to think of Wyatt Edgell at such a moment; there was nothing here to remind her of him.

There was an old disused greenhouse at the end of the Fellows' garden. Nothing had grown in it for years. A neglected vine was dropping down from the roof in one corner, and a great deal of the glass was broken, and the woodwork was decayed and rotting. The Tutor shook the door as he passed, and it opened, and he paused and looked in.

'I think we must have this place rebuilt,' he said, thinking aloud. 'You would like a greenhouse. We must get some ferns and palms and foliage plants. Do you like foliage plants?'

'Not much,' Lucy said. She could not think what he meant by appealing to her. 'I like flowers best. I don't care for leaves. I'm afraid my taste is very vulgar. I like geraniums, and mignonette, and camellias; I am very fond of camellias. We used to have some in our greenhouse at home.'

'You can keep as many as you like here,' he said. 'We will get all the varieties there are, and you can have geraniums in flower all the year round.'

He shut the door, and they walked down the path together, while Lucy wondered what he could mean. It would be scarcely worth while to do up the old greenhouse and fill it with flowers when it was not likely she would be there another spring to see it.

In the long path they met Cousin Mary coming towards them. She looked rather pale and worn in the sunshine, and she had on a most unbecoming garden-hat. It had been hanging up in the hall all the winter; it might have been hanging there for years, and it was battered out of all shape. There was not a bed-maker in the college that would have worn it.

The Tutor had never noticed before how gray her hair had grown, and that there were crow's-feet round her eyes, and that her cheeks were faded. She had not changed lately. She had looked like this for years, getting a little grayer every year, and adding a line or two beneath her eyes, but he had never noticed it before. He was very fond of her still; he had the highest opinion of Mary Rae, but he was very glad that Lucy had come in time—just in time—to save him from throwing himself away.

'Mr. Colville is going to have the old greenhouse done up, Mary,' Lucy shouted to her when she was quite a dozen paces away. 'He's going to have camellias and geraniums all the year round; but perhaps you don't like camellias.'

The Senior Tutor for once in his life blushed. It was not for Mary he was going to have those geraniums in perennial bloom.

'I don't think it's worth it,' said Mary bluntly—'at least, not for us. We shall soon be going away.' And she looked in the direction of the walnut-tree beneath which the old Master and his wife were still sitting.

'That should make no change,' the Tutor said awkwardly; 'the lodge would be still your home.'

He grew ridiculously red, and he did not dare to look Mary in the face.

'We need not talk about that yet,' she said with a smile; 'the dear Master is still with us. I came to ask you to help him in; he has sat there long enough. He is not so strong to-day; I can't manage him alone.'

'I should think not!' said the Tutor, and he hurried off across the grass and took the old Master back to the lodge.

Lucy did not go in; she slipped through the garden-door into the court, and hurried back to Newnham. She had promised to drink tea in a girl's room, and she was already half an hour late.

She went back by way of the Fens, and when she was near the bridge she saw some figures she thought she knew crossing it, and they stopped while she came up, and looked down into the water.

It was Pamela Gwatkin and her brother, and there was another man with him. She had never seen Pamela with her brother before, and she was struck as she came up to them with the points of difference between them.

Being twins, they ought to have been exactly alike. Eric was short, and Pamela was tall—tall and graceful and slender, as a girl ought to be, with a proud, self-reliant bearing that is peculiar to the students of a college for women. Eric was not only short, but he was stout, and not at all graceful, and he had no bearing to speak of. He was an awkward, well-meaning, commonplace fellow. There was nothing remarkable about him whatever, except that he was Pamela's twin brother. This in his case was a decided disadvantage—the ingredients hadn't been properly mixed. All the masculine characteristics had gone to Pamela, and the tender, endearing qualities to her brother. He saw Lucy come tearing along across the Fen, and he took off his hat as she came up to him.

'You have met Eric before,' said Pamela, by way of introduction.

She was looking very pink and white and cool as she stood there on the bridge looking down into the dark shady water, and Lucy had run herself into a fever, and was hot and flushed, and looking 'hideous,' as she told herself.

'Oh yes,' she panted—she was quite out of breath with running in the hot sun—'I have met Mr. Gwatkin before.'

She didn't see, until Pamela's brother introduced her, that the other man leaning over the bridge was Wyatt Edgell. She was so flustered with running, and so taken by surprise, that she blushed like a peony.

She felt she was blushing furiously, and that Pamela, cool and critical and self-possessed, was watching her. Oh, how she hated herself for not being cool and dignified and self-possessed like other people!

They walked back over the Fen and through the lane to Newnham in couples, Lucy and Wyatt Edgell in front, Pamela and her brother behind. Lucy would have given the world to have reversed the order, but the man took his place by her side, and he wouldn't go away until he left her at the gate of Newnham.

'You have met me before, Miss Rae, as well as Gwatkin,' he said, as he walked by Lucy's side. 'I believe he invited you in to see the spectacle.'

'He didn't invite me in at all,' Lucy said hotly; 'I came in. You were very ill when I saw you; I did not expect you would get well so soon.'

'No?' he said indifferently, 'I suppose not. It did not much matter either way.'

'It mattered a great deal!' she said sharply. She was very angry with him for speaking in that absurd way—absurd and ungrateful—considering what a trouble he had been to his friends. 'It mattered a great deal to Mr. Gwatkin. Oh, you don't know how anxious he was about you! He saved your life.'

'Yes,' he said in his slow, indifferent way, flicking with his cane at the nettles in the hedge; 'I believe he did. It was rather a pity he should have taken so much trouble, but I suppose he liked it. I believe he didn't get off his knees all one night. He's always glad of an excuse for getting on his knees.'

And then he laughed. It was such a delightful laugh that it ought to have been infectious, but Lucy looked grave.

'I suppose he was on his knees when you came in?' he said.

'Yes,' said Lucy shortly, but she didn't tell him that she had knelt down beside Eric and prayed that the life he valued so little might be spared. She was very angry with him; she could only trust herself to say 'Yes.'

'Oh, he is a good fellow is Wattles, but he has his little crazes.'

'He is a splendid fellow!' said Lucy warmly.

She was ashamed of her warmth the moment after she had said it, but they had reached the gate of Newnham by this time, and she was glad to say 'Good-bye' and run away. She left him standing at the gate waiting for the others to come up, while quite a dozen girls on the lawn were looking at him and admiring him, and making up all sorts of fine stories in their heads about him.

If they had only known what Lucy knew about him they would have made up a great deal more.

CHAPTER XII.

AN UGLY FALL.

There was a row royal when Pamela got back to Newnham. She told Lucy that her conduct was disgraceful, and that if it came to the ears of the Dons she would be 'hauled.'

There had been several girls 'hauled' lately for the same offence—walking with an undergraduate to the very gate of the college.

Lucy mildly suggested that she was not exactly alone, that Pamela and her brother were with her, and that she herself, when she came up to her on the bridge, was walking in the young man's society.

'You forget that Eric was with me,' Pamela replied sharply. 'It makes all the difference if you have a brother, or any male relative, with you; but to be walking alone, tearing along at the rate you were, and talking confidentially—anyone could see that you were talking confidentially—dozens of girls have been sent down for less than that!'

Lucy wasn't 'hauled,' and she wasn't 'sent down'; but Pamela behaved like a bear to her for the remainder of the term.

Lucy was so anxious about the Master that she went over to the lodge the next day directly after lunch. Cousin Mary was out; she had left him sitting in his chair taking his after-dinner nap as usual, and she had gone out. He woke up directly Lucy came in, and began to talk to her about her father and the old time. She was very glad that she had not brought Pamela in with her, or any of the Newnham girls, as she sometimes did. He would have told them that ridiculous story that was running in his mind, how his brother Dick had met her mother at a dancing-booth at the fair. He would have dwelt on all the homely details of their humble history. It would have been all over Newnham the next day that her father was a ploughman, and her mother kept a stall in the butter-market. Annabel Crewe, who had a fine taste for caricature, would have drawn delightful pictures of Lucy's progenitors—a lovely old man in a smock-frock with straw round his legs, and a milkmaid with her pail!

She couldn't divert the Master's attention from this ridiculous topic. He had forgotten all about the things that had happened in later years, and had gone back in memory to the old familiar scenes and faces of his youth. His eyes were brighter to-day, and he was more restless than usual; he wanted to go out into the garden and sit in his accustomed seat on the lawn. It was such a perfect May day that no wonder he wanted to get out of that dark, gloomy old room, with the stuffy moreen curtains over the windows, and the faded carpets, and the worm-eaten, old-fashioned furniture, and the musty old books, into the sweet summer sunshine, where everything was fresh and new.

There was nothing dark and gloomy and oppressive out there in that sweet leafy Fellows' garden. The lilacs were in their prime, pale puce and white and purple, every delightful indescribable hue, and the laburnum was dropping gold upon the grass. There was a cuckoo somewhere, calling, and the thrushes were singing, and the blackbird's note was still shrill and clear. It would soon be hoarse as a raven's, and the thrush would be silent, and the cuckoo would have altered his tune, and the lilac would have faded, and the gold of the gleaming, down-dropping laburnums would have turned to gray—and—and he might not be here to see it. If he wanted to enjoy the fleeting sunshine and the flying blossoms of the year, there was no time like the present.

The Master didn't exactly put it in this way, but he was impatient to be out in the garden, in his old seat, and he wouldn't wait a minute longer for anybody.

If Mary wasn't there he would go without her.

There are none so impatient as the old. The young have plenty of time to spare—they have their life before them; but the old have not a minute to lose. The Master went out as usual, leaning on the arm that had supported him so many years, that had never failed him yet. Mrs. Rae and Lucy took him out between them. He walked in his slow accustomed way, leaning rather heavily on these two frail props until he reached his seat beneath the walnut-tree, and here he ought to have sat down.

But he didn't sit down. He insisted on going farther; he insisted on going down the path to the greenhouse. Mary had been saying something about it, repeating what the Tutor had said yesterday about having it done up and turned to some account, and the Master would not be satisfied until he had seen it. He must be consulted about it; nothing should be done in the gardens without his consent. He had been worrying about it all night.

He had got half-way down the path, when Lucy fancied he was beginning to lean heavily, more heavily than she could bear, though she put out all her strength. There was not a seat near, but she stopped and begged the Master to rest awhile. He was so anxious to see the greenhouse that he would not listen to her. He never thought of the women who were being weighed down with his great weight. He was as eager and determined as a child.

'I am sure, aunt, you are not strong enough to keep him up,' Lucy said in despair; she was getting really frightened. 'We must get someone to help him back. Oh, if someone would only come in!'

There was not a gardener in sight, and it was not likely that anyone would come in. Nobody but the Fellows ever walked in that garden.

The Master tottered on, feebler at every step; but he would not be kept back, and the two frightened women held him up as well as they could. He seemed to want more support every step he took; he was as feeble and helpless as a child, but still he pressed on. Lucy was sure she couldn't bear the strain a minute longer, and the dear old mistress was straining with all her might to keep up with him. She was putting out all her strength. It wasn't much to put out at the best, but she didn't keep back a feather weight. Oh, if someone would only come!

They came in sight of that wretched greenhouse at last, and here the Master stopped. He didn't exactly stop, but he tottered forward, and Lucy with a supreme effort kept him up, and with all his weight upon her he swayed to and fro, and before she knew what was happening he had slipped through her arms to the ground. He lay on the path, as he fell, all of a heap. He had no power to help himself, and he lay panting and breathing heavily as he had fallen, and the women stood beside him wringing their hands.

Lucy didn't stand beside him long. There was a door in the wall beside the greenhouse that led out into one of the courts, and she flew over to it. Fortunately the door was unlocked. Lucy looked eagerly round the deserted court and raised her feeble cry for help. It was such a feeble, piteous cry; it was like a wail. A man sitting reading at an open window looked out at that strange sound, and Lucy called to him: 'Oh, come, come, do come!'

The man didn't stay to ask what had happened; he was at Lucy's side in another moment, and she took him in through the open door to where the Master lay. It was Wyatt Edgell. A gyp coming across the court had heard the cry for help, and between them they bore the Master back to the lodge.

When Mary Rae came in she found a little anxious group gathered round him, and Wyatt Edgell was trying to reassure the frightened women. Nothing very serious had happened. No bones were broken, but the Master was very much shaken, and he was not quite himself. Wyatt Edgell stayed with him until the doctor had come, and had ascertained that things were not very bad—not so bad as they might have been—and had calmed the fears of the women; and then Lucy was so shaken that he walked back with her to Newnham.

Lucy certainly would have been 'hauled' if the Dons had seen her walking back leaning heavily on an undergraduate's arm. She would have been invited to an interview with the authorities in the Principal's room, and she would have received a caution, perhaps a reprimand, and she would have been very lucky if nothing worse had happened. Lucy forgot all about the Dons and Pamela's warning. She only thought about that poor old man at the lodge.

'I don't think he will ever get over this,' she said, or rather sobbed. She was not herself at all. She was such a tearful, frightened little Lucy. She was not in the least like a Stoic.

'I am afraid not,' said Edgell. 'The Master has been failing for some time. The men all remarked that he would never read the Litany again in chapel.'

'You think he is so bad as that?' Lucy said tearfully.

'Yes, quite. Think of his age. His time must come some day, and he has lived longer than most men. You could not expect him, in any case, to live for many months longer.'

'No,' said Lucy sadly; and then he saw the tears dropping down her pale face. He could not believe she was weeping for that old, old man whose time had come, and who was a stranger to her till yesterday.

'What will you do when he is gone?' he asked abruptly.

'Do? I don't know—I have not thought. I shall stay at Newnham, I suppose, two years; I shall not be able to afford three; and then—and then I shall go out as a governess.'

'You shall never go out as a governess!' said Edgell with an oath.

Lucy looked at him, frightened and bewildered; she couldn't think what he meant, and then she broke down and began to cry.

'Dear Miss Rae—Lucy!' he said, and then he stopped and looked at the girl. He would have liked to take her in his arms, but there were several Newnham girls all hurrying down the road, and they looked at him, and they looked at Lucy. Some of them blushed, and some turned pale, and all were shocked. It was a dreadful precedent.

The atmosphere of Newnham revived Lucy, and she paused at the gate and looked up into his face with a little white smile.

'I am very stupid,' she said, 'but the Master frightened me so much, and I am not quite myself.'

He held her hand longer than he need have done, and he looked down into the small white face with a smile of ownership and protection that was quite new to Lucy. Nobody had ever looked in her eyes like that before, and, instead of drawing her hand away, Lucy hung her head and blushed like a poppy.

'Shall I bring you word how the Master is the first thing in the morning?' he said, still holding her hand; 'how early will you be out in the lane if I come?'

'Oh, as early as you like; seven o'clock!'

And so Lucy made her first appointment to meet Wyatt Edgell.

CHAPTER XIII.

SLIPPING AWAY.

When Lucy went out into the road outside the gates of the college, before seven o'clock the next morning, Wyatt Edgell was already there waiting for her. It is a short, narrow road, or lane, and it leads to nowhere, unless Selwyn College be considered anywhere. It has been the privilege of the students of Selwyn to use this road as a shortcut to their college, but it will not be their privilege much longer.

The road is now the private property of the authorities of Newnham, and a new wing connecting the old and the new halls will be built across the road, and the jealous walls that shut out the grounds from masculine eyes will be thrown down, and the old dusty lane will be covered with smooth, green turf, and it will be a thoroughfare no longer for the foot of man to pass over.

Perhaps they will restore again the old fortifications. There was a Roman camp here once, and a battle ditch running all the way to Grantchester. Every inch of ground here is classic, and strewn with remains of those old Romans who brought us all the gentler arts. Perhaps they brought the Muses with them and planted them at Newnham?

There was an old Roman dug up the other day, four feet beneath the surface, a noble skeleton, six feet six in length. The whole earth teems with ancient coins and pottery and Roman relics. They will have to build a museum in the new wing to preserve the 'finds' that are unearthed in digging its foundations.

Lucy was quite indifferent to the Romans. She would rather, if she had had the choice, have met one of their old ghosts in the lane than one of the Dons of Newnham taking her morning walk. She looked fearfully up and down the road when she got outside the gate, but there were only some Selwyn men going down to the bathing sheds; there was not a girl in sight.

Wyatt Edgell was walking up and down the path flicking at the sweetbriar hedge as he passed, and his eyes were looking down on the ground. He was so lost in thought that he did not see Lucy till he heard her little cry, and she ran to meet him.

'Oh!' she cried, a little pale and breathless, 'how is the Master? Is he worse this morning?'

She augured badly from Edgell's downcast look.

'Not worse,' he said; 'at least, I hope not worse, but I fear not better. When I inquired at the lodge when the gates were opened at six o'clock, they told me the Master had had a very disturbed night, that he had not slept at all, but that he did not appear to be in any pain. Your cousin has been up with him all night, and Mrs. Rae.'

'I was sure she would not leave him,' said the girl, the tears filling her eyes. She was thinking of the anguish in that kind old face when the Master slipped through her feeble arms. 'I think I ought to go over at once and relieve her; she must be worn out.'

Lucy didn't stay to think. She walked back to St. Benedict's with the undergraduate who had brought her the news; she didn't even stay to fetch her gloves. She walked down by his side in the morning sunshine, just as she had hurried out of her room, with a ridiculous little tennis-cap on her head and her ungloved hands. Two Newnham girls who were returning from an early—a very early—walk looked shocked, as well they might be, and some rude Selwyn men whistled as they passed. They were only jealous that she was not taking a morning walk with them.

Lucy found the watchers still up when they reached the lodge. Mrs. Rae would not be persuaded to lie down, and she was looking dreadfully tired and worn out. She looked ten years older, Lucy thought, this morning, and her poor face was as white as her hair. Mary looked pale, too. Perhaps it was the air of that close room that was still darkened; and there was a shade of anxiety under her eyes, but she would not own to being tired. She could stay up a week, if necessary.

The Master had fallen into a doze; but Lucy's light footstep or the whisper of their voices reached him, and he woke up when she came in. Lucy went over to him and laid her warm, moist hand on his, and the touch seemed to revive him.

'Is the milking over?' he asked, turning upon her his pale-blue eyes with that strange brightness in them that is peculiar to the very old. 'I have heard the cows lowing all night for the calves. You have taken the calves away?'

'It is Lucy, uncle,' she said, stroking his hand softly—'little Lucy, not Lucy's mother——' She was going to say 'grandmother,' but she thought 'mother' would humour his fancy best.

'Yes, yes: I know you, my dear. I have been watching for you all the night. You must not go away again for so long; they don't understand me here as you do. Where's Dick?'

'He is gone, uncle,' she said softly. She did not like to say that he was dead.

'Gone? Where is he gone? He was here just now. Is he in the field or in the barn? Send him to me when he comes in, my dear.'

Lucy turned away pale and trembling. She could not bear it; he did not recognise her in the least.

The Tutor came in while she was there, and went over to the bed; but the Master took him for Dick—the brother who had died fifty years ago.

His eyes lighted up when the Tutor came in, and with a strange, eager interest he asked him questions about the crops and the farm. All the later associations of his life had quite faded from his memory, and he had gone back to the scenes and faces of his youth.

The Tutor turned away from the bed with a sigh. He had waited for this half his life. He had looked forward so long as he could remember to being Master of St. Benedict's, and now, when it seemed within his grasp, he turned from it with a sigh. What was it, after all, this shadow he was grasping? Wealth, honour, position, it would all slip through his hands by-and-by, as it had slipped through the hands of the old scholar on the bed: all, everything, that had taken a lifetime—a long lifetime—to gain, would slip away, and there would be nothing left but old memories. Everything would fail; and he would go back to the old humble time, and the dear faces—if happily he had dear faces to go back to. There would be nothing left—nothing that he could carry away with him—but those old tender memories.

The Tutor turned away from the bed and went out of the room. On the landing outside he saw Lucy sitting in the window-seat weeping. The tears were in his own eyes, and he could not trust himself to speak. He went over, and took Lucy's hand, and drew her towards him.

'Oh,' she murmured through her tears, 'he does not know me the least bit. He thinks I am his brother Dick's wife.'

'And he takes me for Dick,' said the Tutor, with an involuntary smile, pressing the little warm hand he held. 'We shall all come to it, my dear, some day—to the vanishing-point, where everything slips away from us but the memories of our youth. Well for us at that time if we have nothing but innocent memories of kindly deeds and loving faces—if we have no regrets, no sorrow, no remorse! Perhaps it is the happiest lot to have the slate wiped clean of all the storms and passions of later years, and to go back at the last, and to take away with us only the memory of the old innocent early days.'

He was a good deal moved. He might have committed dreadful crimes since the days of his innocent youth, instead of being a grave, sober, reverend Tutor of a college.

'You don't think he will ever be better?' Lucy sobbed.

'I don't think, even if his life is prolonged, that his mind will ever be clear again. I fear it has gone, quite gone. Perhaps it is better so: he will pass away happier; he will have no regrets; he will leave nothing behind.'

Lucy sat sobbing in the window-seat. If she had been older she would not have wept so freely: the young have so many tears to spare.

''There is nothing to regret,' he said tenderly, bending over the hand he still held. ''The dear Master has lived his life—a good life, and, I think, a happy one—and he will exchange it for a better and a happier. We have only to concern ourselves about those who are left—Mrs. Rae and your cousin. They must stay with us, Lucy; they must make the lodge their home. You must let them understand, dear'—here the Senior Tutor really pressed Lucy's hand, that he had held all the time he had been talking to her, and she had never once thought of drawing it away: he would have taken her in his arms, but the servants were coming up and down stairs—'you must let them quite understand,' he went on, 'that their home is here with us. I am sure we shall do everything to make them happy.'

Lucy hadn't the least idea what he meant.

She would have stayed at the lodge and taken her share of the nursing night and day, but the Tutor would not hear of it.

'You have got your work to do, my dear,' he said. He called her 'my dear' now quite naturally. 'You have all your work cut out before you to be ready for the examinations in June. You can't afford to risk breaking down for the sake of doing work that any woman can do. A trained nurse from Addenbroke's will do all, and more than all, you three dear anxious women together.'

He sent in a nurse from Addenbroke's during the morning, and Cousin Mary and the Master's wife were turned out of the room. It was quite time the Master's wife was turned out of the room, or there would have been two to nurse instead of one.

The nurse who had been sent from Addenbroke's Hospital to nurse the Master was the little fluffy nurse that had been brought by her brother to Wyatt Edgell's rooms after that miserable folly, and had kept his secret.

If Lucy didn't like trusting a foolish young man she knew nothing about to this flighty nurse, she was much more unwilling to trust this valuable life in her hands. She watched with mistrust, and a certain dull glow of impatience, this little bit of a creature turn the Master's wife out of the room, and reverse everything that had been done under Cousin Mary's directions.

The nurse from Addenbroke's pulled up the blinds and threw open the windows, and let in the balmy air of the sweet May morning, that everybody had been so anxious to keep out; and she threw off the heavy quilts, and took away the pillows, and did everything according to the latest fashion in nursing. If people do not choose to get well when all this is done for them, it is their own fault, and not the fault of the system.

Before Lucy went back to Newnham she went into the little room—her own room till she had left it for Newnham—where the Master's wife had gone to lie down to rest. She had chosen this room because it was near the Master's, and she would be within call.

Lucy insisted on undressing her and putting her to bed, and perjuring herself with fibs of the deepest dye to set her mind at rest.

'I never thought he would go before me,' the dear old soul murmured, when Lucy was undressing her. 'I always thought I should go first; and it has been such a comfort to me to think that Mary could fill my place so well. And now to think that he should be called away first!'

'Who said he would go first?' Lucy said in her reassuring manner. 'He is not at all likely to go before you, you poor dear! If you had been yourself, he would not have fallen. You had no strength left, so he slipped through your poor arms. You hadn't the strength of a baby. Anyone can see how you have been failing lately, and you think it is the Master.'

'And you think it was my fault he fell—that the weakness was not in him?' the poor trembling old creature asked eagerly. She was so anxious to believe Lucy, and the faint colour flushed up under her white skin.

'Of course it was. The doctor will not tell you it was, because he doesn't want to frighten you. Anyone can see that you are much weaker than the Master.'

There really seemed some truth in what Lucy said. The Master's wife was trembling all over like a leaf—she couldn't have got into bed without Lucy's help; but she was trembling with joy.

'God bless you, my dear!' she said, when the girl went away. 'You have made me so happy!'

Lucy went back to Newnham with a heavy heart. It seemed as if everything were slipping away from her. It is so hard for the young to realize the great change. She felt dimly that it was not far off—that this was, indeed, the beginning of the end. Anyone could have seen that.

But it was not the personal sorrow of it that moved her; there was a deeper pathos than death in the fidelity of the dear woman who clung to the old Master with a love stronger than death itself. She could not but think of the look of relief on the old tired face as she walked back to Newnham.

The girls remarked that Lucy looked pale at Hall—that is, those who took any interest in her. Pamela Gwatkin never looked her way. She sat at the 'High,' among the Dons; she never condescended to look down the hall to the table where the freshers sat.

Capability Stubbs came into her room after Hall, as she sat trying to work, and brought her in a cup of tea. The tea was very grateful to Lucy's overwrought nerves: it was the only thing that was nice about Miss Stubbs. Pamela Gwatkin had given her a cup of tea once or twice, but it tasted of tooth-powder. She had packed the tea and the tooth-powder in a biscuit-tin when she came up, and the lid had got off the tooth-powder box, and it had got mixed up with the tea. It would not have been political economy to have thrown it away.

'Nice scandal you've been making in the college!' observed Miss Stubbs cheerfully, as she handed Lucy the teacup. She had only brought a teacup; she considered saucers superfluous, unless one happened to be a kitten.

'Scandal!' said Lucy, aghast. 'What scandal have I been making?'

'Oh! it was rumoured you had eloped with a Selwyn man. Somebody saw you going off.'

'With a Selwyn man!' said Lucy with fine scorn. 'As if I should elope with a Selwyn man! If it had been St. Benedict's it would have been different.'

'Or Hall?' suggested Miss Stubbs, who was rumoured to have a cousin at Trinity Hall, or to know a girl who had.

'Ye—es; even Hall would have been better. Who set the ball rolling—Newnham Assurance?'

Lucy was much too angry with Pamela to call her by her name.

'No, it wasn't Assurance. She took the other side. She said if you were going to run away with—with a man, you would have had the self-respect to stop and put your gloves on first.'

CHAPTER XIV.

WYATT EDGELL.

Late on the evening of the day when Lucy was supposed by the students of Newnham to have eloped, the man she was said to have eloped with sat working in his college-room.

It was not a Selwyn man. The crest on the pocket of the blazer he was wearing was the crest of St. Benedict's. It was nearly the eve of the Mathematical Tripos; there were only a few days more, and, having lost all the early part of the term, Wyatt Edgell was sitting down now at the last minute to recover by a tremendous effort the ground he had lost. He had always been sure of a first; he had never yet taken a second class in any examination at school or college, and his name had generally stood first in the lists. The authorities of St. Benedict's had predicted that it would stand first now in the coming Tripos.

There would have been no doubt about it but for that ugly 'accident'—he called it an 'accident'—in the beginning of the term. He had not been himself since he came up this May term. He had been moody and taciturn, and subject to fits of depression. He had given up his wine-parties, and his club suppers and breakfasts, and he had shut himself up in his rooms and sported his oak. Everybody, Tutors and all, said he was working hard, and they 'let him alone'; but his bed-maker knew better! Bed-makers know so much more about a man than anyone else.

She fetched Gwatkin to him one morning, when she had come in and found him lying on the floor in a fit of delirium tremens. They kept the matter quiet between them and put him to bed, and the bed-maker gave out to all the men on her staircase that 'he was a-readin' hisself to death.'

It was not a very bad attack—it was not the first, but Gwatkin didn't know that at the time—there were no violent ravings, only mutterings and depression—dreadful depression. Gwatkin and the bed-maker looked after him during the morning, and towards noon he fell into a deep sleep. It didn't seem at all likely that he would wake for hours. The bed-maker had had some experience of such cases, and she knew that the fever would take eight or ten hours' sleep to spend itself, and then he would awake with shaking hands and a splitting headache, and have a fine time of it for a week.

Leaving him as she thought sleeping soundly, she went about her work. She had to clear the tables of the other men on the staircase, but before she went she took the precaution to fasten his oak, and to take the key to Gwatkin's rooms.

Gwatkin ran over as fast as he could to Edgell's rooms. He had given such strict injunctions that he was not to be left alone on any pretence. Run as fast as he could, he was only just in time. Had he been a minute later he would have been too late. He took the razor from the poor fellow's hand, and he bound up the wound he had made with it as he best could without assistance. He had not the heart to call for help, to reveal his miserable secret to the whole college. He did for him as he would have wished others to have done for himself if he had been in his place. He kept his secret.

There was a man on his own staircase who had a sister a nurse at Addenbroke's, and when he had done all he could for Edgell, and fastened his arms down to the bed, Gwatkin ran across the court and brought Brannan over. He had to let him into the secret; there was no help for it. He saw exactly how matters stood. He was in his third year, and it was not the first time that he had helped to cover up an act of undergraduate folly. Brannan went away to fetch his sister. He could promise her silence. Phyllis Brannan was as true as steel; but in his haste and agitation he had left the outer oak open, and Lucy came in.

Wyatt Edgell's secret had been faithfully kept by these men and women. Only one of them had committed a breach of trust—Lucy had told Pamela. She couldn't help it, she explained, if she had had to die for it the next day; but Pamela had held her tongue. Not a soul in the college guessed his secret—his dreadful secret. Everybody looked up to him, and praised him, and expected great things of him—everybody but his bed-maker.

She knew something about that last orgie. She had helped to put him to bed, and she had cleared away the small sodas the next morning. She smiled when she saw him settling down to work on the evening of the day when he had brought Lucy to the lodge from Newnham. 'A lot of readin' 'e'll get through,' she said, shaking her head as she went down the stairs with her basket under her shawl. "E'll be under the table, I reckon, when I come in in the mornin'.'

Eric Gwatkin was doubtful about him, too. He was more anxious about Edgell's Tripos than he was about his own Special. He couldn't rest before he went to bed without coming over and seeing if he was all right. He found his oak sported, and he had to knock a good many times before Edgell would let him in.

'Confound it——' he began, and then he saw Eric and stopped. 'Oh, it's you, Wattles!'

He didn't say it very graciously, and Eric was sorry he had disturbed him. He really looked in working trim. He had thrown off his coat, and he was sitting in his shirt-sleeves. He wore a flannel shirt, and the collar was open and showed his white throat and chest, as it had showed it that day when Lucy leaned over the bed and put on the wet bandage. It showed, too, what it had not shown on that day, when a scarf was thrown over the throat—an ugly scar extending for some inches beneath the left ear. It was still purple and red and discoloured—a hideous livid mark on the beautiful white skin.

Eric shuddered when he saw it. The sight of it always made him shudder to think what a near thing it was—what might have been! He could not understand how Edgell could bear to see it in the glass, could bear to uncover it, that others coming in might see it.

'I am sorry to disturb you, old man,' he said, looking round at the work on the table, and the books lying open before Edgell. 'I only looked round to see—if—if you were all right.'

'To see if I had cut my throat again,' said Edgell calmly.

There was a shade of bitterness in his voice, and his lips curled slightly with amusement or scorn, or both. They were beautiful clear-cut lips, full and tender as a woman's, and they had a way of curving when he spoke. They never quivered, they curved; and his nostrils dilated. It was a strong face, with a massive square jaw, but it had these nervous tricks.

'Very kind of you, Wattles,' he went on with a laugh; 'but I'm not going to repeat that performance again—at least, not for the present. I'm going in for my Trip—and—and I'm going to marry Miss Lucy.'

Gwatkin's face fell.

'I don't think this is a time to talk of marrying,' he said, with a certain hesitation in his voice, and the cloud on his plain, homely face deepening. 'The poor old Master is dying.'

'So much the more reason to talk about it. Lucy will want a home. She won't be able to stay up at Newnham, she tells me; she will have no one but her cousin Mary when the Master is dead, and the old lady. I think I shall ask her to-morrow. I should like her to feel that she will not be left friendless when the end comes.'

'I should wait till after the exam., if I were you. I shouldn't let anything interfere with the exam. You will have all your life to marry in.'

Edgell lay back in his chair and laughed good-naturedly at his Mentor.

'Anyone would think, Wattles, that you wanted to marry her yourself.'

There was no occasion for that very common-place-looking young man to blush so dreadfully.

'I only meant to advise you for your good,' he said awkwardly, and then he went over to the door and said good-night, but when he reached the door, and he had the handle in his hand, he paused irresolutely, and looked across the room at the man with the scar in his throat leaning back in the chair. The scar was dreadfully visible in that light. It seemed to have a charm for Gwatkin. He couldn't keep his eyes off it.

'What's up?' said Edgell, seeing that he paused by the door.

Eric came back to the table where Edgell was seated, and laid his hand on his shoulder, a friendly, unmistakable grip.

'Dear old man,' he said in a broken voice, and the other could see that his foolish weak lips were quivering, 'you won't mind my speaking my mind to you; you will forgive what I say?'

'Fire away!' said Edgell; but he didn't look at Gwatkin, he looked at the opposite wall.

'Before you go any farther—before you ask Lucy Rae to marry you—pause and consider——'

'I've already considered,' Edgell interrupted impatiently, and with his face still averted.

'You have not considered everything. You have thought only of yourself. You have not thought of her.'

'I have thought of her!'

'No, no; you have not thought of her in the way I mean. Bear with me, dear fellow. God knows I am saying this for your sake and hers. You have not thought of her as orphaned and friendless, having no one but you in the world, being bound up in you, having all her happiness dependent upon you. A little, tender, delicate creature, with no spirit of her own, who would suffer, and break her heart, and never complain——'

'What would she have to complain of?' Edgell interrupted savagely.

'God only knows!'

'You—you think I shall go over the old thing again—that——'

'Hush! For heaven's sake don't let us even suppose it! You haven't got to consider yourself in this matter, you have to consider her. Do you think it fair to ask her—to—to—forgive me, dear fellow—to ask her to risk it?'

Wyatt Edgell bowed his head.

'You have no faith in me,' he said moodily, with his head upon his breast and his brows knitted.

'I have every faith in you, dear fellow; but I want you to think of her. It is the chivalrous thing to do. Forgive me for saying it. Unless you felt that you could make her happier than any other man in the world—and—and ensure her happiness, you have no right to ask her to marry you!'

Eric Gwatkin was quite astonished at his own temerity—astonished and frightened. He was a weak, nervous, emotional fellow; he couldn't trust himself to say another word. His voice broke, and his eyes were clouded, and he was afraid he had said too much, and with a grip of Edgell's great muscular shoulder he went away and left him sitting in his chair, with his head on his breast, and that ugly scar gleaming like the dark blade of a knife across his white throat.

END OF VOL. I.

CHAPTER XV.

IN THE LANE.

'The rain was raining cheerfully,
As if it had been May.'

Lucy was five minutes late the next morning in keeping her appointment—at least, her understood appointment—in the lane. There was a reasonable excuse for it. It was not a morning fit for a dog to go out in. It was a shivering, blowy, rainy morning. There are not many trees at Newnham, and what few there are tossed their arms wildly in the air, and sighed and moaned as the wind whistled through the leaves. They had not shed many tears as yet; they were fresh young leaves with the tender green of the year upon them, but they were shedding a great many to-day.

After this night of weeping they would never be the same leaves again; they would have grown darker and sadder; they would have begun to shiver by night and whisper by day. They were whispering overhead as Lucy stood beneath them, with her umbrella turning inside out, looking up and down the lane.

The man she was looking for was not there. His bed-maker, who was certainly a seer or a sibyl, had found him an hour before under the table of his room, with his lamp still burning, and the liqueur-case in his cellaret—at least, it was on the table—empty, quite empty.

She had fetched Eric, who was up betimes reading for his 'special,' and between them they had put him to bed, and Eric had come out in the wind and the rain to keep his appointment.

Lucy wasn't looking for Eric. She took no notice of the little fellow in a covert-coat who was sheltering behind the hedge. She was looking for a splendid manly form, clad in a big Inverness coat, perhaps, and indifferent to the wind and the rain.

Eric joined her directly she got outside the gate.

'I have just come from the lodge,' he said. 'The Master has passed a better night. He has had several hours' sleep.'

Lucy looked at him with a question in her eyes that had nothing to do with the Master.

'Why didn't Mr. Edgell come?' she said almost sharply. 'Why did he send you?'

Eric couldn't look into her eyes and tell her a fib. They were such clear, straightforward eyes, they seemed to look quite through him.

'Edgell is working for his Tripos,' he said evasively. 'He has only a few days longer before him.'

'He isn't working at this time in the morning?' said Lucy, looking straight at him.

He couldn't meet her eyes. He looked up admiringly at the red-brick front of Newnham as if he had never seen it before.

'No,' he said; 'he is not working now—he is——'

'I know what he is, without your trying to shield him,' Lucy interrupted with fine scorn. 'He is lying most likely drunk and incapable on the floor, or he is raving on his bed, and seeing hideous things. Oh, Mr. Gwatkin, what is the good of your friendship if you cannot keep him from this?'

Eric hung his head.

'He is beyond my keeping,' he said sadly. 'He is beyond the reach of my poor prayers. God knows I pray for him night and day!'

Lucy didn't say that she had been praying for him that very morning, that she had only just got off her knees, and come out in the rain to meet him.

'Will nothing save him?' she said, wringing her hands.

'Yes,' Eric said slowly, looking at her with troubled eyes; 'there is one thing that would save him.'

She looked up at him, and their eyes met, and her heart gave a great bound, and something seemed to surge up in her ears, and swim before her eyes, and choke in her throat. She wasn't quite sure for a minute if anything had happened to her; and when her heart beat again, and the wave went back, and the trees and the college ceased to go round, Eric was looking down at her with his troubled eyes, and his weak lips quivering as he spoke.

'The one thing that would save him would entail sacrifice—the sacrifice of a life—and only a noble woman could make it——'

'You mean,' she said, speaking hoarsely—that lump in her throat hadn't gone yet—'you mean that a woman could save him?'

'Yes,' he said, almost with a groan; 'but it would be at her own cost.'

'Not if she loved him?'

'Yes; all the more if she loved him.'

Lucy turned away, and the wind got under her umbrella and turned it inside out, and made a diversion.

'There is no other way?' she said, when Eric had brought it back into something like shape, and returned it to her.

'No,' he said, 'there is no other way.'

Lucy put down her umbrella—she would battle no more with the storm—and the rain came down in a sheet and wetted her through and through as she walked slowly back to the college.

There was a crowd of girls round the table in the hall when she came in. The postman had just been, and the letters were lying on the hall table, and the girls were crowding round. Among the girls standing by the table was Pamela Gwatkin. She looked up when Lucy came in wet and draggled, and a dull red flush crept up under her skin, and her lips tightened.

'Wherever has she been such a morning as this?' said one of the girls aloud as Lucy passed them.

She didn't pause at the table and look for her letters like the rest. She didn't expect letters by every post like other girls; the coming of the postman never stirred her pulse the least. She had no one to write to her.

Pamela didn't vouchsafe Lucy another look, but went back to her room with her head lifted high, and her letters—she had quite a sheaf of them, letters and papers—clutched to her bosom. She didn't attempt to open them when she got back to her room. She went straight to the window and looked out at the blinding rain.

'She has been to meet him again,' she murmured; 'and such a morning as this! She must be very far gone. Oh, it is outrageous! It is quite indecent!'

Another girl who had seen her come in followed Lucy back to her room, and just as she had reached it Lucy shut the door in her face.

Nothing daunted, Capability Stubbs tried the handle of the door, but Lucy had locked it on the inside; no doubt she was taking her wet things off. One doesn't take the occasion to hold a levee when one is wet to the skin.

Lucy did not appear at breakfast. Nobody missed her but Maria Stubbs; everybody else was too much occupied with her own affairs.

The very air of the place was full of examinations, and the loss, the total disappearance, of half a dozen girls, more or less—freshers—wouldn't have been noticed at this exciting moment.

Before she went to her morning's work Miss Stubbs tried Lucy's door again. It was open this time; the housemaid had just come out, and there was that silly little Lucy sitting at her table with her wet things still on. There was a strained look on her white face, as if she had been working at a problem all night, and it hadn't come out right yet.

'Oh, good gracious!' Miss Stubbs exclaimed, when she came over to the girl and put her hand on her wet shoulder. 'Whatever are you sitting here for?'

Lucy looked up with a faint look of wonder in her eyes, and then, finding she had forgotten to take off her wet things, she began slowly to peel them off one by one.

Maria Stubbs had no patience with her. She pulled and dragged at her clinging wet garments, and tore off her shoes, and wrapped her up in a warm dressing-gown of her own that she ran across the passage to fetch. When she had got her out of her wet rags, she fetched her a cup of hot tea from the hall, where the tea-urn was still steaming, and then she began to bully her.

'A fine cold you will catch,' she grumbled, 'and give no end of trouble. I dare say you'll expect us to stay up of nights to nurse you. I give you notice, it's no use to expect me to nurse you; I've got my own work to do.'

Lucy feebly protested that she didn't expect Miss Stubbs to make a martyr of herself, and that she had no intention of being ill, but Maria was not so easily appeased.

'It isn't as if it were an examination,' she said in an aggrieved tone; 'then we could understand it. There'd be an excuse for a girl making an idiot of herself if she had been ploughed in an exam. I've known a girl refuse to eat anything for a week, because she failed twice in her additionals; and another girl—but this was a more serious case; her mind gave way quite on the last day of the exam., and she had to be sent to an asylum. I shouldn't be at all surprised if they were to send you to——'

'Not to the asylum!' said Lucy, in a sudden fright.

She was so bewildered she felt very much like going there already.

'I didn't mean that, silly!' Miss Stubbs said scornfully. 'I was going to say the infirmary. If you will go and get influenza, you can't expect to stay among people who are going in for examinations. Suppose I were to catch it—or Assurance! I'm not sure that Assurance hasn't caught something already. She begins her Tripos on Monday, and she's about as amiable as a bear.'

Maria Stubbs went back to her work—she was going to be shut up four hours in a laboratory among delightful smells—but before she went she made Lucy promise that she would ask the housekeeper to give her some breakfast.

Later in the day Lucy went over to the lodge to see the Master. The wind had gone down, but a gray mist hung over everything, and the trees were no longer rustling their leaves overhead. The branches were drooping with their own weight, and the leaves were limp, and dropping slow tears upon her as she passed beneath.

The Master was better to-day, decidedly better. He had slept several hours during the night, and he looked quite himself, Lucy thought, when she went into the room and saw him propped up in his chair. He was up and dressed; he had insisted on being dressed; they could not keep him in bed; and his chair was wheeled over to the window, where he sat looking out on to the river, and the path beneath the trees where an old, old philosopher used to walk long ago.

He had always loved that path by the river-side. It had been his favourite walk once. Perhaps the old associations had something to do with it; they have with most of the things men value in Cambridge. A great past seems to meet one at every college gate. Every inch of ground has its own sacred memories, and the path beneath the trees had echoed to the tread of generations of poets, sages, and scholars since the old philosopher walked there.

But it was not of the philosopher that the Master dreamed, as he sat looking out on the gray path and the blurred river. It was no longer the Cam he saw; it was the babbling trout-stream that ran by his father's farm—the gray shallow river that skirted the meadows, and swept beneath the arches of the old bridge, and roared in a torrent over the weirs.

'You are better to-day, uncle,' Lucy said, as she stood beside his chair and looked down at the worn old face, and the white hair on the pillow.

'Better? I am quite well, my dear. I have just come in from fishing, and I am tired. I have caught quite a large basket, and I have walked a long way beside the river. Dick wouldn't wait for me. He went home early. Perhaps it was as well.'

Lucy looked anxiously at the nurse.

'He is better in himself,' Nurse Brannan said softly. 'He has had a good night, and has awoke much refreshed, but his memory is gone. I don't think it will ever be better.'

Nurse Brannan had made a great change in the sick-room; it didn't look like a sick-room. It was as light and bright as it well could be on such a dull day, and there was a small fire burning in the grate, and a big bowl of lilac on the table—the Master was very fond of lilac.

Lucy ran her fingers through the sweet pale-purple buds as she stood beside the table. She was not fond of picking things to pieces like the Science girls, who can never see a flower without tearing its heart out. She was content to bury her face in a posy and drink in its sweetness and beauty. She buried her face in the bunch of lilac as she stood beside the Master's chair, and the old man watched her with his dim eyes.

They suddenly brightened as he watched her; they were dim no longer; they were bright and shining. Something in her attitude, or in the smell of the flowers, had brought back to him the old time: the old lane that skirted the farm with the blossoming hawthorn-trees on either side, and the orchard with the smell of the apple-blossom, and the lilac hanging over the garden-wall.

'Ah,' he said, 'you picked this from the old tree by the gate. I noticed it was coming into bloom this morning when I passed, and the pink thorn is in bud, and the orchard is a sight to see.

The fragrance of the old days was about him, and its colours were unfaded. Lucy left him babbling to the nurse about the flowers that used to grow in the old garden of his childhood. His heart, like that of a little child, had gone back at the close of the journey to the place from which he had first set out.

Cousin Mary was with Mrs. Rae; she had been up with her all night. There was as much need for nursing here as in the Master's room. Lucy was quite shocked at the change that a few hours had wrought in the Master's wife. She looked years older to-day, and her face had changed. All the cheerful brightness that had given an air of youthfulness to it into extreme old age was gone now. It was placid and resigned, but it was youthful and bright no longer.

There was nothing the matter with her, Cousin Mary said, but the shock had been too much for her. A few days' rest and quiet, the doctor thought, might bring her round.

'You have seen the Master?' she asked Lucy eagerly when she came into the room.

Lucy noticed that the voice, like the face, had changed, and grown feeble and old.

'Yes; I have seen the Master. He is so much better to-day. He is sitting up by the window. He is quite himself.'

She didn't say anything about that fishing excursion of his, nor how tired he felt now the day's work was done.

'He is really better?'

She asked this with a strange eagerness, and laid her thin hand on Lucy's.

'Yes, dear, really better. He will soon be quite well. It is you who are the invalid now. You must make haste and get well, too.'

'Thank God!' said the feeble voice, and the thin hand relaxed its hold, and she fell back on the pillow. 'Someone told me he was wandering,' she said—'that he did not know anyone. But perhaps I am mistaken. It may be in me. I may have dreamed it.'

'Yes, dear,' Lucy said reassuringly, 'it is in you. You have certainly dreamed it.'

She left the old woman quite happy, but tears were dropping from her own eyes as she went slowly down the stairs of the lodge. She was not quite sure in this tender casuistry if she was not giving the Master's wife the sentence of death.

CHAPTER XVI.

THE OLD, OLD STORY.

What on earth possessed Lucy to go out into the lane again the next morning at that ridiculously early hour, before seven o'clock, she could never tell. She was not anxious about the Master. She had left him in good hands, sitting beside the window babbling about the lilac-bushes in the old garden.

Perhaps it was because it was such a lovely May morning that Lucy went out into the lane; it was a shame to stay indoors a minute longer.

A change had come over the scene since yesterday. The clouds had all passed away like magic, and the sun was shining, and the sky was blue above, and the earth was green beneath, and, oh, how the birds were singing! There was no excuse for Lucy being in bed. Most of the girls had been up working hours ago, and some had not been in bed since daybreak.

She didn't expect to meet anyone in the lane; she only went out, and looked round, quite by the way, and—and she saw Wyatt Edgell coming to her, up between the green hedgerows, where the hawthorn was in bloom, and beneath the blue sky, where a lark—where a dozen larks were singing, and she had never seen so delightful a picture before in her life.

Like the storm of yesterday, all traces of that midnight debauch had passed away. His face ought to have been pale and soddened, and his eyes dull and heavy, with great bags beneath them, but they were not the least changed. The fine intellectual beauty of the face was finer than ever, and the mere physical beauty, which no girl could look upon untouched, was seen to its best advantage on this sweet May morning.

Wyatt Edgell wore a straw hat with the ribbon of his college around it. He had just come from the river, fresh from his bath, and the sun had dried his hair as he had come along, and it curled all over his head in short crisp curls like a god. His face was glowing and his eyes were shining; he looked a picture of perfect health and manly beauty.

We have had so many studies of Venus rising fresh from her bath, but the artists have not been so keen on Adonis.

A sweet thing in oils, not 'The Bather,' but 'The Bathed,' would be a novelty on the walls of the Academy.

There are no baths at Newnham, only six feet of zinc to splash about in, and that one has to take in turn at the end of a lane of girls waiting in the passage. Lucy wouldn't have had her turn for another hour this morning, so she had dressed without it, and had come out into the lane to take a bath of sunshine instead.

She looked paler than if she had had her turn of splashing in eighteen inches of water, but her hair wasn't limp and wet and untidy.

Her heart couldn't help beating a little faster as Wyatt Edgell came towards her, and her face burnt hotly. She could feel that she was blushing like a milkmaid.

'Oh, you here!' she said in quite a tone of surprise. 'I didn't expect you this morning.'

He didn't believe her. He couldn't look down into her glowing face and believe she had put on all those blushes to meet the burning gaze of Apollo, unless, indeed, she expected Wattles.

'No?' he said with a smile, and he imprisoned her hand; 'but I couldn't keep away. I had something to tell you this morning.'

'About the Master?' she said, turning pale.

'No; it has nothing to do with the Master. I asked for him at the lodge as I came out, and they told me he had had a good night. Phyllis Brannan is with him, and she is a host in herself.'

Lucy tossed her head.

'Oh, you know Nurse Brannan?' she said coldly.

'Yes,' he said gravely; 'I have reason to know Phyllis, best and kindest of nurses. If ever there was a woman true as steel, it is Phyllis Brannan.'

Lucy sniffed impatiently. She hadn't come out without her bath at seven o'clock in the morning to hear the praises of Nurse Brannan. She was quite sure she would be quite as good a nurse after a reasonable probation, and she wouldn't keep her hair so untidy.

'What had you got to tell me?' she said shortly.

It was not exactly encouraging; but Edgell smiled and drew her away from the gate and up the lane, and then she discovered that he still held her hand.

She drew it away sharply and stopped. She really didn't care to walk any farther with him if he were only going to talk about Nurse Brannan. She had been fighting a dreadfully hard battle with herself all night, all the previous day—ever since that conversation with Eric—and she had worked herself up, like the martyrs of old, for a big sacrifice, for the stake, if need be; and now, after all that struggle, there wasn't going to be any stake at all.

Nurse Brannan was going to the stake, perhaps. She was ready at any time to do all sorts of disagreeable things without making any fuss about them.

'Would you mind walking this way?' he said, and he led Lucy unresisting up the lane into that narrow part, past the posts, between the high hedges, that shut them out from all curious eyes.

'I have come to ask you a question,' he said, speaking low, with a little catch in his voice, 'and I want an answer before I go back to work. The Tripos begins on Monday. Will it be worth while to go in for it?'

'What do you mean?' she said; but she knew very well what he meant.

'I think you know what I mean, Miss Rae—Lucy. I think you know more about me than any other woman. If you will tell me I have anything to work for, I will go back and work, and—and some day I will come to you again; but if—if there is nothing to work for, I shall go down to-day.'

'You would not throw up your chance?' she said. She was quite pale, and she was trembling all over.

'I should certainly throw it up. What would be the use of a degree to me with that before me? There is only one thing, Lucy, to stand between me and it. My sentence must come from your lips. Am I to go back and work?'

No one looking at him standing there in the sunshine, with that smile on his face, would have dreamed the issue that hung on the girl's lips. She couldn't realize it herself; she could only gasp and tremble. He had quite taken her breath away. She would have given the world to run away without giving that fateful answer, but the lane was narrow, and he stood before her.

'Well,' he said, watching with his eager, questioning eyes the changes on her face, 'am I to go back to work?'

What could she say? Her lips faltered, and the words would not come; again she tried, but his sentence lingered.

There was a merle singing in the elm-tree above, and a thrush was calling for its mate, and the wood-pigeons were cooing softly in the orchard over the hedge; everything was so glad and happy and full of life and love on this May morning; every voice in nature was pleading for him.

Her face was dreadfully pale, and her lips were quivering, and her heart was beating like a hammer. She looked up into his face with a strange white terror in her eyes, and she saw the scarf round his throat. It was the coloured striped scarf of his college, and he wore it twisted on that balmy morning round his throat. The sight of that scarf decided her.

'I think you must go back to work,' she said softly, with just a little wan smile.

He caught her in his arms, to his heart, and kissed her on the forehead.

'God bless you, Lucy!' he said—'God bless you, darling!'

The pressure of his arms, the strange, sweet pressure of his warm lips on her forehead, brought the blood back to her heart, to her cheeks, and she drew herself away, flushing scarlet.

A Newnham girl came in at one end of the lane, and a Selwyn man came in at the other, and they went back to their respective colleges and told the tale. It was all over Newnham at breakfast-time that Lucy had been seen kissing a man in broad daylight just outside the walls of the college.

The old, old story has been told a great many times, in a great many ways, but it had never been told at Newnham before or at Girton in such a barefaced way. It will be told in the public streets next, or perhaps in the Senate House.

CHAPTER XVII.

IN THE PICTURE-GALLERY.

The term wore on, and there was nothing talked of in Cambridge but examinations. How could one talk about anything else when it was the subject uppermost in everybody's mind? There were the boat-races, and the college balls, and the concerts, but exciting as these were to the sisters and cousins of the men, they were of secondary importance to the exams.

The nearer the day approaches for the dreaded trial the more dreadful seems the finality of the approaching result. Nobody questions the finality of the sentence at the time, and when it happens to be adverse men go away and hide their heads and think that all things are at an end for them. By-and-by the gates of Hope are opened afresh and things don't look quite so bad, and in nine cases out of ten nobody knows out of Cambridge whether a man has taken a high degree or not.

Perhaps it is different with women, the cases being more exceptional; a girl who has done well usually goes through life with an affix to her name, spoken with awe by her admiring friends—'Fifth Wrangler,' 'First Class Moral Science,' 'Senior Op,' and so on.

There would be a good many girls do well at Newnham this term. There would be several first-classes, and some good seconds, and a few, very few thirds. Women never take Poll degrees, so that all, every one, would go out in Honours.

There was a great fuss made with the girls who were going up for the exams. They were fed and petted and looked after just as if they were in training. There were special dishes for them at the High, and they were taken out for exercise, or driven out for airings, and put to bed at given hours. It was not the fault of the authorities if they did not reflect honour on their college.

The men were not the objects of such tender solicitude to their Tutors and Deans. They were left pretty much to themselves, and went to bed when they liked, and got up when they liked, and took their food or left it. Those who liked took exercise, and those who didn't sported their oak and worked until they were deaf and blind, and their brains were so addled that they could hardly find their way into the examination-room.

Wyatt Edgell sported his oak from morning till night during those few days preceding the Tripos examination, but he didn't addle his brains. They were not brains easy to addle by work. The men remarked that this close application, which would have made most men seedy and stale, seemed to agree with him. His eyes were brighter, and his step was lighter, and more assured than heretofore, and he held his head like a man who was going to win, and he hummed snatches of songs—love-songs mostly—as he crossed the courts or climbed his staircase, taking two and three steps at a time, as a man of his youth and strength should do.

A change had come over him since that morning when Lucy had told him to go back to work. He had not seen her in the lane since, though he had gone up to Newnham every morning, and stood staring at the gate until the bell rang for prayers, and then he had gone up the narrow little path between the hedges, and visited again the spot where he had taken her in his arms.

If she had been there when he made these matutinal pilgrimages to the spot, he would surely have taken her in his arms again, and great would have been the scandal at Newnham.

Lucy didn't go out in the lane again alone after that morning. She was quite frightened at what she had done. She couldn't very well have done otherwise. What woman would? She had saved him—at least, she told herself she had saved him. He would go back to his work now, and he would take his degree, probably a very good degree. She didn't dare to speculate any farther; she stopped at his degree. She never said a word about what she had done to Cousin Mary; she wouldn't have told her for the world. Mary had only pointed Wyatt Edgell out to her on the steps of the chapel a month ago. She didn't know him from Eric Gwatkin a month ago, and now she was engaged to marry him!

No wonder Lucy was frightened, and wouldn't have run the risk of meeting him alone for the world. She developed suddenly a violent affection for Miss Stubbs, and used to implore her with tears in her eyes to accompany her in her visits to the lodge. She was such a dreadful little coward, she didn't dare to go alone.

The Master was no worse; his memory had gone, and his physical powers were weakened, since his accident in the garden, but there was no immediate danger. He might go on babbling in his second childhood for weeks or months.

Lucy met the Senior Tutor at the lodge sometimes when she paid her afternoon visits, but she never went to his rooms again. She wouldn't have risked meeting Wyatt Edgell on the stairs for all the coaching in the world. She would rather have been ploughed.

The Tutor couldn't say any more to Lucy about Cousin Mary and the Master's wife making the lodge their home when he met her at these times, as Maria Stubbs was always with her. It seemed likely that the Master's wife would have a home elsewhere before long, and the arrangement would fall through.

Maria had fallen in love with the long gallery of the lodge, as everybody does who goes to St. Benedict's, and she used to wait for Lucy there while she paid her visits to the invalids. Miss Stubbs never did things by halves, and she made herself acquainted during these visits with all the old portraits on the walls. She knew every one of them, from the pale foundress in her sober pre-Raphaelitish dress, to the old Master in his scarlet gown. She had established quite a nodding acquaintance with all of them, and she had got up most of the facts of their history. She knew more about them than Lucy, though she had lived among them for months.

One day while she was poring over the old portraits in the gallery a man came in. He had come up the stairs two at a time, and he had looked eagerly round when he got into the gallery.

There was nobody there but a red-haired girl in spectacles, and the old dead and gone Masters. Yes, there was the foundress, but he didn't care a button for the foundress. He was looking for a real flesh-and-blood woman; his pulses were leaping, and his heart was thumping against his side, and his eyes were shining—he had just finished the first part of the exam.—and just at this moment the fairest creation of the finest master on canvas wouldn't have satisfied him.

He walked to the end of the gallery looking for Lucy—she might be hiding away in any of the little oriel windows—and Miss Stubbs watched him.

She was so glad to see his countenance fall when he couldn't find her. A woman would not have shown her disappointment in that transparent way. She would have made the best of it, and talked to the man who was there, but Edgell glared at Maria savagely, and didn't seem inclined to talk.

'Lucy Rae is with the Master,' she said sweetly; she knew instinctively that he was looking for Lucy. 'She will be here presently.'

Edgell tried to look as if it didn't matter, and he wasn't particular whether she came now or at midnight, but he didn't take Miss Stubbs in.

He fidgeted up and down the gallery, stopping every now and then before a picture, but never looking at it, or staring out into the court below from the old latticed oriel window. He was standing in the recess of the window idly tattooing on the pane when Lucy came in.

She didn't see him until she reached the window, and she came running down the gallery in that energetic way peculiar to the students of colleges for women.

'I'm afraid I've kept you a long time, M'ria; I hope you don't mind——' and then she paused, and Edgell came towards her with his hands outstretched.

He would have taken her in his arms, but there was that hateful Maria at the end of the gallery. He came to Lucy as a lover should come to his mistress, with the love-light in his eyes, and his whole being quivering with passion.

'My darling!' he said, and he took her hands.

Lucy had no idea of being kissed like a milkmaid with Miss Stubbs looking on, and she drew her hands quickly away.

'You here?' she said.

'Yes,' he answered, looking down upon her with that warm light in his eyes and his lips smiling; 'where else should I look for you? I have waited in the lane every morning in the week, and you have never come since—since that morning——'

'The Master is better,' she said, dropping her eyes; they were such sweet, shy eyes they could not meet the hot flame in his.

'And was it only to hear about the Master you came?' he said in a low voice that thrilled her and brought the colour into her cheeks.

'It was to tell me about him you came.' Her voice trembled in spite of herself, and her heart was beating tumultuously.

'It was because I loved you I came, Lucy—darling! I could not live without a sight of your dear face. I have lived a whole week without you, and it has seemed a year. You must not leave me alone again so long, darling!'

There was more in the tone than in his words, and Lucy looked up anxiously into his face.

He read the question in her eyes and he smiled gravely, almost sadly.

'No,' he said, 'thank God, not that!' and he stooped and kissed her forehead reverently between the bright brown ripples of her hair.

Her face grew warm under his touch, and she trembled and drew back. Suppose that girl in the gallery had seen him? It would be all over Newnham. And the servants might come in at any time, or Cousin Mary; and Mr. Colville might walk into the gallery unannounced, as he was accustomed to do. Oh, it would be dreadful to be caught kissing like a housemaid!

'And you have been working hard all this time?' she said, when she had got the little oak table that stood in the window well between them.

'Yes, I have been working pretty well. I shouldn't have done a stroke if you hadn't given me something to work for. I should have thrown it all up, and gone down.'

'Oh, it would never have done for you to have gone down—you who are expected to bring so much credit to the college! It would have disappointed everybody, and your own people most. What would your people have said?'

'They would have been disappointed—and—and I think my mother would have been sorry. She is such a tender, indulgent mother; she has never refused me anything. She has always stood between me and my father, and covered up all my shortcomings, but she couldn't have covered up this, and—and there would have been a row. Yes, I think it would have disappointed her.'

His eyes were tender and softened as he spoke of his mother, and Lucy thought as she stood there of that dreadful scene when she found Eric on his knees beside the couch, and she wondered how his mother would have covered up that.

She looked up at the warm, tender face of the man bending over her—he had got round the table—and with a sudden terror she saw the mark on his throat—he had not covered it; he wore no scarf to-day, and his collar was open, and the purple mark was visible on the white skin.

He saw her eyes travel to—not to his face; they stopped short at his throat, and a white look of terror came into them.

'Yes,' he said, reading her thoughts—her transparent thoughts—'she would have covered up this, but it would have broken her heart.'

He drew his collar up round his throat as he spoke and Lucy's eyes filled with tears.

'It is all over and past,' she said bravely; 'there will be no need to "break her heart" now. You will fulfil all her expectations; you will make her happy and proud—oh, so proud! If men who are tempted to do silly, selfish things would only pause and think of the people who love them!'

Edgell drew her nearer to him.

Maria Stubbs was not looking that way; she really was a most sensible girl, she was entirely absorbed in the pictures.

'I will think of you, then,' he said in a low voice that vibrated with passion, 'when—when I am tempted; but I must be sure of your love, Lucy, or it will be no good; there must be no mistake about it. It must be the real thing; a make-believe, a sham, would never save a man! Tell me if—if at such a time, darling, I may think of you?'

He put the question solemnly, though his lips were smiling, but his eyes were looking down into hers as if they would read her soul.

Lucy's face grew pale and troubled; she knew exactly what his question meant; she felt limp and frightened, dreadfully frightened. Anyone might come into the gallery at any moment, and he was holding her in a grasp of iron and reading her little transparent soul through and through. She could not escape from him.

She had no alternative.

'Yes,' she murmured almost inaudibly; 'you may think of me if—if it will help you.'

He took her in his arms for one brief moment—he forgot all about Maria Stubbs—and kissed her lips and her eyes.

'My darling!' he murmured—'my darling!'

Lovers have such a limited vocabulary, they are obliged to have recourse to unmeaning repetitions.

Miss Stubbs had behaved beautifully till now—no Newnham girl could have behaved better; but there is a limit to all human endurance, and the limit of Maria's endurance had been reached.

'I hope you are nearly ready,' she said in a most unpleasant voice; 'because if not I must go.'

'I am quite ready, dear,' said Lucy, nearly crying. 'I have been ready a long time.'

She could have blessed Miss Stubbs for taking her away. She was dreadfully frightened, but it was with a strange, delicious terror that stirred her pulses like a tumult of joy.

CHAPTER XVIII.

CAPABILITY STUBBS.

It was clearly Lucy's duty not to go back to Newnham, whatever Maria Stubbs' hurry might be, until she had told her Cousin Mary what had passed between her and Wyatt Edgell in the gallery.

It is not usual, even at Cambridge, where there have been so many social revolutions of late, for young women to receive the visits of gentlemen, and exchange the privileged amenities of engaged persons, without acquainting the elders of their household.

There was no one to acquaint at the lodge but Cousin Mary. It was no use telling the Master, he would confuse it with Dick's courtship that had been over sixty years ago, and he would be telling Nurse Brannan that Lucy's mother first met her lover in a dancing-booth at a fair. The Master's wife was almost past telling; she had been growing weaker day by day ever since that accident; the world had been slipping away from her ever since. She had ceased to take any interest in anything that was going on around her. She seldom spoke now; sight and strength and speech were all failing. When she did speak, she had only one question to ask: 'How is the Master?'

But Lucy would not admit that she had any engagement yet to tell anybody about. She had only told Wyatt Edgell that he might go back to work, and she had further told him that he might think of her at certain times.

This was all; no promise, no real engagement. Of course he ought not to have taken her into his arms until he was properly engaged. He had been premature, but Lucy had no one but herself to blame for it.

This is how Lucy reasoned as she walked back to Newnham with Miss Stubbs. She went straight back without seeing the Master's wife or Cousin Mary; she positively crept out of the lodge as if she had done some shameful thing, and was afraid of being found out. She was very nice to Maria on the way. She called her dear, which is quite an unheard-of thing among the Stoics of Newnham, but Miss Stubbs was not to be taken in.

'It's pretty far gone,' she observed with a sniff, when Lucy made a timid little allusion to Edgell's visit to the gallery.

'Oh dear no, not at all!' Lucy said sweetly.

Miss Stubbs raised her red eyebrows. It was those dreadful red eyebrows and red eyelashes that made her so—so unlovely.

'Oh,' she remarked in her unpleasant way, 'I thought I heard—ahem!—some—some kissing. I may have been mistaken; perhaps it was the wind.'

'The wind was very rough this afternoon, dear; it was rattling the shaky old lattice dreadfully.'

Miss Stubbs smiled scornfully. There hadn't been a breath of air all the day.

'I suppose it's a settled thing?' she said presently.

'Settled? Oh no; not at all!'

'Then it ought to be!' Maria said sharply. 'You've given him encouragement enough. He's been hanging about the lane every morning this week. It's known all over the place that he's waiting for you.'

'But I haven't met him!' Lucy said stoutly. She wasn't going to be sat upon by Maria.

'No; oh no! you haven't met him this week; we should all have known it if you had, because we've all been on the look-out since that day when you were caught kissing in the lane. I shouldn't have mentioned it—though it's not good form in a woman's college—if it hadn't occurred again to-day. It's all right, I suppose, if you are engaged.'

'But I am not engaged!' said Lucy impatiently.

She was not going to be lectured by Maria. Nobody would ever think of kissing Maria in the lane.

'Then I don't understand it,' Miss Stubbs said stiffly.

'Oh, you poor creature!' Lucy said with a weak attempt at a laugh, and her cheeks scarlet. 'I am only encouraging him for his own good. I have only told him he may work; he is sure to take a high place, but he would not do anything if I did not encourage him. Think: all his life depends upon it. You would do the same if you were in my place.'

Miss Stubbs did not say she wouldn't, but she blushed beneath her freckles, and her eyes softened beneath the red lashes. There were depths in her eyes that Lucy had never seen in them before, and she was looking at Maria sharply—unfathomed depths, for nobody had tested the depths and height of Maria's love. Perhaps a brave man, who does not look on the outward appearance, or who prefers red hair, may some day, and he will have no cause for regret.

'And what will happen when—when the work is done, and he has won the high place?' Maria asked softly.

She was thinking how she would love above all things to fire a man who loved her with ambitions. She would fill him with the noblest ambitions, and when he had climbed the ladder, when he had realized all his dreams, she would not cheat him of his reward.

'And what then?' she repeated, when she found Lucy did not answer.

'Oh, I don't know. I have not made up my mind. Whatever happened, it would be a great thing for him to have done the work—to have taken his degree, that could never be recalled. I am sure I have done right—in—in encouraging him, as you term it.'

'I think it would be base—and mean—and unworthy—an unwomanly thing to throw him over in the end!' Maria said, with a little catch in her voice. She couldn't find adjectives strong enough, and she had to pause between each.

Wyatt Edgell went back to his rooms across the court with great swinging strides, and he climbed the stairs three at a time. He met the Senior Tutor coming out of his rooms at the top of the stairs, and the little snatch of a love-song he was singing died on his lips. Still, his lips were smiling, and his eyes were shining, and his face was earnest and set. It was the face of a man who was going to do something—who was going to win.

'How have you done?' the Tutor asked, stopping him. He asked it with a smile; he hadn't any doubt about how he had done.

'Not so well as I could have wished, sir. I shall do better in the next part.'

There are two 'parts' in the Mathematical Tripos. If a man gets through Part I. he is allowed to proceed farther; he is allowed to go in for Honours. There could be no doubt about Wyatt Edgell being 'through' in the 'first part.' He was quite safe in going back to work for Honours. There is a week between the end of one examination and the beginning of another. There is time to pick one's self up and prepare afresh for the fight—the real fight this time.

Wyatt Edgell went back to his room and 'sported' his oak. It was open just for a minute after Hall, and Eric Gwatkin came in.

Eric had been working at his Special—he took theology, about as stiff a Special as a man can take—all the week, and he had just come to the end of his exam. There would be Hebrew on the Monday, about which he knew very little; if he should make a stray shot it would count, but the real work of the exam. was over. He was looking limp, and used up, and dejected. His eyes were dull, and his cheeks were flabby, and his hair, which he wore long, hung down in a spiritless way. He was the greatest possible contrast to Edgell.

'Well, Wattles,' he said, looking up when Eric came into the room—'well, have you floored the examiners?'

Eric didn't exactly turn green, but his flabby cheeks turned a shade paler.

'It's all over, dear fellow,' he said with a gulp—he hadn't got anything to swallow. He had just come in from Hall, but he gulped down something. 'The examiners have floored me. I'm ploughed, to a certainty.'

He sat down as he spoke on the couch where Edgell had lain on that day, and tried to look cheerful.

'Nonsense, old man! it isn't so bad as that. You are through, for certain.'

'No; I don't think I am through.'

'Well, suppose the worst, if it gives you much pleasure to anticipate it; you can come up again in October.'

'No; I shall not come up again. I shall go down and try something else. Remember, I have already tried two professions. I shall take it, if I fail, that—that the Church is closed to me. I have an offer of something in the City, and I should have to go abroad for a time, and then settle down to work. Perhaps it's the right thing for me, after all.'

'Nonsense, Wattles! What would you do stuck on a high stool in the City? You'd be getting off it half a dozen times a day to go on your knees. It's no use your choosing a profession that isn't very near the ground, where you could be on your knees all day long. That's the only profession you've got any chance in, Wattles.'

Eric smiled, and if Edgell hadn't been looking straight before him in that way he had of not seeing anything within a hundred miles he might have seen that his eyes were red, and that there was something very suspiciously like a tear in the corner of one of them.

'You are working in earnest,' he said presently, nodding towards the table where Edgell was seated, which was covered with books and papers.

'Ye—es,' said the other with a smile, still looking out of the window at the patch of sunset sky over the gray battlements of the college—'ye—es; I've got something to work for. I didn't do half well in the first part; I wasn't sure—quite sure—but it's all right now, and I shall go in and do my best. You have never seen me do my best, Wattles; you will see me do it now—for—for Lucy's sake.'

His face was very noble and tender. It was an ideal man's face—strong, and self-reliant, and masterful, and inexpressibly tender. It moved Eric watching him from that couch, and knowing so much about him.

'It is settled, then?' he said presently, again swallowing something unsatisfactory that seemed to stick.

'Yes; it is settled. She has given me an antidote, a charm, against that accursed thing. She has told me to think of her.'

He was thinking of her now as he lay back in his chair watching the sunlight steal along the roof, and up, up, up the spire of the college chapel. He was thinking of Lucy's sweet eyes, and her blushing cheeks, and the golden ripples of her hair, and he was telling himself that the thought of her would be a tower of strength to him in the future, that he would never, never fall again. When the old temptation came, let it take what form it would, he should be able to meet it. He would only have to think of Lucy.

Eric watched him as he sat on the couch opposite. He guessed what was passing in his mind. His own mind travelled over the ground with him, and presently he paused and sighed. He had come to a cul-de-sac.

'Well,' Edgell said, looking round like one aroused from a day-dream, 'what are you croaking at, Wattles?'

Eric made a feeble attempt to smile; it was a very poor attempt, and it only made his poor tired face look more ghastly.

'I only hope, dear fellow, it will answer,' he said huskily.

'Of course it will answer. It is the only thing in the world for me, and for such as me. There is nothing but the love of a woman that can hold a fellow back when—when he has gone so far as I have; there is nothing but a woman's love that could reach down, down—God only knows how deep—and pick a fellow up who has fallen into the pit, that can drag a man out, wounded and maimed, from under the very wheels of Juggernaut at the risk of her own life and reason. There is only one kind of love that can do this.'

Eric looked at him with a strange pity in his eyes.

'You think it is right to put her to such a test?' he said.

'I do not think anything about it. If she loves me, she will not think any trial too hard. Tush, man! you know nothing about love if you do not know that love delights in sacrifice. It must have its altar—the rites could not be celebrated without an altar—and it must have its offering—its free-will offering—its victim. It withholds not its dearest—how should it? Love has no self.'

Eric groaned. He knew nothing about a woman's love. He didn't believe that little Lucy could ever love a man like that.

'My dear fellow,' he said, 'you judge a woman's nature by your own. All women would not rise to such heights.'

'The woman that I loved would,' said the other confidently. 'You will have a chance of putting it to the test before long. If—if I am kept, it will be Lucy's love that will keep me; but if—if it happens again, it will be as you say—I shall have judged a woman's nature by my own.'

The smile had faded from his face, and his eyes were cold and hard, and his lips were pressed tight together. It was not the same face that had smiled upon Eric when he came into the room.

Eric was ashamed of himself, and hung his head. He ought not to have questioned Lucy's love. Nobody had ever loved him, nobody but Pamela, and she was always bullying him. He ought to have been silent until he had found out for himself what a woman will do for the man she loves.

'It must never happen again, dear old man,' he said, laying his hand affectionately on Edgell's shoulder. 'Remember, you have vowed——'

'I know all that,' Edgell interrupted impatiently. 'Do you think all the vows in the world would hold me back, when—when that accursed thing came upon me? You have never been tried yourself——'

'No, no, no, thank God!'

'You may well thank God. I tell you, if the breaking the oath I have sworn—the oaths I have sworn—I have sworn dozens—hundreds—would lose heaven itself, I should still break it—I should not be able to resist when the temptation came upon me.'

'You are right to mistrust yourself,' Eric said sadly. 'Oh, my dear fellow, if you would only trust Him who is the unfailing Strength of all them that put their trust in Him, and who would be a Strong Tower to you in the face of the enemy!'

'Dear old Wattles!' Edgell said good-humouredly. 'I knew you only wanted an excuse for going on your knees. I'm awfully busy now, old man. I'm going to work till daylight—and—and if the Enemy, as you are pleased to call him, should come—I'll think of Lucy!'

He looked past Gwatkin to the blue sky over the roof of the chapel. The sun had all but set, and the vane at the top of the spire had caught the last remnant of fleeting sunshine and rent it in twain.

CHAPTER XIX.

A STRONG TOWER.

'Weakness to be wroth with weakness.'

It was a dreadful time of heartburnings at Newnham through all the next week; not at Newnham only, but all over Cambridge. So many Triposes were on, and the week's interval between the first and second parts of the examination for the Mathematical Tripos was being made the most of by the coming Wranglers and Senior Ops.

There were half a dozen girls at Newnham going in for Honours in mathematics, but there was only one that was expected to take a high place—a very high place—among the Wranglers of the year. There would be several Senior and Junior Optimes, but there would be only one Wrangler this year.

The hopes of Newnham were set on Pamela Gwatkin, who was expected to do such great things, to win such honour for the women's college. A dark rumour had reached St. John's and Trinity—who like to divide the honours between them—that they were likely to be left behind in the race—far behind. They were uneasy and anxious, though they wouldn't have owned it for the world, for—

'At times the high gods, who o'er papers preside,
Send a lady from Newnham to chasten their pride.'

The rumour caused a great deal of midnight oil to be burnt in Cambridge during the first week in June. Wyatt Edgell never went to bed till daylight; not that the rumour disturbed him, he only laughed gaily when he heard that 'the lady from Newnham' was Wattles' sister. Perhaps, being twins, he measured them by the same standard.

He never saw Lucy all through that week, though he went every morning at the usual hour up the lane. He didn't linger at the gate now—he had no time for lingering at gates; but he looked up at her window. He had found out which was Lucy's window, and he paid his accustomed pilgrimage to that sacred spot in the narrowed lane between the hedgerows, that were all white with May now, and then he would hurry back to his work. He would take back with him from Newnham, as a memento of his visit, a bit of sweet-briar from the hedge, and he would lay it on his table before him, that something of the fragrance of his love might be about him while he worked.

He wrote to her during the week a little letter that would have set any other woman's pulses on fire, but it only frightened Lucy. She couldn't understand the vehemence of a man's love. She didn't answer it—she couldn't without compromising herself completely; but she sent him a message by Eric.

It was not often that Eric Gwatkin visited his sister at Newnham. She did not encourage his visits, and she was always too busy to talk to him. He came up one day in the middle of the week; his examination was over, and he had nothing particular to do, and he came up to see his sister. He had been slumming all the afternoon in that odorous district round Magdalen Bridge, and he had come up to Newnham to see if Pamela would give him some tea.

Pamela was not in her room, and Eric had leisure to look round and see how his sister amused herself. One can tell so much from a room in daily use what people's occupations are.

Pamela did not amuse herself much, unless she found recreation in the higher mathematics.

Her table—it was an eight-legged affair in old oak—groaned beneath the weight of the books on mathematics that were piled upon it. It was as much as the eight legs could do to support it.

Eric quite shivered when he saw those books and the problem papers that were scattered about; the ink was still wet on some of them. He couldn't have worked out one of those problems to have saved his life. Oh, Nature had made a great mistake! She ought to have made Pamela the man. What was the use of giving all that brain to a woman?

Perhaps Eric thought so; not for the first time, indeed; he may have got used to the thought as he moved uneasily about Pamela's books. There were shelves and shelves of books in this girl's room, and there were not a dozen in Eric's: a Bible and a few theological books, and some Church histories, and nothing more; no poetry, or travels, or philosophy, or fiction—oh no, no fiction!

There were books on Pamela's shelves that made his hair stand on end. He groaned as he read the titles, and he had cold shivers down his back.

To think they should be twins! Oh, Nature had made a great mistake!

He was still reading the titles on the backs of Pamela's naughty black books, and cold shivers were running down his spine, when the door opened and a girl came in.

He looked up, with mild reproof in his eyes, expecting to see Pamela; but it was not his sister, it was Lucy.

Lucy had not come into Pamela Gwatkin's room by choice. She had been sent with a message from one of the Dons, and she had come under protest.

She forgot all about the message when she saw Eric.

'You here?' she said.

There was no reason why he shouldn't be here, in his sister's room. She had just received that letter from Wyatt Edgell, and she was wondering how she should answer it, and the sight of Eric seemed to bring a feeling of relief to her mind.

'Oh, I have been wanting to see you so much!' she said eagerly; she was so afraid Pamela would come in and interrupt them. 'I want to know—how—how Mr. Edgell is going on—if—if anything has happened since——'

Eric understood what she meant, though she spoke incoherently; and he understood her agitation and reluctance.

'No,' he said slowly, looking at her with a strange pity in his eyes, 'nothing has happened in that way, thank God! He is working hard; I am afraid too hard.'

'Oh, I don't think work will hurt him!' she said scornfully. She remembered how the girls worked here. What the men called 'work' was only play to them. She wasn't at all afraid that her lover would work as hard as Pamela, for instance.

'I don't mean that,' he said; 'I'm not afraid of his breaking down. I'm only afraid that when the strain is over—he—he will feel it—he——'

He was a very awkward young man; he could only stand there stammering and stuttering, while the girl looked at him with dilating eyes.

'You mean,' she said with a shiver, 'that when the strain is over he will go back to his old way—that he will not be able to withstand——'

She could not finish the sentence; there was a strange sinking at her heart—a dreadful unutterable loathing and sickness that she could not overcome—and she sank down white and trembling in a chair and covered her face with her hands. The sight of Eric had brought back that awful scene, and she was thinking of that gap in his throat; she could never get it out of her mind.

'No, no, by heaven! not that!' he said almost fiercely. 'He will never, never fall away again in that way, please God; but it is you alone that can keep him. His salvation—heaven forgive me for saying it!—is in your hands.'

'My hands?' Lucy repeated feebly.

'Yes,' he said gravely, almost sternly, 'in your hands. Your love can hold him when nothing else can; it is to him a strong tower against the face of this enemy. You must not fail him in his need.'

'A strong tower!' Lucy moaned. 'Oh, you don't know what you say! I am such a poor little thing—you don't know how weak I am. Oh, why did he choose me?'

She sat with dilated eyes and white stricken face, moaning and wringing her hands. He was very sorry for the girl, but he couldn't spare her. He was thinking of that look on Edgell's face when he had said what a woman's love could do for him.

'Why do men choose women?' he said almost harshly; 'perhaps it is fate, who can say? He loved you, or he would not have chosen you. Oh, you don't know what it is to win the love of such a man!'

'No—o!' said Lucy meekly, with her little smile—her tiny white smile—'I'm afraid I don't. I'm such a little thing! I could not have a large soul like—like Pamela. Oh, why didn't he choose Pamela?'

'It is too late to ask that question now; he has chosen you. Are you going to be true, and loyal, and put yourself aside, as some women do, or are you going to fail him at the last moment?'

It was a hard question to answer; Lucy could not have answered it if she would. How could she tell—she who had never been tried—to what great occasion she might rise? She might be a heroine yet, though she didn't look like one, sitting there weeping and wringing her hands.

'You will not fail him now; remember his future is in your hands. He will do great things with a woman by his side to encourage him to noble aims, to fire him with noble ambitions. Oh, you do not know what your love will do for him! He will have a great future with you by his side.'

Still Lucy moaned and wrung her hands.

'I shall be always afraid,' she said; 'I shall never feel safe. I shall always be thinking day and night of—of what may happen.'

'It will be your own fault if it happens. It is only your love that will keep him; if that should fail, God help him!'

'I am such a poor little thing!' she moaned.

While she was sitting weeping there, Pamela came in, and Lucy jumped up and brushed the tears from her eyes, and puckered her little level brows, and tried to look as if she hadn't been crying. She forgot all about the message she had to give Pamela, and when the sister and brother were talking she slipped out of the room.

'What's she crying about?' Pamela asked him as Lucy closed the door behind her. 'Has anything happened to that—that Mr. Edgell? or is the Master worse?'

'The Master is no worse; but Mrs. Rae is ill, very ill,' Eric answered. He was not at all disposed to talk of Wyatt Edgell's love for Lucy to his agnostic sister.

'And Mr. Edgell, has he been having another attack? Has he been attempting suicide again?'

'Hush, Pamela!' Eric Gwatkin exclaimed almost harshly. He could not bear to hear his sister speak of Edgell in that way. 'You don't know what you are saying. That was an accident, and he had been ill. If you only knew Edgell, you would not say such things. He is the best and noblest fellow in the world, and he is the dearest friend I have.'

'They say he is to head the list this year; that he is to be Senior Wrangler,' Pamela said in her cool, contemptuous way.

'Yes, he is sure to head the list. There is no one to touch him in the 'Varsity.'

Pamela smiled.

Eric had forgotten what rumour was saying about her—that it would be a neck-and-neck race.

'He is working hard, then?' she said indifferently.

What could it matter to her if he were reading hard or raving on his couch with delirium tremens?

'Yes; he's working like a horse—like a giant, rather. He can do six days' work in one every day. No one can have any chance with him.'

Pamela didn't ask Eric to have any tea, and he went away as he came. She didn't even go to the front door with him. She said good-bye, and sat down to the eight-legged table among her books, and left him to find his way out by himself.

He knew his way pretty well. It was not the first time he had been there. When he was nearly at the end of the first passage a door opened and a girl came out and stopped him. It was Lucy.

'I have been thinking of what you said,' she whispered, with a little break in her voice, 'and I will do what I can. Tell him from me not to work too hard; to—to take care of himself—for my sake.'

Her voice broke down entirely, and she went into the room and shut the door.

He hadn't got to the end of the passage before another door opened, and another girl's head was put out—the head of a girl with red hair. It was Maria Stubbs. She watched him to the end of the passage, and then she sniffed in her unpleasant way and went into Lucy's room.

She went in without knocking, and found Lucy on her knees. She had flung herself on her knees beside her couch, and was wildly imploring Heaven to make her love strong enough and tender enough to keep this man safe who trusted in her.

She looked up when Maria came in, and stumbled up from her knees, pretending she had been looking for something under the couch, as she had been pretending just now she hadn't been crying; but she didn't take in Miss Stubbs.

'Who was that man you were talking to in the passage?' Maria said bluntly. 'It didn't look like Mr. Edgell.'

'No,' Lucy said meekly; 'it wasn't Mr. Edgell. It was Pamela's brother.'

'And he brought you a message from your lover? Of course he is your lover. I like to call things by their right names. I prefer to call a spade a spade.'

'No, he didn't bring me a message,' Lucy said, with some spirit.

She wasn't always going to be trampled upon by Maria.

'But you sent a message by him. I heard you give him a message. Oh, it's no use trying to deceive me!'

'I couldn't help it—indeed I couldn't help it!' Lucy moaned; and then she sat down upon the couch beside which she had been kneeling, and began to cry.

She was feeling so dreadfully in need of sympathy and advice that she was bound to tell somebody. She couldn't bear all the burden of this terrible secret on her little weak shoulders. The great terror that haunted her would not be so dreadful to face if she could share it with another.

She told Maria Stubbs the whole story from the beginning; she kept nothing back.

Maria listened in silence to the end. Once or twice she was surprised into an exclamation, and her face grew pale beneath the freckles, and if Lucy had been looking at her she would have seen the tears gather in her eyes and Maria furtively brush them aside with the back of her hand. She would not have let Lucy see that she was crying for the world.

'What would you do if it were you, dear?' Lucy said with a little sob, when she had finished her tale.

'Do?' said Maria, and then she paused, and recalled the face of the man who had been waiting for Lucy in the long gallery of the lodge.

She had seen a good deal of him in those few minutes. She had seen quite enough of him to make up her mind what she should do if he were her lover instead of Lucy's.

'Do, dear?' she repeated, and her eyes beneath their pale lashes grew inexpressibly warm and tender, and her whole face softened and changed. It was plain and freckled no longer; at least, the freckles were there, but one did not notice them in that new wonderful beauty and exaltation that had come into her plain face that was plain no longer. 'I would be a strong tower to him against the face of his enemy!' And she meant it.

CHAPTER XX.

NO FOLLOWERS ALLOWED.

Lucy neglected those dear old people at the lodge shamefully. She was afraid to go to St. Benedict's lest she should meet Wyatt Edgell in the courts, or in the cloisters, or even in the gallery of the lodge itself.

They were well looked after in spite of her neglect. They would have been very badly off indeed if they had been dependent upon her. There was Cousin Mary, who was a tower of strength to everyone who trusted in her. Not a showy, pretentious tower with a flagstaff on the top, but a plain solid structure, against whose granite girth the storm of time and disaster would beat in vain.

Cousin Mary was the presiding genius at the lodge through all this sad time. She ruled the household, received the visitors—and there are always a good many callers at a college lodge in May term—and went from one sick-room to the other all day long, and often all night.

Nurse Brannan was still in attendance on the Master; it had been hard work to get the authorities of Addenbroke's to give her up so long, but the 'Heads' have a special claim upon the hospital staff.

The Master was gradually growing weaker day by day—weaker and more childish. He had forgotten already, in this short time, all that store of learning that had taken him years to collect. He had disencumbered his mind of a useless load of lumber—dry, musty old languages, Hebrew and Sanscrit and Syriac—which would be of no use where he was going. It had taken him a lifetime, a longer lifetime than most men, to accumulate it, and now, in a moment, it had been shot out in a load like useless rubbish. It had answered its purpose—it had advanced him in the world, it had won him repute and distinction, and it had made some money; and now, when its end was served, when it was only an encumbrance, it had all been shot down.

Perhaps other minds would pick it up, would select from the heap the things that were best worth preserving, and so the lamp of learning would be handed on to another generation.

Lucy came upon the Master once in one of her rare visits to the lodge—it was during the hours set apart for the Tripos Examination, when Wyatt Edgell would be away—and found Nurse Brannan reading to him.

She had opened the door softly and come in unobserved, and the curtains of the big, old-fashioned four-post bedstead concealed her from view. Nurse Brannan was reading the Bible to him. She was reading a parable; the words and the imagery took hold of him more than precept and promise; he had been expounding them all his life, and they had dropped from him with those other things.

She was reading the parables of the Lost Piece of Silver and the Prodigal Son, and every now and then she would stop and explain. She had a good deal to say about them, and the old Master listened meekly.

It quite took Lucy's breath away to hear that little bit of a nurse explaining the parables to the Master of St. Benedict's. He had preached hundreds of sermons in the college chapel from that very chapter; it had always been a favourite subject with him. It had always had a fitting application to those fresh young minds in the benches beneath him that were perennially engaged in wasting their substance in riotous living. He had read it in every ancient tongue in which it had ever been written. And now a little nurse-girl, who couldn't even keep her hair tidy, was explaining it to him.

'Yes,' he was saying in his slow, quavering voice; it was weaker now than when Lucy last heard it faltering over those closing words in the Litany in the college chapel—'yes, I mind it quite well. I heard it when I was a boy standing at my mother's knee. She was a poor woman; she would have searched for it all night if she had lost a piece of silver, she would not have rested till she had found it. I was the youngest of all her sons, and when she read that chapter to me as a boy standing there, I used to think that I was the Prodigal, and that by-and-by, when I had wasted all my substance in a far country, I should come back like the Prodigal to my father's house, and ask to be taken in. I've been wanting to go back a long time, my dear; I'm getting tired and old, and I should like to go back. Do you think he would take me in?'

'We will see what the Prodigal's father did when he went back,' said the nurse; and then she read in her soft, slow, earnest voice the concluding words of the old, sweet story.

Nurse Brannan had a wonderful power in reading God's Word, giving by tone and accent a new bearing to the familiar words of Scripture. Lucy had heard the words hundreds of times before, and had hurried over them in her scrambling way of reading her morning portion; but to-day they seemed to convey a special message. She stood there, behind the curtain, while Nurse Brannan read and the old Master listened.

'It seems very clear,' he said, when she had finished. 'It seems just as my mother said. I will arise and go to my Father—I have nowhere else to go—I have changed a good deal in all these years, but—but He would not be likely to change——'

'No,' said Nurse Brannan; 'He has not changed!'

Lucy's tears were dropping fast; she could not trust herself to go in. She crept softly out of the room and shut the door, and went across the landing to Mrs. Rae's room.

The Master's wife was always glad to see Lucy; she gave her better accounts of the Master than anyone else in the household. She looked up when Lucy came in, and noted with her failing eyes, instinctively sharpened by love, that Lucy had been crying.

'Have you seen the Master?' she asked, with a little catch in her voice.

'Yes, oh yes! he is better to-day, and giving the nurse quite a discourse upon the parables. You remember what lovely sermons he used to preach upon the parables?'

The Master's wife smiled; she remembered every word of them. They were her comfort and stay now, those old sermons of the Master's; they made the way quite clear before her; they removed all the difficulties. She would have been shocked if she had known that that nurse from Addenbroke's had been so presumptuous as to attempt to explain the parables he knew so much about to the Master.

'You must get me a volume of his sermons, my dear—his first sermons; I may have forgotten some of them; and Mary shall read them. It will not be like hearing his voice, but—it—it will bring back something of the old time.'

Lucy stayed longer than she had intended at the lodge. She had only reckoned to look in and pay a short visit to each sick-room, and have a chat with Cousin Mary, and go away; but she had to go to the Master's library and fetch that volume of sermons before she went.

The Senior Tutor was sitting down in the Master's place at the Master's writing-table, answering the Master's letters, when Lucy went into the library. It would be his own place soon. He usually came over to the lodge for an hour in the afternoon now, and attended to whatever college business there might be to attend to, and look through the Master's college correspondence. He used to go through it with Mary once, when she opened the Master's letters; now he went through it alone.

He rose when Lucy came in, and made her sit down in her old seat by the window. He wanted her to talk about herself. He was sure she missed his help; she would never be able to pass the Little-go without some more lessons.

They taught beautifully at Newnham. They teach conscientiously at women's colleges: they don't believe in tips and short-cuts, and mere getting up of likely passages; they plod industriously through the dull, dreary round. The Senior Tutor didn't believe in Lucy's plodding; he would have liked to give her a tip or two.

Lucy declined to talk about herself; she was full of the dear old people upstairs, and the affecting scene she had witnessed in the Master's room.

'He is getting weaker every day, in body as well as mind,' the Tutor said thoughtfully. 'He has not had nearly such good nights lately.'

Unconsciously he was keeping a barometric measure of the Master's increasing weakness. It is not an ennobling thing to wait for dead men's shoes.

'No-o,' said Lucy, 'but I hope she will go first;' and then she burst into tears. 'Oh, I don't know how we shall tell her that he is gone!'

'Do you think at her age she would feel it so keenly? The separation could not be long.'

'Oh, you don't know what her love is. It seems only to have grown with the years.'

The Tutor sighed, and looked out of the window into the garden beneath, and his thoughts wandered away to a time long past, when such a love might have been his. Perhaps his fancy had gone back to a brown-haired girl, who had waited for him until her face had grown wan and her eyes sad with waiting, and who had not had Mrs. Rae's patience. Well, she would have been old and florid and stout now, and her sweet face—it was sweet once—would have been seamed and wrinkled with the cares of, oh, so many children!

Well, it was just as well as it was. The Tutor recalled his wandering thoughts, and looked at Lucy.

She was quite worth looking at as she sat in the window-seat. Her face was graver and sadder, and her eyes were steadier, and her lips were not so loose as they once were. It is astonishing how girls' lips tighten after six months in a women's college. Perhaps this is due to their difficulties with mathematics, and to the anxiety that ethics and Latin prose give them, to say nothing of modern languages and natural science.

She had certainly grown more womanly since she had been at Newnham: that added seriousness supplied just the charm that was lacking. Perhaps it was quite as well that brown-haired girl had not waited.

'Do you think you could love anyone so long, Lucy?' he said presently.

It was not the words, but the voice in which he said them, that made Lucy look up and her face grow warm beneath his eyes. She was dreadfully angry with herself for blushing. It was quite idiotic for a girl to turn as red as a poppy when a man old enough to be her father addressed her.

She shook her head.

'Not a man you loved very much, Lucy? Mrs. Rae must have loved the Master dearly for her love to have lasted so long. I'm afraid to say how many years she waited for him.' And again the Tutor sighed: that brown-haired girl had soon grown sick of waiting.

Again Lucy shook her head.

'I am not like the Master's wife,' she said.

She was thinking of Wyatt Edgell. Why would men make such large demands upon a woman? All women were not made on such large lines. Why would they not be content with a little reasonable love—the calm, steady flame that would burn very well if nothing happened to put it out? What more could they want?

'I think you would make quite as good a Master's wife,' he said, bending over her with that warm light in his eyes that had brought the poppy-colour to her cheeks; and he had taken her hand. 'I think your love will be quite as well worth winning. I hope yours will be as happy a life, dear Lucy, as hers, and that it will be crowned with a fuller and more perfect joy——'

There is no knowing what would have happened if Lucy had not at that moment suddenly remembered that Mrs. Rae was waiting for the book of sermons she had sent her to fetch. She snatched her hand away from the Senior Tutor's just in time, and made a hurried excuse that Mrs. Rae was waiting for her to read to her; and she took the first volume of the Master's sermons she found on the shelf, and ran out of the room.

She could hardly trust herself to read to Mrs. Rae. She made a dreadful mess of her favourite sermon. Whatever other talents she had developed at Newnham, she had not developed a talent for reading sermons. It brought the tears into the dear woman's eyes to hear her; she thought of the kind voice that was so sweet to her ears, that she had last heard breathing those well-remembered words, and she turned her worn white face to the pillow to hide her tears.

'You are sure the Master is no worse to-day?' she said to Lucy as she came away.

'Oh yes, quite sure. He was preaching quite a sermon to nurse on the Prodigal's return.'

Lucy was just in time as she hurried out of the college gate to meet the men coming in from the examination.

They were looking worn and tired, and some were looking glum, and others had assumed an air of cheerfulness that sat ill on their anxious faces. One or two had the examination papers in their hands, and were adding up with their friends the questions they had scored off. The process did not seem to give them unmixed satisfaction.

Lucy thought that her lover must already have passed through the court, as he was not among the crowd at the gate, and she was congratulating herself on having escaped him, when she saw him coming across the road.

She couldn't run away; she was obliged to stop in the face of all those men at the college gate and shake hands with him. She wasn't at all sure he would not take her in his arms before them all. There was no saying what he would do. He never did anything like other men; he did not measure the world and its customs with the impulse of the moment. Was not the world made for him?

Wyatt Edgell didn't take her in his arms, and he didn't kiss her in the face of all the men assembled at the college gate, but he walked back by her side to Newnham.

'Well,' she said eagerly, 'and how have you done?'

He was glad to see she was flushed and eager; he didn't know it was the fear of what he was going to do that had moved her and heightened her colour.

'I have been thinking about you every day,' he said. 'If I have not done well it will be your fault, not mine.'

She would much rather he had been thinking about his work, but she did not say so.

'It is nearly over,' she said, with a little catch in her voice; 'only one day more. What will you do when it is over, when you have nothing more to work for?'

'I shall come to you for my reward.' His eyes were blazing down upon her with a sudden heat of passion that made her tremble. 'I shall come to-morrow night, after the exam. is finished. I shall come to the old place in the lane.'

He did not tell her that he had been there every morning of the week.

'It is so hard to get out of nights,' she said. 'We are not expected to go out after Hall.'

He stopped in the middle of the path and laughed.

'Ah!' he said. 'No lovers allowed, and all that sort of thing; no whispering beneath the moon. Never mind, my dear; if they won't let you whisper beneath the moon, I've no objection to lamplight. If you must not meet me in the lane, Lucy, I shall come up to the front-door.'

'Oh, I'm sure that will never do!' she said, almost tearfully; she was dreadfully afraid he would keep his word. 'They wouldn't let you come in, I'm sure. You are not a brother—or—or a cousin——'

'No, my dear, thank God! I am neither of these undesirable things. I am a lover—my darling's own true lover!'

'Then I'm quite sure they won't admit you!' Lucy said very decidedly. 'Lovers are not even mentioned in the rules.'

'Well,' he said, shrugging his shoulders. They were such handsome, manly shoulders. They didn't stoop, or droop, they were not round or misshapen, or one an inch higher than the other, like so many scholars' shoulders. They were broad, and square, and manly, and they had the strength of a giant. He rowed five in his college boat, and was the best 'forward' in the 'Varsity football team. 'Well,' he said, looking down at the girl's dainty profile, and the curve of her soft cheek, and the dimple in her chin—he had looked at them afar off across the benches in the college chapel every Sunday since Lucy had first come up—'well, my dear, if they won't admit me at the front-door, I must find some other way. "Love laughs at locksmiths."'

He was still looking down at her profile—it was not very far off now, it was very near his shoulder—and he had possessed himself of her hand, when three girls came slowly up to the gate where they were standing.

Lucy saw Pamela's face a long way off, and her heart sank within her. She remembered suddenly that she was late for tea, and she snatched her hand away, and ran hurriedly down the path, and left him standing there to meet Pamela, and Maria Stubbs, and one of the younger Dons who had a deeply-rooted prejudice against lovers.

CHAPTER XXI.

A BLOW TO NEWNHAM.

Lucy saw no more of Pamela until after Hall. She thought she had escaped—quite escaped. After all, Pamela had not seen much; she had only seen Wyatt Edgell talking to her at the gate. Other girls talked to men at the gate—brothers, cousins, even coaches sometimes—when they had anything particular to say that couldn't wait for the proper opportunity, but lovers never.

It had gone so far that Lucy was obliged to admit that he was a lover. She admitted with a sigh what other girls—what Pamela Gwatkin, what Maria Stubbs—would have given anything—everything, even renounced the higher culture—to have been able to admit.

Capability Stubbs was walking with Pamela when they came across the lovers at the gate of Newnham. Capability took in the whole scene in a moment: perhaps she took in rather more. She coloured it with her own vivid imagination; she surrounded it with an atmosphere entirely her own. There was not a detail in the picture that was not brought out distinctly by this mental process and stamped upon her memory.

She was thinking about it all the time she was at Hall. She had no appetite for her dinner. She couldn't get the picture of the lovers parting at the gate out of her eyes. She sat staring across the soup, and the entrée, and the gooseberry-tart, at the white wall opposite. Perhaps it was all photographed there: the manly figure with the great square shoulders; they were stooping now, and the head was bent—it was almost touching Lucy's hair—and his eyes were looking into hers, and his lips were smiling——Pah! what is the use of describing the lips of another girl's lover?

Miss Stubbs broke off abruptly, and began to press the gooseberry-tart upon her neighbour. She had quite forgotten until now that it was her duty to look after Pamela. All the girls who go in for a Tripos are under special surveillance during the time of their examination, and a keeper is deputed to watch over them and see that they take their food properly and go to bed at ten o'clock. It was Maria Stubbs' duty to look after Pamela. The soup had gone by and the meat, and she had never once thought about her charge. Perhaps she hadn't eaten a morsel. She was looking white and hollow-eyed, and had that starved appearance peculiar to scholars whose brains absorb all the material intended for the body. She did not look as if she had eaten a good dinner, as if she had gone conscientiously through the menu. In point of fact,

Pamela had only trifled with her plate, and finding that her keeper was not watching, had not eaten a morsel, and now there was only the gooseberry-pie left.

Maria Stubbs pressed the pie upon her with tears in her eyes. She entreated her, if she valued her place in the Tripos, if the honour of Newnham was dear to her, to partake of that pie; but Pamela was not to be persuaded.

Conscience-stricken, Maria got up from the table and retired to her room. Half an hour later she emerged from it with a tray, and hurried down the corridor to Pamela's door. She didn't find her working as she expected—it was the very last night for work; to-morrow the examination would be over. She found her sitting at the window looking out at the sunset.

Pamela was not generally fond of sunsets, and she never sat at the window like other girls. She had no time to spare for sunsets, and she preferred the Windsor chair at her writing-table to any other chair in the room. It was empty now, and her books were closed, and her papers were all put tidily away. She had quite done with them, and she was looking out of the window.

Maria put down the cup of cocoa and the cake she had brought on a little table by Pamela's side, and watched her while she took it. She took it obediently. It was less trouble to take it than refuse it, but she didn't put any heart in it.

'It will all be over soon, dear,' Maria said by way of encouragement.

'Yes,' Pamela said wearily, and she looked out at the white gate which someone had left open. Perhaps she was thinking that she would soon pass through it, and her life here would be ended.

Maria looked in the same direction; but the gate brought something else to her mind, and she forgot all about Pamela and the cocoa.

'Oh, the pity of it!' she murmured; and her eyes lingered on the spot where Wyatt Edgell had last stood.

'The pity of what?' Pamela said impatiently. She was nervous, irritable, over-strung, and everything jarred upon her.

'Nothing, dear, nothing,' Maria said soothingly. 'I was only thinking of the man that girl is fooling. Oh, what idiots men are! Fancy a man—a real man, not a fool—throwing himself away upon that pink-and-white baby!'

Pamela was listening with an abstracted air, but the colour crept up under her skin, and her lip curled.

'You mean the St. Benedict's man?' she said, smiling with a sort of contempt.

'Yes; the man that was talking to her at the gate. Oh, Pamela, did you see his face?'

'Ye—e—s; I saw his face. I have often seen him before. He is Eric's friend. I have known him ever since he has been up.'

'He has known you—you, Pamela—for years, and yet he has chosen her?'

'There is no accounting for taste—at least, for men's taste,' Pamela said scornfully; but she did not look at the girl she was speaking to; she looked out at the sunset.

'I tell you what it is,' Miss Stubbs said with an air of conviction. 'He has been dreaming all his life about the ideal woman, and what his fancy has painted her; and with this myth, this creation of his own heated imagination in his mind, he has met this—this baby, and he has invested her with all the attributes of his ideal. It isn't Lucy Rae he's in love with; it's the ideal woman that he has been all his life imagining.'

Pamela smiled in a dreary way, but she still watched the sunset.

'Perhaps the circumstances—the very unusual circumstances—under which he first met her had something to do with it,' Maria went on in a lower voice. She was thinking of that scene in St. Benedict's that Lucy had described to her. 'Oh, you don't know what a meeting it was, Pam!'

'Yes,' said Pamela, with a little break in her voice, 'I know what it must have been to her; but no one can tell what it was to him.'

'You have heard, then! How did you hear?' Maria asked breathlessly.

'She told me. She told me the first night; she could not sleep, and I found her wandering about the corridor in a panic of fear.'

'Did she tell you all—quite all?'

'She told me everything,' Pamela said; and again her lips quivered.

'Has she told you she has promised to marry him?'

'No, she has not told me that,' Pamela said with that rising tell-tale colour in her cheeks, and a hard steely light in her gray-blue eyes, which were no longer watching the sunset; 'but I don't think she will marry him.'

'I am sure she will not marry him,' said Maria hotly; 'she will fool him and ruin his life. She is too great a coward to marry him!'

'She would be a brave woman to marry him, knowing what she knows,' Pamela said with the hot blood in her face again; 'but I don't think she will spoil his life.'

'Oh, you don't know! How should you know, you who are made on such large lines? He has placed the keeping of his life—think of it: of his life, body and soul!—in her hands. He believes that nothing but the love of a woman can save him; and he has implored her—that poor thing—to be a tower of strength to him.'

'Her!' Pamela murmured with her scornful lips, and the rising colour in her face.

'Yes, dear, he has asked her. He has made the mistake that men always do make: he has asked the wrong woman. He ought to have asked you or me. I don't think we should have failed him, Pam. We should not stop at the tower; we should have gone down—down into the mud and the mire. There is no depth so deep where our love would not have followed him, and we should have lifted him up. I am quite sure we should have lifted him up; we should have dragged him out of the very jaws of death and hell itself, if we had perished in doing it. Oh, I am sure that our love would have saved him! We should not have stopped at the tower.'

Maria stopped, not at the tower, but for want of breath. The red sunset light had quite faded out of the sky, and the gray night was closing in, and already the shadows were filling the silent room.

Pamela drew back from the window into the shadow.

'No,' she said hoarsely, 'we should not have stopped at the tower.'

The next day was the last, the very last, day of the examination for the Mathematical Tripos. It was the last, the very last, opportunity of making up for all the failures and mistakes of the past week. The front place of the year was to be won or lost on that last day. Its result would be final, quite final.

No wonder Maria Stubbs' conscience smote her when she remembered how she had neglected Pamela at Hall the previous day. She tried to make up for it at breakfast. She plied her with eggs and ham and porridge, but Pamela had no appetite for these dainties; she implored her with tears in her eyes to consume at least a spoonful of porridge, but Pamela was not to be moved. She went fasting to the exam., and Maria went with her so far as the door. She went quite early—girls always do go earlier than the men; they are always in their places, calm and collected, five minutes before the time, when the men generally arrive breathless at the door just as the hour is striking.

As Pamela walked up King's Parade in the sweet June sunshine, Wyatt Edgell passed her on the way from St. Benedict's to the Senate House. He was swinging along at a great pace, with the bearing of a man who was assured of an easy victory. His eyes were shining and his lips were smiling as they had smiled at Lucy. He had no eyes for any other woman; he passed the Newnham girls without seeing them.

His mind was full of the ideal woman who had promised to meet him in the lane when the exam. was over.

Maria Stubbs remembered the tower, and flushed scarlet; but Pamela shivered. She was looking dreadfully pale when Maria left her at the door. She would have liked to have gone in with her and sat by her side and held her pens, or picked up the blotting-paper, or collected her papers; but the examiners were inexorable, and Maria came sadly away.

Pamela pulled off her gloves and glanced over her paper; it was about as nice a paper as the last day's paper of the Mathematical Tripos usually is. There were several questions that Pamela had got at her fingers' ends; they would have puzzled the men, doubtless, but to a Newnham girl, who had worked for her Tripos as conscientiously as Pamela had worked, they were a mere bagatelle. She pulled off her gloves and glanced over her paper, and began work in the quiet, methodical way in which the students of women's colleges take their examinations. There was no heat, no excitement, no hurry whatever, nothing to disturb or bewilder.

She ought to have done uncommonly well with those nicely fitting questions; but instead of working she sat staring at her paper. The examiner, walking up and down the room, between the tables, noticed her abstraction. Once he paused and asked her if she was not feeling well; and then suddenly it dawned upon her that the time was going on, and that she had not yet begun. She had never felt it so hard to begin before; she had never felt that strange reluctance, like a clog upon her memory, that made the wheels of that fine bit of machinery drag heavily.

The reluctance—it was nothing more—grew and grew upon her. The questions were quite easy; she could have answered them with the smallest effort, but her mind refused to grapple with them.

It was like bringing a horse to the water; the water was cool and delightful, and it had only to stoop and drink; but it would not stoop. Pamela could do nothing as she sat there with the time slipping by but think of the man she had met in King's Parade, and wonder how he was getting on at the Senate House over the way with the paper that lay before her. She followed his progress question by question, and when she had come to the end of the paper she gave a sigh of relief—a big sigh, for the examiner who was at the other end of the room heard it, and the girls sitting opposite heard it and looked up.

They saw a very common sight in an examination-room—a girl with a gray dead face slipping off a chair to the floor. Pamela had fainted.

They brought her to, somehow, though everybody was begrudging the time she spent upon her; and then somebody took her back in a fly to Newnham.

It was an awful blow to Newnham. Everybody reproached Maria Stubbs. She hadn't half looked after her. Nothing that anybody said hurt poor Maria like the prickings of her own conscience. She was guilty in the matter of that last Hall. She had forgotten all about her charge until the gooseberry-pie!

She nursed Pamela tenderly all through that wretched day. She did what she could to atone for her past neglect. She brought her little messes of Liebig and arrowroot every hour; she watched beside her with the patient fidelity of a dog, while Pamela would have given worlds to be left alone in her darkened room. She locked the door against her officious nurse once, when she had gone out to fetch the everlasting beef-tea, and Maria made such a ridiculous noise outside, that threatened to bring all the Dons upon her, that she was obliged to get up and open it again. There was nothing to be done but to turn her face to the wall, and let the faithful creature potter about her to her heart's content.

CHAPTER XXII.

READING THE LISTS.

It was the oddest state of things that can be imagined at Newnham all through that next week. The order of everything was reversed. It had been all work—real, desperate work—now it was all play.

It was hard work enough to get through the days. The exams. were all over. There was nothing for the girls to do but to wait with what patience Heaven had given them for the lists to be out. Some of them were already quite indifferent to the lists, and when the strain was over had gone to bed, like Pamela, and turned their faces to the wall. Others had locked their doors and gone through their papers over and over again, and had made up their minds exactly where they should be placed when the lists came out. Some, more wise than the rest, had put their papers in the fire, and relieved their overburdened minds with large doses of fiction.

There was not a book opened in Newnham through all that week but yellow-backs. Annabel Crewe declared that she had read eleven before the week was half out, and a Natural Science girl had discovered that an infallible method for distracting one's thoughts from 'ologies' was to keep three sensational novels going at once.

One by one the Tripos lists came out, and the girls who had gone to bed for good thought better of it, and got up again, and came down to be congratulated, and admired, and made much of. The foolish virgins who had burnt their papers, and behaved with corresponding frivolity through all their University career, received the due reward of their folly, and were snubbed and condoled with in the most approved fashion. If one is down one must expect to be sat upon, or what would be the advantage of success?

The women's colleges had nothing to complain of. They had more than one first-class in every Tripos. They had beaten the men on their own ground; they had not only kept their place, but they were coming more and more to the front every year. They will win their degrees soon. Already the opinion of the Senate is equally divided; very soon the balance will be in their favour, and then all things will be possible.

The list of the Mathematical Tripos is read out last of all. It is not read until May Week has well begun, when the boat-races are half over, and the college concerts are in full swing, and picnics on the river and luncheons in college rooms are the order of the day.

The list is read out inside the Senate House, as befits the dignity of the occasion; but this particular year it was rumoured that the lists would be read out from the steps. Some distinguished visitors were expected at noon, and the Senate, in their zeal for the encouragement of learning and other virtues, were about to confer upon them Degrees of Honour, and the Senate House was full of carpenters preparing for the auspicious occasion.

Half an hour before the appointed time for reading the list the girls of Girton and Newnham and the men from every college in Cambridge assembled on the clean-shaven lawn before the south door of the Senate House. It was a glorious June morning, and the crowd could afford to wait. Having waited so long, they could wait a few minutes longer. To some those few minutes were a boon; the delay enabled them to pull themselves together, and bear with what courage and resignation they could call to their aid the fateful verdict they would presently hear read out.

The girls were more impatient than the men. They had reached the spot a quarter of an hour earlier, and had secured all the front places. They crowded the steps of the Senate House to the very doors, and they filled the broad path beneath the windows. A cool, compact, delightful crowd—a bevy, one might almost say—a bit of bright refreshing colour amid the rusty gowns and limp, disreputable caps of the undergraduates.

But the lists were not read out from the steps, and the girls crowded round the Senate House doors in vain. When it wanted a few minutes to the hour a window was opened just above the heads of the girls on the path, and a man looked out. He wore an M.A. hood, and there was a Proctor hiding away behind him in a white tie. The men sent up a shout and a howl—a shout for the examiner and a howl for the Proctor, who happened to be unpopular. The faces of the girls who had crowded up the steps and round the doors fell. They had expected to be in the very best place, and they were quite out of it. They could look on the eager faces of the men below them and the girls in the crowd, if this was any compensation. They could see how vainly the men strove to hide their anxiety beneath a veil of indifference or careless hilarity, and how the girls made no pretence at all of concealing their feelings, but looked as if they would like to tear that bland little examiner at the window limb from limb.

Among the girls who thirsted for his blood was Maria Stubbs. She had come quite early—one of the first—and she had settled herself on the top step just outside the Senate House door, and she awaited with devouring anxiety the reading of the list. It was not her list; it was Pamela Gwatkin's list. She had left her at Newnham in bed, with the curtains drawn to keep out the daylight, and she had taken away her watch, that the dreaded hour should not disturb her, and she had gone in at the last moment, and found her broad awake, with her weary eyes watching the door. She need not have troubled herself to take away the watch. Pamela knew the time to a second. She had been counting the hours all the night, and now she was counting the minutes.

'You are going to the Senate House?' she said, looking up. 'You needn't hurry back. I know exactly where I am.'

'We all know where you ought to be,' Maria said, hanging her head. 'The men would have been nowhere if it hadn't been for my wicked neglect!'

She was so angry with Lucy for being the innocent cause of her preoccupation that she wouldn't let her walk with her to the Senate House. She would hardly let her stand on the steps beside her, but Lucy wasn't to be pushed aside. She had as much interest in the list that was about to be read as Miss Stubbs.

There were a great many mothers and fathers and sisters and cousins there of the men whose names would presently be read out, and there might have been some sweethearts present; but there was not a single girl in all that crowd of sweet young English womanhood that did not envy Lucy.

'Time, sir, time!' the men shouted, and the examiner smiled benignly down on the crowd beneath.

'Time! time!'

How eager the men were! They couldn't all be Senior Wranglers!

Perhaps there were not many expectant Senior Wranglers there. It is not often that a man whose name is on every lip has the courage to face the ordeal. There is always a chance of disappointment. Wyatt Edgell was not among the crowd. Lucy must have seen him from her elevated place on the steps as she looked down at the upturned faces of the men, had he been there. Eric Gwatkin was close beneath the window among a crowd of St. Benedict's men, but Edgell was not among them.

'Time! time!' the men shouted, but the examiner only smiled and looked at his watch.

The minute-hand of the clock of great St. Mary's had travelled round to within a few seconds of the hour. A Proctor who was standing near the examiner, with the list in his hand, looked down at the crowd of undergraduates beneath with an eye to business, and took down the names of the men who were making a row.

It was the unpopular Proctor, and at the sight of his unwelcome face at the window the crowd beneath set up a groan, and in the midst of the groan the clock of the University church struck nine.

'Time!'

It was time indeed. The examiner opened the list, and held up his hand for silence. The men were still groaning as he read out the first name on the list:

'Senior Wrangler—Wyatt Edgell, St. Benedict's.'

The St. Benedict's men set up a great shout, and Eric Gwatkin waved his cap in a ridiculous manner. Lucy would have liked to wave her hat, too, she was so absurdly elated. She hadn't thought what a great thing it was to be Senior Wrangler until she saw how the crowd applauded. She quite flushed with triumph; it was her victory—hers! If it had not been for her, her lover would not have thought the prize worth winning. He had won it for her sake!

She was so proud and happy she did not hear another name in the list. What did the disappointment of others matter to her? Her cheeks were flushed, and her eyes were dancing with triumph. Oh, it was a proud thing to have a lover a Senior Wrangler!

Pamela Gwatkin was only equal to fifth—fifth Wrangler—and when Maria Stubbs went down the steps of the Senate House Lucy saw she had tears in her eyes. Of course, she was crying for Pamela's defeat. As if Pamela could have had any chance against her lover!

Lucy ran nearly all the way back to St. Benedict's. She wanted to be the first to congratulate her lover. Fast as she ran, Eric Gwatkin was there before her.

There was a strange hush in the outer court as she entered the college gate. There was no shouting like she had heard in the street and in the Senate House yard. There was a strange, ominous silence. The men were standing about the court in knots, and the porter was talking to a little group of men at the gate.

Lucy's heart sank within her. Had anything happened to the Master or Mrs. Rae? She thought the men looked at her with a strange kind of pity as she passed through the court, and they took off their caps as she passed. It was quite an ovation. Her lover was Senior Wrangler. She was quite in a flutter of pride and expectation; still, her heart sank within her.

Eric Gwatkin met her in the cloister; he was hurrying across to the lodge. She thought he was coming to tell her. What else should he come to the lodge for? The Master was past telling.

'Oh!' she cried, running to meet him, 'how does he bear it? You have told him——'

She paused, and her voice faltered with the question on her lips. Eric's face was white and anxious, and he was not smiling. He was not the least like the man who was waving his cap under the window of the Senate House.

'You have not heard——' he said.

'Heard what?' she cried impatiently. 'Is the Master——'

'No—no,' he interrupted; 'it is not that—it is not the Master.'

'It is Mrs. Rae?' she said, with a chill feeling at her heart. She was sure something had happened.

'No, it is not Mrs. Rae. Oh, Miss Lucy! how can I tell you?'

'It is he!' she said in a stricken voice, and with that dreadful feeling at her heart. 'Oh! what has he done?'

She was standing wringing her hands in the middle of the cloisters, and the men were passing through, and everyone could see her.

'Hush!' Eric said almost harshly; 'he has not done anything—at least, he has only done what others do at this time. There was a bump supper last night, and—and Wyatt was there; and when Mr. Colville went in this morning to tell him of his great success, he was on the floor in one of his old attacks. It is all over the college, and everybody is dreadfully shocked—that is all!'

'All!' Lucy said bitterly. 'You speak as if the shame and exposure were nothing. Oh, I shall never be able to face it!' She only thought of herself.

Eric Gwatkin was very sorry for her. He would have spared her if he could. It was better for her to hear it from his lips than from others.

'He has done great things,' he said. 'It was enough to turn anybody's head. He will go down in a day or two, and the temptation will not occur again. You do not know—how should you?—how great the temptation is—what a supreme moment this is in a man's life!'

'No,' Lucy said, with a shiver, 'I do not know.'

They had reached the door of the lodge while they were talking together, and Eric had rung the bell.

'Why do you ring?' she said sharply.

He hung his head.

'I came over to see if Nurse Brannan can be spared for a few minutes,' he said guiltily.

'Is he so bad as that?' Lucy asked; but she did not offer to go to him.

'Ye—es; he is very bad. Mr. Colville is with him, and he thought that the nurse ought to be with him until the doctor comes.'

'You have sent for a doctor?'

'Yes; the Tutor has sent for a doctor, and—and he has noticed that scar.'

'And you have told him?'

'Yes; I have told him. How could I help it?'

Lucy went into the lodge covered with shame and humiliation. She was so proud and happy when she entered the college gate. She had made up her mind to tell Cousin Mary all about her engagement. She was going to her to be congratulated—to be envied and congratulated by everybody in Cambridge. Now she wouldn't have owned it for the world. How lucky she hadn't told Mary!

CHAPTER XXIII.

'GOING DOWN.'

It was rather hard to spare Nurse Brannan on this particular morning; harder than usual. The Master had passed a bad night; he had not slept at all, and he was decidedly weaker. He had been wandering all through the night, and he was still wandering feebly when Lucy came into his room in the morning. He had been going over the old scenes of his youth; he had been travelling back to the sweet green fields and the hills and valleys of his earliest recollections.

When Lucy came into the room he was propped up in bed, babbling about the old scenes and the old places. The blind was drawn up, and the June sunshine poured into the room. Nurse Brannan never denied her patients sunshine. 'Let them have it while they may,' she used to say; 'they will have no need of it by-and-by.' The sun was shining into the room now, and on to the bed, and on to the face of the old Master.

Lucy had not seen him for several days; she had been busy with her examinations, and she was struck with the change in him—an indefinable change that sharpened his rugged features as if a chisel had been passed over them. They were rugged still, but with an added nobleness, and there was a light upon them that Lucy had not seen there before. His dim blue eyes were looking up at the window, and he did not see her come in the room. They were looking with that shining light in them above the gray battlements of the old court to the bright bit of blue sky beyond.

'I think he can be safely left,' Lucy said; 'he is very quiet. I will stay with him till you come back. You must not be long; I have an examination at ten o'clock. You must not stay more than half an hour.'

Nurse Brannan promised to come back within the half-hour, and Lucy took her place beside the bed. She had a dim idea that she ought to have gone herself to Wyatt Edgell in his humiliation, not have sent a hired nurse, but she put the thought away from her. It was not a real engagement, she told herself. She had only consented to it to give him a motive for work. He could not hold her to it now; no one could expect her to be bound by a promise given under such conditions. How lucky it was that no one at St. Benedict's knew of her engagement!

The Master would not let her thoughts wander long. His hands were feebly groping about the coverlet of the bed, and Lucy saw that he was making an effort to get up.

'No, dear Master,' she said; 'no, I wouldn't get up yet. I would wait till nurse comes back; she will be here soon.'

'I was going to meet her, my dear,' he said; 'I have been travelling all night. I came by the coach to the cross-roads; it is a long journey from Cambridge, and I am very tired. I thought it would never end, and the morning was slow in breaking. It broke at last; I never saw a finer sunrise, a higher dawn. The coach put me down at the cross-roads; I had nothing to carry—I had left everything behind—and I have been walking over the hills since daybreak. It's wonderful how little they have changed: I knew every field and hedge on the way; and the old trees and the mile-stones in the road, I knew them every one; and the broken cross in the churchyard, and the old gray tower. The tower looks taller now than it used to, and the vane was shining in the sunlight as I came along; I could see it a long way off, gleaming like gold, and pointing the way.'

The old Master paused for want of breath; he had worn himself quite out. He lay back on the pillow, with the sunshine streaming on his worn face. Lucy could not help noticing how shining it was—shining like the old vane.

'Strange,' he went on presently, talking to himself in a lower tone—'strange! the cross was there, and the church, and the tower, and the old elms in the yard, and the rooks cawing in the branches—I knew the cawing of those old rooks again—but I could not find the Vicarage gate.'

Lucy was beginning to get impatient. Nurse Brannan ought to be back by this time. Her examination would begin in a quarter of an hour. She didn't care anything about that Vicarage gate; there was nobody waiting for her at the gate.

The Senior Tutor came in while she was fuming and fretting about the time.

'I thought you would want to get away,' he said to Lucy, 'so I came over to sit with the Master. We can't spare Nurse Brannan just yet.'

Cousin Mary came in, too, just after him; she generally came into the room a minute or two after the Senior Tutor. She had not been able to come in before, she was in such close attendance on the Master's wife. Mrs. Rae had had a restless night, but had just fallen asleep, so Mary had stolen away.

'This is a dreadful thing about Mr. Edgell,' she said. 'The college was so proud of him; it will be a terrible blow.'

'Yes,' said the Tutor; 'it will be a great blow. It is unfortunate it should have happened just now; it will get so talked about.'

He was thinking of the credit of the college, not of Wyatt Edgell.

'What will he do?'

'Oh, he will go down with his friends. I have telegraphed for them; they will be here by noon; and when he can be moved they will take him away. It appears this is not the first time. He attempted suicide the other day; I saw the mark on his throat——'

Lucy did not wait to hear any more. She ran away as fast as she could, and left Cousin Mary and the Tutor talking by the Master's bedside.

They took no notice of her. They did not even look at her. Oh, if they had only known!

Wyatt Edgell's people came at noon. Lucy saw them crossing the old court when she came back from her examination—an elderly man with a striking resemblance to her lover, and a tall stately woman with a pale beautiful patrician face.

They ought to have been proud and happy people. This should have been a red-letter day in their lives—a day of thankfulness and congratulations and unutterable joy; a day when the tears come with the smiles, and the glad words falter on the lip, and there is a strange catch in the voice, and a dimness before the eyes, when the most eloquent speech begins and ends with a 'God bless you, my boy!' uttered in a very shaky voice.

There were no congratulations to-day and no smiles. If there were tears no one saw them—only a hard break in the voice when Wyatt Edgell's mother thanked the Tutor for his interest in her son. She didn't even look at Lucy as she passed. Something in the rustle of her rich trailing skirts as they swept over the stones of the court brought to the mind of the Master's niece those old stories the Master was so fond of telling—of the stall in the butter-market, and the meeting of her grandfather with her high-spirited ancestress in the dancing-booth at the fair.

It was quite as well that nobody knew about that engagement.

Lucy had another examination in the afternoon—her last. She hastily swallowed some cold luncheon that was laid for her at the end of the long dining-table at the lodge. There was no one present but herself. Mrs. Rae was not so well, and Cousin Mary had a tray carried up into her room, and Nurse Brannan could not leave the Master.

Lucy had no appetite for the solitary meal. Something was choking in her throat all the time she sat at the table, and she could not swallow anything.

She looked in at the Master's room before she went off to her exam. He was still searching for the Vicarage gate. Mrs. Rae was asleep or dozing; she did not appear to notice her when Lucy opened the door of her room. Cousin Mary was still with her—she seldom left her now—and she was looking tired and worn out for want of rest. It did not occur to Lucy to offer to take her place; besides, she had to go to her exam.

'I can "go down" to-night, dear, if you like,' she said to Mary, before she went away, 'if I can be of any use here. A lot of the girls have "gone down" to-day. Term is quite over. I can either come home to-day or Monday, which you think best.'

'Nurse Brannan has not been to bed for a week,' Cousin Mary said wearily, 'and—and I'm afraid I am getting worn out; but you must do as you like.'

Lucy went off to her exam.; but for all the good she did she might just as well have stayed away. She was very sorry for those old people at the lodge, but what else could be expected at their age? She was more distressed about her lover. Nurse Brannan had stayed with him until the paroxysm had abated, and he had sunk into a deep sleep.

He would probably awake from it, the doctor who had been called in said, not very much the worse for the carouse, and unconscious—quite unconscious—of what had happened.

What would he do when he awoke? Lucy was pondering this question in her mind all the time she was in for her exam., when she ought to have been occupied with the questions on the paper before her. She hadn't answered it when she got back to Newnham. She had only gone back to pick up some things she needed and to get her exeat, or go through the ceremony that takes the place of an exeat at a college for women.

She had to say good-bye to two or three of the girls who were going down; some were going down altogether, and their paths were never likely to cross again. Among these last was Pamela Gwatkin. She was going down, broken in health and spirit, and she had no present intention of coming up to Newnham again.

She was up and dressed when Lucy went into her room to say good-bye. She was sitting at her old place at the table, tearing up some papers. She had torn up a lot already, and they were lying in a heap by her side, and Maria Stubbs was on the floor packing her books.

Pamela looked up when Lucy came into the room.

'Well?' she said, with a large look of scorn in her eyes that made Lucy's cowardly little heart sink into her shoes. 'Well?'

It wasn't very much to say, but a great deal can be got into a word of such varied meaning. Lucy saw in a moment that Pamela knew all.

'I don't know what you mean,' Lucy said with some spirit.

'No,' said Pamela scornfully; 'I suppose not. You have not seen him then?'

'Seen him?' Lucy exclaimed, flushing scarlet, and her eyes smarting with tears of anger and humiliation. 'I never intend to see him again! His own people are here.'

'What has that got to do with it?' said Maria, sitting down on the floor in the middle of a heap of books.

'Everything. He doesn't want me if he has got his people.'

Lucy was thinking of Wyatt Edgell's mother. She had been haunted by her pale patrician face all through the exam.

'I don't see that,' Maria said hotly. 'He will want you more. You ought to stand between him and them, and see they are not too hard upon him. I think you ought to have gone to his mother at once, and told her everything.'

'I?' Lucy gasped—'I?'

'Yes, you. Who else should take his part at a time like this? Oh, you are a poor coward! You are not half good enough for him!'

The tears were in her eyes as she spoke; she had to put up her hand and dash them off her hideous pale lashes. She looked as if she would have liked to have taken Lucy in her strong arms and shaken her.

'I'm afraid I am a coward,' Lucy said humbly; and then she began to cry.

She wasn't content with crying, she began to sob hysterically. She had gone through a great deal that day, and her nerves were shaken. Maria got up from the floor and came over to her. She put her on the couch, and took off her hat, and stroked her hair back, and soothed her, but Pamela took no notice of her; she only sat tearing up her papers.

'You would do the same if you were in my place,' Lucy sobbed; 'you would be afraid to venture. What girl in her senses wouldn't?'

Miss Stubbs smiled.

'I know some girls who wouldn't,' she said.

She was very angry with Lucy—angry and impatient; but that did not account for the hard break in her voice.

'Hush!' Pamela exclaimed harshly; 'it is not her fault she has so small a soul.'

'I am sure you would not do otherwise,' Lucy sobbed, not heeding the interruption. 'You would be afraid to—to marry him. Oh! who could marry him?'

Maria's eyes were shining, and the hand that was stroking Lucy's hair trembled; but Pamela's face was hard and stony as she sat tearing up her papers, and her thin lips were pressed tight together.

'You would never be safe,' Lucy went on, defending herself. 'You would never know what he would do. He might break out at any time—he might kill himself, he might kill you!' The picture was too appalling, and Lucy subsided into a fresh passion of tears. 'Oh, I could never run the risk!' she said with a shiver; 'I should never be safe!'

'Not if you loved him?'

Pamela asked the question in a low voice—low and vibrating with passion. She had not intended to give a voice to her thoughts. She would have given the world to have recalled the words after she had spoken.

'No,' Lucy exclaimed passionately; 'not even if I loved him!'

'Oh, you poor thing!' said Maria Stubbs, with her eyes flashing, and her freckled face all aglow with a strange fire.

'Let her alone,' Pamela said wearily—'let her alone. How should she do otherwise? It is not her fault that she has not a large soul. Let the poor little thing alone. She can only act according to her lights. Let her alone.'

They let her alone—at least, they said good-bye to her in a strained, unemotional way. They didn't shed a single tear in that parting. Maria Stubbs kissed her on both cheeks, and told her to write to her and say how the Master of St. Benedict's was. She didn't say a word about her lover. Pamela kissed her on one cheek—at least, she made a peck at her, and said some cold, formal words of farewell, and went wearily back to tearing up her papers.

When the good-byes were said, the poor thing with a small soul crept humbly down the stairs. Everybody cannot be made on such large lines as Pamela Gwatkin.

CHAPTER XXIV.

THE VICARAGE GATE.

The old Master of St. Benedict's had not found the Vicarage gate when Lucy got back to the lodge. He had been searching for it all through the long June day, and he had not found it yet. He was lying back propped up with pillows when Lucy went into his room, and the sunset light was falling on his face. All the hard lines had been smoothed out of it; the furrows that years of work and thought had stamped upon it were all smoothed out, and it was like the face of a little child.

His eyes were open, and Lucy thought he was watching the sunset. It had already slipped off the grass in the court below, and it had climbed the chapel wall and reached the gray battlements at the top, where the bits of blue sky could be seen between. She went to the window and drew up the blind that he could follow it still higher, and he watched it with a strange wistfulness as it slid off the chapel roof, and lingered for a few moments on the spire.

Everything had slipped out of his life like the sunset light, and now that, too, was fast slipping away. He watched it until it had faded quite away, and then he closed his eyes with a sigh. Lucy watched beside him through the early part of the night; she was to call Nurse Brannan at daylight. He lay very quiet, wanting no watching, until past midnight, and Lucy thought he was sleeping. She was conscious of no overwhelming sorrow. Perhaps she could not feel things deeply like some people. He had lived his life—his useful, honourable life—and now he would pass away full of days and honour.

She wondered vaguely as she sat beside the bed in the silent room—so silent that she could hear the ticking of the Master's watch on the dressing-table—what would become of her. Things might have been different—so different; but she did not dare to think of that now. It was unreasonable of Pamela Gwatkin and Maria to blame her. No one in their senses would blame her.

Lucy could not help repeating to herself, as she sat there thinking over the events of the miserable day, Pamela's question, 'Not if you had loved him?' 'No,' she told herself impatiently, 'she would not be justified in making such a sacrifice, however much she loved him. Nothing could justify it. Girls were not expected to make such sacrifices for their lovers. No girl in her senses would think of it.'

Lucy's meditation was disturbed by the Master's rambling monologue. He had been dozing through all the early part of the night, and about midnight he awoke and began talking to himself in low, disconnected sentences, his mind wandering off in strange fancies and old recollections, which escaped from his lips in broken sentences. He had forgotten the Vicarage gate now, where Rachel used to wait for him in those far-off days when he came back term after term from college. He had gone back in memory to an earlier time. He was a boy again in his father's fields; the old faces of his infancy and childhood were about him. He was a boy again in the old humble home, among the old humble folk.

He babbled in his rambling, disconnected way about things and people that Lucy had never heard of, only now and then she caught a familiar name that his memory had gone far back to seek. She didn't shrink now from the mention of her humble progenitors: the dear old rustic with a hayband round his legs, the dairywoman who kept the stall in the butter-market. At this solemn time these distinctions seemed but a small matter. The years had rolled back, and the rustic in his furrow and the Master of St. Benedict's were again boys together in their father's field. There were no distinctions now to separate them; there would be no distinctions ever again. They had all slipped away with the labour and the learning of the intervening years; with the well-earned honours—the scarlet gown and the doctor's hood; they were all among the things that had been. There was nothing left but love and tender trust—the heart of a little child.

The hours dragged wearily on; it seemed to Lucy as if the sweet June night would never end. There was not a light in a single window in the college court, and there were no stars in the sky, only the clouds hurrying on their noiseless way. The silence of the darkened room seemed to the frightened watcher to grow more oppressive as the night wore on. She could hear the rapid tick, tick of the Master's watch on the dressing-table; it could not beat the moments out fast enough. Oh, it was dreadful to hear it hurrying on, and to know that it was ticking off at every beat the few remaining moments of a human life!

Lucy listened to it until she could bear it no longer. Should she call Cousin Mary, who was with the Master's wife in the room across the passage? She had got as far as the door to call her, and then she recollected that Mrs. Rae was always listening for any sound from the Master's room, and that she would be disturbed.

The thought of the watchfulness of the Master's wife, and the love—the faithful love that had stood the shocks of more than sixty years, and had only grown truer, and deeper, and tenderer with the years—smote upon Lucy like a blow. Oh, she had never known what love was, if this was a woman's love!

She asked herself, as she sat beside the Master's bed watching the feeble, groping hand straying over the coverlet, as if it were searching for something, what the Master's wife would have done if she had been in her place. Would her love have stood the test? It had been all fair sailing with her—a long, long sequence of success, distinction, and honour. There had never been a cloud upon the horizon of her love; there had been no harder test than the test of years of patient waiting, and the happy fulfilment of all her dearest hopes. There had not been a single disappointment. Her love had never been tried like Lucy's.

Oh, it was too cruel that this blow should have fallen upon her! Lucy was quite sure that if her lines had fallen in such fair, still places as Mrs. Rae's, she would have made quite as devoted a wife. She would have been the tenderest and most loving wife to a successful man—to a man without any moral or mental taint, to a man of stainless reputation; but to a poor, miserable wretch, who had no control over himself, who wanted to be watched, and guarded, and restrained, who might at any moment do some dreadful thing——Oh, no, no, no!

Lucy couldn't finish the picture, it was too terrible. She could only throw herself sobbing on the floor beside the Master's bed and grovel on the ground with her face in her hands in a paroxysm of humiliation and despair too deep for words.

Oh, why had she such a small soul? 'I am made on such small lines,' she moaned in her self-abasement. 'I am such a mean, pitiful creature. I want to be happy, and safe, and prosperous, and everything to go smooth. I cannot rise to great occasions like other women. I cannot make sacrifices that other women would love to make. I am not Pamela—I am not even Maria Stubbs!'

Nurse Brannan came in while Lucy was on the floor beside the bed. She pretended that she was kneeling—Lucy was always pretending things. There was quite sufficient reason to account for her tears and for her kneeling beside the Master's bed. All who loved him in life should have been there, where Lucy was, kneeling and weeping. There was no one else left to kneel and weep but Cousin Mary, and Nurse Brannan fetched her presently, when she saw how near the end was.

They watched beside him until the dawn, and then the nurse drew the curtain up and let in the faint gray light of the new day. Lucy sat sobbing miserably beside the bed, and Cousin Mary held the feeble hand in hers—it was too feeble to grope any more; and the rapid beat of the Master's watch on the table beat out like a swift shuttle the solemn closing moments of the Master's life.

The sky above the chapel roof turned from gray to rose, and rose to gold. The vane on the spire caught the first gleam of the rising sun, and at the same moment the Master opened his eyes. He looked round on the group by the bedside with a glad, dazed expectation in them that had caught the brightness of another morning. He was looking round for someone; perhaps if she who he was looking for had been there he would not have seen her. His lips were moving, and Lucy bent down to hear what he was saying.

'I shall meet her at the gate,' he said. 'She is sure to be waiting at the gate.'

The sweet June morning broke, and the sun rose over the gray battlements of the old court and the roof of the college chapel; but to the old Master there was a newer day and another morning.

When Lucy came in to see the Master's wife later in the day she found her still dozing. She had not taken notice of anything or anyone all through the night. She had not missed Mary from her side; but when she heard Lucy's voice in the room—she was only speaking in a whisper—she opened her eyes, and Lucy thought she knew her.

'It is I, dear,' she said in a shaky voice. She could not keep her voice steady or the tears out of her eyes. 'It is Dick's little daughter.'

The patient face on the pillow smiled, and she moved her hand towards her—a little thin, shadowy hand, that was feebly groping about the coverlet, oh, so like the Master! Lucy took it in hers, and smoothed it between her own soft, warm palms.

Her lips were moving, and the girl bent over her to catch the words. It was the old question; she had never anything else to ask.

'How is the Master?'

Lucy ought to have been prepared for it; but she wasn't. She was so broken down and unstrung and worn out with that night of watching that she was not prepared for anything.

'Oh, you poor dear!' she said. 'Don't you know that the Master is well? He is quite—quite well!'

'Quite well?'

'Yes, quite well.'

Then Lucy began to cry. She could not keep her tears back any longer, and Cousin Mary turned her out of the sick-room. Nurse Brannan found her sobbing in the window-seat, and ordered her to bed, where she soon cried herself to sleep.

With the unimpaired appetite of youth for sleep, Lucy slept through all the long June day. She slept until the sunset light again touched the roof of the college chapel.

It would be slipping off it presently, like it had slipped off the day before, when the Master was here to watch it.

Perhaps he was watching it now.

Lucy would not have awakened even then, if Nurse Brannan had not aroused her.

'Come,' she said, shaking her; 'get up at once. Mrs. Rae is asking for you. Come at once, or you will be too late!'

Lucy did not stay to dress. She hurried across the passage with her hair falling over her shoulders and her dressing-gown, which she did not stay to put on properly, trailing on the ground behind her. Her nerves were so over-strung that it seemed to her that its rustle on the floor sent a whisper after her the whole length of the passage. It was like the Master's voice.

The face on the pillow had changed since she had seen it last. It was sharper and grayer, and the breath came shorter and at longer intervals.

The shadows were already closing around her when Lucy came into the room. She no longer opened her eyes when the girl spoke to her—she would never open them again here—but her lips were moving.

Lucy bent over her with her ear to the failing lips, but she could not catch the faint, broken words.

'I cannot hear you, dear,' she said, while her tears fell on the meekly folded hands that were groping no longer. 'I cannot catch what you say. Is it about the Master?'

She had touched the right chord—the only chord that stretched across the gulf—and the feeble lips moved. They only framed a single word:

'Where?'

'Where is the Master?' Lucy said eagerly. 'Oh, he is waiting for you at the gate. His last—last message was: "I shall see her at the gate!"'

The face on the pillow changed. It changed as Lucy bent over it.

The great, solemn change! Over all the weakness and the weariness came, not a shadow, but a light—the wondrous light of the full fruition of her changeless love.

CHAPTER XXV.

THE STALL IN THE BUTTER-MARKET.

The Senior Tutor took all the trouble of the funeral—or the funerals, rather—off the Master's nieces. He came over directly he heard that the Master was dead, and arranged everything. He knew his last wishes, expressed long ago when he was in health and the end seemed a long way off.

His wishes had been so clearly expressed that there could be no doubt about them. He had provided for every contingency. He was to lie beside his wife. If she preceded him, he was to be laid by her side wherever she was laid. If he should happen to die before her, he was to be carried back to the old place, to the old churchyard where all his humble forefathers lay, to go back to where he had started, and find his last resting-place where his life had begun. In no case was he to be buried in the college chapel. They might put up a brass for him on the old walls, among the carven tombs and tablets of the old Masters and Fellows, but the dust of his bones should not mix with theirs.

The Senior Tutor carried out his wishes faithfully. He arranged everything. There was nothing for the Master's nieces to do but to see to their own humble mourning. He came over directly he heard of the Master's death, and he was coming backwards and forwards to the lodge all the day. He wanted to get a sight of Lucy; he only wanted to see her for a few minutes; he would have preferred to see her alone. He had arranged exactly what he should say, and the time had come for saying it.

Whatever it was he had to say he had to put it off, for Lucy did not make her appearance all through that sad day.

She was so nervous and overwrought when all was over that Nurse Brannan had to put her to bed; and when she came in in the night, finding that the girl was awake and weeping, she came into her bed and lay down beside her.

Lucy could not go to sleep until she had poured out all her trouble into her sympathetic ear. She wouldn't have told Cousin Mary for the world.

Perhaps Nurse Brannan knew all about it without being told. She knew more about Lucy's lover than Lucy herself knew.

'Do you think I could do otherwise?' Lucy asked, weeping, when she had told her all her sad little story.

'Not unless you loved him very much,' Nurse Brannan said promptly. She could understand a girl doing a great deal for a man she loved.

'No—o—o,' Lucy said hesitatingly. 'I don't think I ought to marry him even then. One never knows what he may do. I should never feel safe.'

If the room had not been quite dark, Lucy would have seen that Nurse Brannan was smiling with a contemptuous sort of pity; but, whatever she felt, she only soothed and petted the weeping girl as if she had been a little child.

'You are quite right, dear,' she said; 'one never knows what such a man will do when there is no influence strong enough to restrain him. I don't think you would be strong enough to hold him back. He ought to marry a woman with a large nature, who loved him devotedly—and I think he would tax her devotion to the uttermost.'

Lucy turned to her pillow with a sigh.

'Ah!' she murmured, 'it is the old story. I am a poor thing with a small soul!' Still, she was helped and comforted.

Eric Gwatkin came over to the lodge the next morning and asked for Lucy. He was charged with a message of condolence from her lover. She saw him in the long gallery among the pictures of the old Masters. It was such a grave and stately place, there was no room for sentiment here. She knew the trial had come, but Nurse Brannan had helped her to meet it.

She looked such a white, weeping little Lucy as she came down the long gallery to meet him. She seemed to have grown so small, to have shrunk into herself with this sorrow that had fallen upon her, that Eric Gwatkin hesitated to deliver the message that had been committed to him. She had been so sorely tried within the last two days, how could he add to her pain? He would much rather have taken her in his arms and comforted her, and offered her their safe, sure shelter from all the storms of life. He would have given the world to have the right to take her in his arms, but he had to deliver his message.

Perhaps Lucy would have preferred it if he had. She wanted to be loved and comforted, and, above all things, to be safe.

But Eric Gwatkin had not come courting on his own account. He was only the bearer of a message of sympathy from her lover. It sounded cold and formal as it fell from Eric's faltering lips. If he had come himself and taken her in his arms, if she had felt the warmth of their strong pressure and his breath upon her cheek, it might have been different—it might have been quite different.

After all, it is the occasion that makes the heroine.

Eric delivered his message of sympathy, and Lucy stood white and downcast, with wet eyelashes and trembling lips, waiting for that other message that she knew was coming. He looked at her standing there—he was only a man—and he hadn't the heart to deliver it. He was so sorry for her. He was conscious of another feeling besides which he would not have owned for the world, but he couldn't keep it out of his eyes.

His eyes were full of tenderness, but his lips were faltering in a most absurd way while Lucy waited.

'You have another message for me,' she said presently, seeing he faltered and hesitated to speak.

'Yes,' he said, 'I have another message.' But he didn't attempt to deliver it.

If he had had no tenderness for the girl he would still have hesitated. How could he, looking at the white, shrinking little figure, lay this heavy load upon her?

'What has Mr. Edgell asked you to say to me?' she said in a thin, reedy little voice that she couldn't keep from shaking.

'You have heard,' he said huskily, and with a voice low and ashamed in his throat; 'everybody has heard what has happened. Knowing this, he has sent me to ask you if you will give him another trial. It is never likely to happen again—God helping him, it will never happen again—but, knowing this, and what has gone before, he has bid me to ask you if you will give him another chance.'

He paused and looked above Lucy's head; he could not look her in the face.

'His fate is in your hands,' he went on, without looking at her. 'It depends upon you whether a happy and useful life is before him. If you are true to him he will have the strongest motive to lead an honourable and honoured life that a man can have; but if you refuse to give him a chance, he will abandon all hope—he will have no inducement to make a stand.'

He said nothing about risking her happiness. It might not have occurred to him that he was asking her to risk the ruin of her young life on the chance of saving his friend. Still, he did not look her in the face.

'How can I answer him?' Lucy said, wringing her hands.

'You can only answer him as your heart dictates,' he said huskily. 'Remember, in refusing him this last chance, you are snatching away a rope from the grasp of a drowning man.'

Oh, what a coward he was: he could not look the girl in the face!

'Oh, this is horrible!' Lucy said, with a moan, and then she sat down on one of the high-backed chairs against the wall and began to cry. Her nerves were so shaken that tears came readily now.

If there was one thing more than another that Eric Gwatkin hated, it was to see a woman cry. Pamela never cried. Perhaps these foolish tears showed him more than anything else the girl's weakness. He was dreadfully sorry for her; he was sorry and ashamed of his errand. How could he press this sacrifice upon such a little weak creature?

'I am such a poor thing!' Lucy moaned, wringing her hands. 'I should never be able to influence him. Oh, you don't know how weak I am!'

Eric smiled sadly, and sighed. He knew exactly how weak she was; he would not have had a woman stronger.

'I am not like Pamela,' Lucy went on, with her little feeble moan.

'No,' he interrupted her hastily, 'thank God! You are not like Pamela.'

Lucy looked at him with wonder, through her tears, not unmixed with reproof.

'If I were Pamela,' she said, with some dignity—'if I had a great soul, and were made on larger lines, like Pamela, I should give you a different answer.'

'I must tell you,' he said hastily, interrupting her—'I must tell you, before you give your answer—your final answer—that Edgell releases you from your engagement; that he reproaches himself for having ever asked you to risk your happiness in his keeping. He begs me to say that if you have any fears or misgivings, if you have no confidence in his resolution—if you doubt him or yourself—it would be better for you to give him up.'

Lucy sighed.

'But if you can be so generous as to give him another chance, he will never, never, God helping him, betray your trust!'

Lucy looked at him with a break in the dull misery in her face. Why hadn't he delivered this part of his message first? Why had he talked about snatching away a rope from a drowning man?

'I am very grateful to him,' Lucy said, in a small shaky voice; 'tell him I am very grateful to him. I do not deserve so much love. Ask him to forgive me if he can; I am such a poor thing. I have no courage—I cannot even be generous!'

She broke quite down. She could not trust herself to say any more. She took her lover at his word. Eric Gwatkin gave her one more chance before he went away.

'Remember,' he said, 'it is his last hope of reform.'

But Lucy only moaned, 'I am such a poor thing—I have no courage!'

He went away, and left her weeping in the gallery, under the picture of the Old Master. Surely he would have approved her decision.

It was a dreadful time at St. Benedict's all through that sad week. The boat that was going to do such great things—that was going to make a bump every night of the races—did not row during the three succeeding nights.

Perhaps it was quite as well that it did not; the bumps might not have come off, and, at any rate, it had the credit of them. Most of the crew had gone down; there was nothing to stay up for. All the men, indeed, who were not staying for their degrees, or who had not people up, went down at once. There was nothing to keep them here: the college concert had been put off, and the boat ball, and the supper that was to celebrate the bumps. There was not a single festivity to celebrate; there was nothing but a funeral to stay up for.

A few men stayed up for it, and all the Tutors and Fellows. There was quite a large muster in the college chapel at the early service, when the coffins of the old Master and his wife were brought in and placed in the clear space in the body of the chapel, between the long rows of benches. There were no flowers to hide the dreary outline of the coffins—nothing to cover up their nakedness; there were no flowers heaped up in the Master's empty stall beneath the organ-loft, but someone had laid on the seat of the adjoining stall, which was draped with black, like the Master's, a wreath of immortelles. Someone—no one seemed to know who—placed the little solitary wreath on the coffin of the Master's wife, and it travelled with her down to its last resting-place.

Not a few of the Fellows of other colleges, and all the 'Heads,' followed the little sad procession to the railway-station. There were but two mourners to follow: Cousin Mary and Dick's little daughter. There were no other relatives left. The Old Master had outlived all his kin.

The Senior Tutor went down with the women to Northwold. He had made all the preparations. And as the sun was sinking at the close of the sweet June day he stood bareheaded beside the open grave, where the Master of St. Benedict's and his wife lay side by side.

They buried him in the old churchyard where his humble forefathers slept. Their stones, aslant now, and overgrown with moss and lichens, were all around him. Lucy could not help reading their rudely-carven names and homely epitaphs, as she stood listening to the solemn words that were being read over the Master's grave.

There was a Richard Rae among them who had 'died in sure and certain hope of a joyful resurrection.' What could he have done more if he had been Master of a college?

She lingered among the graves with the Tutor, and read the simple records of her humble race. She could trace her family back to the seventh generation; it was quite a long line of descent: Davids and Nathaniels and Marthas and Marys, but there was only one Lucy, the high-spirited ancestress who had kept the stall in the butter-market, and met her lover at a dancing-booth at the fair.

They left the old Master sleeping among his kinsfolk, in the old churchyard that his memory had gone back to, close to the Vicarage gate. The setting sun was shining on the church tower and on the old vane that had lingered so long in his memory, and the rooks were cawing in the old elm-trees overhead, as they turned away and left him to his rest. He would sleep more peacefully here under the daisies and beneath the dewy heavens than amid the scenes of his learned labours, under the stones of his college chapel.

The mourners returned to Cambridge the next day; there was nothing to keep them here. Before they went Lucy asked the Tutor to take her to the butter-market. Everything had changed, but the old market still stood where it had stood for centuries, with the quaint stalls and the old brown awnings, and the rude boards spread on trestles where the country folk displayed their homely wares.

There was an old woman sitting behind that corner stall now, lean and brown and wrinkled as an autumn pear. Lucy bought some flowers of her before she went away; it might have been her namesake.

It was among these homely surroundings, in this morning walk, that the Senior Tutor asked Lucy to be his wife. He knew all about her birth, and those old stories of the Master's—he had heard them dozens of times—and he had just taken her to the stall which that other Lucy Rae had once kept.

He couldn't have chosen a happier moment to press his suit. Lucy's heart had quite failed her. It had been failing her ever since that morning when she met Eric

Gwatkin in the cloisters, and at the sight of that stall in the butter-market it was at its lowest ebb. She had no spirit left in her; she had no one to cling to. She wanted to be loved and comforted and petted, and Cousin Mary was not good at petting. The Senior Tutor's offer came at the right moment; he couldn't have chosen a more auspicious time.

Lucy didn't exactly jump at him. She was too bewildered and broken down and upset generally to jump, but she asked him to give her time—to give her a week to think about it.

When a girl asks a man to give her time, he generally knows beforehand what her answer will be.

CHAPTER XXVI.

COUSIN MARY.

Lucy couldn't do things like other girls. She couldn't go straight to Cousin Mary and tell her that the Senior Tutor, the new Master of St. Benedict's, had asked her to be his wife. There was no reason why she shouldn't have told Cousin Mary. She had no one else to tell. She wouldn't have dared to have told Pamela Gwatkin or Maria Stubbs.

They had gone down now; everybody had gone down. Wyatt Edgell had gone down the day that Lucy sent back that answer to his message. He had gone without taking his degree.

Everybody was crying out at his folly, and a great many people—wise people—thought they knew the reason why, but no one guessed the real cause of his hasty departure from Cambridge.

Lucy was not sorry that he was gone. She could not have met him again in the court in the cloisters. She would not have been sure that he would not have taken her in his arms, and that all her fine resolutions would not have melted away. But he was gone down. She had nothing more to fear from him. She had an ugly dream about him the night he left Cambridge, a dream that haunted her still.

She dreamt that Wyatt Edgell was falling over the edge of a precipice, and that he held out his arms to her, but she would not reach out a hand to save him.

There was a great deal to be done in these lonely days of the Long Vacation. There was a good deal to be done, and now it could be done quietly, with no lynx-eyed undergraduates looking on.

Of course, they would have to turn out of the lodge—at least, so Cousin Mary said, when they were talking things over a few days after the Master's funeral.

The Master had behaved very generously to his niece; he had left her all the furniture of the lodge and what little money he died possessed of. He had made no mention whatever in his will of his nephew Dick's little daughter. The will had been made years ago, when Lucy's father was living, and she was not dependent on his bounty.

It was really very lucky for Lucy that the Senior Tutor had made her an offer at such a time.

'We shall continue to live together, of course, dear, if you have no other plans,' Mary said, and she paused to see if Lucy had any plans about her future, but Lucy was silent.

'I suppose you will give up Newnham now?' she continued presently, and Lucy thought there was just a shade of derision in her voice; but this was only fancy.

She might be excused for fancying it, for she had been plucked in both her examinations. She had failed in both parts of the Little-go. There was quite reason enough to account for her failing at such a time that she need not have fancied that Cousin Mary underrated her powers.

'No, I shall certainly not give up Newnham,' Lucy said with some spirit. 'I shall go in for the examination again in October. I shall continue at Newnham until—until——'

She couldn't finish the sentence, but stopped short in the middle, and blushed delightfully.

'Until what?' Cousin Mary said bluntly. She hated to see girls blushing; she never blushed herself.

'Until I am married,' Lucy said softly, and her eyes fell and her colour rose.

It was a great pity that the new Master of St. Benedict's was not there to see her.

'Married?' Mary repeated, with a little break in her voice. 'Whoever are you going to marry, child?'

She had a vision of Eric Gwatkin; she had often seen him looking at Lucy in the college chapel, and she remembered that he had called to see her several times lately. Why hadn't Lucy told her of it before?

'Mr. Colville has asked me to marry him,' Lucy said humbly.

The room didn't turn exactly upside down; if it had, all the books would have tumbled out of the shelves, and the old Worcester vases on the mantelpiece would have been broken to pieces, which would have been a thousand pities, and the furniture of the room would have been generally disarranged.

Something happened—Mary Rae never exactly knew what; she was only conscious of a band tightening round her heart, and that when she tried to speak her voice sounded a long way off.

'Mr. Colville?' she repeated in her distant, faint voice.

'Yes,' Lucy said bashfully, as if it were the first time any man had asked her to marry him; 'but I have not given him an answer yet. What answer do you think I ought to give him?'

Cousin Mary was not going to advise Lucy on this point. She knew what answer she had been prepared to give him the last twenty years.

The Master of St. Benedict's came over to the lodge for his answer the next day. He hadn't been formally elected Master yet, but the matter was practically settled. He and Mary had been doing the Master's work together for years past.

But it was not to see Mary he came to the lodge now; he asked to see Lucy, and she came to him in the gallery.

Lucy knew exactly what he had come for, and she had his answer ready for him—quite ready. It had cost her something to make up her mind. She couldn't marry a man with gray hair—only iron-gray as yet—and with a bald spot on the crown, and with a big red throat, and bushy eyebrows, and a crop of wrinkles round his eyes, without a pang. She was only twenty—sweet and twenty—and her life was before her. Yes, it cost her a pang to accept the Senior Tutor.

Perhaps it would have cost her more to reject him. He had a good deal to offer. Lucy did not lose sight of that in making up her mind. If she refused him she would have to toil through life as a governess—possibly a nursery governess. One cannot teach what one doesn't know, and a term's residence at Newnham had taught Lucy one thing: that she knew very little, and that that little was not worth much.

Perhaps if she had passed her examinations with honour—had come out in the first class—she might have given the Senior Tutor a different answer. Immense possibilities would have opened before her. She might be Senior Wrangler, Senior

Classic, Senior Theologian—oh no, women are never theologians; she might have been a first class in any Tripos, and by-and-by, when the way was made clear, she might take a high degree, and wear a scarlet hood, and—there will be such things—she might be a female Vice-Chancellor!

Now all these dreams were over. That Little-go examination had nipped her hopes in the bud. There was no other way of enjoying the highest dignity the University has to bestow than by marrying the Master of St. Benedict's. He would be Vice-Chancellor some day, and she would rule by proxy.

Lucy lay awake all one night thinking over these things. She would have preferred to marry Wyatt Edgell, all things being equal, and she shed a few small tears at giving him up. In fact, her pillow was quite wet in the morning.

She accepted the Senior Tutor the next day. She told herself that she had no more love to give away to any man: that her heart was dead within her, and that the tender dream of her youth was over, and that henceforth her life would be a dreary round of duties—perhaps dignities—but there would be no pleasure in it.

Nevertheless, when she had accepted Mr. Colville, and he had kissed her in a paternal way, and she had gone through the gallery with him, and the big drawing-room—that had been so little used during the life of the late Master—and had discussed the alterations and improvements he was going to make, she felt quite interested in life—interested, if not animated. There is nothing like furnishing for giving one an interest in life.

Mary came upon the lovers while they were discussing these details. Lucy's eyes were shining, and there were two pink spots on her cheeks which Mary had not seen there for many days, when she came across them in the big drawing-room. Mary quite understood the girl being moved, she would have been moved herself; but she did not know that the burning question that had moved Lucy so deeply was the upholstery of the drawing-room.

The new Master of the lodge had set his heart on yellow—yellow satin and dark oak. He had seen a yellow room somewhere. Lucy loved pinks and blues, and delicate creamy tints that would match her complexion; she would not have had a yellow drawing-room for the world.

Mary came upon them when they were discussing this burning question. And then Mary had to be told.

The new Master told her in as few words as he could, and about as awkwardly as a man dealing with a new subject and addressing an unsympathetic audience. He got over it as quickly as he could. He was sure Mary would have no sympathy with him. He was sure that she despised him for his ridiculous infatuation for this little bit of a girl. He was rather ashamed of himself.

'I hope you will continue to make the lodge your home,' he said to Mary, with an awkwardness that was quite new to him; 'there is no reason why you should leave it. There is plenty of room in it for all. You will keep your old room'—'and your old place,' he was going to say; but he checked himself in time, and said: 'I am sure your advice will be everything to Lucy.'

Mary Rae smiled; not scornfully, not even proudly, but with a sort of pity in her eyes, and her face was grave, and her voice was steady.

'No,' she said coldly; 'I could not continue to make my home here. My plans are all settled—quite settled. Lucy will stay with me—until—until she marries'—she could not help a little break in her voice—'and then I am leaving Cambridge altogether. I am going back to my old place, to my own people.'

The Senior Tutor had heard nothing about Mary Rae's people until that day; he never knew she had any people; he had forgotten all about her mother's relatives.

Cousin Mary began to make her preparations for leaving the lodge at once. She was only taking with her to the little house she had engaged at Newnham a few necessary things. She was leaving a great deal of the old furniture behind. It had been at the lodge for over a century. It was heavy and clumsy, and some of it was worm-eaten; it was ill suited for a modern residence. It had been taken off by one Master after another, and now, unless the new Master turned it out into the court, or threw it out of the windows into the Cam, it would remain where it had so long stood.

Lucy consented to its staying almost unwillingly. She had no idea how valuable those precious old relics of carved oak, and Chippendale, and old Sheraton furniture would have been in the eyes of a connoisseur.

She didn't mind the old blue Worcester vases remaining on the mantelpiece, where they had stood so many years; but she would have preferred some modern gimcrackery for the drawing-room. Her heart yearned for little satiny chairs with gilt backs, and plush five o'clock tea-tables, and all the latest abominations of the modern upholsterer.

It was very sad work turning out all the old Master's papers, going through all his drawers and turning out all the private records of his life.

Mary never knew until she went through his papers how generous he had been to all those poor relations she had left sleeping beside him in the churchyard at Northwold. Some of these old letters she turned out from their hiding-places, yellow with age, written by hands long folded, touched her deeply. Some were from her own kin, and some, most of all, from Lucy's father, grandfather, great-grandfather, three generations, all telling the same story of benefits received, of the unfailing liberality of that generous hand.

Mary did not know what to do with the papers. The Master had left little else—an old scholar's wardrobe, a rusty gown and hood, an old-fashioned silver watch; no rings or jewellery or knick-knacks; nothing but books and papers, everlasting papers.

Lucy would have burnt them all unread—nothing would have given her greater pleasure than to have put all the musty old lumber in the flames; but Mary would not destroy a single line.

She gathered the old family letters together and took them away with her to the little house at Newnham; but she left all the old scholar's papers, his Semitic manuscripts and pamphlets in crabbed characters that she could not understand a line of, behind her. The labours of his long useful life she left behind to the college that had enabled him to pursue these studies. Perhaps a younger scholar coming by some day may look over the heap, and pick out from it what is worth preserving.

Mary was in a great hurry to get out of the lodge. She need not have got out until the end of the Long Vacation, but she chose to clear out at once. Lucy was a little angry at all this haste. She would much rather have stayed at the lodge than have gone into a small, uncomfortable little house at Newnham.

She wrote bewailing her lot to Maria Stubbs, but she didn't say a word about her engagement to the Senior Tutor.

Maria answered her letter by the next post. She was staying up in town in a small lodging in Bloomsbury, in order to be near the reading-room of the British Museum, and she wrote and begged Lucy to come up and share her poor rooms. Her letter touched Lucy, and brought the tears to her eyes. She remembered how she used to hate Maria, and wouldn't notice her in the street. Her letter contained some information that interested Lucy, and may have had something to do with her tears.

Pamela's brother had gone abroad with Wyatt Edgell; he had been engaged by his family to travel with him and look after him. Pamela had only heard from Eric once since he had been away, and he had not written hopefully of his charge; but Maria did not give any particulars.

Lucy would have given the world to have seen that letter of Pamela's. She remembered what Eric had said about taking away a rope from a drowning man, and she recollected that dreadful dream.

Oh, if she could only have seen that letter! Perhaps even now it might not be too late.

The Master—he was really Master now—came in while her eyes were yet wet with tears. He had brought with him some patterns that had just arrived for the hangings of the new rooms. It was really a serious question. The effect of everything would depend upon the colour of the hangings. In deciding this important point Lucy forgot all about Pamela's letter.

CHAPTER XXVII.

OCTOBER TERM.

October had come, and term had begun again, and Cambridge was full of new faces—fresh young faces that would soon lose their smoothness and roundness, and that delightful ingenuousness that distinguishes successive generations of Cambridge freshmen.

There were a great many girl freshers at Newnham this term, and several of the old familiar faces were no longer seen. Pamela Gwatkin had come up for another year. A scholarship, the Grace-Hardy Scholarship, which is only given to girls in their fourth year, who have done well in a Tripos, had been awarded her to enable her to proceed to the second part of the Mathematical Tripos. When women year after year stand first on the list of the Smith's prizemen, it will be necessary to create a third part, when probably the majority of the candidates will be women.

Pamela Gwatkin had been working hard all through the Long Vacation, and she had come back pale and hollow-eyed, and oh! so lean. She will be like a deal board by the end of the year, and her beautiful, serious eyes will have nothing but mathematics in them.

Lucy had come back to work, too, but there were no mathematics in her eyes. She had just been plucked again in that horrid Part II. of the 'Previous,' which takes in Mathematics and Paley; but she had passed the classical part. She had only come up for one term. She was to be married in the spring, and she was quite, quite determined to get through the Little-go before she took her place as the wife of a Master of a college. She wouldn't be pointed at by everybody in Cambridge as a Failure!

She had got her old room next to Maria Stubbs, and she told Maria all about her engagement the first night after Hall.

Maria didn't bully her as she expected she would, perhaps she would have done the same thing herself had she been in her place.

She thought Lucy a very lucky girl; nobody had ever fallen in love with her, and asked her to preside over a college lodge, though she was twice—a dozen times, at least—as clever as Lucy. She couldn't, for her part, think what men saw in Lucy. Cousin Mary often—indeed, she had always—wondered what the Master of St. Benedict's saw in Lucy. Mary had quite given up the lodge long ago. The shabby, old-fashioned bits of furniture that she had taken away with her had all been carried over the college bridge to the little house at Newnham. She had only taken the oldest and the shabbiest things away; she had left everything that was worth leaving at the lodge.

People who had known her well remarked when they came up in October how much she had aged during the Long Vacation. She was not only looking, but she was feeling old and changed. Something had gone out of her life.

The Master of St. Benedict's noticed the change with a little twinge of conscience, but his hands were too full just now to think very much about any other woman than the woman he was going to marry.

The lodge was full of workpeople; the old place was being turned upside down. The plaster and the paint and the whitewash had been scraped off the old oak, and, oh, what a lot of beeswaxing it took to make it brown and mellow with that delightful old dull polish upon it that antiquaries love! There were all sorts of discoveries made during this pulling down and building up of old panelling. Rooms were unearthed, and musty old cupboards and passages laid open, and no end of old windows that had been blocked up for centuries brought to light. Lucy had to come over to see all these discoveries, but Mary never came to the lodge again after the day she left it. That chapter of her life was closed.

Not many people congratulated Lucy on her engagement. Very few people in Cambridge knew of it. Everyone had been expecting the Senior Tutor for years to marry the Master's niece; and when, after the Long Vacation, the engagement was spoken of, nobody ever dreamed it was Lucy.

Mary had very properly gone away from the lodge until she could return as its mistress; and Lucy—well, Lucy had gone back to Newnham to fit herself for her work as a governess. Under these circumstances she got very few congratulations.

Everybody would congratulate her fast enough when the time came. She was not doing a thing that there was no precedent for. Nearly all the heads of the Colleges in Cambridge had married young wives. It was quite the fashion.

It was not so long ago that Fellows of colleges could not marry at all, but now the order had been reversed, and the first use the dear old things made of their new liberty was to marry wives out of the nursery. As the Poet of the University touchingly put it:

'It hath been decreede, that ye Fellowes may wed,
And settle in College walls;
And wake ye echoes of cloistered life,
With their lyttel chyldren's squalls.'

There had been no children's 'squalls' heard in the lodge of St. Benedict's within the memory of the oldest Fellow in the college; no pattering footsteps on the stairs, no children's voices in the long dim galleries, had disturbed its monastic quietness. The Fellows who in their turn had been Masters of St. Benedict's had been old, old Fellows when their turn came, and one only of all their number that anyone living could remember had taken to him a wife.

Perhaps other women were not so patient and faithful as the old Master's wife.

Lucy would not have been so patient; she was getting impatient already, now the novelty had worn off. She was not sure that she was doing the best, the very best thing she could with her life; that she was making the most of it, that she was 'arranging' it aright, as they put it at Newnham.

Her heart misgave her as she pictured her future, her prosperous future, as the wife of the Master of St. Benedict's. The quiet, stately life of a college lodge oppressed her. She was sure she should soon weary of its stateliness and its loneliness. She pictured herself sometimes standing at the old oriel window and looking down at the lusty young life in the court below and longing to be in the midst of it. She was longing already. The sight of young lovers in the college Backs filled her heart with a strange tumult, and the sound of a fiddle coming from the open window of a man's room as she passed through the court set her feet twinkling. There is a great deal in heredity.

The Master met her at the lodge one day when she was in this mood. She had been working at mathematics all the morning, and she was nervous and overwrought; she had been feeling a strange depression for several days, and had come over to see the alterations at the lodge in order to shake it off.

The Master took her out into the Fellows' garden to see the new greenhouse. It had been rebuilt, and, late as it was in the season, it was ablaze with Lucy's favourite geraniums. He had considered her taste entirely, and filled it with the flowers of her choice. She ought to have been grateful, at the least, and expressed her gratitude in any of the little pleasant ways that engaged people are wont to express their feelings.

She ought to have gone round sniffing the flowers, and picked the choicest red geranium and stuck it in the Master's coat; but she did nothing of the kind. She sat down on a bench and began to cry. She couldn't keep the tears back.

Perhaps the sight of the new greenhouse had brought to her mind that scene when the old Master had fallen in the garden, and Wyatt Edgell had carried him back to the house.

Lucy couldn't account for her tears. She said it was the air of the greenhouse had made her faint, and her lover walked back with her to Newnham.

'You are sure there is nothing the matter?' the Master said before he left her; he didn't leave her at the gate, he went straight up to the door of Newe Hall with her. 'You are sure that the faintness is quite gone?'

'Yes,' she said, 'it is quite gone. It was only the heat and the smell of those horrid geraniums.'

This was rather hard on the Master, as he had gathered them together for her benefit.

There were still traces of tears on her cheeks when she got back to Newnham, and her eyes were red, and everybody could see she had been crying. Maria Stubbs saw her coming up the path with the Master, and she saw in a moment, directly she came into the hall, that there was something amiss. Nothing escaped Maria.

She followed Lucy into her room and shut the door behind her.

'You have heard, then?' she said.

Lucy noticed that she spoke in a more subdued tone than was usual to her, and there was a catch in her voice that jarred upon her ear.

'Heard what?' she said wearily. 'I have only just come back from the lodge. I have heard nothing.'

She was not very anxious to hear Maria's news. She thought it was one of the old things that was always happening: someone had passed an exam., or someone had been plucked, or someone had broken down. She was so used to these things that she did not care a straw which it was, and she began drawing off her gloves, and threw her hat down on a chair. When she had done this she became aware that Maria was looking at her with a strange pity in her eyes.

'And you have not heard?' she said with a little hard break in her voice.

'I have heard nothing,' Lucy said impatiently.

'Oh, you poor dear! How can I tell you?'

Lucy looked at her startled and amazed, with a sudden terror in her eyes.

'It is about—about——'

Her lips grew suddenly white, and refused to pronounce the name of the man who for so short a time had been her lover.

'Yes,' Maria said softly, 'it is about Wyatt Edgell.'

'He—he—oh, don't say he is dead!'

Lucy fell on her knees beside the couch and clutched Maria's gown. She was white as a sheet, and her lips were quivering.

Maria Stubbs threw her arms around her, she thought she would have fallen, but Lucy pushed her aside.

'Oh, don't tell me he is dead!' she moaned. 'Don't tell me I have killed him!'

'Hush!' Maria said almost fiercely, but her own eyes were full of tears, and her voice faltered as she spoke. 'It isn't your fault that he is dead. He would have died just the same whether you had given him up or not.'

She spoke to unheeding ears, for Lucy had fallen with a little cry to the floor.

She tried in vain to rouse her. Her face was perfectly colourless, and her lips were white, and she lay like a log where she had fallen.

Maria undid her dress and loosened the things about her throat, and threw some water over her face and hands, and then, finding she didn't revive at all, she got frightened and ran to get assistance. Pamela Gwatkin was the only girl who was in her room at that hour, and Maria implored her to come at once.

Pamela was sitting with her hands clasped before her and an open letter in her lap. She looked up when Maria came in with a bewildered look in her eyes, which were heavy with weeping.

'You must not ask me,' she said harshly; 'I would not put my hand out to save her. You must ask someone else. I can never, never forgive her!'

If Pamela could not find it in her heart to forgive the girl who had ruined Wyatt Edgell's life, it was harder for Lucy to forgive herself.

As she lay tossing with fever in her little darkened room for weeks after that miserable day, she reproached herself a thousand times for having murdered her lover. The shock of Wyatt Edgell's death had told on her already overwrought nervous system, and it had given way, and she had been struck down with brain-fever.

It was not an unusual thing in a women's college.

No one but Pamela Gwatkin and Maria knew the real cause; everyone else, doctors and all, put it down to overwork—to the mathematics she was getting up for the Little-go.

Nobody attached any meaning to her wandering, not even when in her delirium she called herself a murderess; she didn't mince matters, she shocked Cousin Mary by declaring that she was a murderess. She was for ever raving about that dreadful scene, when she had found Eric Gwatkin on his knees beside the couch, and in her dreams she was ever helping him to sew up that awful wound. She couldn't get that gaping wound out of her eyes.

Nurse Brannan came over from Addenbroke's to Newnham to nurse Lucy. Perhaps she could have thrown some light on the girl's wanderings, but she was silent. She nursed her back to life, and soothed her and comforted her in the first wild abandonment of her grief and remorse, as she had comforted the old Master. She had only one kind of medicine for all the diseases of the mind. She had only one set of old-fashioned remedies. She read Lucy in those first weak days of convalescence the same, the self-same, words from the same old Book that she had come upon her reading to the Master at the lodge. She had only one story to tell to all her patients—an old, old story. It seemed quite new to Lucy as she sat listening to it in those weak tired days; it seemed to her that she had never heard it before.

When she was well enough to talk about anything, Lucy insisted upon talking about the subject that was uppermost in her mind. Nurse Brannan let her have her way; she could not have stopped her if she would.

'You have nothing to reproach yourself with, my dear,' she said to her when she found there was nothing to be gained by silence; 'it would have happened in any case. With that tendency and that awful heritage, you could not have prevented it.'

Then Lucy learned, what she had only surmised before, that Wyatt Edgell had died by his own hand.

'You must tell me how it happened,' she said, 'and who was with him; you must not conceal anything.'

'There is very little to tell, dear. Eric Gwatkin was with him. He could not have had a truer or more devoted friend.'

'No,' said Lucy with a sigh; 'he loved him more than I loved him; he would have laid down his life for him.'

'Yes, I think he would. They were away alone together in Scotland, on some shootings that Mr. Edgell had taken, when it happened. He had been moody and out of sorts for several days, and had stayed indoors wrestling with his disease. Eric did not leave him day or night during this dreadful time, and on the fourth day the temptation seemed to have passed, and he went out on the moors. Eric was with him alone when it happened; there was no keeper near. It was all over, and—and he was quite dead when the keeper came up. There was only Eric to witness that it was not an accident. Oh, he behaved splendidly! He did everything. He brought the dear fellow back to his people; he covered up all the dreadful part of the story; and no one—no one belonging to him—will ever know that it was not an accident. It would have broken his mother's heart; it would have killed his old father, who was so proud of him; it would have been a crushing blow. Oh, Eric was quite justified—

it must have cost him a great deal to cover it up, but he was quite justified; he behaved splendidly!'

When Lucy got well enough to see anyone, the first person she saw was the Master of St. Benedict's. He had inquired for her every day during her illness, and he had sent daily messages by Mary. He reproached himself for letting her walk back on that last day he had seen her. He ought to have known that she had broken down when she fainted in the greenhouse.

He was not at all prepared for the change in her. She had not only grown thin and white, but her eyes had changed; they were graver and steadier, and something that used to be there, he didn't know what, had gone out of them.

'The lodge is quite finished,' the Master said cheerfully, as he took his seat by her side; 'your home is quite ready for you, my dear.'

Then Lucy had to say to him what she had sent for him to say. It was rather difficult to say, and she said it in her little weak, faltering voice.

'I have found out,' she said, 'while I have been lying here, that I have made a mistake. It is not the first mistake I have made—and—and thank God I have found it out in time!'

Her voice broke, and her lips quivered, and a faint flush of colour came into her cheeks.

'We have all made mistakes, my darling,' the Master said, stroking her little thin hand that lay on the coverlet. 'Don't let this little mistake you have made, or fancy you have made, trouble you; you have all your life to set it right. You have only to get well as fast as you can; your new home is ready, quite ready, for you.'

Lucy shivered.

'That is it,' she said eagerly; 'I want you to help me to set it right. I have ruined one man's life; I will not ruin another. I—I want you to give me up.'

She did not tell him she was not worthy, she knew that would be of no avail; she only asked him to give her up.

'You do not love me, Lucy?' he said reproachfully, when he found that all other arguments failed to move her.

'No,' she said sadly, 'I do not love you enough. I never, never could love you enough to marry you for yourself. I should have married you for—for the sake of your position—it is a great thing to be mistress of a college lodge—and, and I wanted a home, and to be taken care of—and loved—and I had nothing to give in return.'

It took a long time to convince the Master of St. Benedict's that Lucy hadn't accepted him for himself. He hadn't looked in the glass lately, or his eyes had grown dim—he hadn't seen that the brown locks of his youth were turning gray, and that he was getting bald, and fat, and florid. There were plenty of women in the world who would have loved him for himself still; there was a dear woman in the adjoining room who had loved him for twenty years, and who would go on loving him in spite of his baldness—who rather preferred it, indeed.

The Master couldn't conceal from himself that the girl really desired to be free. Her words, her eyes, her manner, all showed him that she desired to break off her engagement. He had no alternative but to give her the release she sought.

CHAPTER XXVIII.

A COLLEGE 'PERPENDICULAR.'

A whole year had passed. There was quite time enough in a year for things to straighten themselves—for things that had gone wrong to get right again.

One thing that had once threatened to go wrong—very wrong—had righted itself. The new mistress of the lodge of St. Benedict's was in her right place.

The lodge had taken months to restore and refurnish, and the work had been carried out quite regardless of expense. It only wanted one thing when it was finished—a mistress to preside over its stately hospitality.

The Master had not far to go to find one. He did not go so far as Newnham College; he found what he sought at an unpretentious little house in the village, furnished with very shabby old furniture.

He ought to have been ashamed of himself to have gone back to Mary. No doubt he was ashamed, dreadfully ashamed; but he went back, nevertheless. He did what is always the wisest and the noblest thing to do; he went back and confessed his folly, and asked to be forgiven. He did not ask in vain.

Mary is now the most popular mistress of a college lodge in Cambridge, and the handsomest. She has grown quite young again; the ordeal she has passed through has only added a tender, pathetic nobleness to her beautiful grave face. The hope of her youth, of her mature womanhood, is fulfilled. She cannot help looking prosperous and handsome.

And Lucy? Well, Lucy went back to Newnham when she was well enough—when she had quite recovered—and passed the Little-go with distinction. She worked at her Tripos all through the next year, and Pamela Gwatkin was her coach.

She was about as unhappy as a girl with a 'small soul,' as she still described herself, would be, after what she had gone through; but her mathematics diverted her thoughts, and the prospect of her coming Tripos sustained her.

At the end of the year an event happened which affected Lucy's views on the subject of her Tripos; that cut short, in a not wholly unprecedented way, her University career.

At the close of the October term, the Master of St. Benedict's gave what is known in undergraduate parlance as a 'Perpendicular.'

At this particular 'Perpendicular' all the Dons and Donesses in Cambridge were present to do honour to the new mistress of the lodge, and the whole suite of reception-rooms, that had been the subject of such heartburnings to Lucy, were thrown open.

It was the first time that she had ever seen them lit up and filled with such a goodly company. She was there with Maria Stubbs and Pamela Gwatkin, as her cousin's guests. She had not altered much during the year; only her eyes were steadier, and she did not blush so readily.

She ought to have been blushing now, for she had just met an old friend who had taken her hand when they met and had forgotten to give it up again.

It was Pamela Gwatkin's brother.

He was in Orders now; he had been ordained nearly a year, and held a curacy in a village in the West-country, with the magnificent stipend of one hundred and fifty pounds a year.

He had gone through all the familiar rooms of the old lodge with Lucy, but he had hardly recognised them again. Only in the long gallery the faces of the old Masters looked down on him as of old, with a stately welcome in their grave eyes.

He had no idea that the dark, musty old place could have been so changed. He passed through room after room, with Lucy's arm in his; and presently, when she was tired, he sat down in the deep-recessed window of the oak-panelled saloon, where the Masters hold their annual feasts and eat their state dinners.

Full-length portraits of old Masters and Fellows hung on the walls, and above their massive gilded frames—they had been regilt lately—a rich carved frieze of oak went round the room; and above the great open fireplace was a quaint carven mantelpiece that was a sight to see. It was a room to delight the soul of an antiquary.

Lucy watched Pamela's brother as his eyes travelled round the room and took in all these things. He was such a simple, transparent fellow that she could not help reading his thoughts.

'What are you thinking of, Eric?' she asked him presently. She called him Eric.

'I—I?' he said, with a blush. 'I was wondering why you gave up this—how you could give up this!'

'Did you wonder?' she said softly, and her eyes, he saw, were very sweet and tender. He thought she lingered on the 'you,' and he looked at her with a strange trouble in his eyes.

'Yes,' he said with a sigh, 'I don't think many women would have—have given this up lightly. You must have had a reason?'

'Yes,' she said in her low voice, with a quiver in it, and that droop of her pretty mouth that he remembered so well; 'I had a reason.'

Something in her manner more than in her voice struck him, and the trouble in his eyes deepened.

'May I know—will you tell me the reason, Lucy?' he said hoarsely.

'I could tell anyone but you,' she said passionately, and then she turned away her face from him, but not before he had seen that her eyes were full of tears.

Then a strange light came suddenly into his eyes as he looked at her as she sat there in her soft white clinging gown, with her bosom heaving, and the rich colour sweeping over her neck and face.

'You do not mean——Oh, Lucy!' he said, and his voice shook, and the trouble in his eyes gave place to the light of a sudden wild hope.

Whatever she meant, it was whispered so low that it reached no other ear than his.

Before Lucy went back to Newnham that night with her friends she had a little interview with her beautiful hostess. Cousin Mary looked like a queen with her gleaming jewels and her rich dress.

It was not a dress intended to be crushed; it was intended to be put away carefully, and to be worn at no end of grand University receptions and dinner-parties; but Lucy threw herself upon it in the most unfeeling way, and let her foolish tears—they always flowed very copiously—stream down the beautiful satin bosom and over the lovely real lace.

'Oh Mary, congratulate me,' she murmured; 'I am going to marry Eric Gwatkin!'

She was going to marry a curate with one hundred and fifty pounds a year. She had thrown over the Master of a college, and she was asking Cousin Mary to congratulate her!

What can be expected of the children of such a union? They will neither be beautiful nor clever. Probably in a generation or two they will go back to the low estate from which they sprang, and another Lucy may keep the old family stall in the butter-market. Heredity has so many vagaries it is not safe to predict.

The success of the old Master may repeat itself in the male line, and another Anthony—Lucy's boy is called Anthony—may occupy with equal distinction as a Church dignitary another stall elsewhere.

Who can tell?

Meanwhile Lucy is famous for her poultry, and, like her distant progenitor, prides herself on the excellence of her dairy.

THE END.

IT WAS MEANT TO BE

K.M LOWE

Author History

Kelly McMullen Lowe was born on 19th March 1986, to the proud parents of Christine Greenlees Beaumont Steedman and Hugh Patrick McMullen. My parents taught me the true value of life and they showed me how to succeed. I married my husband David Lowe, on 30th December 2006 and we have two wonderful children named Dylan and Tianna. Over the last couple of years I was unwell and I put all my time into my family and books. However, in 2012 I wanted to commit myself to writing my own novel. I have put a lot of time and effort into this new book. I hope that you all enjoy it, as much I did writing it.

Acknowledgements

First of all, I would like to thank Kellie Dennis, for helping mc to create a beautiful cover for my third novel. You have helped me through a difficult time when I couldn't see forward and I will always be grateful to you.

Secondly, I would like to thank Alan Riehl at Riehl Faith Productions, for editing my book. This process has been so much easier with you guys on my side. You answered all of my questions when I had any. I hope to have you as my editor for a long time to come.

Also, I would like to thank my family and friends for putting up with me over the last couple of months. My husband will get some sense out of me for a couple of weeks, until I start writing again. This book would not have been possible, if it wasn't for the support of my husband. I love you to the moon and back.

Next, I would like to thank my children for being my little angels. I love you dearly and you mean the world to me. I hope that one day you will be able to read mummy's work. In the meantime Dylan, you can read the blurb. My son is my very own book worm. I hope when he gets older, he will still enjoy reading.

Finally, to my readers. Thank you all, for purchasing my books. It means a lot to see so many of you reading what I write. All of your lovely reviews and comments make everything worthwhile. Your

encouragement to buy the Smile series, gave me the nudge I needed when I was at a low point in my life. I have made lots of new friends from all over the world. That wouldn’t have been possible, if it wasn't for my writing.

Thank you!

Dedications

I would like to dedicate this novel to my wonderful husband, David. He isn't just my husband, he is my best friend. Without him I would never be able to write. He has shown me so much support over the last couple of years and I can’t thank him enough.

PROLOGUE

Leela Park thought she had her life worked out. She was a straight A student, with a wonderful career ahead of her. She had everything she ever dreamt of and more. She spent four long years studying at the University of Stirling, where she finally achieved a degree in Psychology. Her life was on the up. She never thought that anything could knock her off of her pedestal. Up until ten days ago, she was the happiest that she had ever been. She had everything. A life. A job. A partner. A future. It was so easy how quickly things changed. Leela was always hoping and praying for the best out of life. Could she find a happy ending when she least expected it?

CHAPTER 1
Life is like a piece of string!

Leela's boyfriend Mark was a constable in Strathclyde Police force. She was thinking of how lucky she was, because they had been dating each other for the last ten months. They've been together without any downward spirals and they've enjoyed many high moments as a couple. Everything was great. So great at times, that she had to pinch herself on many occasions. Mark called her that afternoon and asked if she would go for dinner with him that night. He was always showering her with gifts and taking her out to lovely places. No one could ever imagine how much she loved him. He was her Mr. Right. She couldn't ever imagine life without him.

That day flashed by quickly. Her thoughts were never far away from him. Many things always remind her of him and lately it was

trivial things, like a smell or someone talking. Thinking of her loved one always got her through her day. Especially since her morning routine never changed. She was always glad when lunch time arrived, because her afternoon clients were a mixed bunch. She even had a group session, with a bunch of ex-soldiers that day. That always made her afternoon eventful. She loved to see how far her heroes have come since they enrolled in her programme for Post-Traumatic Stress. They were like her babies and pride beamed from her on those occasions.

When she made plans with Mark early on, something always crept up on her. She always got side tracked and time was never on her side. However, everything happened when it was supposed today. No one was late for appointments and Leela managed to leave work on time for a change. Normally something would go wrong, or they would get called out to emergencies on the wards, but that day was a good day. She had to stop thinking negative and accept that good things really did happen.

Leela's Story

I came home from my placement at the local hospital to get ready for my date with Mark. I had a smile from ear to ear just thinking about him. I loved how he made me feel inside. All I could feel was warmth and love. All I could think about was that my bad day was over and it was about to get much better.

As I pottered around tidying things up, I glanced up at the clock. I quickly realised my lovely Mark was late. I got that weird feeling in the pit of my stomach, because Mark was one of the most punctual people I had ever came across. My gut told me there was something wrong, but I didn't want to overreact. Especially when my house was empty. It could just mean he was working overtime, because everyone was late coming home and they all work together. My mind was beginning to imagine all kinds of things. I was always a worrier. Even more so, because most of my family work in the police force. I know how quickly things could crop up. Then before

you know it, hours have passed without them even realizing. They only realize that everyone's been a nervous wreck when they come home. I nag in their ear about a simple text message. It's not hard to let your loved ones know what's going on. I groan about the long hours they work, but if it wasn't for my brother being a constable, I wouldn't have met Mark. I would never forget that either. That was one of the only things I had to thank my brother for. He was twenty-seven years of complete and utter nonsense. No one would ever believe he was a police man, because he was a complete laugh a minute. Craig and Mark became good friends when they got paired together over a year ago. I was glad that my brother had finally found a good friend. We were all beginning to settle after the horrible few years we've had.

Even when I started dating Mark, I was a bag of nerves, because I've always seen Craig as the joker. I thought I would have been too grown up for him if he could relate to Craig. However, to my shock, Mark never had a bad word to say about Craig. He always told me he was a great officer and there was no laughing or joking on the job. Mark always praised my brother and I loved to see how close they were. I was happy to see their relationship bloom in and out of work. My dad was a D.C.I. at the same station. Even he had to laugh at the fact, that Craig was paired with Mark. But to be honest, they were excellent at their job and no one could take that away from them. It was at home that we got to see their true personalities. I suppose when I thought about it, I was different at work as well. If someone at my work had to describe me in three words it would be quiet, timid and reliable. My family would probably beg to differ with those characteristics. However, we looked at one another as a close knit family.

I managed to snap out of my over active thoughts for a few moments and I could see there was no need for any of it. The fact that the whole house was empty only meant that they were all still caught up at work.

Pacing around was only making me worse. The bottle of red wine on top of the worktop caught my eye. It was the perfect cure to calm the nerves. The moment I poured my glass, I saw the reflection of lights in the window. It was good timing on their part, because I

knew alcohol would never cure anything. Besides, I wasn't supposed to be drinking anyway. My heart stopped beating, as I saw that my dad was home. He was about to tell me I was a born worrier, but there was no need for me to worry about them. I moved slowly into the hallway to see my dad coming in through the door with Craig tagging slowly behind him. The looks on their faces let me know that there was something wrong. Their faces were like stone with no sense of expression. I really was worried. Craig went right through to the study and I heard the lid getting lifted from the crystal decanter. Whisky wasn't a drink Craig ever touched, but at the moment I could see it didn't matter what the drink was, as long as it was alcohol.

"Hey sweetheart." My dad's arms wrapped around me and I instantly knew that whatever was going to come, was bad. Craig never walked off without acknowledging anyone in the house, let alone me, his sister.

"I take it you guys had a bad day? I've been waiting for Mark for the last hour. I guess he's been tied up with Craig?" I said it with the hint of sadness in my voice. I was waiting for someone to tell me that he would only be five minutes, but no one was telling me anything. I was screaming inside to know what was going on. I was doing a good job not expressing my feelings. They would be worried if they could see my insides being ripped to shreds.

"You better come and sit down sweetheart." As my dad took my hand, he led me into the study. I could see Craig sitting with his head in his hands, with a glass of stiff whisky touching his head. It was evident that I had every right to be worried about something. I just wanted answers, because I was going out of my head with worry and fear.

"Dad. You're scaring me. Will you tell me what's going on?" He sat me down beside Craig, and he perched on the table in front of us. My eyes darted from Craig to my father and back again. While my dad started to squeeze my hand, I could feel the pain build up inside me. The silence was killing me piece by piece and someone needed to start talking. Sooner rather than later.

"Have you seen the news today, Leela?" I could only shake my head. Work kept me busy today, just like any other day. There was

no time to stop and see what was on the news. Not that it was something I would normally do in my spare time anyway. "There was an accident at about 3pm today." My father's shaky voice made me feel worse. I could feel my body shaking underneath his hand, but I needed to know about the accident. Where was Mark? I was shaking from the unknown.

"Accident?" My voice was shaking, as much as my legs. I managed to bring myself together just to find out what was going on.

I looked at Craig and immediately thought it had something to do with him. He was in some state and that had me concerned. I had never seen him like that before. "Craig? What happened?" Putting my spare hand on his shoulder, let me see how tense he was. I needed to know why he was like that, because nothing looked like it was going to shake him out of it.

"Mark and Craig were called out to a disturbance today. When they got there they had to go up to a top floor flat. They had no idea what they were going to be faced with. It was a 999 call and they were in the area. But..." My dad stopped in his tracks and I knew that it was bad. I couldn't take the suspense anymore.

"But what, dad? What happened?" My patience was wearing thin. I needed to know everything.

"As they got to the door two men were running out. Craig chased them like any other officer would have done. Mark on the other hand, was the one that went into the flat to see what the disturbance was. Two people had been shot dead!"

Shot dead. Other people. My head was going crazy. I needed to see Mark. He must be going out of his mind after seeing that.

"So, where is Mark now? I need to see him. To see that he's okay." The silence was agonizing. That was worse than hearing words I didn't want to hear. "Why are you like this dad? I mean, you work in Glasgow! You see this kind of crime every other week!" I knew there was going to be more. I didn't know if I wanted to hear it now.

"He's dead, Lee." My brothers voice rung in my ears. I could hear it over and over again. My dad was going into detail after detail, but I was glad that Craig just told me straight.

The tears started to roll down my cheeks as I took it all in. I couldn't stop hearing Craig's words repeating in my head. It was like

a stuck tape recording. "I should have stayed with him, but I didn't. I should've been shot with him." I could hear my brother's words, but my mind was still stuck on the fact that he was dead.

"Leela. Did you hear what Craig just said?" Again, I could hear my father speak, but I didn't want to hear any of it. I wanted this to be some kind of nightmare.

"I am so sorry, Leela. I should have been dead with him. I wish it was me." Craig's sobs started and I didn't quite know what to do. I wanted to comfort him but I was stuck in my seat. I was afraid of approaching him, just in case I blamed him for everything.

"Craig. Don't think like that son. No one knows what they would have down in the same position. Mark was a fantastic officer and he went on without you. I know you would have done the same if he went after the runaways." The conversation was going around in my head. I wanted it all to be one big joke. I was listening to *partner this* and *partner that*. What was his real life partner going to do now? What was I going to do without him?

"We should have waited for back up." I watched my brother jump up. It brought me out of my trance, but I still couldn't speak. The shock had stunned me into silence. "Because of it, so many people are going to pay the price." Anyone could see how much Craig blamed himself. I could see that he would trade places with Mark if he could. He now had the job to help me grieve for my partner and that was going to be a difficult job to do.

"This can't be happening!" I flew off of the couch and went to get my mobile phone from the kitchen. "He can't be dead! He just can't be gone! We need him here!" I was frantic. All I wanted was Mark to answer my call. I wanted him to tell me that it was all a big mistake. He should be on his way to pick me up for a lovely evening. I didn't need this. Then I heard his voice come over his voicemail and I crumbled into pieces. Craig came in and caught me as I fell into his arms.

Reality suddenly hit me like a tonne of bricks. I sobbed until my body went still and quiet. I felt safe in Craig's arms. I never wanted to leave him. I never wanted to face another moment without him around. Everything about Mark went round in my mind and I wasn't grasping anything around me. My body was here but my soul

seemed vacant of substance. I couldn't believe I was never going to see or hear him again.

Craig did what anyone would have done in his situation and comforted me for as long as I needed him. He held back his tears and pain, just to let me get it all out in the open. Bottling everything up would be the worst thing for me to do. I hoped that I would feel better getting it out. I knew all of this, because it was the same thing that I spouted every day to my clients. I never thought for one minute I would have to use therapy on myself.

Craig and I were crumpled together for about an hour. He sat in complete silence, until I felt ready to move.

"We were talking about our future just last week. Why does everything in my life have to turn out like this? What have I done, Craig?" My head was all over the place. Nothing was going to make any sense to me for a while. Maybe it never would. I knew Craig would make sure he was here for me whenever I needed him.

"You will still have a future, Lee. You're perfect in every way and I'll be here for you. Mark wouldn't want your life to stop." He knew that wasn't what I wanted to hear, but he was just trying to give me a sense of hope.

"I don't want anyone else, Craig. I wanted to marry Mark and spend the rest of my life with him." Still clasped in my brother's arms, I was about ready to get everything off my chest.

"Look sis. I know for a fact that Mark would want you to be happy. He wouldn't want to see you like this." I stood up and went over to my glass of wine. My body felt like it was floating in mid-air. All I wanted was to feel stable.

"You don't know anything Craig." I poured my glass of wine down the sink and put the lid back on the bottle. I was thinking clearly enough to know drinking myself into oblivion wasn't going to help me.

"I will be here for you. I will always look out for you, Leela." Craig was hoping I could get through this, but after the ordeal it was going to be a hard one.

"Craig..." Craig knew that there was more to my shock, but he didn't want to push me into anything. He let me know that he would always be here for me and the rest was up to me. I knew he would be

around when I wanted to talk. He would be there to listen to me scream, shout, and just let it all out. It was the least he felt he could do for me. Although, I didn't want him to blame himself.

"Leela. I'm always going to be here for you, no matter what."

"No matter what?" I spoke with a hint of sarcasm in my voice. My tear stained face looked out over the sink and my reflection in the window said it all. My life was never going to be the same again. I was facing all of the facts now, instead of dragging everything out.

"No matter what, Leela." Craig's hand went round my waist and the tears flowed down my cheeks. I felt his big bear frame wrap around me and I felt myself at ease. "Even if I'm pregnant?"

The silence in the air made me turn round to face my brother. As the tears rolled down his cheek, I reached up and wiped them away. I didn't tell him to make him feel worse. I told him so he could be there to help me.

"Did Mark know?"

"He knew that I did a home test. He just didn't know that I got it confirmed today. He was over the moon when I told him this past weekend. I was shocked that he took it so well, because we never really spoke about kids." My mind felt ten times lighter, getting the baby news off of my chest. He looked grateful that I could confide in him. He now knew that I would confide in him if I needed to.

"He would have been a good daddy." Craig stopped me from going any further and he felt like he had the weight of the world on his shoulders. He didn't just lose a work colleague or a friend. His sister lost her partner and the father to their unborn child. We were a great pair.

"What am I supposed to do, Craig?" He looked stunned that I was asking him his opinion. He was never the level headed guy that I would usually ask. He knew that he needed to be strong for me. All the joking was put a side.

"Get some sleep. Take care of yourself and we will talk about all of this when you get up. I've been given a week's leave, so I'll be here to help you get through this." I was honoured that I had a great family. It would have been a lot worse if I was on my own.

"I should tell dad about the baby, but I don't know how to. I felt okay about it before, because I had a good job and a wonderful

partner. We were ready for a baby. Now that's all shattered." I was frightened of everything and I wasn't sure that I would ever feel okay again.

"You have me and dad who will always be here for you. Scott and Sheree will be back from university at the end of June. They'll be here to help you as well. I know that you've always been closer to Scott, but I will do anything I can until he gets home." Just as Craig finished talking, he placed a piece of hair behind my ear. There was a knock on the door and we both looked in the direction of the front door. We knew that our dad would do the honours, so neither of us moved. Then I heard him showing someone through to the kitchen. I was stunned to see Mark's mum and dad.

"Mr and Mrs. Mackinnon. I'm so sorry for your loss." Craig was first to offer his condolences, while I was still stuck on the spot. The tears were still rolling down my cheeks and I couldn't stop them just because I had visitors.

"Thank you Craig! We just stopped by to make sure that Leela was alright." Everyone's eyes were on me. I wanted to say that I was fine, but I couldn't. I wanted my Mark to walk back in behind everyone.

"I don't know what to say." My body felt empty. "I'm shocked beyond belief, to be truthful. I crumpled to pieces when my dad and Craig came home. I knew something wasn't right, because Mark was meant to pick me up after work. When his usual time came and went, my mind started to play tricks. I know Craig and Mark usually take the piss about me worrying about them, but I just had an awful feeling in the pit of my stomach." My voice ran thin, as I couldn't contain my grief anymore. I felt like my whole body was getting ripped apart, piece by piece.

"Will you promise us that you'll take care of yourself?" As Mrs. Mackinnon spoke to me, I had a funny feeling that she already knew about the baby. I looked at Craig to help me out but I wasn't sure he knew what to say. I couldn't handle the big talk about all the pros and cons of the first stages of pregnancy. Not right now, anyway.

"I will do whatever I can. I'm not promising anything. Mark promised me at the beginning of the week that we would spend the next eighteen years caring for our son or daughter. We laughed and

joked about what he would be like with a teenage daughter. I can still hear his voice. Our laughter." A smile crept up on my face, as I could see and hear Mark's reaction to a baby girl. Why was life so cruel? Why did this happen to us?

"Am I missing something here?" My dad was a detective and he could pick up on anything. Somehow he never sensed any of this before tonight. He used to drive us all crazy when we were kids. We could never keep anything from him, because he knew us too well. It was good in a way, because we never got bogged down with anything. We never stressed over things and we lived a happy life.

"Dad. I didn't know that Mark had told his parents anything. I wanted to get it confirmed first."

"Leela. You're worrying me. What are you talking about? We've all had enough shocks for today, so please don't keep anything from me, sweetheart." My father's voice had a pleading tone to it. That was the moment I had been waiting for. I hoped that Mark and I would be telling him this together, but now I was left on my own.

"To set the record straight we only found out, because I got to see Mark on Monday night after you left. He was on cloud nine." I couldn't help but smile at Mark's mum, because I knew exactly what she meant. He was like a child with a new toy when I told him.

"I'm 7 weeks pregnant dad." My hand rested over my stomach and I leaned back in toward Craig. I could feel my brother's warmth and love and it eased my pain. I desperately wanted my dad to say something, but he stood there not saying a word. "Dad. I know a week ago we had it all. We just had a house to buy. Now everything seems so bleak. I don't want you to be disappointed in me."

"That was one of the things Mark wanted to show you tonight." We all looked back over at Mrs. Mackinnon, because none of us knew what she was talking about. "Mark had stupidly bought a house for you both, sight unseen. I say stupidly, because I know if it was me, I would want to see it first. But Mark…well…he wanted to show you how much he loved the idea of you having a baby together." Again, the tears rolled down my cheeks. It was just another thing that showed me how much I had lost today. "I will leave these here for you." I watched her lay a set of keys and papers down on the work top. I couldn't believe that this was happening.

"No!" I couldn't help but yell out. I didn't feel like I could accept the deeds and keys to a house I never paid for. "I can't accept them! I won't accept them!" I knew I must have sounded ungrateful, but none of it was mine. Mark bought it for us, but there wasn't going to be any *us* anymore.

"Mark wanted you all to be comfortable and happy as a family."

"I will never feel comfortable and happy again, Mrs. Mackinnon. Your son was the only thing I ever wanted and we are never going to be a complete family now. I'm going to be a single mum bringing up this baby to the best of my ability. How am I supposed to tell him or her, that they'll never see their daddy, because he's with the angels? No house is going to bring him back and no house is going to make us a family again!" I realised how childish I must have sounded, but I wasn't going to lie about something so big. We had everything twenty-four hours ago and everything had a meaning. Nothing made sense anymore.

"Nothing is ever going to bring him back my dear. This is what Mark set up for you and the baby. I'm not forcing you to take it, but just think about it when you've had time to calm down." I didn't want to hurt anyone else, so it was easier for me to shrug my shoulders and agree that I would think about it. "We will organise the funeral as soon as Mark's body is released. We will let you know when and where it's going to be held." Another knife struck my body. I felt like I was never going to be a part of arranging his funeral. My head was full of mixed emotions and I just wanted to close my eyes and never wake up. I wanted to know what we had done to deserve any of this. Life has a mind of its own and we never know how long we have on this earth. Mark and I were living life to the max, because we thought we would be around to see our grandkids grow up. We had everything to live for, but now I was going to be mummy and daddy. I had to find the inner strength from somewhere.

"If we can do anything to help you, please let us know. Craig has been given one week's leave and I am sure he would be happy to help with anything you need." I saw my dad looking over at Craig. I carefully nudged him without anyone noticing.

"Yes, of course. I would be honoured to help. My main concern at

the moment is my sister, but I am yours for anything you need." It was hard to see Craig so grown up, while not having a laugh and a joke. We've all had a big wakeup call today. They go out to work to keep us all safe, but who's keeping them safe?

"Thank you Craig. My wife and I appreciate that very much. Leela? Will you keep us posted with the progress of the baby?" I wasn't about to be mean and cut them out of their grandchild's life. They lost just as much as I did and Mark would want them to be a part of the baby's life.

"Of course I will, Mr. Mackinnon. Mark isn't here and it's not going to be the same, but we will always have a part of him with us." I had to have them in my life. They both meant a lot to Mark. Yes, they had their disagreements just like any family did, but they were going to mean a lot to me for my unborn baby.

"I think we all need to get some rest," said Mr. Mackinnon. "It will help us take it all in properly. We will leave you now, but we'll keep in contact if need be." Mr. Mackinnon looked emotionally drained, as he made his last comments. I felt sorry for them both. It was every parent's worst nightmare, to bury their child before them. I could only imagine how they felt. I felt bad enough. I didn't want to move away from Craig. I knew that he would look after me. It was a good reminder of what Mark use to do for me. I stood and watched, as my dad let Mr. and Mrs. Mackinnon out. I knew our conversation wasn't over with. Since my mother passed away three years ago, my dad had done everything. He was mum and dad to us all. I was so glad I still had him. I just wasn't sure what he was going to say. I was a twenty-eight year old woman. I was ready to settle down and have a baby. Nothing was going to stop me. This baby was going to be my little piece of Mark and I would cherish every moment we could share. He or she was going to be my little miracle gift, no matter how bad the grief was. My dad has been a true inspiration to us all. I know that I'll be able to do this, because he had done it for us. I might have a head full of bad things floating about, but I knew that I would be okay.

"Dad. Before you start, I'm not in any mood to get a lecture from you." I had to get my neb in first. However, I was surprised when he came right up to me and Craig. I was sandwiched in between them

both. I felt the love and warmth of both of the male role models in my life. With them on my side I would get through almost anything.

"I wish that you had told me about the baby sweetheart. Now that we all know and everything is out in the open, we're all going to be here to support you. Mark has provided for you both, but you have your family for support darling. To answer you from before, I could never be disappointed with any of you. Don't you ever forget that. Okay?" I was amazed at how well my dad was taking the news. I was lucky to have a family like these guys, especially when some people have nothing. We were always brought up to look after one another and I was glad they were here for me now.

"I don't know if I can do it without him dad." I wanted to be brave, but my strength was gone. I know the baby and I will be looked after and we will get through all of this with my family's support. But without Mark, it was going to be a very hard road.

"Shhh. You've just been dealt a rough hand, but you're always going to have us. There are plenty of single parents in the UK, and they manage just fine. You will manage just fine. Let's get the funeral and the inquest out of the way, then we will give you some time to come to terms with everything. It's going to be stressful, but you will need to take things easy. None of it matters apart from you and this little one and you're going to let us take care of you."

The feel of my dad's hand on my stomach made me tear up again. Mark did the exact same thing when I told him. He said that he was going to talk to my stomach every day until I gave birth. It was all the silly little things that were going to play on my mind. Little things that I was never going to forget.

"I love you guys." That was the only thing that I could say at the moment. I was usually chatty and full of beans around my family, but *that* Leela was gone tonight. I had to try and find the new grown up me that was going to be strong for me and my baby. I knew it was going to be difficult, but I was up to the task.

"We love you darling, and we will always be here for you. If you need anything you just need to ask." I didn't want to leave my dad and Craig's comforting hugs at the moment. "The press is going to try to get a story. They're going to love getting their teeth into it all, but they will go away in a couple of weeks." I suddenly realised that

I wasn't going to get the peace and quiet I wanted. I suddenly felt uneasy and awkward about it all. I hated confrontation with anyone and I just knew that the press would push me into a corner. I wish that my dad never mentioned the press. It was like I was getting hit with one thing after another. I was never going to get any peace.

"I'm off for a week anyway. Just let them come anywhere near you and they'll have me to deal with." I couldn't help but smile, because that was the Craig that I needed right now. I could deal with anything, if everyone I cared for backed me up. "I've always wanted to punch one of them. They thrive off of grief and it makes me sick." I could sense my brother's anger. I have never been on this side of the press before, but I had a funny feeling it would only be a matter of time before I got a view of what they were like.

"They have a job to do Craig." My dad always saw the best in people. "Although, they could go about it in a better manner."

"They can't come into the gardens though. Can they?" I was a nervous wreck and I was only getting myself worked up.

"No. They can't, sweetheart. They can't come passed the gates, which will be shut, unless we're going out." I calmed down slightly, because I knew that my dad wouldn't lie to me. I trusted him with my life. "Go and get a nice hot bath and try to get some sleep. We will be here whenever you need us." I liked the sound of everything my dad said. I wanted to relax and get my head around it all. For the first time in my life I was mixed up and I didn't know whether I was coming or going.

"Thanks Dad. I think I'll do as I'm told." Hot bath and rest sounded like bliss. However, I didn't think I would be able to switch off my emotions any time soon. I wanted to wake up and realise this was all one horrible nightmare. That was never going to happen. This was something I was going to see through and I had to hope for the light at the end of the tunnel.

I kept thinking about my mum's death. This was different. My mum was ill for a start. We had three weeks to come to terms with losing her to lung cancer. We knew that she was dying from the start, but it was extremely hard when her eyes closed and her heart stopped beating. We were all left to pick up the pieces and had to try and move on. With Mark, no one expected him to go anywhere. He

was young and had the rest of his life ahead of him. Life and death are so very close together. It just takes that fine line to snap, leaving everyone in turmoil. Life really was like a piece of string. It can be as long or as short as God decides to give us. We only realise we are no longer on this earth when we turn into an angel in Heaven. We are then on the other side looking over our loved ones. That was something I could take from this situation. My Mark was our guardian angel and he was up there looking after us. I could only hope that he could guide me down the right path and I do what's right by me and our baby.

CHAPTER 2
The Dream That Felt Real

"Wake up sleepyhead." Rolling onto my back I could feel a huge smile on my face. I just loved getting woken up by Mark. It's been the first morning, since I was pregnant that I've woke up last. I was feeling refreshed this morning and that's all thanks to a good sleep. His soft kisses trailing down my shoulder, made me giggle. His hand rested on my stomach, as I felt the baby kick. It was saying to him clearly to get off my mummy, because you're crowding my space.

"This little one is going to be a footballer, Lee."

"You're just hoping for a boy. I hope she is a girl and you'll have to take her to dance classes." I loved having these conversations with him. I would just be glad when he or she makes their appearance. "Today is D-Day. What do you think?"

"He's going to be stubborn like his mummy and make us wait as long as he possibly can." We both laughed, as he sounded like a spoiled child getting told, no. I have laughed and cried for the full nine months and now I was getting fed up. We wanted our baby here, so we could finally be a family together. "I have to go to work as well. I can't get my maternity leave until this little one graces us with his presence. Are you going to get Scott over to sit with you? It's good that he's home from university at a time like this."

"Will you stop fussing over me! I will be absolutely fine. I will have my phone with me at all times. Any sign I get, I will phone you. If I can't get you, I will call my dad. He always has his phone with him and he is the boss. I am sure he can get you to me." I felt like a child again. I was really hoping the baby didn't go overdue, because I would crack with all the fussing and mollycoddling.

"You can still get Scott over, or I can drop you off at your dad's and I'll pick you up when I finish." I was never going to hear the end of this.

"Will it keep you off my case if I go to my dad's?" His nodding head was like one of those nodding dogs with the sad puppy eyes. "No hundreds of phone calls and text messages, because your head needs to be on your work."

"I'll wait for you to phone me. I promise" I knew for one moment his promise would be void. He wouldn't even be able to get until lunchtime, without sending me a message. I loved him for his kind heart and warm personality, but he's changed into baby-zilla. "I'm going to go for a shower. I'll leave the water running for you."

"Thank you!" I rolled back onto my side. I could quite easily close my eyes and go to sleep. But oh no, my other half thinks it's a good idea to drag his heavily pregnant fiancée out at seven o' clock in the morning, because it's my due date. I was groaning, but then I would be groaning if he didn't show me any love and affection. It was crazy how quickly these nine months have flown by. Although, now that my due date was here, I wasn't sure if we were one hundred percent ready, or if we were ever going to be ready.

***

I woke up out of breath and soaking with sweat. I had no idea what had just happened. I couldn't stop myself from crying and it was so soar. Everything that happened earlier all came flooding back to me. Only this time it was harder. The dream that I had felt so real that I thought I could still smell Mark around me. I was a psychologist and I knew only too well that the mind is a wonderful thing. I was in no mood to sit and analyse my dreams, but I knew that I was dreaming what I wanted to happen in the future. I didn't usually dream and I didn't want to start now. That was the only way I was going to see Mark. It just wasn't fair. I was going to have to try and relax and hope that nothing like that ever happens again, because it was going to knock me for six every time. I didn't even recognise the room or my surroundings that I was in. Nothing made any sense. I sat on the edge of my bed and wiped the sweat and tears off of my face. I did wish the dream was real, but I felt like I was waking up out of a nightmare. I would have done anything to have Mark here right now. He would have wiped away my tears and cuddled me until I fell back to sleep. If only that was the case.

"Lee!" The knock on my door made me jump. I hoped it was Craig.

"Come in." I tried to make myself look presentable, but there was no point even hiding it, because both of my brothers know me too well.

"I thought I heard you. Are you okay?"

"I think so. It was just a bad dream." I was only too willing to let him wrap me in his arms. I needed to feel like I was safe and right now that was one of the only places that I could feel safe and calm.

"You're shaking, Lee. Are you sure you're okay?"

"I'm better since your here. I'm exhausted Craig. I can't shut off from everything. When I do close my eyes, I have weird dreams. They feel so real."

"What are the dreams about doll?"

"One was my due date and Mark was fussing over me. He woke me up that morning to get me to come and stay here with Scott. He was concerned about me being alone when I went into labour. The strangest thing is, the dreams felt like they were happening now. I feel like I am actually living that moment." I knew how ridiculous I

was sounding, but I knew that Craig would listen to me without nit-picking at me.

"You know better than anyone that the mind can make you believe wonderful things. You've told me that millions of times." His big soft hand moving my hair out of my face, made me realise how stupid I actually sounded. "Don't quote me on anything, but I think your mind wants to see Mark so badly, that it would do anything to let you think the dreams are real." I knew he was right. I knew that I had to stop being so silly. I knew that I needed to get a grip before I lost my mind.

"I am just so tired, Craig."

"Get back into bed and get comfortable." I wondered what he was doing when he placed the covers over the top of me. I watched him kick his slippers off and take his jogging top off just to leave himself in shorts and t-shirt. "I know this seems a little weird, but I'm going to be here all night." I couldn't help but smile, as he climbed into bed. "I'm not Mark, but I'll do anything to get you to relax."

"Craig. I don't know what to say."

"Don't say anything. Just close your eyes and get some sleep." I sat up and placed a kiss on his cheek and laid my head back on his chest. I could feel my body relax and my eyes felt heavy. I knew that I was going to drift off into sleep and I just hoped that there would be no more dreams, because they were knocking me further back in my healing process. I didn't want to think about my due date or Mark fussing over me. I wanted to try and get on with my life and make the best out of a bad situation. However, that was never going to happen if my mind kept playing tricks on me.

CHAPTER 3
Reality Strikes!

After a long night of tossing and turning, I decided to get up for a coffee. I felt like I had gone ten rounds with Mike Tyson. My body was sore and exhausted. I was all cried out. I had to stop thinking about Mark dying alone, because I was just driving myself crazy. I heard about murder all the time, but I never expected it to land on my doorstep. I had to stop getting worked up. I had the baby to think about and that had to be my main concern. I had done really well and had no morning sickness before all of this, but there I was this morning feeling nauseous. It was typical. I knew Mark would want to be there to look after me. He would have fulfilled his role as a husband and a father, because he would have been there in sickness and in health, through thick and thin. Now, I was on my own and I had to figure out a perfect way to get through the rest of my life

without him. It was seven o' clock in the morning and I had to phone my work to explain everything.

Today was going to be the worst day of all. Everyone was going to know about Mark and the news reporters were going to love the story. I was going to have phone calls and text messages from all of my friends and family, to send their condolences. Even Facebook and my e-mails were going to be overrun with well wishes. The best thing I could do was phone work and turn off all the technology. No phones, no computers, and no iPad. I was going to shut myself off from the outside world and hoped everyone would just leave me in peace.

"Leela. Sweetheart." I jumped out of my skin, as my dad came into the kitchen behind me and put the big light on. I was quite happy walking around with just the light coming from the kitchen cabinets, but now I was blinded. Hardly any sleep with tear stained eyes and big bright lights didn't mix well.

"Dad. Please put the light off." It was too bright for that time of morning and my eyes were aching with all the crying I had done the previous night.

"Leela? Have you had any sleep?" I watched my dad come over to me and take the kettle from my hand. I was going to get fed up with everyone treating me like I was fragile. But right now, I was too weak to protest.

"I just can't shut my eyes, dad. Every time I try, all I can see is Mark's face. I can visualise him lying in pain and scared to death of being alone." I couldn't keep doing that to myself. I pulled out the stool from the breakfast bar and tried to sit, but fell over instead.

"Leela. You need to put all of that out of your head, sweetheart. I can tell you truthfully, Mark did not suffer in any way. He wouldn't have felt a thing, because it happened very quickly. No one would have been able to save him darling." I know that my dad was trying to help me, but I wasn't sure how I felt hearing information like that. It was good to know that he never suffered. I should have been grateful for that. The fact that it happened so quickly and there was no chance of him getting help, made me feel sick to the pit of my stomach. "I've made you a cup of tea, because coffee isn't going to do you any good. It will keep you from sleeping and you need your

rest for the baby's sake as well, as your own."

I might have guessed that my dad's head would be screwed on no matter what he was going through. I should have been relieved that one of us was thinking about me and the baby, because at that moment my head wasn't in the right place for me, or my unborn child. "After you drink this, I want you to try and get some sleep."

"Its pointless dad. I have tried all night." I got more sleep when Craig came in and cuddled in beside me. It was a little weird, but it was comforting. He was my brother and my best friend.

"Well, let me phone the doctor. He might be able to give you something."

"I'm pregnant, dad. I don't want to get hooked on sleeping tablets. Once I get today out of my way, I might be able to sleep." I would say anything to get my dad off of my back. I didn't need everyone fussing over me, because they were all going to suffocate me.

"I will give you one more day, but if you don't sleep I'll call the doctor with or without your approval. There's got to be something you can take that won't affect the baby." I could only roll my eyes at my dad, as I took slow sips of my tea. It wasn't what I wanted, but it did hit the spot. I actually felt relaxed, as the hot liquid hit my stomach. I could feel the warmth radiate throughout my body. It was nice. "Do you want anything to eat? I can make you whatever you fancy." Normally I would have jumped at the chance to let my dad cook for me, but not today.

"Not just now, dad. I feel sick as a pig this morning." Of all the mornings to feel sick it had to be today. I hated being sick at the best of times. Hopefully with a bit of luck it wouldn't last too long.

"Your mum had bad morning sickness with you and Craig." I looked up at my dad, as he started talking to me. "It was so bad with you, she had to be admitted into the hospital, because she was dehydrated. I felt bad, because I was to blame for her condition." I thought it took two to tango, but I loved how much my dad loved my mum. I hung on my dad's every word, just because I loved listening to stories about my mum and the past. I could do with her here. She would have known exactly the right words to say.

"I haven't had any sickness at all. It's strange, because I've been feeling fine until this morning."

"You've had a huge shock darling. None of this will be helping you either." I knew my dad was spot on. Everything had emotionally buried me from last night and I was paying the price.

"Did mum have sickness for the full nine months?" I wasn't sure if I wanted to hear the answer. However, I enjoyed the distraction talking about my mum. It made me feel a bit more relaxed.

"No, no! Not with Craig. It eased off after twelve weeks. She did with you. It was horrendous to watch her suffer. She had no symptoms with Scott. She was afraid that she lost him at one point, because she didn't even feel pregnant." I never heard any of those stories before, but it was a good time to hear them.

"I wish she was here right now." I always felt her presence around me, but it wasn't the same as having her in person.

"She would have been over the moon about the baby. She would have spoilt you and the baby rotten." That I knew for sure. She would have loved to help me shop and set up the nursery for the baby. "She would know exactly what to say and do right now. Just don't forget that I will be here for you all the way, Leela. If you need me to come to appointments or antenatal classes, you know where I am. I'm not saying I will be any good at seeing you uncomfortable and in pain, but I will be there for you." I never expected to hear my dad say any of that. I was honoured to call him my dad. I never thought any further than the present. Although, I *was* going to need someone with me at appointments and at the birth. My dad would be perfect with me and the baby. He was kind and strong willed. I'm going to need someone to be harsh but kind with me when I am in labour.

"Thank you dad! It means a lot to me to have you on my side." I felt my usual connection to him and I loved him so much. The pride rushed through me, as I thought about everything he has done for me over the years. Even though my life was falling apart, he looked so proud of me. I just hoped and prayed to God that I can be the best mother to my child. If I am half as good a parent as my dad, I will be perfect. He doesn't know it, but he taught me how to do all of this on my own. I will be entirely grateful for his help and support.

"Anytime, day or night, Leela. You're my only daughter and I will do anything I can for you. I am so proud of you and your brothers,

because you have grown up to be great adults." I wasn't sure how much praise I could take. I didn't feel great at the moment and I think it was going to take some time before I felt like an adult again. However, with my dad and brothers by my side, I could get through everything.

"Will you come with me this afternoon to see Mark's mum and dad? I want to be able to help them organise Mark's funeral. I don't want them to pay for it all on their own." It was going to be small things like helping to arrange the funeral that was going to get me through everything. I needed to feel like I was helping and hopefully it would make me more at ease.

"Of course I will. I wouldn't let you go by yourself anyway." He gave me a huge hug. I felt the love and warmth radiate from my dad and I knew that I was lucky to have him. "Why don't you try and get some sleep? Leave your phone here and I will phone your work for you." My dad was like a mind reader. I was glad that someone was going to take care of my phone call, because I was dreading hearing the shock and pity in their voices.

"Thank you, dad! I wasn't looking forward to phoning in. My phone is on charge in the living room." I placed a kiss on my dad's cheek and lifted my cup to head back upstairs to my room. I really needed to try and get some sleep. Even if it was only for an hour. It would give my body some chance to refuel. I was glad when Craig was still sound asleep. I knew that I would be able to cuddle back into him and sleep peacefully for a little while. I just wanted to shut my mind off from thinking, because that was the only thing that was keeping me awake. While lying down, I felt how heavy my eyes were. I was determined to sleep and wake up a lot fresher to face another day. We were going to be here for one another and that helped me relax with peace of mind.

***

Getting ready to go and see Mark's parents was another step forward. I never had much to do with them before, apart from family gatherings. I only stayed over at their house a few times. If we weren't here, we were away for the weekend having fun. Mark got

along with his mum and dad in small doses. His mum was always a *bossy boots*, as Mark would describe her. He would always say that his dad was like her *lap dog*. He would nod and say all the right things just to keep the peace. I could never imagine living in that kind of relationship. I was brought up in a 50/50 environment where everything was shared. Still to this day my family is united. I was glad that my family was here with me last night and that my dad was going with me.

I had butterflies floating around my stomach and the grief was tearing through my body inch by inch. I would just be glad to get it all over and done with and maybe my mind and body could relax a lot better.

"Are you ready, Leela?" My dad's voice was soft and caring all the time. I could never imagine life without him.

"Yeah." I didn't sound confident. I knew I looked exactly how I felt. "If I don't go now then I never will." I had doubt coming from somewhere and I had no idea why. Mr and Mrs. Mackinnon were sincere when they came round last night. I just hoped they would be the same when we called round to their home. I knew it must be difficult for them to bury their son and I just hoped they could let me be a bigger part of their life.

"I will be waiting for you. Just take it easy, Lee," said Craig. I've seen a different side to my big brother over the last twelve hours. I hated to see him so upset and hurt. But his big strapping frame took me in a bear hug. I got that sense of love and warmth every time he hugs me. I was going to get used to having him around. I had no idea how I was going to get through everything when he went back to work.

"Thank you for coming to my rescue. You've helped me get some rest and I will never be able to thank you enough."

"You don't need to thank me, Lee. Just go and do what you have to do. I'll be here when you come back."

"We won't be long." I was hoping that I wouldn't be long, but I suppose I would be as long as it took me. I had to leave with my dad before I changed my mind. Then as soon as I was outside, I saw the press by the big iron gates at the front of our house. They certainly didn't take long to pounce on innocent people. Even if it is their job.

They will get paid for the best story and right now the pregnant fiancée of the dead policeman is the topic of conversation.

“Get in, sweetheart.” My dad knew exactly how to handle the press. I was glad, because I was frozen on the spot. He ushered me into the front seat of his jeep. I felt the tears roll down my cheek, as everything chipped away at me. I wanted to stay strong but I had a feeling that everything was going to overpower me. “They’ll get fed up at some point, sweetheart. Just ignore them and they’ll get bored.” I hoped I had the strength to keep strong until they gave up.

“When? After the funeral? After the trial? When the baby is born? They’re going to find a story at every stage dad.” I was shaking with a mixture of shock and anger. I had seen things like this on the television, but I never expected it to be me one day.

“They can’t come anywhere near you. They wouldn’t be allowed on our property, at your work, or anywhere near the cemetery.” That was something, I suppose. There should be a law made that we go to the press to give our side of the story. They shouldn’t be allowed to pester us and make up stories. Half the time, what they publish is far from the truth and then you have people believing what they read. I know why celebrities get stressed out, because none of this would be any fun every day of the week.

“Great!” I didn’t mean to speak out loud and sound sarcastic, but I couldn’t help it. The drive was going to take forever and everything was going to rattle around inside my head. “Will there be more at Mark’s parent’s house?”

“Probably, but I won’t let them anywhere near you. I promise you that, Leela.” I knew my dad would do everything in his power to protect me and that was something I would never doubt. On the other hand, I had also seen how hungry the press was for a story. They wouldn’t give up without a fight.

I should have been relieved when we pulled onto Mark’s parent’s street, but I was more shocked when I could see how many press vans there were. We were never going to get a break. Even if we managed to pick up courage to move on from Mark’s death, we were going to be tortured everywhere we go. “Does Mark’s mum have a driveway that we can pull into?” My head was all over the place. I was stupid to think I would be strong enough to get through today.

“Leela.” I heard my dad, but I was too busy thinking about all the crazy shit in front of me.

“Aye. Aye, they do, but the gates are closed.” I pointed my dad to the right house, not that you could miss it. I looked at him to see what we were going to do, because I certainly didn’t know. I don’t know why I sounded shocked about the gates being closed. Why would they be open with this mob taking over the street? “What are we going to do dad?” I could feel the nerves kicking in and my head was beginning to blur with the stress of everything. Then to top it all off, I couldn’t believe that my dad was pulling up further down the street and parked. “You can’t be serious dad. We are never going to get passed them. They will know you, because of press conferences. They’ll put two and two together and guess who I am.” Why was this all happening to me? Why couldn’t anything be straight forward for me and my family?

“Leela. Calm down, sweetheart.” My dad’s hands cupped my face, as he made me look him in the eyes. I could feel my body relax, as my breathing returned to normal. “We can go home if you want and come back tonight.” I somehow managed to shake my head while I was still in my dad’s grip.

“No! If I don’t do it now, I will never do it.” I took my seatbelt off and took a deep breath. I wasn’t going to be bullied by those pests. Not today. Not ever.

“I will come round for you. Don’t get out before I do.” I had never felt myself panic before and I didn’t like feeling that way. I teach people not to panic and give them techniques to help them, but there I was panicking like crazy. “Just don’t run. We’re going to take a casual walk over the road without drawing any attention to ourselves. I will have my arm around you at all times. Leela, look at me.” I did manage to look at my dad and his soft face made me settle down slightly. “This is my job and I will keep you safe, if you hold onto me tightly.” I managed to nod in unison with my dad and got out of the car. My legs felt like jelly but my dad’s arm came around my shoulders. I wrapped my arm around his back and clenched his jacket. I could feel the blood drain from my clenched fist, which clung onto my dad’s jacket, but I felt safe. No one had spotted us yet and we got over the road with no hassle. Suddenly, we were

surrounded by cameras and people shouting at me from all angles. Mark this and Mark that. They were even shouting about the baby. I became angry, because someone had told them about the baby and they had no right to bring that up. My baby had nothing at all to do with any of it. However, putting all of my anger aside, I was more relieved once we got into Mr. and Mrs. Mackinnon's garden. I felt like I could breathe again.

"How did they know about the baby? It was only me, you, Craig, and Mark's mum and dad that knew." I don't know why I was surprised, because I knew they would leave no stone unturned.

"They can find out any info, Lee. They will find anything out if it is compulsory to the story." The press was horrible. I hoped I never had to be around them again after this. I knocked on the door and hoped for a quick answer. I was surprised when the door opened before I stepped back. My face told the story.

"Oh. Leela. What can we do for you?" asked Mrs. Mackinnon. I thought I would have gotten a warmer welcome from her. "You shouldn't have come out here with all the press about." I was gobsmacked at the reception I was receiving. I couldn't even speak.

"We are sorry to drop by unannounced Mrs. Mackinnon, but Leela wanted to see if she could help with any of the funeral arrangements. She feels like she needs to be doing something to help." I was glad that my dad was there or I would have crumbled to pieces.

"Has the cat got your tongue?" I managed to look up to the woman that was my mother-in-law. I felt like I could have slapped her for the way she was treating me.

"I'm just overwhelmed by it all. The press has knocked me off balance." Why I even felt the need to explain myself after the response I was getting from her, was beyond me. Mr. Mackinnon joined us at the door. He was so different.

"Hello my dear. How are you?" How could they be married? They fit together like chalk and cheese?

"She wanted to help with the arrangements, but I was just about to tell her that everything was taken care of." I couldn't believe that was happening. Mr Mackinnon looked just as shocked.

"So, you know when the funeral is?" I managed to hold back my tears, but I felt like I was choking on them as I spoke.

"Not yet, but we will." She was so cold towards me. I didn't deserve any of it.

"I err…I…" I was speechless.

"If that was all, I have to get back to my guests."

"Can I ask if it will be okay to go ahead and order flowers? I know that everyone will want to know if you're accepting flowers and Leela will want to know as well." My dad was not showing any signs of losing patience, but I was getting angrier by the second. My lack of speech was a sign to my dad. I was glad when he spoke for both of us.

"You can do what you like. All the main family flowers are ordered. Now, if you excuse me…" It felt like another nightmare. I never expected to be treated like that.

"I'm sorry Leela. My wife is grieving and she doesn't know what she's saying." I lost respect for Mr. Mackinnon, as he stood by and tried to make excuses for his wife's behaviour. Any decent person would have told her how wrong she was. He was her *lap dog,* like Mark said.

"She doesn't look like she's grieving to me. In fact my daughter has been up the whole night and fought through crowds of press here and at home, to come and offer her help. Your wife might not like it, but Leela and Mark were engaged to be married, and Leela is carrying your son's child. My daughter has been made to feel like she was nothing to Mark. We all know that none of that is true, because Mark adored Leela." I was proud of my dad for sticking up for me. He even managed it in a diplomatic way. No one could say he was out of order.

"I am sorry," was the lame apology we received from Mr. Mackinnon, before the door got shut in our face. I couldn't hold my tears back any longer. My dad, being the gentleman that he was, wrapped me up in his arms and we turned away. I felt like the air was being pulled from my lungs.

"What have I done, dad?"

"Don't think like that. You've done nothing. That woman is just an evil bag that will get her day." It wasn't like my dad to speak about anyone like that, let alone a woman, but he was right. I hoped I would be around to see her get her day.

"Leela." We stopped and turned around to see Mark's brother Brian, walking down the driveway to greet us. I was petrified. I didn't know what I was going to say to him. I was taken aback when his arms wrapped around me. I broke down in tears. "I can't apologize enough for the way my mum just treated you. Believe me, she will be told exactly what I think when all her guests leave." As grateful as I was for Brian sticking up for me, I didn't want him to get involved in all of this.

"Don't Brian! I can't take any more of it, because it will be me that cops it all in the end. I welcomed her into my home last night and she told me to keep her posted about the baby. She can go and whistle for it! I didn't want to take over anything. I just wanted to feel like I was doing something." I sobbed the words out. Both Brian and my dad had their hands on me for support.

"Listen to me, Leela. You're doing more than enough. You take care of yourself and look after my niece or nephew." I somehow managed to smile, as Brian reminded me about the baby. "Please don't let my mum get to you. Don't let her feel like she's won. You don't need all of this stress." I could understand what Brian was saying, but I was too weak to respond and pull myself out of the hole I was just knocked into.

"Brian is right, sweetheart. Forget about her. You have the baby to think about."

"Let me take you home and it will save you going out the gates to the press." I was grateful that Brian was treating me with the respect I deserved.

"Thank you Brian, but I will get back to my dad's car the same way I came in here." Brian gave me one last hug and kissed my cheek. He was so like Mark in every way. I honestly didn't know where they got their manners from. It certainly wasn't their parents. "Thank you. Goodbye."

"Take care, Leela." My dad wrapped his arm back around me and my hand clenched his jacket again. I just wanted to get back to the car in one piece without any missing limbs. The press there was worse than the ones back home. They were like a pack of lions set on their prey and they were not going to stop until they got their teeth into something. They just didn't care who they hurt, as long as

they got their story. Thankfully, my dad got me back into the passenger seat and locked into the car. The flashes of cameras and people knocking on the window, made me burst out in tears. I gave them exactly what they wanted, but I couldn't help it. The relief washed over me, the minute the car started to move. I wished dad might have knocked a few of them down.

I wanted to get home to my own comforts. I wanted to forget that today ever happened and I just wanted to close my eyes and never wake up again. I felt bad before I left my house, but after that I felt a hundred times worse.

"We will be home in no time, Leela. I just texted Craig to watch for us and buzz the gates open. That way I don't need to leave you." I could see that my dad and my brother were only doing their best to look out for me. I was honoured to have a family like mine. Especially when I just witnessed what Mark's parents were like. We loved and cared for one another and we would be there if one of us needed them. That's all anyone could ask for. My baby and I were better off on our own with the people that loved us. We were not going to have room for anyone that disrespected me. We deserved to be loved.

***

I got out of my dad's car and headed straight into the house. My tears didn't stop and my anger was beginning to boil over. The more I thought about it in the car, the angrier I became. I really didn't know why I was letting Mark's mother get to me. I got inside and I flung my bag down without looking to see where it was going to land. I went straight into the kitchen. I was so glad I couldn't drink alcohol for the sake of the baby, because I would have drank myself into oblivion. I poured a glass of water instead and I hoped no one would speak to me, because they would cop all the pain and anger I was feeling. I would be glad if no one spoke to me until I managed to calm down.

"What has happened now?" The concern in Craig's voice made me stay quiet. I just looked out the window hoping for a magic spell to erase what happened. I could see all of the press just waiting for

something to happen. It was times like that I wish that I would have taken a gun to them all. How they could prey on people's misery made me sick and even angrier. "What happened dad?"

"Mark's mum wasn't very pleasant."

"She's grieving just like us." That was all I needed to hear when I turned around and looked at my brother leaning across the breakfast bar. How dare he stick up for her when he has no idea what she has done to me?

"Grieving? Grieving like us? Have I kept you at the fucking door? Have I practically told you not to have anything to do with the funeral? Have I been damn rude? No! I bloody haven't!" I banged my glass down on the work top and it smashed in my hand. My dad and Craig came to my side. I sobbed while Craig hugged me again. I just wanted to know what I had done to deserve all of that. All I wanted to do was be a part of the plans. What harm would that of done? "Wh…what have I done?" I managed to stutter out with tears.

"Lee. You haven't done anything wrong." My dad was back with a first aid box, but even I could see it was just a scratch. "You're my sister and I would never lie to you. You're one of the kindest people I've ever met when you're not smashing glasses." We all managed to chuckle at Craig's sarcastic comment. Somehow we could always count on him to bring us out of a mood. "I know that Mark thought the same as us. He adored you, Lee." I knew that Mark adored me, but it still didn't make his mum treat me any better.

"I must have done something, if his mum treated me like that. She left us on the door like some Jehovah Witness. She looked down her nose at me, like I was some snotty child." I just couldn't believe it and I couldn't take it all in.

"It's her loss, sweetheart. She's missing out on you carrying her first grandchild. This baby is her last piece of Mark and she doesn't deserve to be a part of your life. You're my daughter and I am so proud of you. I am proud to tell everyone that you're mine and I will be proud to tell everyone that I'm going to be a granddad. That woman was mean and horrible, because that's her way. It has nothing to do with you. She deserves to be alone and she deserves to have no part of this baby's life. My concern is you and the baby. Craig and I will be here by your side every step. Scott will be home

at the first chance he gets. You and the baby will not need the Mackinnons for anything. I would even give birth for you if I could." I was still sobbing, as my dad put a plaster over my hand. Craig didn't let me go and my dad was looking me square in the eyes. Even he had tears waiting to burst through, but it wasn't because of Mark's death. It was because he saw me hurting so much.

"Why don't you and Craig go through to the living room and I'll make us some tea. Mrs. Knight next door, gave us your favourite cake. She said if you weren't eating properly, she knew you would at least eat her cake." I put a slight smile on my face. I loved Mrs. Knight's baking. She was so good. She used to be a baker before she retired. When we were kids, she would give us all sorts of baking goodies. She even gave mum lots of recipes. Between the two of them, we were never short of home cooked food. Even with mum gone, we knew when Mrs. Knight was baking, because we always have a kitchen full of cakes and pastries. I let Craig lead me to the living room and I sat beside him with my head leaning on his chest. I was physically and mentally exhausted. I knew that I was going to have to sleep at some point, because it wasn't healthy for me or my baby to stay awake so long. I had to put everyone else's problems out of my head and think about me and the little one. My priorities were going to be changing. I knew my dad would breathe a lot easier hearing that. I was going to start as I meant to go on and my baby was going to be my first priority followed by my family and the people that care about me. I had no room in my life for ignorant people.

***

Day's had passed since my world came crashing down and I still felt lost. I felt like I was going around in circles. No matter what I was doing it felt all wrong. Each morning that I woke up, I thought about Mark. I realised that Mark wasn't going to walk through the door at any moment. While all of that hit me, I quickly came back down to earth with a bang. I realise there's been no nightmares. It's all real and so unfair. I try to pick myself up and make myself look human, but flowers arrive or sympathy cards and I'm knocked right back to

square one. I just couldn't wait to get the funeral over with, because then I would never have to see Mark's parents again. I didn't even want my baby to have any part in their life after the way they treated me.

Craig found out the funeral was taking place in the Holy Trinity chapel next week. I was upset that we still had a week to wait, before we laid Mark to rest, but I was devastated that we had to find out through a social networking site. It would have taken mere minutes to lift a phone to keep me updated, but she was that evil she couldn't even do that. I didn't know why I was surprised after what happened lately, but I was pleased in a way. It has made my decisions easier. My baby and I would live our life just as we please. We wouldn't need them for anything, so we might as well cut them out now.

"Morning, sweetheart. How are you feeling?" I was walking around on a different planet lately. I never expected to see anyone up just yet. I was a little surprised when I saw my dad making breakfast, when I entered the kitchen. I did a double take to see if I was still dreaming. I was in shock to see everything going on around me. I was the only one that couldn't move forward and get on with things as normal.

"I'm okay dad. I actually got better sleep last night."

"Good. You look a lot fresher this morning. I'm making a fry up. It's about time you and Craig eat something, instead of picking." I knew what he meant, because I couldn't remember the last time I sat and ate a decent hot meal.

"Dad. It isn't even 8am yet." I wasn't a morning person at the best of times and I never normally ate breakfast until ten or eleven o' clock when I'm taking my break at work.

"I know. Craig is away for a shower. I wouldn't have woken you. I would have stuck it in the microwave and you could have gotten it when you got up. Now, we will be able to eat a nice hot, home cooked breakfast, together as a family." I didn't want to burst my dad's bubble, because he had been fantastic with me. I didn't know where I would have been without him and Craig. They've been there through my tears, tantrums, smashing glasses, and now just my general support blanket. I pulled out a glass and poured myself some milk. I was trying to cut the tea and coffee out and there was no time

like the present to start. I was determined to change my habits, before the baby came along. I knew the months would fly by in no time at all.

"I've made fresh coffee in the machine, sweetheart."

"I'm good dad. Coffee isn't what I need right now and it isn't good for the baby." I was amazed at how much I would change for the sake of my unborn child. It overwhelmed me, the love and passion I had already for the tiny foetus inside me. I could only imagine what I would feel like when he or she was born. I've heard people saying they never knew they could love something as much, but the minute they saw their baby for the first time, it was like every emotion rolled into one and the sheer love and passion shined through them. I couldn't wait to have my baby in my arms. It was going to be my little piece of Mark. My little miracle.

"Morning, sis. Did you get a better sleep last night?" My brother laid a soft kiss on top of my head.

"I did."

"I checked on you a couple of times, but you were sound asleep. You surely don't need me to cuddle anymore." I was amazed to hear my brother had checked on me through the night. He is a star. He will make the perfect husband and father one day.

"I missed you last night. I feel a lot fresher this morning though. I will hopefully be even better after a shower." I was lucky, because some siblings never get along. My mum and dad brought us all up to love and respect each other. No matter what has happened between us, we always go and make up. Even when we were teens, we looked out for one another. I was so glad the bond was just as strong. "Dad. I will never eat all of that." I don't know who my dad thought he was feeding, but even on a normal day I would never eat all of what he had on my plate. Bacon, sausage, haggis, black pudding, hash browns, beans, and toast. I would like to know when he had the chance to go shopping, because I didn't see him leave the house. It just shows that I've been in a fantasy land lately.

"Just eat what you can. Make your old dad happy and try something. You're eating for two now." I did actually forget that I had to eat properly for the sake of the baby. I actually felt so stupid. "So, what do you two have planned for today?"

"I have to go and order flowers. Will one of you be able to come with me?" I had to go and order flowers for Mark. That was another step forward for me, because days ago I would never have managed to even think about flowers.

"I'll come with you, Lee. I wasn't doing anything today and dad has to go into the office for a couple of hours." I was surprised and wondered what dad had to go into work for.

"Is everything okay dad?"

"Yes, sweetheart. I've got some reports to fill out concerning Mark's death. There isn't going to be any internal investigation, so it's just to put it all to bed. Craig. You'll have to figure out what you want to do when your leave runs out. You'll either come back at the end of your leave, or you'll have to go to your doctor and get a sick line." I was listening to my dad keeping us all organised. It was a good thing he was there. We wouldn't know what we were doing and we would be more than lost. "No hurry, son. Take your time. There is no point rushing back to work, when you're clearly not ready. You'll just come to regret it and your love for your job will be non-existent." My dad knew everything and he seemed to know exactly what Craig was going through. I did think he had been through something like that before, but I didn't want to ask him any questions. I knew he had been in my shoes before, because he lost mum. I don't know how I would ever live on if I had been with Mark for twenty or thirty years. I felt bad enough and it was still early in the grieving.

"Thanks, dad! I don't know what on earth I'm going to do when I go back. I'm going to have no partner and even when they allocate me one, no one is ever going to be Mark. I'm not sure if I will ever feel the same at work." I felt my heart ache for Craig. He was never going to get away from his thoughts and feelings. When was he ever going to get the chance to break free again?

"When you're ready to go back, you'll be able to answer your own questions. Right now, you're still grieving and it's understandable. No one in the force can fault you for that. You and Mark were partners, best friends, and nearly family. It's understandable why you're feeling like this." Sitting in between my brother and dad, listening to their conversation, I could see it wasn't just me who was

grieving. It's not just my life that had been turned upside down. One death was like an earthquake and everyone was left in the aftermath to pick up the pieces.

"What flowers have you decided to go for, Leela?" My dad's question brought me back to the here and now. I was glad of the interruption, because my mind was dangerous.

"I'm going to order the Stairway to Heaven tribute. I was going to go for his name or fiancé. However, I've been left out of the preparations and I don't want to step on anyone's toes." I was the type of person that would stay away from conflict and I wasn't going to change my ways now.

"You do what you want, Leela. Mark loved you and nothing is going to change that." I was a bit surprised at my dad's response. But saying that, my dad always got on well with Mark. He approved of our relationship from day one.

"Thanks, dad." I knew that if the tables had been turned and it was me that died, my dad would have let Mark be there taking part in all of the preparations. It just shows how no two people are the same. It would be a better world if everyone was like my dad, there would be no bickering, arguing, or fighting. Everyone would be tolerant of one another and would get along regardless of the situation. I knew in time I would learn from the experience. At the moment, I was just trying to put everything into perspective and be strong. I wasn't a strong individual at the best of times. As long as I had my family by my side, I knew I would be able to come out at the end with a smile on my face.

CHAPTER 4
The Funeral

Just as I stood up to look out of my bedroom window, I suddenly realised my life was as bleak as the weather. Today was going to be one of the worst days of my life and it was one that would stick with me until the day I died. No matter how hard I was going to try, I would never get over the ordeal. Saying your final farewell to anyone is hard, but it's even worse when you have lost someone.

Going back twenty years, there would have been none of this. One could leave their doors and windows open without the thought of someone stealing something. Now a days, everything has got to be bolted down. Drug's, alcohol and violence were there, but not on my doorstep. Everyone could go out and be safe. My family can't even go to work without getting killed. It's a crazy world we live in. The probability of it being Mark walking into that building, was low, because the Strathclyde Police Force is very big. His time was marked and he had to go. It was hard for me to think like that, but it

was one of the things that kept getting me through this. I wasn't getting a chance to forget him, because every time I closed my eyes I could see his smiling face. The joy that he expressed when I told him about the baby was priceless. He was over the moon about becoming a daddy and I was overjoyed to see him so happy. How could we be so happy one minute and then it was all snatched away the next? It left me heartbroken.

Life seemed so bleak and it was going to be like that for the foreseeable future.

None of us were looking forward to Mark's funeral, but we could only hope for the best. No press and no headlines. Everyone showing their condolences and remembering what we no longer had. It was going to be hard for us all.

I was lucky to have found Mark. He was my first true love and was going to be mine for the rest of my life. We liked and disliked pretty much the same things. We shared the same views on religion and politics. Most of all, we wanted the same things out of life. I never believed in soul mates before I met Mark, but it was clear to both of us that we were true soul mates. If ever two people were meant to be together, it was me and Mark.

"Leela." Craig's voice startled me. I realised it must have been time, but I didn't want to leave the comfort of my room. He slowly came over to me and gave me a hug. I was getting so used to Craig's support, that I was frightened of being alone when he went back to work. I was over the moon when Craig went to see the doctor about the stress he was under, because he came home with a sick line for four weeks.

"How's my favourite sister and niece or nephew today?" Everyone was being great to me. I was honoured that everyone had accepted my baby news. It should have been the happiest time of my life. I should love my brother touching my stomach, but I just couldn't get today off my mind. Although it wasn't just today, it was every day after this one. There was always something taking my mind off of my baby and I didn't always want it to be like that.

"We are much better, now that I've stopped throwing up my breakfast. I'm sure this little one is just going to make the rest of the pregnancy horrific." My voice was as dull as the weather and anyone

that knew me well enough could hear that. I could feel Craig's heart pounding on my back. My pain and groaning weren't helping him.

"Here I was, thinking that you were feeling better, because I was here." Craig knew that today wasn't a time for jokes, but he wasn't about to let me crumble into tiny pieces again. "I know that Mark would be holding your hair out of the pan or rubbing your back, but dad and I can't help you if you lock the door." I was surprised to be hearing any of that. I felt bad for shutting them out, but there were some things I was meant to do alone.

"You really don't want to be holding my hair or rubbing my back."

"Said who? Is this in Leela's head or is it in someone's manual?" I couldn't stop myself from laughing at my brother. He just had a funny way with words. "Dad and I want to be here for you. If that means holding your hair, letting you scream at us, or wiping the sweat off your brow in the labour suite, we will be there, Lee. Got it?"

"I get it. I get it."

"Now that we have got that sorted…"

"Craig. I haven't thanked you for everything you've done for me, since Mark..." I paused as I made eye contact with him. He knew that I had to say *died* at one point, otherwise I was never going to come to terms with Mark's death. "Well you know what I mean, Craig. I don't know what I would've done without you. Everyone else can't even speak to me and I would have gave up at the beginning if it wasn't for you and dad."

"Leela. You don't have to thank me. I'm your brother and I love you too much to give up on you, but I need to say something. Please don't think that I'm being an arrogant prick." He took my hands and sat me down at my dressing table. I stayed quiet and squeezed his hands, as he knelt down beside me. "You know that I love you and you know I will be here for you no matter what, but you need to accept that Mark is gone. Just by keeping quiet and never saying *death* or *died*, it isn't going to bring him back." His head bowed, because he didn't want to be harsh with me. He needed to let me know what he thought and I was glad in a way, because I was sick of people walking on egg shells around me.

"I'm coming to terms with Mark not being here. Just because I

can't say that he's…dead, doesn't mean that I think he's going to walk through the door." I had tears held back and my breath was held back for a second. "If I say that he's dead, I just break down in tears and it isn't good for the baby. I don't want to be a blubbering wreck every day for the rest of my life. It's bad enough seeing Mark's face plastered all over the news, papers, and the television. They even know about the baby thanks to Mr. and Mrs. Mackinnon's interview." I wanted to keep the baby to myself for the time being, because it's still early. I don't want to hear people saying *that poor girl,* or *that poor child is going to grow up without its father.* I'm never going to get peace from the press. Am I?"

"Just ignore them, Lee. Something else will come along next week and Mark's murder will be last week's news." I wanted to believe him, but I've seen so many people's worlds turned upside down by the press.

"I wish for that every day, Craig. Right now, I just want to get today over with." Craig stood up straight, dressed in his police uniform. Without letting my hands go he gently pulled me up so that I was standing beside him. He looked very smart. "Why do you have to be so bloody tall?" Craig's lips placed a soft and tender kiss onto my forehead and he smiled softly at me.

"I'm not that tall. It's you! You're a midget." I had to smile at him. He was my rock. I was glad he didn't pussyfoot around me. He had always called me a midget since we were at primary school. It was always his little joke with his friends. Thinking back, we always wished that we were adults. Now that we were adults, we would give anything to go back to being kids again. No worries or cares. Just fun and laughter.

"Thank you for just being you. You're going to be my rock today and every other day afterwards. Do you know what you're letting yourself in for?" His arms wrapped around me and I could have stayed here all day with him.

"I know what I'm letting myself in for. Do you?" That's what I liked about my brother. We just bounced off of one another no matter how bad things got. "We really should go and get dad. He'll be waiting for us, Lee." Craig said it without hesitating. He knew what he had to do in order to get his family through today and that

was the only thing that was going to keep him going. I knew with him and dad by my side I would be fine.

***

Just as my dad pulled up outside the church, I could see how busy it was. My heart sank and my head was spinning with the thought of greeting everyone. I wondered how many people were there just to be nosey. Just to say they were at the *dead policeman's funeral.* Then Craig opened the car door quickly. I knew only too well that I had to get out of the car, but I felt like my body was glued to the seat. I was leaving my comfort zone and entering the unknown.

"I won't leave your side at all today, Lee." Craig held his hand out to me and with relief, I took it. While I stood looking in the opposite direction of the church, my dad closed the door. Both Craig and my dad were dressed beautifully in their police uniforms. As I turned around clasping Craig's arm, I could see a large group of officers standing in the church yard. My feet started moving, but again I felt like I was stuck. I felt like a knife had struck my heart when I could see Mark's family getting out of the funeral limos. I was so hurt that I wasn't included in any of the preparation. I knew if I was married to Mark, I would have included his family out of respect. "Don't let them get to you, Leela. You are by far, better than them." The tears had already started rolling down my cheek, when I saw the coffin inside the hearse. I couldn't come to terms with Mark being inside that coffin. He hated confined spaces. My hand touched the window of the car and I sobbed uncontrollably. My head rested on the glass and I felt close to him again. I would have done anything to have Mark with me for just five minutes to say goodbye.

"Leela." I heard my name behind me and I wiped my eyes. I turned slowly to see my brother Scott with his girlfriend Sheree. I didn't expect him coming home today, but his arms wrapped around me and I sobbed on his shoulder. It was the best thing that could have ever happened. I missed Scott so much, since he's been away. I would have done anything to have him there with me throughout the previous week.

"I didn't expect to see you until the end of term," I sobbed.

"I couldn't stay away, Leela. You're my big sister and I love you more than anything in this world. I was just upset that I couldn't have gotten home earlier for you." As I pulled away from Scott, I felt happier surrounded by my whole family. Scott took my hand and we went to move on into the church, but we were stopped by a group of officers approaching us.

"Leela. This is Sergeant Graham." Craig spoke proudly, as he shook his hand.

"Hello Leela. I just wanted to tell you how sorry I was about your loss. Mark told me on many occasions how much he loved you." I was proud to hear someone else tell me how Mark felt about me. "I worked with Craig and Mark and I lost count how many times I heard your name mentioned." I managed a smile at the sergeant. I was shocked that Mark spoke about me all the time. But on the other hand, I was honoured that he loved me so much.

"Thank you! All of you, for coming. Mark would be grateful to see you all here." I tried my hardest to stand there and be strong. I thought I was doing really well considering the circumstances.

"He was a great man and officer. It breaks my heart that he never got around to marrying you, or seeing his baby." Again, I was honoured that this sergeant was speaking to me like that. He was the first person that truly treated me like Mark's partner. But now I felt uncomfortable, because I could feel some of Mark's family staring at us, trying to hear the conversation.

"Before we go inside, I have a couple of things to tell you. If you don't mind?" My legs felt like jelly, as I stood among all of the officers. Now was as good as any time, to hear what he had to say. I managed to nod my head. "Mark had you down as his next of kin and there is a box of his things that we have for you. The day that Mark died, he had this in his pocket." I held my hand out, as the officer gave me a small jewellery box. "As his fiancée and his next of kin, you will receive a bereavement payment that will set you and the baby up. Mark wanted to make sure that you and the baby were looked after." I couldn't speak. I was dumbfounded and stunned to be holding my engagement ring.

"You can't be serious?" I moved over a step, as Mark's mum butted her nose into our conversation. I wondered when she was going to

appear.

"I don't know what to say to you Sergeant Graham." I was still trying to get my head around all of it.

"Mark made it clear to us months ago, that you were his next of kin and you would be in receipt of everything." He was confident, as he explained everything to me.

"He was our son and we arranged his funeral," Mrs. Mackinnon burst out. I was livid.

"Just hold it right there, Mrs. Mackinnon! You made it perfectly clear that I wasn't a part of the funeral arrangements! You came to my house the night Mark died and showed concern for the baby, but the next day when my dad and I came to your house, we were left on the doorstep. You told us you didn't need help and that Mark was your son and I was only his girlfriend. I cried for days. He was going to be my husband and the father of my child. You made me feel like scum. I felt like my heart had been ripped out for a second time. Then to top it all off, we found out through Facebook when and where the funeral was. So you carry on, but don't you dare say I didn't want to be a part of the arrangements." I stopped speaking and had no idea where my courage came from. I wasn’t one for confrontation, but I wasn’t going to stand and be bullied anymore.

"I don't know what my son ever saw in you and your family!" I had absolutely no idea why she was so bitter towards me.

"Meg! Enough!" Mr. Mackinnon finally stepped in, but the damage was already done.

"Sergeant Graham. I’m grateful for you telling me all of this, but I want you to pay Mark’s funeral off with the money. Anything else that is left, you can make out to his family. I loved Mark for his love, his personality, and the friendship that we shared. The house that he bought for us, you can sell. I don't want it without Mark. I don't need a penny from you or what Mark left for us. Mrs. Mackinnon. You’re welcome to it. I hope you have such a miserable life with every penny! I’m a doctor! I am not the scum that you’ve treated me like. I can provide for me and my baby and I don’t want you in my life! You’re horrible and spiteful! If Mark was here right now, he would have been livid at your behaviour.” I stopped, because I knew that I could say much more. I had over a week of mixed emotions and was

ready to get everything off my chest.

"That's all very well, Leela. I'll get the forms over to you and you can sign everything over to Mark's family." I nodded courteously to Sergeant Graham and noticed that, apart from the officers and Mark's family, everyone was inside the church. "One last thing, Leela." I stopped dead and turned back around to the sergeant. I wasn't in the mood for any more surprises. "We all had a collection in the station for the baby and this is a cheque made out to you. I'm sure that you won't need it, but it is from all of us. We all know that it isn't going to bring him back, but it's to show you that we all cared for him and wanted his baby and you to be comfortable." Another shock to my system. Today was going to be a long day. I could feel it inside me. It was nice to see that Mark was loved by all of his colleagues.

"Thank you! Mark would be grateful to you all. It's nice to see that you all cared about him." I held my hand out and took the envelope from the officer. I slipped it into my bag and walked past Mark's family to take my place in the church. I didn't want to cause any more upheaval today. I sat at the front of the church in the side pews that wasn't reserved for his family. I was so hurt that I was made to feel like I was nothing. I hoped that his family would get their day. I was seated in-between Craig and Scott, just like a sandwich. Once the church organ started playing, the coffin was led to the front of the church carried by different family members. Some, I had never seen before. I just wanted to close my eyes, forget where I was, and forget why I was there. I was startled when I felt someone touch my hand. I looked up to see Mark's brother Brian standing in front of me.

"Come over and join me. You have more right being over there than any of us do." I was pleased that Brian was treating me like I mattered, but I couldn't move now.

"Thank you Brian." I whispered. "I am okay here." I was even more shocked, when he sat at the end of our pew beside my dad. He was showing us that he didn't approve of the way I'd been treated by his family. Again, I was shocked at the scene that had unfolded in front of me. Now I was desperately waiting to get out of there. It was getting harder to breathe by the second. I felt like the walls were

closing in and I needed to get out. The only thing I could do was place my head on Craig's shoulder and close my eyes to block out the next hour.

***

Standing outside in the cemetery, I was surrounded by a mix of people I didn't know. I felt like an outcast. No one even gave me a rose to throw down on the coffin, when it was lowered. It was like they were trying to hurt me in every way possible. After today, I wasn't going to let Mark's family bother me. The tears that I shed, wasn't just because I buried my fiancé, it was also because I had been treated so badly. I was relieved when the priest stopped talking, because I had to walk away and get a seat on the bench stuck in the middle of the cemetery. Each and every one of my family members followed behind me. I knew I didn't feel very well, but I thought that it was because of my mixed emotions. I was drained by the whole experience and it was beginning to show.

"Leela, sweetie. Are you okay?" My dad knelt down in front of me, while my brothers sat at either side of me. I could feel the concern from them all, but there was no need.

"You don't look well Leela." I looked up at Scott's girlfriend, because I didn't instantly recognise the voice. She was always nice and polite. It was weird to hear her express concern.

"I'm going to go home for a lie down. I feel exhausted. I couldn't keep anything down this morning, so I think it's all caught up with me." I was hoping that was all that was wrong with me. I had never felt so weak in my life and I was starting to get a bit worried. I haven't been pregnant before and I had no one to compare notes with. For all I knew, it was normal pregnancy symptoms. I was going to have to grin and bear it for the duration.

"I think we should get you to a doctor, just to make sure that you and the baby are okay," said my dad. I could hear the fear in his voice and I didn't want to hurt him.

"Dad. Stop fussing. We'll be fine after a good sleep." As strong as I wanted to sound in front of my family, I knew that deep down I wasn't going to succeed.

"It's my job to fuss over you. You really don't look well. Sheree is right." I could see the concern in my father's face and I quickly realised that he really was worried. Did I look as bad as I felt? Was that even possible?

"What harm will it do, Lee? You've been through so much the past couple of weeks. Let's take care of you both the way Mark would want us to do." Scott knew that he was playing the Mark card, but it was the only way I would let them take me to hospital.

"If it's going to get you all off of my case, I'll make an appointment for tomorrow." It was the only thing I could think of and I hoped it would work.

"Okay. Let's get you back to the car then." My dad stood up and they all followed his lead. I really felt weak, as I tightened my grip on Scott's arm.

"Leela." As I heard my name being called out, I stopped and turned to see Mark's brother Brian walking towards me. He was much like Mark in so many ways. It didn't make sense that they were both part of such a horrible family. I thought the same thing, every time I saw him, but I couldn't believe it. "I just wanted to tell you that I don't agree with the way you've been treated. I'm not getting spoken to, because I voiced my opinion on several occasions this week. Please keep in touch with me. I want to be a part of you and my niece or nephew's life. If you need anything or just want to blether, you know where I am."

It took me a few moments to register his words. I hated to think he had pushed his family away because of me.

"Thank you Brian!" I walked forward and hugged him. I kissed his cheek and felt a little light headed. Lucky for me, Brian caught me from falling.

"Leela! Are you okay?" Everyone was concerned about me, but I just wanted to get home. I didn't want to make a fool of myself.

"Falling for Mark's brother already and Mark isn't even cold in the ground." I wanted to find some energy to hit his mum, but right now I didn't even have the energy to walk.

"Mum! Shut the hell up! Leela isn't feeling well and anyone can see that!" I managed to lift my hand and rubbed my head, as I somehow steadied myself.

"Look here, Mrs. Mackinnon..." Brian still had his arm wrapped around my waist and I was relieved, because he wouldn't let me fall and hurt myself. "…I don't know what I have done to you or your family, but you don't know anything about me. Just stop with the digs! I loved Mark more than any of you know! He was everything to me and more. You don't have to care about the funeral bill, because it's all paid for! I just want to get on with my life the way that Mark and I discussed. He will be turning in his grave at the way I've been treated by you since he died!" I stopped in my tracks, because my legs were like jelly. My head was spinning and my vision was blurred. I fell slowly to the ground, without any injuries. Luckily. I could hear people all around me, but I was too weak to keep my eyes open. Suddenly, a sharp pain soared through my stomach, causing me to moan in pain.

"It's okay Leela! Help is on the way, sweetheart!" I heard everyone fussing around me full of concern. I managed to open my eyes wide to see Brian still cradling me in his arms, as the pain got worse. "Everyone get back and give her space! All she needs is her family." I was out of it, but I felt so proud of Brian.

"We *are* her family." I heard Mrs. Mackinnon say sarcastically. She surely wanted to be my family now.

"Mum! Get the hell back! If anything happens to Leela or this baby, I will never forgive you! Leela is right! Mark will be turning in his grave at the way you've treated the only woman he has ever loved!" The pain cut me in two and although I wanted to be strong, I cried out in agony. The pain was so intense that it took my breath away.

"The ambulance is coming, sis." Scott's soothing hand wiped hair off of my sweating face. I was surrounded by the people that mattered and I knew they would all take care of me. "Has anyone got cold wipes?" Wipes was the last thing that I wanted. I needed to know what was wrong with my baby.

"It's the baby Brian. She's dying." I sobbed the words out, as I came in and out of consciousness. The pain was so bad, that I would have been better out cold.

"Don't think like that. She'll be a fighter like her mummy and daddy." I wanted to believe everything Brian said, but I knew it was

the baby. My heart was racing and I felt cold. I knew my baby was dying and there was nothing anyone could do.

"I can feel it. I'm losing her…just like Mark. I can't hold on to anything that I love." Self-pity seemed like the best cure. I couldn't say too much, because I was out of breath.

"Neither Mark nor the baby is your fault. "Brian and Scott could see me slipping in and out of consciousness. I was getting weaker by the second and there was nothing anyone could do. Call it a mother's instinct.

"Someone phone for another bloody ambulance! She needs medical attention now if she's going to make it!" My poor father knelt beside Scott, keeping vigil at my side. He unbuttoned his jacket and took it off to cover me. It was scary and I was too weak to communicate anymore. Everyone could see how bad the situation was and fear filled the air. I was hearing things, but my body felt dead. Then nothing.

"Should we not put her in the recovery position?" Scott was probably right, but no one heard him. "Yes. No. Maybe." Everyone was trying to think of something useful to help, but they weren't paramedics.

"I think we should leave her in Brian's arms. If that's okay Brian." Craig answered his anxious brother and looked to Brian for a response. "Brian is that ok?"

"Sorry. Of course it is. Don't even try taking her away from me now." Anyone could see that Brian felt a huge connection with Leela. But in all honesty, none of them wanted to think of what was happening in front of them. All they could do was hope and pray for the best possible outcome.

"She's a fighter!" Of course he wanted to believe his words. "She has to be okay. I can't lose her. Not now." Sheree put her hands on her future father-in-law's shoulders in order to try and calm him down. It wouldn't be any good Leela or the boys, if their dad couldn't be strong for them.

"We can't lose her or the baby!" Brian spoke with tears running

down his cheeks. Suddenly, Leela managed to stir with the pain soaring through her again. Brian bent down and laid a kiss on her forehead. It was hard for anyone to stay positive.

"The ambulance is here!" The priest was out of breath, as he ran back to the crowd. They were in an awkward location of the cemetery and it was going to be hard for the paramedics to bring the ambulance any closer.

"Mark!" Everyone could hear Leela call for her dead partner, and everyone's heart was breaking for her. She was so clammy and sweaty, that she was delirious. Scott went to tell her that Brian wasn't Mark, but he was crying so hard that he couldn't.

"It is okay, Scott. If her thinking that I'm Mark, is going to get her through this, she can call me what she likes." Everyone surrounding Leela knew that only a decent genuine guy would say something like that.

"Can everyone give us some space please?" The paramedics pushed through, as they were told and moved back. "What's her name?"

"Leela." Brian, Scott, and Her father answered at the same time, as the paramedics smiled.

"Can you tell us quickly what happened?"

"We just buried Leela's fiancé and she walked over to this seat. She was feeling tired. Within minutes, she stood up talking to Brian, her partner's brother. Then she went light headed. She had a disagreement with her fiancés mum and she passed out. Brian caught her though."

"So, she didn't hit her head in the fall?"

"No, I caught her. She's what…9-10 weeks pregnant?" Brian filled in for my father, since he was stressed out.

"Has she been unconscious since?"

"No. She's been going in and out of consciousness. She was in a lot of pain gripping her stomach." Brian forgot about his mum, but was being everything Mark would want him to be.

"Can I ask you all to take a step back? Brian? Are you okay to stay there until we get her on the trolley?"

"Of course I am." Brian kept Leela warm and comfortable in his arms. Everyone watched in fear, as the paramedics hooked her to

monitors and gave her fluids through a drip. They managed to get her onto a pat slide board for transfer. She was cautiously moved and wrapped up warm on the trolley. It was now obvious that she had been bleeding quite a lot, because there was a puddle of blood on the ground. Everyone knew what that meant. Tears of sadness washed over the crowd of people still gathered.

"We need to get her to hospital A.S.A.P.! We shouldn't take anyone with us under the serious conditions, but we will take one member of her family."

"I'm her dad."

"Okay. Let's go." Everything was hurried up and everyone knew how critical things were. The paramedics knew what was going on.

"Dad. Keys. We'll meet you there." Just as Craig caught his dad's keys, he could see the urgency as the paramedics started running. Craig always liked to see the positive side, but he even knew it wasn't good.

"Do you mind if I follow you guys to the hospital?" Brian was being polite. No one could tie him in the same boat as his parents.

"Of course you can, Brian. Leela would have been worse if it wasn't for you." Craig wasn't about to punish Brian for his parents.

"Thank you!" Just as Craig, Scott, and Sheeree ran to their car, Brian did the same.

"Brian? Can we come with you?" Mrs. Mackinnon said, surprisingly. Brian actually thought he was hearing things, as he turned slightly.

"You're not coming with me, mum. You should go to the reception and put your tears on for attention. You've caused enough trouble today! You have no ties with Leela anymore, so just stay away from her!" Brian jumped into his car feeling relieved that he spoke out to his mum again. He was right after all. His parents gave up all rights to be a part of Leela's life, when they pushed her out the day after Mark got killed. But looking around us now a day's, it becomes clear that people only realise what they've got when it's too late. It is a lesson learnt for many, but for some it is like water off a ducks back. But Brian did hope that it would make his mum see that she didn't have to behave the way she did, but he wouldn't hold his breath. She would never admit how wrong she was. He could only hope one day

before she died, or lost someone else, that she would stop being so angry with everyone. . It isn't even if she could blame her son's death for her anger and temper, because she had been like this for years. It was a good thing for Mark and Brian, because they watched her behaviour growing up and they were determined to go in the opposite direction. It just shows that you can be close to your family, but it doesn't mean that you're all tied with the same brush.

CHAPTER 5
Aftermath

Nearly a week had passed since Mark's funeral, and everyone was still keeping a vigil at Leela's bedside. When she got brought into Stirling Royal Infirmary, it was clear she was haemorrhaging. Her gynaecologist got her to theatre as soon as possible. It came out she had suffered an ectopic pregnancy. The small foetus was growing inside of her fallopian tube and it had no chance of survival. While Leela was in theatre, the doctor had to remove one of her tubes due to the damage that was caused. The operation went as well as it could have. However, once she got put to recovery, it became obvious Leela was in a coma due to the quick loss of blood.

***

Six days later, her family was taking turns to make sure there was always someone there just in case she woke up. They didn’t want her to wake up with no one familiar there. She was going to be scared enough being surrounded by strangers. They were all hoping and praying that she would come around soon, because they were at their wits’ end with worry.

Although they were dreading telling her that she lost the baby, they had even worse news. Due to the circumstances and surgery, she may not be able to conceive another child. Everyone knew that Leela never planned a baby, but it was clear she was over the moon when she discovered she was expecting her first child. She was going to be devastated. Not only was she going to be grieving for Mark, but she was going to be grieving for their child.

It was clear that life could be so cruel. Death didn't care who it struck next. It just left a massive hole inside the remaining family and they were left picking up the pieces.

"Hey." Leela's father Frank, turned around at the sound of a voice.

"Hi Brian."

"I’m sorry. I didn't mean to intrude. I just finished work. I can come back later."

"Don't be daft, son. Come on in." Brian came in and threw his jacket on the table in the corner. "I’ll be glad to have some company, to be honest. This room gets quite boring after a while. There are only so many times you can look at the same four walls without going crazy."

"I can only imagine Frank. How is she doing today?" It was a silly question to ask but it was the most obvious one. Brian looked around at all the machines, but he was looking for some good news for a change.

"Well, there isn't much change from the other day, as you can see. There was some kind of neurologist in earlier today and he did some brain function tests." The tears rolled down Frank's face. Brian immediately thought the worst. It was better if he let it all out instead of bottling it all up. Throughout everything, he had been the only one that hasn’t cried. "I’m sorry Brian. I just feel overwhelmed by it all. I’ve been the strong one for everybody. Even though they’ve all doubted that Leela would recover. I just can’t keep bottling it all up.

I can’t give up on my little girl." He was only human and there was only so much that he could take.

"Don't be sorry, Frank. No one could know what you’re going through. I can only imagine. Losing Mark was bad enough, but to be sitting here watching your daughter hinging onto life…It must be torture,” Brian said with compassion.

"The brain tests they did showed lots of brain activity. At least now we know Leela’s brain is okay. Surely it will be a matter of time before she wakes up.”

"That’s fantastic news!” Brian tried not to sound so ecstatic, but he found it hard to control his excitement. “I am sure you must be pleased with the results."

“Honestly? I thought I had won the lottery, Brian. You’re the first person I’ve told, so keep it to yourself until I can fill the family in." Brian used his hands to make the motion that his mouth was zipped.

"I can stay for a couple of hours if you want to go and get something to eat." Frank was exhausted and he needed a break. He was drained, sitting there all day. Sometimes, sitting and doing nothing can be worse than working twelve hour shifts.

"Are you sure you don't have anything else to do?" Frank asked, showing concern.

"Microwave meal for one and boring T.V. I’d rather be here for Leela. If Mark was here, he would have been here around the clock. I’ll always see Leela as my sister-in-law and I want to help when I can. I’m not like my family. I want to be a part of Leela’s life, no matter what is going on.”

"Thank you Brian! When Leela comes around… The doctor said her memory could be blocked, because of the sudden trauma." Frank lowered his head.

"We’ll cross that bridge when we get to it, Frank. You’ll have us all to help out. I promise to do anything I can. Even though the baby is gone, I want to be there for Leela, if that’s okay with you and your family."

“I know that you’ve had a lot of trouble with your family, because of your involvement with Leela. I’ve got so much respect for you son. You could have stood back and let your mum treat Leela like dirt, but you didn’t. Leela wanted you in her life before and I am

sure that won't change." Brian was overwhelmed to hear Frank speak like that. He understood why Mark had so much respect for Leela and her family. They were truly genuine people. He wished his family could have been the same way.

"I appreciate that, Frank.

"Call me if there is any change, Brian. I'll be back as soon as I can." Brian's eyes moved from the door when he realised he was alone with Leela. He didn't feel uncomfortable about being there, because he still felt a connection to her. As he took her hand in his, Brian looked down at her body lying motionless on the bed. She was still beautiful, while fighting for her life. Brian remembered the first time he met Leela. Mark introduced her to him at their dad's 60th birthday party. Anyone could see they were both madly in love. She spoke sweetly and made an effort to talk to everyone, including Brian's mum. They were all glad to see that Mark found someone he loved enough to introduce to his family. He always said police work was his life and he could never have a woman, because it was dangerous and just not fair to them. No one at the time knew that Leela was brought up with a policeman and had a brother who was partners with Mark on the force. They were a perfect match for each other. They made one another truly happy and that's what counted. In fact, I had never seen Mark as happy before. He was head over heels in love with this woman, and I knew she had to be special for that to happen. Brian's mum was quiet toward Leela, but she would have been the same with anyone that Mark or Brian got involved with. Her little boys were now fully grown adults and they had minds of their own.

"Come on, Lee. You can pull through this. I can hear Mark already, *I leave you all for five minutes and my wife to be is fighting for her life and my baby is dead.* We can face life without Mark…together. I was just thinking about the first time I met you. Can you remember? You were the love of Mark's life and I will always be grateful to you for that." His eyes shot up to her face. "Leela! Can you hear me?" He still held her hand and stood looking at her, like she was a picture about to fade. Her eyes opened a couple of times and her hand came up to the tube in her mouth. "Don't touch that, Leela. I'll call for the nurse." Brian felt like he was floating in

the air.

***

"Is everything okay?" said the young nurse, before she was fully in the room.

"No…Yes…she's coming around." Brian was all over the place with excitement.

"I'll get the doctor. Keep talking to her. Reassure her that everything is going to be okay." He heard everything that the nurse said, but all he could do was squeeze Leela's hand. His heart was racing so fast, that felt like it was going to jump out of his chest at any moment.

"You have gave us all a fright, missy." He could see that Leela understood him. It was a worry to see what she could remember from before she took ill. Brian's eyes followed her hand, until she placed it on her stomach. His head bowed slightly to let her know that he knew what she meant. He didn't know what to say. When his eyes moved to meet hers, he could see a tear falling down her cheek. His spare hand instantly came up to wipe her face clear. "Don't cry, honey. You'll set me off. You're made of stronger stuff. You have a fantastic family that will help you get through all of this. I will always think of you as my sister-in-law. Nothing and no one will ever change that." The sincerity in his voice would have made the most cold-hearted person cry. With relief he sighed when two doctors arrived back with the nurse quickly. The doctors had come in at the right moment.

"Hi Leela! It's great to see you back with us." The doctor held Leela's other hand to take her pulse. The tall male doctor that was in charge, seemed to know what he was doing, but his silence was unnerving to Brian. "Leela. I'm just checking you over to make sure you're stable enough, before we take you off of the ventilator. If you understand me, please squeeze my hand." She did. "Good! Now, if you know who this person beside you is, please squeeze his hand." She squeezed Brian's hand as well.

"Thank God!" Brian exclaimed. The relief on his face said it all.

"I know that you want to be with her, but I need to ask you to wait outside. It’s only for a little while." It was clear in the doctor’s voice that he didn't like asking relatives to leave, but it was protocol.

"Of course! I’ll call your dad, Leela." Leela didn’t let go of Brian’s hand. She didn’t want him to leave. "I’ll just be outside sweetheart. I will come right back when the doctors are finished. I promise pal!" It took a good thirty seconds or more for her to let go. Brian didn't want to leave her either. He had a strong bond with Leela since the previous week. As soon as he got to the other side of the door, he fished out his phone and sent a text message to Leela's family. He slowly sank into the chair outside her door. He felt so much love and heartache for Leela, that even He couldn't understand it. He also knew that nothing would or could ever happen between them. They were both grieving for Mark and now they would grieve for her baby. The baby that was going to be the only thing that was left of Mark. That’s what was killing everyone.

The family had nearly a week to come to terms with the miscarriage, but it was just the beginning for Leela. No one knew how she was going to react, but it was all about to be confirmed.

***

Fifty minutes later, Brian was still sitting on the same seat, desperately waiting for the door to open. Just to get some kind of news. Good or bad. It felt like an eternity. He was desperately waiting for something to happen.

"Brian!" He jumped up, as Leela's dad and brothers darted right to him. "How is she? What’s happening? Is she okay?”

"Everyone. Just slow down." Brian held his hands up, as a way to calm the situation down. "Leela was awake when I came out. She could answer the doctor’s questions by squeezing his hands. She knew who I was. I think she is going to remember everything. But whatever happened since I was sent out here, is anyone’s guess."

"Does she know about the baby?" Scott had a valid question.

"I think so… I don't know..." Leela was still on the ventilator when Brian was with her, so he wasn’t sure.

“What do you mean?" It was a terrifying time for the family and even more so for Scott, because he was so close to his sister.

"She put her hand over her stomach, and I bowed my head away. I couldn't bring myself to tell her outright. When I looked back at her, there were tears running down her cheek. I could only imagine the heartache that she was going through. I felt like another piece of me died last week.”

"It’s okay, Brian, son. You were there when she woke up and that’s what counts. None of us would know what to say. The worst is about to come.” Frank looked around to make sure he had everyone’s attention. “With us all rallying around to help her, I’m sure given time, she will bounce back." Frank knew Leela needed love and support. That’s what she was going to get. Then just as the conversation stopped, as the doors to Leela's room opened. The nurse waved for everyone to go in.

Leela sat up in bed and propped up with pillows. She was off a lot of the machines and the room was quiet. Everyone was stunned into silence.

"You all look like you’ve seen a ghost." Just as everyone heard Leela speak with a husky voice, the room started to breathe again.

"Leela. We’ve all been so worried about you." Leela's dad stepped forward and took his daughter in his arms. He was out of his mind with worry.

"As you can all see, Leela has made a remarkable recovery. She is still very sore from the surgery, but she will make a full recovery in time. We have offered Leela a councillor to help deal with the grief, but she turned it down." The doctor seemed disappointed in her decision.

"She is a psychologist herself, doctor. I’m very sure she would know what the councillor would do or say." The doctor had no idea that Leela was a doctor herself. No one thought to tell the staff. It just shows that grief and heartache makes your mind forget all the little details.

"Leela should have doctor before her name. That will gain her preferential treatment. Just don’t tell anyone I said that." The doctor’s sarcasm certainly lightened the mood. "We’ll keep a close eye on her for a couple of days and make sure that she improves.”

"Thank you doctor! You have been marvellous with my daughter! I don't know how to repay you for this." Frank shook the doctor's hand.

"No need for repaying me Mr. Park. I'm just glad that she's on the mend. I can see that she has a wonderful family. That's what she needs for a decent recovery." The doctors then left the room. It was a weight of everyone's shoulders to know she was on the mend.

"You better never frighten us like that again, Lee. We've been going out of our minds with worry." Craig rattled on. The situation could have been different. They could have been burying her beside Mark if the staff here didn't act quickly.

"I can't remember much, but maybe that's all for the best," Leela said, trying her hardest to be brave. Her throat was sore and her body tensed up.

"How are you feeling, sweetheart?" Asked her concerned father. He knew his daughter would tell everyone what they all wanted to hear, rather than actually how she felt.

"I don't know, dad. I'm soar and tired, but I will be glad to get home and take everything in."

"We will be glad to see you home, hen." The relief in her dad's voice made it clear how happy he was. Just a couple of hours ago, he was an emotional wreck praying that she would come round. His prayers were answered.

"You will be coming home to rest, Lee, so don't you be getting any ideas!" Scott spoke just like he knew his sister inside and out. Everyone stood around laughing and joking with Leela, but she was in no mood for small chat. She needed time to herself, but she was too polite to tell everyone to go home.

"Leela. As much as I am over the moon to see you awake, I have to get going." Brian leaned over her fragile body and placed a soft kiss on her cheek. "If you need anything…anything at all, just give me a phone and I will be here."

"Thank you, Brian! I am grateful to you being here when I came around. It was nice to see a friendly face."

"No thanks needed. Just let everyone fuss over you, and enjoy it while it lasts." Saying goodbye to Leela made it final. Mark was gone and so was his baby. It made life feel so short and cruel. They

were all going to have a huge hole to fill. The problem was, it wasn't going to be filled as quickly as it was made.

***

Forty-eight hours since I woke up out of my comma. My family has been running rings around me. I couldn't breathe, I couldn't move, and I certainly couldn't think straight. I was over the moon to be told earlier that I could go home. I should have felt wonderful, but I was far from it.

My drive home from the hospital began my road to recovery. I wanted to get back to normal, but there was a huge weight sitting on my shoulders. A weight that was too heavy for me to bear. I knew too well I should be grateful to be alive, but I had lost too much to be grateful. I was in a world of my own when my dad opened the passenger door to help me get out. Everything was on my mind. Everything, but going into the house. There was a part of me that was glad to be in the hospital, because there were no memories there. It was a complete blank canvas there and home wasn't where I wanted to be.

"It's good to finally have you home, sweetheart." My dad was so ecstatic to have me home. I knew I was going to have to put a brave face on for his sake.

"It's good to be home, dad." Lying was the easiest option, because I didn't want to go into a huge conversation. As I got out of the car, I felt sore and uncomfortable. I had to take baby steps. I took my dad's arm and let him lead me back into the house. All I wanted to do was get inside and go for a lie down in my own bed. While I stepped over the door step, I saw all of the faces there to greet me. I didn't know whether to laugh or cry, even though I acknowledged them all, by letting them hug and kiss me. Then I reached Scott at the back of the crowd. He gently put his arm around me and led my exhausted body into my once comfortable living room. "Scott. I thought you knew me better than this." I wanted to be angry, but when my brother raised his spare hand, I knew the welcoming crowd wasn't his fault.

"I found out after it was too late."

"I can't be dealing with any of this. I just want to lie down." I felt like I was suffocating with it all. I didn't want to be around anyone. I wanted to be on my own with no one fussing. I wondered when that was ever going to happen.

"Just for an hour and I promise I will get you to your room." My face said it all. It showed Scott that I didn't want to, but I felt I had no other choice. The minute I sat down on the couch, an older woman who I didn't even recognise, handed me a glass of wine. I couldn't even say thank you, because I was overwhelmed. Surely, they all knew that I was going to be on medication and I wouldn't be able to drink alcohol. Everything was like a celebration, but I had nothing to celebrate. My world had crashed around me and I had to pick up all of the pieces.

At the moment, I wasn't ready to start rebuilding my life. It was torture sitting there, but my mouth was clamped shut.

I placed the glass on the table. I did try to relax. I even sat back to get comfortable. While everything else became a blur, I went over all my thoughts. At the moment, my head was the best place to be. It really wasn't good for me, considering it would have made my mood worse.

***

It was an hour later and my patience was wearing thin. All I wanted to do was run away and never look back. When my eyes focused at the door of my living room, I could see Craig shaking hands with who I thought was Mark at first. My head burst and my heart raced.

While the seconds passed slowly, the tall strapping frame turned round to see where I was. Then I quickly realised that it was Mark's brother, Brian. No wonder I thought it was Mark, because they were so much alike. They were like two peas in a pod. Even the way Brian came and knelt down beside me with a huge bouquet of flowers. I had to let a smile form on my face. I knew if Mark was still there, he would have arrived with the same present.

"Hey, Leela! I hope you don't mind me dropping by I thought you could use all the support you could get when I heard about this

welcome home gathering." I was shocked that he knew what I would be thinking. Although, on the other hand I was glad he dropped by.

"Not at all, Brian. You're always welcome here. You're actually doing me a favour, because I need to get out of here." I was going to use him as my get up and leave card.

"Where to, Leela?" He sounded just as shocked, although I knew he would do anything I asked. He was that kind of guy.

"Just follow me." My aching body eased up off the couch and left slowly. It was my perfect excuse to get out of the room and I headed out into the back garden. "I was ready to go crazy in there. Thank you."

"How are you doing?" As I looked up at Brian leaning against the deck, looking over at me. I didn't know what to say.

"I'm good. I'm really not good, but you know what I mean." Everyone seemed to know me better these days and it was weird hearing someone ask how I felt.

"No, I don't know, Leela." It was nice for someone to think about my feelings.

"Why do you have to be so like Mark?" I couldn't believe I had just said that out loud.

"That's why I've been keeping my distance the last couple of days. I think you have enough to deal with without seeing me. I know Mark would've wanted me to be here to make sure you're okay." We all knew Mark too well and I knew Brian was right.

"He also would've brought me the same bouquet of flowers." The tears rolled down my cheeks, as I turned away to look over the garden. I didn't want to cry all the time, but my tears were on a tap lately. I had no control over them and they came and went as they pleased.

"Leela. You don't have to hide your heartache from me. I know what you're going through. I wish I could trade places with Mark. I would do anything to let Mark be here for you right now." Listening to Brian speak like that, made me feel weird, but in a good way. It was also flattering.

"Don't be nice to me, Brian. I don't deserve it."

"Why not, Leela?" I started walking down the garden to a bench under a tree. I needed to sit down before I fell down and I thought by

walking away, I would've gotten away from answering that question. "Why do you feel like any of this is your fault? Mark knew the risks as a policeman. It was the whole reason he never loved anyone enough to take that chance. He doted on you Leela. You never pulled that trigger." It still didn't make me feel any better. I still felt responsible. Every piece of me felt guilty and nothing was going to take that away.

"I lost the only part of him I was ever going to have." That was killing me the most, because the baby was giving me the strength to keep going.

"Again, that was not your fault. My family never made it easy for you. Trust me, my mum is feeling it now. You've done nothing, other than be the perfect person in every way possible. I know this isn't the best time or place to say this, but in a few years' time, you will look back and be able to have some closure." I wanted to believe all of it. I really did, but my heart was broken. I was never going to feel closure over any of it. There was always going to be something keeping the pain and heartache flowing.

"I can't see that far ahead, Brian. I will never move on and forget about Mark. Never!" He was my one and only and nothing will ever change that. I could never love another man like I did Mark.

"We've had nearly three weeks to come to terms with everything and this is your body starting to grieve. Give it time, Leela. I'm not going to call on you anymore. However, if you ever need anything, you know where to find me." I didn't understand why he was saying that. I felt like I was pushing him away for some reason.

"Why? What have I done or said to offend you?" My head fell into my hands, as the tears fell again.

Brian placed his hand over mine. I felt like it was me. It was me that was driving all of my loved ones away.

"You've done nothing wrong sweetheart, so, stop blaming yourself. I'm staying clear, because I could see your face when I turned around today. I could see your heart break all over again. You don't need me constantly reminding you of Mark. I think you have enough support around you, but you have to let them all in to help you. I will always be here if you need me."

"What if I don't want you to stay away?" I didn't want to lose him

as well. I never wanted to feel alone.

"You will always know where I am Leela. My house and office will not change any time soon. I need you to be brave and come back fighting stronger than ever." His gentle kiss on my head was comforting. I couldn't look up to stop him from walking away from me. Deep in my heart I knew he was right. Even though, it just felt like everyone I needed was leaving me alone.

"Leela!" Craig ran down the garden to embrace me. I should have known Brian would send someone out to comfort me. "Come on, sis." I felt secure with him there, as I sobbed. "Brian said that you were upset. This is good for you, Lee. You need to get all of this anger and tension out. It’s only going to eat away at you if you keep locking it in." I wasn’t used to Craig being the one that had his head screwed on right. It was always me that helped my brothers through their difficult times. It felt weird being on the other side.

"What am I supposed to do, Craig? I just can't forget that Mark and the baby ever existed. They’re not anything I can ever replace." That was the hardest part to accept. I was never going to see them and I was never going to feel that love and passion again.

"I never said you could forget, but you can't go on like this. This isn't the Leela we know. Even when mum died, you were the strong one. You kept us all strong." Our mother died three years ago and everyone fell apart. As usual, I was the ball and chain that kept everyone together. I felt different then.

"Mum was different. She was dying from cancer, Craig. She was suffering. I got to say goodbye to her. Mark and the baby were just snatched away from me." Craig couldn't answer me, because he could see what I meant. "I’ll get through it on my own."

“You don’t need to do any of it on your own, Lee.”

“I am not burdening you all with this! You need to move on for work. I will be fine on my own.” I got up and stormed off with Craig coming after me. I didn’t want everyone to feel like they needed to be with me out of sympathy or family loyalty. I just wanted to deal with it.

"Leela! Wait!" As I entered the house, laughter filled the air. I was seething from it all. The anger inside me was unbelievable. I needed to get away, before I said something I would regret.

"Leela. Sweetheart." My dad and Craig were concerned about me, but I took to the stairs and there was no stopping me. My life was being torn to pieces around me and I just needed to be in my own space. I just needed my room. As I slammed the bedroom door, a picture of Mark and I at a wedding fell from the wall and smashed. My body crumpled to the floor, as I gathered up all the pieces. My sobs were unbelievably strong and painful, until there was nothing left for me to give. My eyes grew heavy with tears and I drifted off to sleep around the pieces of the picture.

***

"Dad. I'm worried about her. This isn't Leela. Nine times out of ten she's the strong one that keeps all of us together." Craig and the family were all gathered around in the kitchen discussing how they found Leela crumpled up on her bedroom floor, sleeping with a cut finger.

"Craig. She just lost her partner and unborn child. We will have to be strong for her for a change and be there when she needs us. I have just put in for another week off work, so I'll be here for her this week." Everyone was worried about her, but no one was going to be able to agree on the best action to take.

"Dad. I know you love us all, but it's going to take Leela more than a week. I have got to go back to the university in two days, but I really don't want to leave knowing her state of mind." Scott was always going to know Leela best. They were like twins growing up and Craig often felt left out. They were now a united front and they had a great family unit.

"I'll get more time off if I need to, but I am taking it week to week. The force is deeply concerned about Leela. They'll grant me any time I need for her." Going round in circles was exactly what the three of them were doing, and they all had Leela's best interest at heart.

"But dad, we saw her before the funeral. She wasn't as bad as she is now. She's getting worse!"

"If anything happens to her, I will hold you all responsible! I know

her better than any of you and I know this isn’t her." Scott was seething, because he felt like he was the only one taking the situation seriously. He knew he could give up university for the upcoming year, but he just couldn't do that. Leela wouldn't let him give up his dreams. That would probably make her feel even worse.

"She’ll be fine boys. I’ll make sure of it." Frank was determined to see his daughter through it. He was desperate to let the boys think that he had everything under control, but he had some doubts that Leela might need some professional help. That would be the last possible scenario, if all else fails.

"What about a break away from here?" Everyone turned their attention to Craig without saying a word. They thought about the pros and cons of his statement. "There are reminders everywhere here and that isn’t doing her any good. It might just be what she needs."

"It could be, son. Let’s just see how she goes, because a break away is good but then she has to come back to it all. Leela is a psychologist and she would tell us that quick fixes are never any good." They had heard her talking about cases where she used the term *quick fix*.

"I’m going to go be there when she wakes up. I’m exhausted and I won’t sleep if I’m not with her. We’re just going around in circles here." Craig pushed and headed to be with his sister, who they moved to her bed and bandaged her cut. His head was bursting after the day’s fiasco and a lie down is just what he needed. He carefully opened his sister’s bedroom door. Her unconscious body was curled up in the foetal position. His heart sank, as he laid down beside her. He had a connection with Leela. Other than being her brother, it might have also been because they both lost Mark. Maybe it was the baby. Who knows? He did know he wasn’t going to let her crumble to pieces, because of the multiple disasters she went through. She was a strong individual and her family knew she was in there somewhere. It was just a case of finding out where.

THREE MONTHS LATER

CHAPTER 6
A Long Way To Go

Three long months had passed and I was just starting to pick up the pieces of my life. My job was put on hold and my life was still non-existent. However, I was determined to get back on track, one way or another. I just had to take a few hard steps before I could face the future. One of those steps was going through Mark's things. I woke up yesterday with a new outlook on life. I started off by getting my hair done and generally pampered myself. It was needed badly, because my split ends desperately needed to be sorted. I couldn't remember the last time my hair was coloured. Those were things I used to do regularly, before Mark's death. It was good to feel human again. My head felt a lot lighter. It gave me the courage to start a fresh. That morning, was the morning I was going to go through all

of Mark's belongings from work. I needed to do those things in order to put the past behind me. It was all steps in the right direction. It would seem my family was happy at those steps I was taking. In turn, that made me feel accomplished. They have been so supportive of my thoughts and feelings lately and I know I would have been put in a mental hospital if it wasn't for them. I felt like I was on the right track.

The boxes were in front of me shouting my name. My heart was beating so fast. There I was, opening the first box and I was shaking like a leaf. Just looking into the open box, I felt a sense of relief wash through me. I didn't know what all the fuss was about, because it was the easiest thing that I had done in three months. The box was full of trinkets and pictures dear to Mark. I was so happy I had managed to take that step, because it let me see how much I really meant to him. I had to honour his memory and move forward. It was easy to dwell in the past and have everyone walk on egg shells around me, but I didn't want that. I didn't want to be the weak person I had become after Mark and the baby, even though I couldn't help the way the grief hit me. I wanted to be the strong and confident person Mark fell in love with. The fun loving woman that was always classed as *the ray of sunshine.* I couldn't remember the last time I smiled. I was sick of all the gloom and doom. I wanted to get some kind of normality back in my life and that was only going to happen in my future, not in the past.

I put aside, the things that Mark's family would want to keep. I hadn't had any contact with Mark's brother, Brian, since the day he told me he wasn't going to be around anymore. He was the only one of his family I would feel comfortable seeing. I could take the items to his mum and dad's house, except I didn't want to see them. I was doing so well taking baby steps and they would only drag me back again. A quick look at my watch and I could see that it was just about lunch time. I grabbed my jacket and bag and headed for my car. I knew if I left now, I would be at Brian's office at 12:30. I had to face Brian at some point. If I couldn't do it then, I wasn't ready to move forward.

***

I surprised myself, because I hated driving on the motorway. Yet, I had to drive to Cumbernauld to get to Brian's work. I was full of surprises that day. I took it as a good omen. However, walking into Olympia's building where Brian worked, I felt like it was the biggest step I had taken. I felt accomplished that I had come so far in such a short time. All I had to do was figure out a way to see Brian.

Without thinking, I walked up to the receptionist's desk and a young blonde woman was sitting there and on a call. I took the opportunity to take a look around the ground floor. I had never been in there before. I wondered what it was like one day when I was sitting in the car, while Mark dropped things of to Brian. It's a huge glass building on the outskirts of Cumbernauld. No one could miss it, even from a distance.

"Hello Miss . Can I help you?" I was disturbed by the receptionist talking to me, because I had to have the courage to go through with the rest of my visit.

"Sorry. I was in a world of my own. I'm wondering if you can tell me how to reach Brian Mackinnon?"

"Mr. Mackinnon is on the twelfth floor. He's in now." I didn't know if that was what I wanted to hear.

"Thank you!" I couldn't believe how easy that was. I wasn't sure if I was happy he was in. It would have been easier to leave the things for him with his receptionist. But I was there now and I picked up the Dutch courage and took the lift to the twelfth floor. My heart was pounding yet again, but I wasn't letting it stop me. I had gone that far. I was a lady on a mission and I would only be happy if I hit all of my targets. I looked at my reflection in the wall mirror in the lift and I looked like the usual Leela. Especially since I had gotten my hair done yesterday. I looked and felt human again. I thought that Brian would see a difference in me from the last time he saw me. Which could only be a good thing.

The lift halted on the twelfth floor and I left it with less confidence. I walked over to the next receptionist's desk before I ran for the hills. The woman there was older than the blonde and much older than I expected.

"Can I help you, my dear?"

"Yes. I know Mr. Mackinnon must be very busy, but is there any chance I can speak with him?" I sounded confident. I tried to hide any nerves I had and be nice and polite.

"Of course you can. What company are you from?" I didn't make myself clear and I got flustered.

"I am not from any company. My name is Leela Park. He'll know who I am." I did expect to get told he couldn't take personal visitors. I waited and waited, but it never came.

"Okay. I'll let him know you're here when he comes out. Please take a seat, dear." I was shocked that it had been so easy. I walked over to the glass window and looked out, because I was too nervous to sit down. I stood with my back to the receptionist's desk, until I heard some laughter when a door opened. I turned slowly and saw Brian shake hands with another gentleman. He headed for the receptionist. But before he could be told about me, he spotted me standing a few feet away from him. His face lit up when he saw that it was me. I didn't expect such a response after so long. The courageous me met Brian in the middle of the waiting area, as he placed his arms around me tenderly.

"Leela! This is a lovely surprise. Are you okay?" It wasn't a surprise. He thought there was something wrong. I haven't had any contact with him for three months and here I am in his office.

"Yes." I managed to smile. "I know you must be busy. Is there any chance I can speak with you for five minutes?"

"Of course. You know that I will always make time for you. Cath? Can you put my status as *out* for the time being please?" The receptionist looked flustered. I knew she thought there was something going on between us, but I shook it off and followed Brian to his office. "I didn't expect to see you. I mean…I always wanted to. I spoke with Craig several times and he told me how you've been." I could only smirk. I might have guessed Craig couldn't keep his mouth shut.

"Craig just can't shut up," I said, trying to sound okay. "I'm much better. Thank you." I wasn't lying. I felt like a million dollars compared to a few weeks ago. It was scary to look back and see how I was.

"Please, sit down. Can I get you a coffee?"

"No. I'm off coffee. I just need to do this before I bottle it." I was starting to get flustered myself. I knew that I needed to get it out of the way. Tea, coffee, and small chat were just going to stop me from doing what I went there to do.

"You're worrying me now. What is it?" Brian sat beside me on a large leather sofa. He was waiting anxiously to hear what I was doing there.

"Well…I finally picked up the courage to get my life back on track. However, in order to do that I had to go through Mark's things from work and what I had at home. Most of it I kept, put it back in the boxes, and stored them for safe keeping, but I came across a few things…"

"What things, Leela?"

"Mostly family photos and trinkets I have no use for. Only a mother should have such things." I handed over the bag of Mark's things. It was clear that Brian wasn't expecting anything like that.

"Cool. I'll pass them on to my mum." I stood up quickly to say my goodbyes, but Brian pulled back on my hand. "Leela sit. Please." My head wanted me to run, but my heart wanted to stay. Neither won, because I broke free from Brian and stood a few feet away from him. "Tea or water? It's lunch time. Can we go for lunch?" Brian's urgency to be with me made my heart melt. I didn't know if it was because I saw him all suited and booted. He looked more like Mark than ever before.

"You twisted my arm. Water will be fine." Relief washed over Brian's face, as he grabbed a bottled water out of the fridge. I felt comfortable standing there, which was a good thing. I didn't want to run for the hills.

"How have you been? Truthfully!" I could hear the sarcastic tone. I knew that was him telling me that I can't hide the truth from him.

"Like Rubbish, but I woke up and smelled the coffee. I was able to get my senses together for the first time in months."

"Good! I'm glad Leela. Have you gone back to work yet?"

"No. I just handed my resignation in yesterday." I knew that everyone was going to think I was crazy, but that was the clearest my head had been in ages.

"I don't understand. You loved your job." I picked up on his shocked expression. It was going to be a doddle compared to my dad's reaction.

"I just couldn't go back to listening to people's problems. My colleagues were going to pity me and my clients were going to know about my life outside of work. I've been plastered all over the tabloids, so it's hard not to know who I am. I can't even go to the supermarket without getting noticed. I need a change, Brian."

"You were a fantastic doctor." I was good at my job and I loved what I was doing, but since Mark and the baby died, they took a piece of me with them. That piece was the piece that I needed to go back to my normal life.

"I still might be good at my job one day, but I'm taking a year off. I haven't told anyone yet, but I'm going to go travelling for a year. I've made my mind up, so please don't try and talk me out of it." Nothing was going to hold me back anymore.

"I wouldn't talk you out of it, not if it's what you really want." I should have known that Brian would be on my side.

"It's what I want. There's nothing keeping me here. I don't want to be here for the trial of Mark's killer. I don't want to dredge it up all over again. For the first time in months, I feel like I'm human again. Having reporters all over me would just set me back again, so I'm leaving next week." That was the first time that I said it out loud and it did sound crazy, but it's what I was going to do.

"Where?"

"I don't know yet. I'm going to the airport next Friday and I'll be going where the first flight takes me. I'm lost Brian. I need to find myself again and this is the most certain I've been, since..." My eyes looked from the ground to meet Brain's eyes. The smile on his face was no longer there. "This has been the biggest step I've taken and I'm glad. I was going to post the things to your parents. I thought it was just what your mum deserved after the way she treated me, but I couldn't be cruel like that." As bad as I felt over the last few months, nothing could make me as cruel as Mrs. Mackinnon.

"Cruel is what you should have been, Leela. I only see my parents at special occasions now. I never forgave her for what she did to you. I still say if they were nicer to you then, we would have been

able to see Mark's little boy or girl in a few months." I didn't think that he still would have been so bitter and angry. It wasn't like him to hold grudges. That was another prime example of death making people react in mysterious ways.

"Don't, Brian. Don't blame them. An ectopic pregnancy can happen for any reason and it would have happened even if Mark didn't die. She was a girl." I felt like I owed him that. I didn't want him to be separated from his family. I wanted them to have a united front just like I had with my family.

"What? How do you know?" I could hear the shock in his voice and I wasn't sure if it would relieve him or not.

"When I got taken to the hospital they took the foetus away in theatre. When I got discharged, they asked me if I wanted the keepsake box. I had no idea what it was, but when I discovered that it was all little details of my little one, I said *yes*. Her box is at home with Marks things. I named her Esme." I surprised myself again, because I was talking about the baby and not crying. That's another first in three months.

"Leela. I'm sorry." I did the courteous thing and walked over to him and wiped his tears away. I didn't mean to upset him. I thought it would be me walking out of there in tears.

"You don't need to hide your pain in front of me, Brian." A smile crept up on his face, because it was three months ago that he said the exact same thing to me. "I wasn't going to tell you about her, because I thought you would have moved on with your family."

"Of course I would have wanted to know I would have had a niece. I will never move on with my family, Lee. There's been too much going on. Not just you and the baby, but going back to other things. You and the baby were the final straw for me. I'm moving on too. I'm looking to buy a company out of here and I can't wait." It looked like we were all finally coming to terms without Mark. It was hard, but we know he would want this.

"I'm really pleased that you're looking to the future, Brian. Mark wouldn't want us to be unhappy. I have got to go now, but I will leave my card. It's got all of my details on it, if you ever want a chat." We both composed ourselves and I opened the office door to leave, with Brian close behind me.

"Leela..." I turned back toward Brian and I could see how torn he was. I walked back and placed a gentle kiss on his cheek. I was amazed at how much I felt for Brian. Feelings that I didn't understand.

"Be strong. If I can do it, anyone can." I knew that he could do it. He was stronger than me. I had faith in him.

"Just take care of yourself when you go travelling. There are a lot of creeps all over the world. Come and see me when you get back. I'll text you with all of my new details when I move." Walking away from Brian was harder than I had anticipated.

Once inside the lift, the doors were closing. I looked back to see him vanish, as I started to move down to the ground floor.

We both shared a lot of heartache. It was reasonable why we felt a connection with one another. I would never forget what Brian did for me since Mark died. He will always be my brother-in-law as far as I'm concerned. Now, I had the great job of going home to tell my dad and Craig, about my plans. I didn't think they would be supportive. But I was happy with my decision and that's all that matters. After all, I think I deserved to take some time out for myself. I needed to care for me. I had a long way to go and traveling for a year is just what I need.

***

I had a productive afternoon. I stopped off and got a few groceries. I decided to make my dad and Craig lasagne for dinner. I was hoping by feeding them, they would be so tired from work they wouldn't have much energy for a heated discussion. It was six o' clock and I knew that they would be home any time. I always felt a sense of relief when their cars pulled into the driveway. That was another reason I was going away. I worried non-stop when they went to work. I couldn't take any more of it. When they were at work, every time the phone or the doorbell rang, I got anxious, because I thought someone was going to tell me that they died. I would be glad when my dad retired and even happier if Craig moved up to be a D.C.I., like my dad. I was never going to stop worrying about them,

no matter how hard I tried. I hoped that travelling would keep me occupied. I wouldn't have time to think about dangers and my past. I could only hope for a fresh start.

Just as I popped the wine open, I heard their car pull into the drive. I was nervous about telling them my plans. I don't know why. My dad would see that I needed to do it. I hoped that Craig would be just as supportive.

"Something smells delicious!" I couldn't help but smile at my dad, as I took the lasagne out of the oven.

"I hope that you're both hungry." It was good feeling to be the mother figure again. I was taking care of them, as opposed to them taking care of me.

"You're just spoiling us. We're going to miss all of these home cooked meals when you go back to work." I was glad that Craig was thinking about me not being there, but I bit my tongue until we were all sitting down at the table.

"I opened white wine, but if you want red, dad, I can open that as well." I knew my dad wasn't keen on white wine, but I knew that Craig took after me.

"I'll get it, sweetheart. You've done enough slaving over the cooker all day." My dad was always grateful for anything anyone did for him, but I always got the special treatment. That was another reason I wanted to take time for myself, because I didn't want everyone to walk on egg shells around me. I was an adult and I wanted to be treated like one.

"I haven't been slaving around, dad. I fancied lasagne, but I wasn't going to buy it ready-made. Can you imagine what mum would say if I bought a microwave meal?" We all thought about that and the soft laughter was enough evidence to prove me right. My mum was a great cook. She would never buy something already prepared, if she could make it. She used to have a three course meal made every night when we were growing up. Homemade soup, followed by a stew or casserole, and then homemade rice pudding or baked cakes. I had great memories of my mum and I was glad that I used to love watching her cook. I knew if she was here today, I would have had no problem telling her my plans. She would have been over the moon for me. I thought my mum was standing beside me when I told

them what I had planned to do.

"I've been out most of the afternoon. I just rustled this up quickly when I came home." I could see that they were both shocked, as I served up dinner. I had been out two days in a row. That was more than I'd done in three months. I had got used to the Scottish air and I don't know how I managed to be cooped up inside all of that time without going crazy.

"What have you been up to, sis?"

"Well…I went through the boxes of Mark's things. I came across a lot of things that his mum should have. However, I wasn't going to go round to their house, because they would just drag me back down. So, I drove out to Brian's office in Cumbernauld. I gave him the things to pass on to his mum and dad." The room was silent as I spoke, but I sat down at the table feeling proud of myself. I had come so far over the last couple of days. I never thought it was ever going to be possible.

"How's Brian doing?" My dad had a huge smile on his face. It felt good to see him smile.

"He's good. He still doesn't see much of his parents. He said he sees them on special occasions and even that's an effort for him to go. He's looking to start working for himself, but he just started thinking about it. I got the feeling that a lot has happened between him and his mum. I tried to tell him not to blame his mum for the baby, but he said that me and the baby was the final straw for him." I didn't like seeing someone I care about breaking away from their family, but I have learned to stay out of people's personal lives, because I didn't know what went on behind closed doors.

"I think you had a lucky escape, Lee." I could hear Craig's relieved tone and I had a funny feeling that he was right. It's just a shame it didn't feel right.

"It's good to see that both you and Brian, are now looking to the future. I knew you would get there, sweetheart. I'm very proud of you. Maybe now you can look at getting back to work." I was glad that my dad brought work up, because it was going to make my task easier. That was the moment I had been waiting for and I was going to pounce while I had the chance.

"I'm glad you have brought this subject up, because I've been

thinking a lot about my future. I went to see my boss at the hospital yesterday. She was very supportive of my decisions."

"Good! So when do you start back?" My heart felt like it was going to jump out of my chest, but I knew that this was my time to tell them my decisions.

"Well…I'm not going back dad. I handed in my resignation yesterday." My dad's eye quickly shot up to me. He placed his knife and fork down, so that he didn't miss a single detail. He wouldn't be mad at me, because it wasn't in his nature. I knew if he had something to say, he would give me his honest opinion whether I wanted it or not.

"Leela. You've lost me, honey. I don't know what you mean. You're doing fantastic!"

"I want to do something different. I don't want to go back and listen to people's problems or work through their mental issues. I handed in my resignation, because I'm ready to take this next step. It isn't an option to go back there for me." Looking from my dad to Craig, I could see that they were both listening to me carefully. They both seemed concerned to see where I was going with this. "I'm going to take a year out from work and I am going to go traveling." Now that it was out, I couldn't take it back. The silence made me nervous. "Say something…one of you."

"Leela. Are you sure you're ready for all of this?" I knew my dad would try to psychoanalyse me, but I wasn't telling them, so that they could talk me out of it.

"Dad…I didn't just wake up this morning and decide this. I've been thinking about it for a while. I'm going to do this and I was hoping that you would both be happy for me."

"Lee. Is this what you really want?" I managed a nod at my brother. I saw the smile on his face, as he reached over and took my hand in his. "You better keep in contact. Skype, text, phone, and write. I'm happy for you, if this is what you want. If you told me this weeks ago, I would have said *not a hope in hell's chance are you going to do this.* But the Leela that we all know, is back. You're looking more content and that's all I can ask for. I know why you need to do this. I thought of doing it as well, but I'm too much of a home bird. You're a free spirit and this will be good for you." I was

grateful for Craig's honest opinion. I expected him to be the one that protested against me going away. However, he got to know me a lot more over the last couple of months and we were more alike than we ever thought.

"Dad. I want to know what you're thinking. I'll understand if you don't agree. I just need to hear it from you."

"Leela, sweetheart. You're my daughter and I don't want to lose you. I know you feel like you have to do this, and I can't…won't stand in your way. Just you remember that this will always be your home and you are welcome here anytime. Like Craig said, you better keep in contact and let us know where you are and what you're doing. I'll always love you no matter what decision you make. Of course, I would love you to be here with me and Craig, but somewhere inside of me, I know why you have to do this."

I could see it was hurting my dad. He was only saying those things to support me. I couldn't thank him enough for his love and support and always being there for me when I needed him. Throughout my life, he had been a tower of strength to us all. He was there to support everything we did. He taught me what it's like to love and cherish someone, because that's all he had ever done with our family.

"I love you guys more than anything in this world. I'll keep in contact all the time and I will let you know everything." The tears were welling up in my eyes, but they were happy tears for a change. I felt happy and relieved that I had my family's approval to go. It was going to be my fresh start and I was going to enjoy every second of it without looking back.

"You won't be going for a while though. Right?" I had another bombshell to drop on my dad. I wasn't sure how he was going to take the next piece of news. I looked back at him and waited until he swallowed the bit of dinner he had in his mouth. I didn't want him to choke.

"I decided to go to the airport next Friday. I'm going to take the first ticket I can get and be on my way to a year full of adventure." I was trying to show them my enthusiasm. I wanted them to both see that I was looking forward to it.

"So soon? I'll miss you, sweetheart, but I can't stand in your way.

I also know why you're doing this all so quickly. I'm so proud of you for coming this far. I'm proud of you all. Your mother would have been proud of each and every one of you." My dad was the most loving person I have ever come across. "You know, I worried when your mum passed away, because she was the one who dealt with this kind of thing. She was a fantastic mum to you kids. I have tried my best with you and hope that you know that I would do anything for you." My dad was one in a million and not many men could do what he has done.

"Dad. You've been the best father that anyone could ask for. I, for one, don't know where I would be without you." I got up from the table and took my dad in my arms. He had been mum and dad for the last three years and had done everything in his power for me and my brothers. "I love you dad. Don't ever forget that. Any man can make a child, but it takes a real man to raise one. I can't ever think of a time when you let us down." I was overwhelmed thinking about my childhood and growing up. We had a perfect life and it was all down to my dad working to provide for his family. He gave my mum the opportunity to quit working and look after us full time and that's what she did. We never wanted for anything.

"I love you too sweetheart. Your mum would be so proud of you both. Especially, how we've all stuck together when we need to the most." I sat back down at the table. I felt hungry after all of this talking.

"You and mum brought us up to look out for one another. There's no doubt about it, we will always do that." My nerves were gone. I was sitting with my family talking about the good things that made a family perfect. There wasn't much more I could ask for.

"So, enough of this smooch talk. Where do you fancy going first?" I wasn't leaving that table, until I knew we were all talked out.

"Honestly, dad? I've got no idea. I just know that I want to take this year out from here and put all the memories behind me. I've seen several places with you guys, but this time I want to take in all the culture and see how different people live and such."

"I'll take next Friday off and take you to the airport." I was lucky to have a dad like mine. It was such a waste, because he was just like

me. He could never love another. He was going to spend the rest of his life on his own with just us kids making him grey and bald.

"I will as well, Lee. I'm not even sure if I'm working, but I'll be there with you." It was going to be hard walking away from those guys, but I would be back and I'd be in touch all the time.

"Thank you, to you both! I would've never gotten through the last few months without you and I am going to miss you all fussing about me." That was going to take me a while to get used to. I always had my family with me through thick and thin, but I was going to be in the big bad world on my own. I honestly had no idea where my courage came from, because I had never been one for doing things on my own.

I remember when I was growing up and even from an early age, I always had to have my friends around me when I was out and about. I could never do anything on my own. Even when I went to Stirling University. I quickly found new friends on my course and we were inseparable in the end. We still keep in contact. I have missed them since Mark died. I have kept myself inside most of the time and I completely kept myself away from my friends. They've visited me a few times mind you and I was grateful to them for thinking about me. I always knew who my true friends were. Maybe that's where my courage has come from. Mark was my world and I expected to have him for the rest of my life. I never expected to do anything on my own, but now I feel like I needed to do this to prove a point to myself. It was something that was screaming at me and I was going to do it. Who knows? It might be the perfect making of me. It was maybe meant to be my direction in life, but only time would tell.

CHAPTER 7
Traveling Where?

I had to say, the last week had gone by quickly. Usually, when I planned something, the time goes slowly. That was something I called a good omen. It was something else telling me I was doing the right thing. I shopped, visited friends, and said my farewells to my nearest and dearest. I even cleaned the house from end to end. I knew that my dad and Craig would keep the place as tidy as possible, but I was giving them a good head start. There was no reason why housework should lag behind, because there are only two adults in there that work long, crazy hours. They really should sleep more than anything else. I even prepared them meals and put them in the freezer. At least I knew they would have decent food for a little while. I realised I was acting like an obsessive parent, but I

was making sure my two favourite men were going to be okay.

Now that they were taken care of, I could show off my excitement of starting my new adventure. Of course, there were still some nerves in the pit of my stomach, but I knew that I needed them. I had to believe what my mum used to say to me when I was growing up. "*Everyone had to have some kind of nerves. It was those nerves that made them the best they could be.*" I had to hope that my nerves were another good omen. Was that my mum trying to tell me that she approved of what I was doing? I believed in things happening for a reason. I was going to believe whatever I needed, to get me through my travelling. I wasn't going back on my decision no matter what. It would be easy for me to say I had changed my mind, although I wasn't the type of person to quit before I started something. It was my fresh start and I was excited to see where it was going to lead me.

"Lee." I smiled, as I heard Craig call me, but when I turned around from my bed I could see him standing in my doorway. "So, you're really going through with this?" Looking at my suitcases on my bed, he still thought I would change my mind.

"Craig. I need to do this." I sat on a spare bit of my bed and tapped it for him to join me. I took his arm and laid my head on his shoulder. "I love you Craig, but I want you to be happy for me. I know that I have worried you all sick lately, but after all that's happened I'm getting back to myself. I need to do this in order to move forward. I've never had the chance to do something for myself before and this is what I want to do." I knew this was going to be hard for Craig, because we've become so close lately. It was going to be him and dad rattling around in that big house on their own.

"I am happy for you, Lee. I'm just going to miss you like crazy." I have moaned and been depressed for all the heartache a death can cause, but on the other hand it did get me closer to Craig. It let me see that he wasn't always a joker. He's kind, loving, and thoughtful. He will make some woman very happy one day.

"A year isn't forever." I had a funny feeling the year would go by in the blink of an eye.

"It's long enough! I just know that you're going to love it somewhere and you're never coming home!" I had no plans of

staying away, but I couldn't promise him that I would be home either. I only made promises, if I knew I could keep them.

"You never know. When I come home you might have a future Mrs. Park on your arm, or the pitter-patter of tiny feet."

"I'll crack the jokes, Lee. It's you and Scott that will settle down and have families. Not me." I knew he didn't mean that. He can't help who he falls in love with and he will come across Mrs. Perfect one day. I would bet my life on it.

"Maybe there would have been a time I would have agreed with you, but that will never be me, Craig. Not again. I'm happy with just me now. I will never be hurt that way again, but you will make a perfect husband and daddy one day."

"Don't make me laugh! This new Leela has lost her mind. Try and bring the sensible Leela back, please." We both laughed. I was happy when I saw Craig laughing with me. I don't know why he has doubts about getting married and having kids. We were brought up in the perfect environment and I thought it would have rubbed off on him.

"Are you ready for me to put these in the car?" I took a deep breath and took one last look around my room.

"Ready as I'll ever be." It was weird to think I had spent most of my life growing up in that room, but it was time for a journey of my own. I would've probably moved out and got a place of my own by now, if my mum hadn't passed away. Craig and I were there for my dad's sake. It was just like having a place of our own, because we had the run of the house. Even when I come home, I'll be happy to come back there. I shook myself out of my thoughts and tried to stop overthinking things. I left Craig to lift my luggage and I headed downstairs. I was like a child with a new toy. I was so excited to see where I was going to go on the first part of my travels. I searched online for a few places, although I still didn't care where I ended up.

"Are you ready to go sweetheart?" My dad startled me as he came out into the hall as I was at the bottom of the stairs. "Sorry. I didn't mean to frighten you, Leela."

"I'm ready dad. I'm more than ready. Much more than I expected anyway."

"Have you got everything?" I was thinking about it. If I had

forgotten anything now, it was just tough.

"Yip! Ready and raring to go."

"Have you said all your farewells?" I was sure that I would have forgotten someone, but it was a bit late, because I was going to the airport. Besides, I was still going to have my phone, email, and Facebook to keep in touch with everyone. It wasn't like I was going to disappear off the face of the earth.

"The important people. I made sure I filled them in on my plans. I even went to the cemetery yesterday. I couldn't have left it to today, because I didn't want to leave feeling down. Will you check Mark's grave every week?"

"We both will, honey. He will always have fresh flowers from you." That's the only thing I was worrying about. I knew that Mark had family, but apart from Brian, I could see the rest getting fed up with jaunts to the cemetery in all kinds of weather.

"Thank you! Right, let's do this. I'm ready!" We were all waiting for the first person to move. I knew I had to do it. I had to prove to my dad and Craig, that this was what I really wanted to do. As I got outside and the air hit me, there was no doubt about it. There was nothing left for me there. It was just bad memories everywhere I looked. I was hoping when I decided it was time to come home, I would be able to put all of those memories to bed.

***

Walking through the doors at Glasgow airport, I felt like I was doing the right thing. I was lucky, because it wasn't busy. I just had the fun task to find out where I was going to go.

"Well, Leela. You still have time to turn around and come home with us." I ignored my brother and walked over to look at the departure boards. There were umpteen flights about ready to leave in the next couple of hours, but I noticed a star beside the flight to France and it kept flickering. I was wondering if it was trying to tell me that was where I was supposed to start my journey. "Well? Where are you going sis?"

"France." I turned around to see my dad and Craig, with the exact

same look on their faces. "I *am* going to France. I'll just have to find out if there are any seats left on the flight." That was my star for a reason and I was following it to see where it took me in France.

"I'll do it, sweetheart. You go and get a seat with Craig." I gave my dad a hug. He then left to find out about tickets for that flight. I was glad my dad was happy for me, because it was making this decision a whole lot easier. I wished my brother was just as happy.

"Look after dad for me, Craig. I want to know how you're both doing all the time. Don't keep anything from me. Promise me, that you'll both look after each other." I knew that I sounded like a mother hen. I had to laugh to myself.

"I promise you, Lee. We'll be okay. We'll be more worried about *you.* You're crazy! You do know that. Don't you?"

I wasn't known for being spontaneous, but something inside was different. I was pleased I started a new lease in life.

"People go travelling with partners, friends, and family. Oh no! Not my sister!"

"Well, I don't have a partner...anymore. My friends are all settling down with partners and kids. Scott is at university and you and dad have your jobs. I think my list of options is gone." There probably would have been someone else that would have been daft enough to embrace the trip with me, but I couldn't think of anyone I could spend a year with, without wanting to kill them.

"I would have done it with you, if you asked." I couldn't believe I was hearing that now. I looked at him to see if he was being serious, or if he was trying to make me change my mind, until he could get time off work.

"Why didn't you say this last week?" His shoulders shrugged and he turned to look over at the check-in desks. "You can come out and get me when you've sorted it out with work." I wasn't putting it off any longer. If Craig wanted to come with me, he could join me when he was ready.

I lost my thoughts when I could saw my dad coming back. He didn't look happy or sad. I didn't know what to think of his expression. "Well? Are there any flights?" I was on edge now. I didn't want to feel like that.

"Are you one hundred percent ready for this?" There was my other

lecture. I was getting used to answering the same questions over and over. I should have gotten a tape recorder and just pushed repeat, because my dad and Craig were like broken records.

"I am dad. I'm one thousand percent ready for this."

"Well then, your flight leaves here in two hours. You can check in at gate three anytime." I was gobsmacked, as he handed me my flight ticket and all of the details. I got up and wrapped my arms around my dad. I loved him dearly and I was much happier.

"Thank you, dad!"

"The travel agent I got your ticket from, told me there are plenty of help desks in France. They can book you into hotels. They have a list of premises that are for let, if you plan to stay for a while. I know you have plenty to keep you going, but if you ever need anything, you know where I am. I'll get the inheritance that your mum left you all sorted out. You can use that for emergencies."

"There's no need for that dad. You know I have worked every hour God sent over the last few years... I wouldn't be doing this if I wasn't financially stable. Just don't forget that I love you both very much. I'll phone you when I get there. When I get settled, I'll send you the address. Just be careful at work and don't take any chances on those low life thugs." I was still worrying about them and I wasn't even out of Glasgow yet.

"I love you, Leela. I know I've said this many times, but your mum would be so proud of the young lady you have become." I didn't want to cry, but I could feel myself getting weepy. "Right. Let's get you checked in." There were more tears than I expected, but I don't know why I ever thought it was going to be easy. My dad's arm was still wrapped around me, when Craig wheeled my luggage behind us. I was still shocked that I had enough courage to make the move, but it just showed how strong I had become. Mark's death made me some kind of blubbering mess. As I came to terms with him not being there, it made the person I am today. Yes, I still miss him. Yes, I will never get over him and yes, the pain and heartache is still inside me. But without any of that, I would probably still be that blubbering mess.

It was my turn to go through check-in, I handed the steward my passport and ticket. I was sure she could see I was upset, because I

was still wiping tears away when Craig lifted my luggage and placed it onto the conveyor belt.

"Thank you, Miss Park. You're all checked in. I hope you have a great holiday."

"Thank you!" I knew that my goodbyes were going to be painful, yet I was going to be strong through it. I had come through much worse.

"Well, it's time." My dad hugged me tight, as my head rested comfortably on his chest. My tears were flowing down and I couldn't stop them. Anyone would think we were never going to see each other again, the way we are behaving.

"I love you, Leela. Take care of yourself and have the best time of your life."

"I will, dad. I love you too." I moved away from my dad and turned to see Craig. He was crying as much as I was. "Are you just going to stand there or you coming to give me a goodbye hug." We both tried to laugh, but it was too hard for it to last too long.

"I'm going to miss you like crazy, Lee." It was normally me that sobbed, but it was my brother for a change. I knew when he got home, he would realise why I had to do it.

"You'll be free from all of my hassle, Craig. Just think of all the peace you'll get."

"Leela. I miss Mark like crazy, but I've loved taking care of you. You've been no hassle." I couldn't let go of Craig. I wanted to leave so much, but I hated to think I was causing my brother more heartache. "Just take care of yourself. When I get a holiday from work, I'll find out where you are and come out for a visit." I was glad I was finally getting his blessing to do this. "Take care of yourself, sis. I love you."

"I will. I love you too, Craig." I managed to pull away from him, as we both tried to compose ourselves.

"Miss? Get ready to board your plane. Call us when you arrive safely and take care." My dad was doing me a favour, because he knew if I stayed any longer, I would never leave.

"Bye, you guys." I put my handbag over my shoulder and started to walk to the checkout gate. That was it. My new journey was about to begin and I was feeling nervous. I got to the metal detector and

was passed to go through quickly. There was nothing stopping me from getting on that plane. I was surprised at how smooth everything was going. I turned around and waved to my dad and my brother still standing in the same place. I could see them both wiping their tears away. But I kept walking until I couldn't see them anymore. It was for the best that I didn't hang around, because we all needed time to compose ourselves and get used to the big change in our lives. We thought it was weird when Scott went away to University, but we eventually got on with life. We will all manage to get on with our lives again. We were brought up to love and respect each other and that's exactly what we've done. We will continue to do it for as long as we all live. It's just a shame there aren't more families like mine.

***

I was pleased when the plane touched down in France, because I was desperate to start my journey. I bought a French guide back in the Glasgow airport. It kept me engrossed on the flight. I was even learning basic French phrases all in the space of two hours. I felt accomplished. I was actually surprised at how much French I still knew. I hadn't spoken an ounce of French, since I left school. I never thought I would have ended up in the city of love. It did seem a little bit bizarre, since I was trying to forget about Mark and the baby. However, I was a firm believer of things happening for a reason. Maybe going to France was meant to be. It was another good omen. I had a sudden feeling rush through me, as I stood in the long line of people waiting to find somewhere to stay. I had no idea how busy that airport was. I was knackered. I just wanted somewhere to lay my head for the night. I felt a little bit out of place, because most of the people in front of me were young people looking for hostels. I never thought I was a cut above anyone, but I wasn't looking for a hostel. I hoped to get somewhere half decent to stay, so I could explore Paris. I also thought that I was a bit old to stay in a hostel.

"Bonjour Madame. Comment puis-je vous aider?" I could only understand some of the words, so I was going to have to guess that she was asking me what she could do for me.

"Bonjour. Parlez-vous anglais?"

"Yes. How can I help you, miss?" I was relieved she could speak

English, because guess work with French wasn't going to be easy. I could have ended up in a pig sty with how little I spoke French.

"I'm taking a year out from my work in the U.K. and I'm looking for somewhere to stay. I am not looking for a hostel, though." I didn't want her to think that I was being snobby, but I couldn't slum it in a hostel. I'm too used to my home comforts to go back to a single room, while sharing bathrooms and toilets.

"Come with me and I will see what I can do." I knew that I could do whatever I set my mind to. It felt so good to be independent, but I didn't want to end up with nowhere to stay. "Take a seat. I thought you might be looking for more than student accommodations." I didn't think I looked much different from the French, but maybe I was wrong. I was ahead of a long line of people and I was too tired to wait at the back. I guess I was glad she took notice.

"I was a student once. It just seems like many years ago." I had no idea why I had said that, but my nerves were making me talk nonsense. I hoped she would be chatty too.

"What did you study?" I couldn't help but smile. I didn't know what her job title was, but she was friendly and seemed right up my street. I was glad I spoke out, because it broke the ice.

"I studied psychology and then I did my training to be a doctor of psychology. So, I'm Dr. Leela Park." It wasn't often that I spoke about myself to strangers, but it might have helped me get something other than a grubby flat or bedsit.

"Well, welcome to Paris, Dr. Leela Park. Let me see what I can do for you. We do have a couple of clients that advertise their accommodations with us. We are only supposed to show to people that look trustworthy and you fit that description." I wasn't sure if I should have been happy or not. I didn't want to come across as being posh, but I was glad that I wasn't going to get a place anywhere dirty or overcrowded.

"I am grateful for you taking the time out, but I am more grateful that you speak English." I laughed at my comment, because I would have been lost if she couldn't speak my language. I was amazed at myself, because the Scottish slang was gone and I was speaking proper English.

"Lucky for you, I am bilingual. We all have to speak the main

languages in order to get a job here." I learned something new, because I always thought women that worked in the travel industry were dizzy blondes. I was wrong. You really should never judge a book by its cover.

"I only have one available now. It is a two bedroom cottage style bungalow close enough to all of the attractions. I'm sorry. Is bungalow the right word for you?"

"Yes, it is. I'll take it." I didn't care about pricing. I just wanted to get settled in one place for a little while.

"It will be 380 euros for the month. Since it is classed as a holiday home, you can rent it again if you haven't decided to move on." I couldn't believe how lucky I was. That was certainly the right choice for me. I was looking forward to tour Paris and see the sights.

"That's great! Thank you!" The next half hour was spent filling out the rental forms and paying the rent. I was very surprised at how cheap it was for a month. I thought it worked out to about £300. I certainly wouldn't get accommodations back in the U.K. for that price. The travel advisor that had been helping me was very good. She wrote the address down for me and arranged a taxi to take me to the property. I never let that piece of paper out of my sight. It was the only thing that got me back without getting lost.

***

I was gobsmacked, as I was driven through Paris. The sights were beautiful and I saw many people having a good time, taking in all of the amazing scenery. I would have plenty of time to visit the amazing attractions. The longer I was in the taxi, the more excited I got. I felt like a child again.

I could remember when I was a little girl, my mum and dad used to book fantastic holidays for us in the summer and we were always excited. We visited Disneyland Paris when I was about ten years old. Everything looked very different to what I could remember.

However, something was making me feel like I had been there before, even if I couldn't recognise what it was. I wished I had done something like this years ago, because it was a once in a lifetime

opportunity. I decided when I was waiting to board my plane back in Glasgow, that I was going to keep a diary of all the things I did and all the experiences I have while traveling. I bought a journal when I bought the book about France. I started, by writing my departure from Glasgow up until I was on the plane. I would make sure to write in it every day. It would be a good thing to look back on in years to come. I quickly realized we were outside of town, as the taxi pulled into a narrow street with lots of lovely bungalows on each side. They were typical French cottages. I saw lots of mosaics and lots of lovely colours. Already, I felt right at home. I felt relaxed and at ease, not like I expected to feel on my first night away from my family.

"This is your home, Madame." I looked at the taxi driver. Even with his French accent, he actually spoke good English. I really expected no one to understand me.

"How much do I owe you?" I felt like I was talking slowly to a toddler, but it was going to be like that, until I could speak fluent French. I watched as the driver tapped the machine and I could see it read 8 euros. I took a 10 euro note out of my purse and told him to keep the change. I was grateful how nice and helpful everyone was being to me. I thought I would have been made to feel like an outcast, but I was wrong. "Is there a shop close by for food?"

"Just down that way. You will see it."

"Thank you!" The driver helped me to the front door with my luggage. I thanked him for his kind service. With all the support I received, it made me see that I made the right decision. I was very excited to see where I would be living for the next few weeks.

As I entered through the front door, I was stunned into silence. Everything was gorgeous. There were stone floors. The colour scheme was different shades of whites and blues. The furniture was all fresh and modern. As I spotted the fitted kitchen, I had to pinch myself just to make sure I wasn't dreaming. It was beautiful. I started to explore and I could see the French patio doors, leading out to a lovely garden. It was going to be perfect for relaxing. Opening another door, led me into a huge bathroom with a shower in one corner and a large Jacuzzi style bath in another. The colour scheme was all white with silver fittings. Bright and fresh. I could see why

they only let those places out to very few people. Coming back out, I opened another door and found the bedroom. “Wow!” was all I could say. It was all white with red and gold spread throughout the room. I knew that was the room I was taking. It was perfect for me. It was like home. The last door grabbed my attention, but it was only me being nosey. I didn’t care what was behind the door, because I picked my room before seeing it all. To my surprise, it was similar to my room, just a lot smaller. I was gobsmacked with my accommodations. I landed on my feet and I just had to get some groceries to save me from eating out all the time. After all, I was there to enjoy myself, but I was also there for a while. I wanted to live like I did back home, but that wouldn’t be eating out all the time and drinking alcohol. I walked back to the kitchen and took in all of the features. I noticed there was tea, coffee, and sugar already in canisters. It was handy, because I didn’t need to rush out. I could get settled in and find a store at my leisure. I had to phone home and tell them I arrived safely. I couldn’t wait to tell them how lucky I was. It was going to take a while for it all to sink in and adapt to the cosy lifestyle. It wasn’t like I was used to living in poverty, because I had a good upper class life back home. I just didn’t expect to be living the same life while I was travelling. I heard of people travelling all the time and I saw them in hostels, cabins, and cheap bed and breakfasts. I was excited to see where the adventure was going to take me.

***

CHAPTER 8
18 MONTHS LATER

Eighteen wonderful months passed, since I decided to take a year out travelling. It was the best decision of my life. My first stop was France and I have taken a full year touring that lovely country. I started in Paris and then visited Cannes, Dijon, Nice, and finished off in Marseille. I came to Marseille, fourteen months ago and settled down to make a life for myself. I used my inheritance money that I received from my mum. I found a perfect French cottage on the outskirt of Marseille, and I bought a share of the new medical centre in the middle of the city. I'm enjoying life, but I miss not seeing my family often. They visit every couple of months and we speak on the phone weekly.

I followed my heart, but hadn't had another man in my life since Mark. I was happy with that. I didn't want to love anyone, but no one would ever come close to making me feel like Mark did. My

brother Craig slagged me off every time we talked, because he thinks it's hard to believe that I haven't fell in love with a French man. My answer never changed. Life in France had been better than I ever could have ever imagined. I felt like I belonged where I was. I could jump in the car and find my way around and nothing fazed me. The French language still baffled me when they spoke quickly, but I haven't let it spoil my time there.

I enjoy many things including, work, nights out, keeping fit, and lazing around my cottage. I decorated every bit of the cottage to my liking. I feel like I have achieved a lot. If I had been back home, I would never have had the time and I would have paid someone to do it. However, since I had been here I have excelled and tried to do a lot of things I would never have done back home. Since settling down in Marseille, I have worked around the clock, but it's different here. I do the exact same job I did back home, but I enjoy getting up in the morning. I love every minute of my day. Even when I come home from work, the day is still young and there's plenty to do.

I've just started two weeks holiday. What a better way to start my break, than a night on the town with a few friends.

***

I had spent the last couple of hours getting ready for my night out. I enjoyed the luxury and comfort of my own home, as I waited for my friends. It was time to pop open the Prosecco. It had been so long since I had a night out and I had a feeling it was going to be a good one. I heard the doorbell ring and rushed off to answer it. I was like an excited teenager to see who was there first.

"Come in! You must have smelled the wine." My friends Sophia, Rosa, and Pierre, were the first people that I met when I came to Marseille. We have gotten close as time went on. I have been honoured to meet so many lovely people that treat me like me for a change. Back home, everyone knew my problems and I felt pitied. At least here, I was free to mingle and have a laugh. That was exactly what I was going to do tonight.

"Give me wine! Give me wine! I had the worst day at work today." I couldn't help but laugh at my friend Pierre. He was always so

dramatic with or without a drink. I heard that all good men were gay, which fit perfectly with him. Pierre was fantastic in every way possible. "Leela! Why do you always look so beautiful?" Pierre was always praising me. I didn't know if he was just trying to boost my confidence. But he's the only person that knew my story. I trusted him. He worked similar hours with me in the medical centre and we were like family. We came back to my cottage on many occasions and enjoyed some dinner and a bottle of wine. He knew there was more to my story, but he waited for me to tell him in my own time. I don't feel like I have to be a fake around him.

"Pierre. You know me, darling. I'm just beautiful inside and out. That's why you love me." I tried to imitate his feminine tone, but I did it badly and we were in fits of laughing. "Wait a minute! Where's Sophia?" I realised that one of us was missing. It was weird for the three of them not to turn up together.

"She's running late," Rosa said, sarcastically. Rosa and Sophia were always nit-picking at each other, it was amusing at times. "Well, I think it's about time you get a man in your life, Leela." Rosa was always trying to play matchmaker. She always got the same answer from me. You would think she would just give up.

"Oh, give over, Rosa. I don't need a man in my life. I'm too free spirited to settle down. Besides, I have Pierre in my life. What more can I ask for?" I almost always hated the usual girlie chats, because I didn't want a man. I was happy with just me.

"You are right, my darling. You have me and I will love you forever." I loved Pierre, because he didn't put any airs on. He was who he was whether you liked it or not. "Drink up and leave the girl alone! We can't get a shot of a man, because of you, Rosa." Pierre danced around, while having fun winding Rosa up. This is why I loved those nights, because I never stopped laughing. My sides really did ache by the time the night was finished.

"I am happy Pierre. You're just jealous that no one likes you like they do me!" I loved the confidence that shined through from my friends. They made me feel the same way and I loved that.

"Well, girl! I am on the lookout tonight, so keep your grubby paws off! Pierre was fantastic company. He was always on the ball and he was always on my side. I loved the happy atmosphere in my cottage.

"Pierre, sweetie. You can't get a man, because they never get a word in edge ways." Rosa was obsessed with men. She was crazy.

"Rosa. Every man loves me. I don't let everyone in my bed. I'm too fussy. They have got to be a pure breed, honey."

"You guys are crazy." I was only stating the obvious. Anyone meeting them for the first time, would say *what the hell have we got here?* But I have seen their playful side and their serious work side. I loved both sides.

"That is me, my love."

"Oh look! I have a message from Sophia. She's running mega late. She'll meet us in town. So, are we all ready to party?" I started getting my things ready. I wore gold shorts and a cream vest top that trailed down my side to show my glorious figure that I keep getting told I have. Pierre had told me thousands of times how I looked and I was starting to believe it. I knew that I had lost X amount of weight since I came to France, but I've been a lot happier with myself. I was a comfortable size twelve and I had my confidence back. I wasn't afraid to show it anymore. It took many years when I was younger to gain self-confidence, but it wasn't until I started university that my confidence came back. It always seemed like when I got back up, something always knocked me down. I wasn't going to let anything get in my way of happiness. I was up and I was going to stay up.

"Leela! The taxi is waiting, darling," shouted Pierre.

"Coming Pierre!" I was always the last one to leave the cottage. We all bounded into the taxi and were ready for a well-deserved night on the town. It's always work and no play, but I had a feeling in my stomach, that the night was going to be all play and no work.

***

Hours into the evening, each of us was well on our way to being tipsy. We all worked hard and we deserved to let our hair down once in a while. When we do let our hair down, it's well and truly let down. I was happy watching my three friends dance the night away. I came back to sit down, because my legs were aching from all of the shenanigans. It was my own fault, because I never wore heels, until I went out, because they give me a bit of height. So, it was a small

price to.

As I was drinking away at my raspberry cognac sparkler, Pierre came and joined me. I had to laugh, because he was out of puff with red sweaty cheeks. He was always the life and soul of the party. We had to practically shout at each other, to hear over the music.

"Baby girl! Are you enjoying yourself?" Pierre's French accent when he was drunk, always made me laugh.

"I am honey! This has been exactly what I needed!" I was happy and enjoying every moment. There was nothing else that I could ask for.

"I love seeing you let your hair down! I just wish that I was straight, because I would make you love again!" I loved him for his honesty. I did love Pierre. It was the same kind of love I had for my brothers. I knew that Pierre would always be a part of my life. No matter what.

"You know that I would never have met you if you were straight! I won't enjoy the headache in the morning, but you guys are great!"

"I don't know about you, but I am sweating like a bitch on heat!" Pierre exclaimed, waving a hand in front of his face. I was in stitches laughing. I thought I was going to wet myself.

"Oh my god, you get worse Pierre!" There was never a dull moment when we are all together.

"I just love listening to you laugh! You are much happier than when we first met a year and a half ago," he said with a sparkle in his eye. That I couldn't argue with. I felt much happier and at ease. I never thought that I would have been where I was, but I'm happy.

"You certainly know how to tickle my fancy!"

"No one has said that to me for years!" Pierre laughed, rattling his hands on the table. I was glad that I managed to amuse him for a change. "You are on the ball tonight, ma cherie!"

"Good drink and crazy ass friends! What more could I ask for?" I shouted and laughed above the sound of the music. While everyone around us was doing the exact same. Laughing, joking, and drinking. "I'm going to the little girl's room, mon Pierre!" Anyone could see how tipsy I was, but I didn't care. That night was so much fun. I was just managing to squeeze through the crowds of people that gathered. It made me realise how I needed to get out and do this

more often.

I searched my bag for my phone to see if I had any missed calls or messages, because there was no way that I would have heard it over the music. Trying to find it in my bag was proving to be a difficult task with everything that I had inside it. But getting out into the lit hallway, made me see clearer. It also made me feel how tipsy I was. As I turned round a corner, I bumped into a man and the contents of my bag crashed to the floor.

"I am so sorry sir. I wasn't looking," I shrieked, as I picked up the contents of my bag. The gentleman bent down to help me and I felt embarrassed. I didn't know if he understood English for a start. I wasn't sure what language he spoke, but I thought it was typical of me. I was clumsy at all the wrong times.

"No need for apologies, miss." English was much easier to understand and I felt relief, as his face softened when he spoke to me. I just wanted to disappear and fast. I wanted the ground to open up and swallow me.

"Sorry. I'm so clumsy."

"Leela!" I heard someone call my name, as I zipped my bag back up. I had no idea whether to turn around or not. "Leela! Is that you?" I found the courage to look over at the voice and I couldn't believe my eyes. I was shocked beyond belief. The gentleman that helped me pick my things up, looked a little bit shocked at my expression.

"Miss? Are you okay?" I didn't know the answer to that question. I was stunned.

"Brian? I can't believe that you're here." His arms came around me and immediately that connection stirred in my stomach all over again. I pulled carefully away without Brian letting my hand go. I felt like I was blushing.

Was I dreaming? Was I really there standing in France next to Brian? I couldn't believe it.

"Leela. You look fantastic." I was blushing so much that I could feel the heat rise in my cheeks.

"You don't look too bad yourself, Brian. Are you here on holiday?" I wanted to know everything. He was the first familiar person that I had seen since leaving home, apart from immediate family. The shock was sinking in and I was starting to relax.

"No. I took over the renovation programme here in Marseille. I have been out here for nearly a month now. What about you?" Wow! I can't believe that we both ended up here in France. What are the chances of that happening?

"I take it you two know each other?" The gentleman I banged into looked rather confused, as he looked to me and Brian for an explanation.

"Yeah. Leela used to be engaged to my brother." I smiled at Brian, because even he looked shocked that this was happening. I gathered that these two men were some kind of friends.

"This is all good, Brian. Just hold that thought, until I come back from the bathroom." I managed to speak out.

"Sure." I left the two men quickly, because I wanted to get back just as quick. I hoped that the shock would sober me up a little bit. I still didn't believe that I had just bumped into Brian, of all people. I was glad that there was an empty cubicle, because I didn't want to go without seeing Brian again.

I peed and washed my hands in record time. The reflection of myself in the mirror made me smile. I was glad that my hair and make-up were still neat and tidy. I half expected Brian to have vanished while I was away, but when I opened the door I saw him still standing in the exact same position with his friend. It was now obvious to me that the man I had bumped into, was definitely with Brian.

I had the biggest smile on my face. I felt a little bit subconscious, as to what I was wearing, because Brian always saw me as a sophisticated doctor.

"Brian. I don't know what to say. I can't believe after nearly two years, here we are again…In France of all places."

"I'll head back to the guys and leave you two to catch up." I was relieved when his friend wasn't going to drag him off quickly. Since the shock was gone, I wanted to know everything.

"Thanks Sean! I will be going home after here. I'll see you all at work," said a still shocked Brian.

"I am sorry for banging into you Leela. I wasn't watching."

"It's cool. I was as much to blame." I was too busy looking for my phone. It was probably all my fault anyway. I followed Brian

through to the bar and we found an empty booth. It was quieter and lightly lit with sparkling lights. The waiter spotted us coming to sit down and she came right over to assist us.

"Bonjour, monsieur. Voulez-vous un verre?" Brian looked confused. He reminded me of myself, when I first arrived. "Bonjour, madame. Pouvons-nous obtenir une bière et un verre de cognac framboise, s'il vous plaît." I could see Brian looking at me with surprise. I had to smile at him, because it was one up for me.

"Puis-je vous offrir quelque chose d'autre?" asked the sweet waiter.

"Non, merci." I replied. I knew that I had a few to drink, but I liked to think my French was just as good.

"How did you do that?" I smiled at Brian's inquisitive tone. He was shocked that I could speak good French.

"Let's just say, the last eighteen months I had to learn to speak French or I would never be able to communicate. Luckily here in Marseille, there's a lot of English spoken."

"So, you have been here for a long time?"

"After I left home, I told you I would be travelling. I came to France and I never got any further. I started in Paris and did a tour of a few places. I ended up in Marseille and I fell in love with everything. I bought a house on the outskirts of town and a share of the new medical centre. It was built two years ago. It was like I was meant to be here. Everything fell into place and it was so easy to settle down." I couldn't believe how easy it was to talk to Brian after all of the time that had passed.

"What do you do at the medical centre?"

"I'm the head of the psychological services and I have been training in paediatrics for twelve months. I love being a doctor, but I needed a change. When the position came up for training in paediatrics, I jumped at the chance. I do three days as a psychologist and two days training." I felt like I was rambling on about myself. But I was just as keen to know what he had been doing with himself.

"I am so happy for you, Leela. You deserve all of this and I knew that you would be able to settle down again." The waiter cut in and placed our drinks on the table. Brian covered my hands, as I went to pay for the drinks. I should have known that he would be the perfect

gentleman "This is on me Leela. Merci."

"See? You can speak French." I laughed.

"I'm okay, but when they speak fast I'm lost. They always speak like someone is holding down a fast forward button." I had forgotten what it was like to talk with someone that I had known for years. I was pleased to see him.

"So, Brian. What brings you out here?" He knew all about me, but it was my turn to ask questions.

"Well, to cut the story short, I bought into the redevelopment over here. After died and with you leaving, I thought…what the hell? Why not start fresh. I bought a house, but it's taking forever to finalise. I'm staying in the Hilton now, but I can't wait to settle into my own place. I jumped in head first and so far I love it here. I just wish that I did it years ago." It was weird, because I thought the exact same thing when I first arrived here in France.

"I just can't believe that I bumped into you. It's like fate telling us something."

"Leela? There you are!" I jumped, as Pierre came up from behind me. "I was worried about you when you didn't come back." I was glad Pierre piped in, because he stopped me from probably saying something stupid.

"Sorry, Pierre. I bumped into an old friend from back home. Brian. This is my friend, Pierre. Pierre. This is my friend, Brian." I could see Pierre eyeing Brian, as he shook his hand with a sexual overtone. I knew that Pierre would have approved of his looks and build.

"We're heading to the next club, girlfriend."

"Just go on without me. I'm calling it a night. I'll call you tomorrow." I wasn't leaving there, without a full conversation with Brian.

"Baby girl! I am *not* leaving you by yourself."

"Pierre. I'll make sure she gets home okay." I shot Brian a smile. He knew that Pierre was not going to take *no* for an answer. He was over protective of me and I suppose that was a good thing.

"Bien. Fille bonne nuit. Amusez-vous avec ce sexy homme." I was amused how Pierre was telling me that in French. He knew that Brian's French was poor, by taking one look at him. I would have been embarrassed, if Brian knew what he said.

"Se comporter! Il est le frère de mon ex-fiancé!" I exclaimed, in a not so playful tone. It would stop him from having any wild ideas. But who was I trying to kid?

"Ma cherie."

"Goodnight, Pierre!" I was glad to see the back of Pierre. I was also glad that Brian couldn't understand what was said, but my cheeks must have said it all.

"What did he say that has you blushing?" enquired Brian, with a huge smile on his face.

"You don't want to know," I said, smiling while shaking my head. "Don't you need to get back to your friends?" I didn't want to keep him if he was busy.

"Leela. I haven't seen you in nearly two years. I'm not letting you go that easily. Besides, I think your friend will have my guts if I leave you alone." I took a sip of my drink and thought about everything he said.

"I've had enough of pubs and clubs for one evening. What do you say we take this conversation back to my place? I have enough wine back home to sink a ship." I wanted to be casual and not uptight or nervous. I would be able to do that in my own surroundings.

"Sure, why not! At least I won't have to speak French when I am with you."

"C'est ce que vous pensez, monsieur!" I couldn't help but pull his leg. He was so easy to kid. Just like his brother. I couldn't help but laugh at his confusion.

"You aren't going to tease me now. Are you?" As I stood up, I grabbed my bag without answering his question. It was just good to know I had one over on him. He followed behind me that time and I didn't feel uncomfortable. The stunned feeling was gone and I was back to being relaxed. However, when the air hit me, my head felt kind of funny. I flagged down a taxi, as we stood on the path outside the club. I was relieved to see that it was my usual driver that stopped. It was like he was my stalker when I was out, because nine times out of ten, I got the same driver. Some people might think it's just a coincidence.

"Bonjour, Leela. Est-ce que vous allez rentrer à la maison?" asked Fabienne in his cheery tone. I never saw him any other way. I was

always happy to go home alone, when he was taking me.

"Oui. S'il vous plait, Fabienne." I sat opposite Brian in the taxi and was still kind of shocked that the night had turned out the way it did. Never did I expect to go out and bump into anyone I knew from home, let alone Brian.

"I can't believe that you are the same person, Leela." I was surprised at his comment, but I smiled, because I didn't know what he meant.

"Is that a good thing or a bad thing?" I wasn't sure if I wanted to hear the answer.

"It's fantastic, Leela! You look really happy. Stunningly beautiful and so confident. It's nice to see."

"Oh please, Brian. You'll have me blushing before long."

"I mean it, Leela. Mark would be proud of you. I'm proud of how you turned your life around." It was easy to do, when I was comfortable with my surroundings. I had France to thank for my change.

"I keep telling myself that Mark would have approved of my life out here." I looked down at my hands, just to break eye contact from Brian.

"Is there anyone special in your life?" Brian asked a question that I always tried to avoid, but I had nothing to hide with him. We have always been honest with one another and I wasn't about to start lying to him.

"No, there isn't, Brian. In fact, I'm not even going to lie to you. I haven't had anyone special since Mark left my life. In fact, apart from Pierre, you're the only other male to come home with me." I looked up to meet Brian's gaze. He never took his eyes from me, throughout the conversation.

"Why not? That's if you don't mind me asking." I would never mind sharing my life story with him. He was one of the one people who was there for me when I was at my lowest.

"Of course I don't mind you asking. Either I haven't found Mr. Right, or I never will. I have never felt a connection with anyone, since Mark."

"And here I am bringing it all up again." I could hear how pissed off with himself he sounded. I didn't like to hear him like that.

"Don't be silly, Brian. I just didn't want to lie to you. I am more settled now and more comfortable here. I can think of what happened and speak about it without breaking down." I was at ease with my memories and that's what I had always hoped for.

"I would have a cheek telling you to settle down, because I clearly haven't either,"

"Il s'agit de votre maison, Leela," Fabienne interrupted. I was rather annoyed at arriving home, because I was enjoying our chat. I loved talking to Brian. I didn't have to think about what I was saying.

"Merci, Fabienne." I leaned forward and paid for our ride. I was glad that I was quicker than Brian to pay that time. I liked to pay my way. I wasn't one of those women who likes the man to pay for everything.

"Bonne soiree, Leela."

"Bonne soiree, Fabienne." I closed the door and led Brian down my driveway. "Welcome to my home." I felt quite giddy showing him my new home.

"It's beautiful, Leela. You deserve everything that you have here."

"Come in and I'll get us a drink." As we entered the house, I flung my bag down on the entrance table and kicked my shoes off. It was the best feeling in the world to kick my shoes off. The relief was instant. "Make yourself comfortable, Brian. I'll be right back." As I left Brian to make himself at home in my living room, I flicked the switch for the music player and grabbed a bottle of wine from the fridge with two glasses. The soft mixed C.D of love songs, played while I filled our glasses. I flicked the switch for the lights on the artificial fire and took a seat next to him on my huge corner sofa. I felt my heart pounding in my chest. I was happy to have Brian in my living room. I had no idea why I felt the way I did.

"This is all lovely, Leela. Thank you." Brian clinked his glass with mine and I swung my legs up beside me. I wanted to relax and chat away all night. I felt like we had lots to talk about. The conversation should never run dry.

"So, you were in the middle of telling me about Mrs. Right, when the taxi pulled up." I wasn't letting him get away with asking the questions, but not answering. "Well?" I watched him settle back on

my couch inches away from me. His white crisp shirt clung to his muscular frame. The first few buttons were open to show his chest full of hair.

"I guess I never fell in love. I saw what happened to you when Mark died and I don't want to put anyone through that." Mark's death had an effect on all of us in some way.

"Brian. You can't stop your life, because of what happened to me when Mark died." I placed my glass down on the table and swung back round to place my hand on his arm. I didn't care about touching him or feeling any connection, I just wanted to tell him what I thought. "Mark was snatched from us by those scumbags. He knew the risks as much as anyone. I wish our baby survived just so I could have a piece of him. But I believe everything happens for a reason. I came out here, because I panicked every time Craig and my dad went to work. Every time I saw you…I saw Mark. I am not just saying any of this, because of the alcohol, any woman would be honoured to have a man like you in their life." My heart was beating so fast, that I could feel it beating through my blouse. "I left, because I felt a connection with you Brian." I couldn't believe I was finally telling him the truth. "The last time I saw you, it broke my heart seeing you crumble around me. I didn't want to see you suffer because of me. Your family needed you to be strong for them and that was never going to happen if I was dragging everyone's mood down." Brian's thumb rubbed across my lips to quiet me and tingles ran throughout my body.

"Leela. Why on earth did you not tell me any of this?" I was a bag of nerves, because I thought he was going to run away. "I watched you in a comma. I watched you crumble to pieces and return into your little lost shell. I stayed away, because I felt the same connection to you. I thought it was because of Mark, but seeing you again tonight has just stirred up feelings." I thought that I was stunned earlier when I bumped into him, but now I was stunned in a completely different way.

"Brian…" I covered his hand that was on my cheek with mine and looked deep into his eyes. "This would be wrong on so many levels, but I have made a life here and there's no more running." I couldn't run and I wasn't going to run anymore. I was an adult.

"Why run from it, Leela?" I heard his words being repeated in my head and I was thinking of everything over and over again.

"I loved Mark so much that it hurt. Can you imagine what your family would say? I would be all the cows and sluts under the sun. Again." As always I was thinking of everyone apart from myself.

"Leela. Stop thinking about everyone else for a change. I've been in love with you for so long. I have since Mark died. Probably before that, but I just never realised it. It's like I'm meant to love you. Not that you need to be taken care of, but I need *you*, Leela. I think you need me as well." I never took my eyes from his. I could see the same sparkle that Mark had when he spoke to me. The love. The passion. It all sounded so crazy, but it was so real. "Leela? Say something."

"I can't give you everything that you need, Brian. Even if I wanted any of this, I couldn't put you through any of it. You would hate me in the long run." I had loads on my mind that he didn't know.

"Leela. I could never hate you. You are everything I need." His soft warm lips touched mine and the tingles and heat soared through my body. Our tongues touched and I loved every second of being needed again. I pulled away from him to catch my breath and to realise what we had just done. It wasn't just him, because I was kissing him back without even thinking about it.

"Brian. I don't want some one night stand or a fling. I don't want to be hurt. I want to finally be happy and I am here…" I was laying everything down on the table and I wasn't about to change any of my conditions. It was all or nothing.

"Let me love you, Lee. Let me spend the rest of my life with you. We're in the country of love, so let's have some fun getting to know one another." It sounded crazy, but I was intrigued to say yes. Something was yelling at me to say yes.

"You need to know a few things first, Brian, then you can make up your mind to stay or run." I was starting to get everything out in the open. I didn't have the time to love someone, then spill some awkward news and be left broken hearted again.

"Nothing you say is ever going to make me run, Leela." His soft sensual tone, made goose bumps rise on my arms.

"When I lost the baby, I suffered some complications. I was told

that there's a strong chance I will never have another child. I couldn't hold you back, Brian. You deserve to be happy and have a family of your own one day. A full family with a wife *and* kids."

"Leela. You're all I need and want. If we had a child one day that would be great, but if not, then it isn't the end of the world. If there is no me and you, then I wouldn't have a chance of love or happiness. Let's take it slow and see where we go." There was so much going on in my head. I thought of all the things that would stop us from having a happy life. Could it work between us?

"What about your family?" I asked, nervously. His mum and I would never see eye to eye. She would hate the fact of me and Brian dating.

"I don't care what they have to say, Leela. We are adults and we can decide what path we're going to take in life." I was hearing everything that I wanted to hear, but there was one last thing that was on my mind.

"Mark!"

"I think that Mark would be over the moon for us. He knows that I will love, cherish, and would look after you. Stop looking for excuses, Leela. Tell me what you want! Tell me what you're thinking!" I knew exactly what I wanted, but I was scared. I was scared of agreeing to it and being left with nothing all over again. It was all new to me and I wasn't sure if I knew what I would be doing. It would be like a child trying to ride a bike for the first time.

"I haven't been with anyone since Mark and I'm scared, Brian." I felt stupid talking like that, but I wasn't going to lie. We both deserve to have the truth from the start.

"Scared of what, honey?" I shot him a look as if he should have known what I meant. His grin suggested that he knew perfectly what I meant. "I haven't been with anyone either, Lee." I didn't expect to hear him say anything like that, but I felt more relaxed.

"When you're ready, we can learn together." I was the first to lean into his arms and our mouths met again. I felt what it was like to be kissed by this man and it stirred more feelings inside of me. We were both hungry for each other, as the passion soared through our bodies. The feel of his hands on my bare back shocked me into stopping.

"I'm sorry, Leela. I didn't mean to go that far. You get to call the

shots." I stood up and saw the curious look on his face. I took his hand and led him through to my bedroom. I was relieved when he let me take the lead and he followed me through. As we entered through my bedroom door, I felt myself being pulled toward his body. His sparkling eyes danced at me and my heart raced. "Leela. I will never ever hurt you. I'm only going to go through with this if you're sure." I loved the fact that he honoured my feelings and he was going to go as slow or as fast, as I wanted things to go.

"Just shut up and kiss me!" I somehow got courage and ordered him to kiss me.

He slipped my top over my head leaving me wanting more. He caressed my naked breasts with his big, soft hands. I fumbled recklessly at his shirt buttons, until my hands ran through his chest hair. Before I knew what we were doing, he edged me over to the side of the bed and pushed my gold shorts off. He left me completely naked and wanting him. I should have felt awkward, but I wanted him and I couldn't stop this from happening. He stood back and took his pants off, until I saw his well-endowed package spring free.

My body was electric and every inch of me was tingling to be touched by this man. His kisses trailed up my thigh, until his finger entered me. His tongue trailed around my soft spot and made me climax almost immediately. The cries escaped my mouth, as spasms ran throughout my body. His mouth then trailed kisses up to my breasts, as my body arched at his touch. His big warm hand held my back in place, as his tongue invaded my mouth.

I felt tears run down my eyes, as I savoured every touch. He nestled softly inside me and our bodies cried out with pure pleasure. I accepted every thrust as much as the last, until our bodies convulsed around one another. Our powerless bodies laid together, with him still inside of me. Neither of us moved a muscle, apart from my eyes releasing tears. I felt so guilty that I had enjoyed it so much. Since Mark, no one had ever made me feel so loved and alive. I felt Brian lift his head slowly as he kissed from my breasts up to my lips, until he spotted my tears in the dim light.

"Leela, sweetheart. Are you okay? Did I hurt you?" I lifted my hands and pulled his face down to kiss me. I could feel his arousal inside me and I needed him again. "We don't need to be doing this,"

he whispered. I knew we didn't need to be doing it. We could have sat in my living room talking all night, but I wanted it just as much as he did.

"I want you, Brian. I need you. I'm crying out of guilt, because I enjoyed it so much." I sounded ridiculous, but I hoped he understood what I meant.

"You don't have anything to be guilty about, babe." His hips slowly grinded, as he thrust inside of me and out again. I could have screamed in ecstasy, but his slow movement made me whimper all over. "Do you want to stop?" The way I was feeling, I never wanted him to stop.

"No!" is all I managed to say, as his hands gripped my breasts. The electrical charge between us was so powerful and the cries that escaped my mouth were filled by his kisses. I wanted it so much. I had never felt that way before.

"Leela. You're so beautiful." I couldn't stop my body from reaching a climax, as his eyes never left me. I sat up slowly and pushed him to his back. I needed to let him see that I wanted it as much as he did. Straddling his long package, sent shock waves through my body. He sat up to meet me in the middle, as I straddled him. The kisses we shared were so intense. His hands tangled in my hair as we both cried out with the pure electricity of our love making and he climaxed again. We both sat with him still inside of me, tangled in a way that would be impossible any other time. His soft nibbles on my neck made me lift my head to look at him. My long wavy hair fell down around my breasts. That time, there were no tears, just smiles from both of us. It still felt weird, but I didn't care. It had been a long time coming and now that it was here, I never wanted to let it go.

"For someone who hasn't slept with a woman for a long time, you sure make it look easy." I managed to say a full sentence before my lips met his for a soft and tender kiss.

"I told you making love is easy if it's meant to be and I mean it, Leela. I've spent two years trying to forget about you. I've got two years to make up for." His tender words made the tears softly fall from my eyes again.

I held him tightly taking everything in. I wanted to feel every inch

of our skin touching.

"Don't cry, sweetheart. I don't mean to upset you."

"You're not upsetting me, Brian. Tonight has only made me realise that I can't live without you anymore. I blocked it out back then and I was blocking it out here. Seeing you tonight and coming back here with you, has made me realise that I can't block it out anymore." I laid him back onto the pillows and I laid beside him with a hand on his chest looking into his eyes. "It isn't about saying no anymore, Brian."

"Are you happy, Leela? Did you just enjoy me making love to you? Could I walk out that door and never look back? I know that I couldn't, Lee." I never thought I would have been in this position again and I knew exactly what I wanted.

"I don't think I'm going to survive another day without you, Brian, but your family is going to go ballistic." That was the only doubt in my mind. My body tensed at the thought. He was going to feel the differences in me.

"Forget about them, Leela. Just leave them to me. Our life is here now. My family will never be here, so I don't care what they have to say. As long as you can still have a relationship with your family, that's all I care about."

"My family will be happy as long as I am. We can jump any hurdle if we face them together." That was my mum's favourite saying and I would never forget it.

"We will be happy, Leela! I promise that I will be here for you every minute of every day and I will never let you down." I loved listening to him talk. I could see from looking into his sincere eyes, that everything he said was the absolute truth.

"I never thought that I would have felt like this again. One night and you've turned my whole life around. It's weird how we both had the same feelings back then and now here we are in France. Do you believe in fate?"

"I believe that something has been pushing us together. Every omen has lead us to each other and I am truly grateful to have you in my life."

"Finally." I Leaned down to meet him half way and our mouths became one. I didn't know how I was ever going to get used to

feeling the way I did. I didn't even feel that special when I was with Mark. I felt guilty about that. The soft feeling of our skin touching was electrifying and I hated to part from him. I felt like my heart was going to burst out of my chest.

"Are we ever going to get used to the passion between us?" I couldn't help but giggle at his words. "I love hearing you laugh," he whispered.

"I have a funny feeling that there isn't going to be a day that goes by, without you making me laugh." I knew that he was going to do everything in his power to make me happy.

"I'll do my best, Lee. Now come and get some sleep. We can talk as much as you'd like tomorrow, but right now, I just want to curl up beside you and wake up to another brand new fresh start." I laid my head down on his chest. I couldn't believe that I was lying there with him. It's crazy how a couple of hours, changed my life. This time last night I was in bed by myself reading a book. Then I was in Brian's arms. I could think of a thousand positive words that described me right then. But I never wanted to look back.

I felt absolutely shattered after a long day at work followed by a night of fun and passion. I closed my eyes and felt him take my hand. There wasn't a part of our bodies that wasn't intertwined together and I loved feeling so relaxed. The sound of his beating heart was enough to sooth me into a light but peaceful sleep.

***

Waking up to the sound of my alarm, made me jump out of my skin. I managed to lift my hand and hit it off. I couldn't believe I forgot to turn it off since I was on holiday. While the reality of last night's passion just hit me. I laid my head back down on his chest, wondering what the hell I was doing. Yet, I felt like I could sleep in his arms forever.

"Do you have to go to work, Lee?" His voice was still soft that morning and I was hoping he wasn't regretting what we got up to last night.

"Nope," I managed to say, as I lifted my head off of his chest. I

hated the morning after a night out, because my head would always spin. “Can you believe I’m on holiday for two weeks and I forgot to turn the damn alarm off?” I felt totally alive. Just seeing Brian smiling back at me, made me feel warm and tingly. “I bet you have to rush off for work though.” I heard the dread in my voice. I wasn’t ready to let him go.

“Today is your lucky day, Miss Park. I’m off until tomorrow.” I moved my head and placed my lips over his. My nerves were gone when he accepted me with just as much passion as last night. “I could get used to waking up like this.” His soft and sensual voice made goose bumps on my arms.

“Now that the alcohol is out of our systems, do you regret any of this?” I could have kicked myself for asking the question, but I wanted to know that what we said and did last night was for keeps. He wasn’t going to leave and never return.

“Leela. I spent most of the night making love to you. I plan on going nowhere apart from work and home. I’m going to struggle to be apart from you.

To show you how serious I am, I’m going to phone home tomorrow and tell my parents all about us. We’re in a different country and I could keep it from them and continue to sneak around, but I’m not ashamed about falling in love with you. I had two years of pining for you, Lee. The fact that we’ve ended up here together, means it’s our destiny. *It was meant to be*.” I heard his confidence and loved how he thought about me and my feelings.

“I just can’t stop feeling guilty in a way. . . I can’t not have you in my life now. I’m not going to lie to you, Brian. No one has ever made me feel the way you do. I loved Mark and obviously we had a great love life, but last night, you made me feel like a woman for the first time in years.” I could feel my cheeks get flushed. I smiled and dropped my eyes to his chest, but his fingers lifted my chin back up until he could look me in the eye.

“I will always treat you with respect, Leela. I want us together, forever. I know it’s early and we’re in the middle of getting to know each other better, but I really mean that I want us to start as we mean to go on.” I was relieved to hear that, because I couldn’t go back to just being friends.

"So, where do we go from here? I might work twelve to fourteen hour shifts at the medical centre and I know you must work a lot since you're a partner." It was going to be hard to make it work, but I had a feeling that we would do whatever we could in order to be together.

"We will work something out, sweetheart. I'll start taking weekends off, or taking the same days you have off, or vice versa. It'll work, Lee. We'll make it work!"

"I really do hope we can, Brian."

"Well, we have a full day together today. Since you're off for two weeks, I'll take as much time off as I can." I was honoured he was proving to me that this was just the start. We were going to be the talk of our friends and family. That wouldn't have usually bothered me and something about us made me careless.

I was truly happy for the first time in a long time and nothing was going to burst my bubble. I thought that I was happy here before last night, but now I can see I was only comfortable. But right now I'm ecstatically happy.

"What do you want to do today? I'll have to go back to the hotel to get changed, but I'm all yours after that."

"Where's your house?"

"I'll show you when we go back to my hotel. Don't ask me to pronounce streets, because I'm useless with the language, as you discovered last night." We both laughed. I loved his honesty. "The whole process is dragging with the previous owner. I wanted to be in two weeks ago. The hotel is lovely mind you, but it isn't home. I also brought a couple of guys over from Scotland with me. They're staying in the hotel as well. They're all going to be renting a cottage near town and they move in next week. We're working from the hotel at the moment, because our office building is just getting finished off. All the guys like the nightlife here, so the hotel is handy for them. You don't want to listen to my boring work life." I wasn't like all other women. I didn't just want the physical relationship. I wanted it all and that included work and all the boring things.

"Of course, I want to know. I like listening to you talk, but I don't know what you're going to think, when I say this next bit. Please, don't just say yes, because you don't want to offend me."

"Spit it out, Lee. You're worrying me." We were both going to have to stop worrying about things, because everything wasn't always bad.

"I have two spare rooms here, if you want to stay and get away from the hotel. It saves you being stuck in a hotel room." I knew I was rushing into things, but I had a good feeling about us and we *had* been friends for a long time.

"Do you think I would ever be able to sleep in a spare room?" He made me laugh, because I knew he was right. "We wouldn't be able to sleep in separate rooms and you know that."

"Well, you could have a room allocated. It doesn't matter if you find me irresistible and you can't keep your hands off of me. You can think about it for when your guys get a place of their own."

"I don't need to think about it, Leela. I don't want you getting lonely when I get the keys for my house." I never thought about that. It would be just like any other relationship in the early stages.

"We can cross that bridge when we come to it." I didn't want to think about hurdles. I just wanted to let my hair down and have some fun. It had been a long time coming for me and I was more than ready to get the relationship off the ground.

"Come here and give me a cuddle, Miss Park. You've been out of my arms too long." I had no difficulty in doing what he said. The minute I laid in his arms, I felt at peace. He had magic arms. The minute I was wrapped in his arms, everything disappeared. I never had any intentions of being in a relationship, but Brian and I seemed like we are meant to be. It didn't matter where we were or what we did, we ended up together. There just didn't seem like there was any point in fighting it anymore.

Just the feel of his hands running through my hair, made me forget about all the *what ifs.* We deserved to be happy and if that's what it took, then so be it.

"I could lie like this all day with you, Lee." I knew exactly what he meant. I was relaxed and never wanted it to end.

"Tell me about it," I managed to say with a sleepy tone. The lack of sleep was going to tell on me. "We should get up and have breakfast." I didn't know why I had to suggest moving. I was just being stupid.

"Sounds like a plan. You go for a nice shower or bath and I'll rustle us something up." I couldn't believe that I was hearing him right.

"You're just too good to be true mister. What have I done to deserve you?"

"You deserve everything and much more, doll. I intend to give it to you." I lifted my head to place a kiss on his lips. Within seconds, I was on my back and Brian was nestled down nicely between my legs. I could feel his hard package against my stomach, as he kissed down to my breasts. His teeth sent my body soaring, as he gently bit my nipple. His large hands caressed my body, until his finger slid into me. Immediately, my body arched, as the climax from his touch was overwhelming. His lips found mine, as he slowly placed his package inside of me. The cries of ecstasy escaped my mouth. Each thrust made the electricity soar, as we both climaxed at the exact same time. Our sweating bodies laid together, as his kisses trailed up my neck and softly on my mouth. I didn't think I would ever be able to stop feeling so alive.

"Time for a shower, Miss Park. I'll take care of our breakfast." I about choked, as I looked directly into his eyes. He was curious as to what he said wrong, but I couldn't stop smiling at him.

"You mean to say, you've just had mind blowing sex with me and you're now leaving me to get showered on my own."

"Leela. Sex isn't in my vocabulary. I'll always make sweet love to you. If we're just going to end up in bed all day, you need your energy." His sexy smile made me laugh, but the minute he left me lying in bed, I watched him put his boxers and shirt on. I was glad he left the shirt open, because I loved looking at him. I also loved to think about my hands tangled in his chest hair, as he made love to me.

However, as much as I felt like I was floating on a cloud, I still couldn't believe it was happening to me. I was going to have to start believing in myself more. Having Brian in my life was going to be the perfect key. I felt like I had been a closed rose bud lately, but since last night I opened up and flourished into a beautiful flower.

***

The last twelve hours of my life had been on fast forward. I never expected to sleep with any man, never mind Brian. As I was now fed and fully dressed, I walked shyly back into my living room. I could feel Brian's eyes on me and I didn't know why I felt so subconscious after the night of passion we shared.

"Hung-over, lack of sleep, and you still come back looking gorgeous." Listening to him paying me compliments, just made me blush. I was going to have to control my blushing, otherwise I was going to be bright red every minute of every day. "Do you want to come back to my hotel with me? I have to brief my staff at eleven o' clock, because my assistant manager has gone A.W.O.L."

"Sure!" I wasn't ready to let him go just yet. Why shouldn't I go? I was off from work and had nothing else planned. I haven't broken any laws and I was free to do whatever I want with whoever I wanted. "Are you sure, Brian?"

"About me and you? Of course I am, Leela. I want to shout from the roof tops and tell everyone that you're mine!" I instantly melted into his arms. We fit perfectly together like two peas in a pod.

"There's no going back after this."

"Good, because I don't want to live another day without having you in my life." As his words swam around in my head, I turned around and placed a soft kiss on his lips.

"We should go, before we never get out of here." I could feel the chemistry between us again. It was getting stronger by the second. If we didn't move, we were going to end up in a pile on my living room floor.

"Won't we need to order a taxi?" I had to laugh, because even though we spent a full night intimately together, we still had a lot to learn about one another.

"Why do we need a taxi, when I can drive?" I said laughing softly. "That's if you can trust me driving."

"Only time will tell." I thought that he was a cheeky bugger. "If we can get back to my hotel in one piece then I will know if you're a good driver," he said, sarcastically. "Have you ever gotten used to the stuffy weather?" Again, I had to laugh at his lack of enthusiasm about France.

"Yes, it gets easier. Just not when you've got a hangover." We were both full of smiles.

I showed him to my garage and I opened the doors to my Renault Clio. I was really looking forward to spending the day with him. I was like a child going out on a day trip. But, one thing I knew I was going to do was enjoy every minute of and not think of another person apart from us. Life was too short and I had to take everything with both hands to make the most of it.

***

As I pulled into the Hilton car park, I just knew I was never going to get a space easily. It was always busy and generally cars were waiting for spaces.

"You can park in my executive space, because my car hasn't come over here yet." I couldn't believe what I was hearing. I followed Brian's orders and parked into his space. There was no driving around waiting for spaces, because he had an executive space. It all happened quickly, yet I felt like I was on a go slow getting out of the car.

I was nervous as hell about bumping into Brian's colleagues. But reaching the front of the car, Brian intertwined our fingers together and I felt that little spark reignite inside me. I felt like we could face anything, as long as we were together.

The minute we entered the hotel, I could see that we were walking straight toward a group of men in suits. They all turned to greet Brian and I could feel my cheeks flush. I had no idea why, because we hadn't done anything wrong. We were in France and there were couples everywhere who spent long steamy nights together. We weren't any different.

"What's going on guys? Where's Craig gotten off to?" I might not have known Brian perfectly well, but I knew when he sounded out of sorts and I could see that he was pissed off.

"No one has seen him since last night." I quickly remembered the voice from last night. He was the man who knocked everything out of my hand in the club. He looked different in a suit. That's probably why I didn't recognise him.

"I'm going to get freshened up, but I'll be back down at eleven to brief you all. It's my day off and I have plans. If anyone happens to see Craig, tell him to phone me A.S.A.P." I didn't think that my Brian could ever be a boss, because he was too nice. Although, I could see he had one manner for me and another for his colleagues. He was kind of sexy when he sounded angry.

"Yes, boss. Good night last night. It was a good idea to go out." I had a funny feeling that Sean was just as nervous as I was. It was quite amusing listening to him throw question after question at Brian.

"Yes Sean. It would be even better if my team could turn up the next morning. Make sure everyone is there at eleven, because I am not hanging around all day." I was so glad when Brian started moving, because I felt uncomfortable listening to him speak to his team.

"If you need to work, Brian, I'll understand. We can arrange something for another day. I don't want to put you out." I was taken aback when he stopped and placed his lips over mine. Everything else went out of my head and I couldn't care who saw us.

"You will not leave me to work," he said, with his soft hand resting on my cheek. My breathing was all over the place and I was glad that he chose me over work. "This is my first day off in over six weeks and they'll manage without me for one day. I could ring Craig's neck though. I should be able to run things from the office. I shouldn't need to go out into the field." Our hands were placed together, as we started our journey to his hotel room. I just couldn't believe that he kissed me like that in the lobby.

"The joys of being your own boss. I'm the same at the medical centre. I'll be shocked if I get two weeks undisturbed from work." I tried to compose myself and talking about work was taking my mind off of all the sexual tension.

"It's all crazy, because our building is getting equipped with everything and our group is working from here. I think I'm going to have to be tougher on them and make a few changes. We've worked together for years and they know the sweet loving guy that's full of fun." I couldn't argue with him, because he was sweet, loving, and he knew it. "Before last night, I had nothing to take time off for. But now, I have you and I'm not jeopardising what we have. I've waited

too long and now I have you back in my life." Just as Brian finished speaking, the lift pinged open on the ninth floor. I followed him over to his room.

He buzzed us in with one hand and I was relieved, because I didn't want to let his hand go. That probably had something to do with the fact I had hadn't let go of his hand since we got out of the car. But once we were inside his of room, he let me go.

I placed my bag down on the table and took in my surroundings. The room was gorgeous. It was perfectly decorated in reds and gold. I didn't know what to say. I didn't know what I expected to see in a Hilton bedroom, but I could see why they charged what they did.

"No a wonder you're not in a hurry to move out of here," I somehow managed to say, as his arms snaked around my waste. He gently turned me around to face him and I couldn't stop smiling. I didn't think I was ever going to get fed up of being in his arms.

"Leela. I loved being with you last night. I hope I can spend many more nights like that with you. Whether it's here or your house. I will always be happy as long as I'm with you." His mouth was on mine and our bodies were on fire, as I was backed up against the wall. Thinking quickly, I pulled away and caught my breath. I was never going to get used to that. I didn't pull away from him, because I didn't want him. I knew if he was to go to work then he had to go before we ended up in a compromising position.

"You need to brief your men. Go and get changed!" I pushed him in the right direction, because none of us would be able to stop.

I somehow managed to compose myself again, as I walked into the living quarters of the hotel room. I didn't feel much like being nosey, so I sat down on the couch and tried to nurse my aching head. It was becoming apparent that I was getting too old for hangovers. I didn't know why I touch alcohol, because it goes right to my head. Even more so when I mix drinks. I should just stick to white wine and I would be fine. When I was out with my friends, the cocktails just shout to me and I can't resist them. I forget I'm not a teenager anymore.

I could always remember the first time I was drinking with my friends in the park. I was always sensible, but that night everyone was doing it and I thought, *what the hell*. The following day, my

mum was going to visit a family member in England and she made me drive with her. It was a hot summer day and we got stuck in traffic on the M9. As if that wasn't bad enough, she stopped at the services and got a burger. It was safe to say that I didn't touch alcohol again until I was eighteen.

"If you're feeling under the weather babe, we can stay here or go back to your place." I was so comfortable that I never even heard Brian come back into the room. "I just need to go down and make sure the work gets done today." His muscular body leaned over me on the couch and I had no idea what to say. My head was stuck on the memories that had just resurfaced. "I can come back and we can go in the bath and order room service." His lips lingered centimetres away from mine and every inch of my body tingled. "What do you say? Will you let me spoil you today?" The thought of being spoiled made me feel special. My body was on fire just thinking about spending the day with him.

"It sounds good if you're sure you really don't want to go out." I stopped dead in my tracks, as someone knocked on the door. Brian didn't move a muscle.

"Come in!" His lips were placed on mine and I didn't care who saw me and him together.

"Sorry, Brian. I was told you wanted to see me." When the voice paused, Brian stood straight and stuck his hands in his pockets. I immediately saw how pissed off he was and wished I could have been invisible.

"Craig. So nice of you to join us today." I was glad that I had my back to the poor guy, because I couldn't stop myself from smirking at Brian's sarcasm.

"I am sorry, Brian. It won't happen again. You know this isn't like me."

"Listen Craig. When I came out here, I brought my best guys with me. I need an assistant manager that's going to cover my time off. I don't want to have to rush back to cover your arse. My house is going to be outside of town and when I'm off, I should be off! You only work five days and I'm a bloody good boss to you guys!" His tough act was working. Again, I was glad I couldn't see Craig's face.

"You know I'm committed to you and your company. I think I got

drugged last night. After we left you I can't remember what happened to me and I only had a couple of pints." Wow! I was shocked to hear that kind of thing goes on here. I sat forward and looked behind me to see if the poor guy looked okay.

"How do you feel now?" I couldn't help myself. I wasn't at work, but I would never forgive myself if anything happened to him.

"I was bad all morning, but I'm feeling much better. Thank you." I stood up and walked over to him. I checked his pulse and looked into his eyes. He probably thought I was crazy. He didn't know I was a doctor.

"Leela is a doctor, Craig."

"Your pulse is very fast and your pupils are quite enlarged. I would like to say this kind of thing didn't happen here, but I guess it happens everywhere. If you get any worse, get medical help. Drink plenty of water to flush it out your system."

"Thank you, Leela!" I moved back over to sit on the couch and I could see Brian looking at me with that sparkle in his eyes.

"Doctor's orders. Don't be too harsh with him." I couldn't help but stick my nose in. I thought if he had been drugged, it wasn't his fault. I had a smile from ear to ear, as I saw Brian roll his eyes at me.

"I'll be down at eleven. Make sure everyone is ready, because I have plans for my day off."

"Yes, boss."

"This is a verbal warning, Craig. Just be careful in future. Please."

"I understand boss. See you downstairs." Craig took off quickly. I never took my eyes off of Brian the whole time.

"I'm sorry, Leela, I didn't want you to have to get involved with my staff."

I stood up slowly and wrapped my hands around his neck. He was my big softy and I loved every inch of him.

"I would have given a verbal warning myself, but if he has been drugged, then it wasn't his fault." I couldn't get away from work even if I tried. "Just remember me not to get on the wrong side of you."

"I could never speak to you like that." *That*, I was glad to hear. I didn't think I had anything like that to worry about with Brian, because he was a perfect gentleman in every way possible.

"I don't want you to go. You better hurry back, Mr. Mackinnon."

"Is that an order, Miss Park?"

"If you want it to be an order, then it can be." Our mouths met and our bodies became one, but it was short lived when Brian's phone rang. We both sighed at yet another interruption. It was going to be one of those days by the look of things.

"Sorry. It's my mum." I didn't want to stop him from answering his call, so I indicated for him to take it and sat back down on the couch. "Hi, mum," he said, impatiently. "No. I'm not working yet, but I am busy trying to get ready for work." I was smiling at him lying to his mum. He wasn't too busy for me. I wished time would freeze and we could be stuck there for a little while in each other's arms. I was a bit nervous, but he was only on the phone to his mum. I knew the way she treated me before was always going to be at the front of my mind. I was always going to be cautious of her. "Mum. I'm glad you called today, because I have something to tell you. I was going to phone you tomorrow, but you saved me a job. No. It isn't anything bad, but I want you to listen without jumping in. I bumped into Leela over here in Marseille. She's done really well for herself. She has her own house and shares of a medical centre…Don't start mum and just listen to me for a change…I told you to listen and not jump in. Can you do as I ask for once? Leela and I have been seeing each other. I'm not asking for your permission, because I love her and that's it. I just wanted you to hear it from me instead of someone else." I didn't expect Mrs. Mackinnon to approve of us, but I never expected to hear him say how much he loved me either. Our feelings had been locked away for two years. All the doubts were gone. I was feeling happy to be in a relationship again and I didn't care what anyone had to say. "Okay. Speak soon. I haven't forgotten mum, but I'm not sure that I'm going to make it back. The company is so busy and I haven't had a day off since arriving here. It has come around at all the wrong times. I'll let you know next week, one way or another. Bye." I wish the couch would open up and swallow me, because I didn't really want to hear what she said about us. However, I knew I wasn't going to be able to refrain from asking.

"Is everything okay?" I managed to ask, with a shake of my voice.

Brian joined me on the couch and my body relaxed a little bit. I didn't want to spend the rest of my life on tenterhooks every time his mum phoned.

"She took it better than I expected." The amusing ring in his tone made me smile. "She was more concerned to know if I would be going home at the end of the month for the trial." My heart felt like it stopped and I stood up to look out the window. I couldn't believe what I heard. "I take it you didn't know that it was about to start?" My silence was speaking volumes. The next thing I felt was Brian straddling me from behind. I was so happy twenty minutes ago and then I felt deflated all over again. "If it's any consolation, Lee, I doubt I will get away for it. We're finally piecing our life together and I want you in every way possible." I felt like I was going to let Mark down if I didn't go back, but I doubt I could go back fighting again. "Leela. Are you ok? You're shaking." He turned me toward him, so he could see my face. I felt every limb shaking with fear. "I have got to go downstairs for ten minutes, but promise me you'll be here when I get back." I could see how concerned he was about me and I wouldn't have the power to run away.

"I promise," was all I could say. I felt like all the bad emotions had been stirred inside me again. It didn't take much to bring them back to the front of my mind.

"Leela, sweetheart. You're not alone this time round. We have each other and we will get through everything." *That*, I would be entirely grateful for. I was hoping that would make a huge difference to my mental health issues that I suffered after I lost Mark.

"My family never told me." I couldn't quite believe they would keep something like that from me. It would have been better if they had told me, because it wouldn't have come as much of a shock.

"They probably thought it was for the best, Lee. You have a life out here. They watched you crumble. Remember." I could remember only too well, but I still felt like they deceived me. They were my family and we never had secrets between us. We were brought up to tell the truth and to never keep anything away from one another. Yet, there I was in the dark about an important piece of information. I wasn't sure if I was hurt or angry.

"It's still no excuse, Brian. I had every right to know. I should

have been the one to decide if I was going or not."

"The last time I saw you back home, you told me that you were going travelling to avoid the trial." That I could remember only too well as well. That was the day I could feel strong emotions.

"That was then, Brian. I'm a different person now. I'm stable." Well, I thought I was stable. After the way the news had hit me, I wasn't so sure.

"Your family was just trying to look out for you. You would have done the same if the shoe was on the other foot." Maybe I would have, but it didn't make everything okay.

"I just feel so pissed off right now. I was so happy twenty minutes ago and here I am, hating the world now."

"I'll be back as soon as I can and I'll make you love the world again. Make yourself comfortable and help yourself to anything." His warm lips placed over mine and his tongue parted my lips. He made me feel warm and wanted.

As I watched him pick up his phone and badge, I knew I was going to be alone for the next little while. The door shut and I went to get my bag off of the table. I needed to phone home. I needed to know if they were ever going to tell me about the trial.

Scott was my first call. He was easy. He was number one on my speed dial. I thought it was going to ring out, as it continued to ring. But I was about to hang up when he answered.

"Hey, Lee. How are you doing?" I was surprised he answered. Normally, his phone was on silent and he always had to phone me back when he got the missed call. The whole point of a mobile phone is so he could take it around with him, but not my brother, he had to be different.

"I'm good. How are you doing?" I asked, while biting my tongue and giving him the benefit of the doubt.

"Exam season. Driving me crazy!"

"Rather you than me. So what's been happening?"

"Not a lot, sis. I haven't been home in weeks. I've been too busy with work and shit. I'm going to try and get out to you when I'm finished with university. I haven't seen you in ages." I missed not seeing him, as often as I used to.

"That would be great Scott. I look forward to seeing you, but I'm

calling for a reason."

"Is everything okay, Leela?" I heard the concern in his voice. I was letting him squirm a bit after knowing what I did.

"When were you going to tell me about the trial?" The sound of silence made me realise that Scott was shocked I knew. Out of all my family, I was shocked at him the most.

"How? Who told you?"

"Well, I think I should fill you in with what I have been up to. Don't judge me, because I'm the happiest I've been in years."

"Leela. You're worrying me. Spit it out!" The fear and terror rung in my ears and I was glad he couldn't see me, because I was grinning like a Cheshire cat.

"I bumped into Brian out here. He has his own company here in Marseille and he has just bought a house. Strange as it may seem, but we've started seeing each other."

"Wow! I'm acting shocked, but it isn't really strange, Leela. I could see this coming a long time ago, it's just weird to hear it. Is he in France now for good?"

"Yeah, he has a new company starting out on a renovation programme."

"I don't believe in fate or soul mates, but that's crazy. I'm happy for you, Lee. Mark would be too." I knew my family would say that. "So, the trial. Are you coming home for it?" That was a good question, because I was so mixed up. My head was all over the place trying to think about it.

"I'm not sure yet. I feel like I have to go, but it isn't going to bring Mark back. I might sound selfish, but I have turned a corner in my life and I'm happy. The trial will just mess with my brain again." I knew I could speak like that to Scott, because he would listen to me and give me his opinions. He would never judge me and that's why we get on so well together.

"Only you can decide what to do, sis. I don't think it will benefit anything if you come back, but you know what you need to do. Let me know as soon as you've decided. I will be here for you." That I was grateful for. I knew if I went back for the trial, I would need as much help as possible.

"Thanks, Scott. Listen. I have to go, but don't tell dad or Craig,

because I'm calling them next."

"No problem, Lee. I'm going to an exam just now, anyway. Take care and remember that I'll always love you no matter what you decide."

"Good luck. Speak soon. Love you. Bye." I was feeling better already just speaking to Scott. I was glad he understood about Brian. But then again, I never doubted my family for one second. They would always stick by me if it was something I wanted. So, the second person that was going to hear from me was Craig. He really shocked me, because he would have to be a part of the trial. I would hate to see him have no one with him. But yet again, I was surprised when he was quick to answer his phone. "Hey, Lee! What's up?" I loved hearing his lively voice. He always made me smile when I had something on my mind.

"Not much. Just checking in with you guys, since I'm on holiday." I was giving him the chance to tell me first.

"Good for you. Put your feet up and chillax. How long you off for?"

"Two weeks! I was out last night with friends and I'm feeling delicate today." The hangover was getting worse as the day went on.

"My sister has got a hangover! That's something I would love to see." I'm glad that I was surprising my family, because it was letting them see that France was the making of the new me.

"No. You really don't want to see me right now. My head feels like a drum. Anyway…how are you doing?"

"I'm good, Lee. I'm on a break now, sitting in the car with a roll on bacon and a strong coffee." Always stuffing his face. I should have known.

"How's your partner now?"

"I have a new partner now. Her name is Suzanne. I have a female partner for the first time and she keeps me grounded." That I was glad to here. I don't know what I was most surprised at. The fact he had a new partner and was okay with it, or the fact he was partners with a woman.

"Good! That's just what you need mister! Talking about partners, when were you going to tell me about the trial?"

"Err…how do you know?" He went from being that lively

character to being a stuttering wreck.

"I'm in France, not another planet. But since you asked, I bumped into Brian out here. He has a new company over here in Marseille."

"What are the chances of that? Cool!" I could hear the shock in his voice and I couldn't help but smile.

"Speaking of Brian, you should know that we have been seeing one another. Early days, but I don't want you hearing this through the grapevine." The silence between us lasted for a few seconds, but it felt much longer.

"I don't know why I'm shocked. We all saw this happening right before you moved away."

"I must have been the only one that never saw it."

"You were blinded by grief, sis, but I'm happy for you both. You deserve to be happy, Lee."

"What about the trial? What's happening?" I needed to know the details, because one way or another I was going to either be there, or be told what was going on.

"The thug is pleading not guilty and self-defence." I felt like I had been struck a hard blow to the head.

"How? Why? Surely he'll get put away, right?" I had a thousand questions that were jumping around in my head. I could only start with the obvious ones.

"The evidence is all there, but what happens at the trial is anyone's guess. Leela. Stay in France. Please." I was surprised at him trying to tell me what I should do. They were trying to keep me away for a reason. I felt something fishy going on.

"I haven't decided yet, Craig. I feel like I owe it to Mark and Esme to be there."

"Think about it, Leela. Don't jump in feet first." I knew why Craig was worried about my decision. Hearing him trying to tell me to stay, I felt like I should be there.

"I'll see what happens. I have to go. I need to call dad."

"Okay. Let me know what you decide and we can work something out." My brother was talking like he knew my decision already. I think we all knew that I would be there, but they were giving me the benefit of the doubt to stay put.

"I will. You take care. I still worry about you every day."

"I'm made of strong stuff hen. Just don't worry. I love you." He may have been strong, but he wasn't that strong.

"Mark used to say the same thing. You're not untouchable, Craig." The thugs don't fight with their hands, they fight with weapons and in huge gangs.

"You're a born worrier, Lee. I'll speak to you soon"

"I'll call you the minute I know what I am doing. Love you, Craig. Bye." I always hated hanging up on Craig, because I knew how quickly his job could take his life. After what happened to Mark, I have every right to worry myself sick. My dad was the same, but because he was a D.C.I. now, he dealt mostly with the office and crime scenes. He wasn't at risk like Craig. I usually loved phoning my dad, but wasn't so sure that day.

The phone only rang a couple of times, before my dad's cheery voice rang in my ears. It was like they were waiting for my call.

"Hello, my sweetheart."

"Hi dad. How are you?"

"All the better for hearing your voice. You must be psychic, because I was going to call you tonight when I got home."

"Is everything okay?"

"Yes, sweetheart. I was just missing you. So, tell me how life is treating you in France."

"Everything is great dad. I'm on holiday for two weeks, so I had a well-deserved night out with friends last night. I'm paying for it today, though."

"Great! I love hearing you so happy and relaxed. France has been the making of you." That I couldn't argue with.

"I love it, dad. I couldn't imagine my life anywhere else."

"I am happy for you, Leela. I just miss you. Enough of my moaning. What have you got planned for your time off?"

"Zilch. I need rest from the long and crazy hours that I've worked lately."

"Go and treat yourself to something nice."

"Yeah, maybe. Listen, dad. I might be coming home at the end of the month." I was going around it in a different way.

"Really? Are you sure, sweetheart?" My dad's strange response told me that he had no idea I knew about the Trial. He would

normally be so thrilled that I was coming home.

"Dad! Stop it! I know the trial is starting! I just haven't decided what I'm doing yet."

"It's going to be tough, Leela. Are you sure that you're ready for it?" Everyone was concerned about me. I was like a different person and they have all seen it.

"I feel like I owe it to Mark and Esme to turn up, dad."

"Think about it carefully, honey. You know that it would be great to see you, but only if it's what you really want." That's why I loved my dad. He never did something for his benefit. It was always what was best for us.

"I have something else to tell you dad and I don't want you to get funny about it, because I'm happy."

"What is it, Leela?" I hated springing surprises on my dad, but for a change it was all good.

"I bumped into Brian over here. He has a company getting started and he bought property. . We've started seeing each other, dad. I really don't want a lecture." The line went quiet and I wondered what the hell was going to come next.

"Leela. If this is what you want and you're truly happy, then I'm over the moon for you both." For a change it was me being shocked into silence.

"Really?"

"Really. I am. What has the old battle-axe said about it?" Even my dad knew that Mrs. Mackinnon would do her best to keep us apart.

"She probably had her say, but Brian didn't go into it with her. He was going to brief his team and she was the last person that he wanted to talk to. I'm just waiting in his hotel room for him to come back. He's downstairs, so he shouldn't be too long."

"I know that Brian will look after you, Leela. I'm happy you're not alone and glad you have someone in your life now." I was over the moon at my family's response. I felt like I had won the lottery.

"Thank you, dad. You know that having your blessing makes me even happier. I love you more than anything in this world, dad."

"Just like I love you, sweetheart. Are you okay? Do you want to talk about anything?" My dad was always perfect. He always knew me better than anyone and he probably knew it was all turning my

head into mush.

"No. I'm okay, dad. I just found out about the trial today, so it's kind of knocked me for six, but you know me." I heard the door open and smiled to acknowledge Brian coming in. "I'll be fine, dad."

"Just don't rush into anything, sweetie. Is Brian coming back for the trial?"

"He isn't sure yet. His work is crazy busy now. They're working from the Hilton, until their building is finished."

"You know we will keep you filled in if you don't come back." I knew they would only tell me what they wanted me to know. They would hide a lot of the tricky bits

"I know that, dad. I just don't want Craig to go through it all on his own. He was there for me plenty of times Craig told me the guy is pleading not guilty and self-defence."

"Did he now? I could kill him at times." I just opened my big mouth and stuck Craig in. I could tell with my dad's tone, that I wasn't supposed to know any of that.

"I asked him about the trial, dad. It wasn't his fault."

"The judge on the trial is great! I don't think he'll get away with it. I would put money on him going away for a long time. The judge takes this kind of thing seriously. The fact that the flat was full of guns and weapons, just shows they were intending on hurting people."

"I do hope you're right. Well, listen dad. I need to go now. My head is bursting from everything. I'll contact you when I've made my mind up."

"Okay, sweetheart. You take care and tell Brian I said hi. I love you, Leela. Never forget that. If you do come home, you and Brian are welcome to stay here."

"Thank you, dad. That means a lot. I love you, too. Bye." My ears were ringing when I put my phone down, but I headed into the kitchen to find Brian. "Hey! Is that you all finished with work?" I was all giddy at the thought of being together all day. I was glad of the distraction, because I always hated saying goodbye to my family on the phone.

"That's me, honey. Here are some pain killers for your head." I accepted the box of pain killers, as he poured me a glass of water.

"Thank you," I managed to say, as I accepted the glass of water. "I didn't even realise that you were gone. I phoned my dad, Craig, and Scott. The time just flew by."

"I'm glad you had some company, while I was gone. Is everything okay at home?"

"Yeah, everything seems good. My family is over the moon for us, by the way. If we do go home for the trial, you're welcome to join me at my dad's."

"That's very nice of him."

"Craig told me that the scum bag is pleading not guilty, because he's saying it was all self-defence." My blood ran cold at the thought.

"Really? I don't think my mum knows, because she hasn't mentioned it." I wasn't too interested in anything his mum knew. I wouldn't put it past her to keep that kind of news to herself.

"My dad says it doesn't matter, because there's no evidence to show that it was self-defence." I trusted my dad and I knew he wouldn't have said that if it wasn't true.

"I'll be glad to see the back of it, to be honest, Lee. It just seems like we've rebuilt our life and now we are back to square one." I knew exactly what he meant, because I felt the same.

"Tell me about it. I haven't decided if I'm going to go back yet. My head is telling me one thing and my heart is telling me another. Then there's your mum. I'm not sure if I could face her just yet. She's only going to call me all the cows and sluts under the sun." My heart pounded just thinking about her and it shouldn't have been like that.

"Leela." Brian placed both of his hands on my waste. His eye's sparkled at me, but his face was full of concern. "My mum can go to hell and back. She just likes the sound of her own voice. My dad won't be long at shutting her up. As long as your family didn't give you a hard time about us, that's all I care about."

"Each of them said the same thing. They all saw this happening at some point." We were both smiling at one another.

"If you want to go home for the trial, I'll be right beside you. If not, then I'll be here with you also" His head bent into kiss me and my mouth accepted every inch of his tongue. It was like every

painful memory was sizzled away and I was back in the relaxed state that I was before. Brian was exactly what I needed and I found it all unbelievable. It was weird, because all the times that Pierre tried to set me up, I had no intention of getting into a relationship. There I was with Brian after one night of seeing each other again. The love. The passion. The electricity. It was all so powerful. It really felt too good to be true.

"Leela. You make my body crazy for you." I smiled.

"You do the exact same to me, Brian. It doesn't feel wrong in anyway." His warm hands lifted my top over my head to leave my breasts tingling inside my bra. I found the courage to lift his t-shirt off. That time, my hands couldn't be removed from his chest, as he lifted my skirt up. Never in a million years did I expect to have sex on a bar stool, but before I could think straight I was practically naked, as his fingers entered inside of me with slow and soft motions. His kisses trailed up to my neck and onto my mouth, leaving the skin tingling for more. I couldn't get my breath, because the passion was so strong and powerful between us as my legs wrapped around him. As he pushed his package inside me slowly, we both cried out with pleasure. Every thrust, every touch, and every kiss, set me on fire until a climax shuddered violently inside of my body. Then, his body collapsed shuddering inside of me. His head rested on my shoulder, as we both composed ourselves.

Even though it should have felt like a cheap and quick fumble, I could still feel the passion and love between us.

"I'm sorry, Leela." His breathing was just starting to slow down and his sweaty palms caressed my back in a soothing motion.

"Why are you apologising?"

"Because I lost control and you're not just my playmate." I could understand why he thought that way, but none of it felt like I was just a playmate. There was too much love and consideration behind it.

"I'm glad that I'm not just your play thing Mr. Mackinnon, but you have nothing to apologise for. You're one of the kindest lovers I have ever come across and I adore you for it. I could have said no if I didn't want you to. Besides, I'm getting too used to making love to you," I teased.

Trying to straighten myself up and reassure Brian at the same time wasn't easy.

"That isn't a bad thing. Is it?" His soft smile, that broke out of his playful face made me giggle.

"Not right now, it isn't a bad thing. When I go back to work it will be. I'm going to struggle not to have you every minute of every day." I had no idea how I was ever going to concentrate at work, or on anything other than Brian. I was like a love struck teenager.

"Well, we'll have to make the most of it while we can. Do you fancy taking a bath with me? I'll order some champagne and strawberries if you like." Everything always sounded good when it came out of Brian's mouth. It's like he read my mind.

"You don't need to keep spoiling me, you know." I loved how he treated me like a princess.

"I want to spoil you Leela. I'll run the bath."

"Do you want me to order room service, since your French is rubbish?" I couldn't help but laugh.

"Ok, smart arse. Order what you like and put it on my room. Room thirty-five." I felt honoured to be there today. Things like that didn't usually happen to me and I was going to enjoy it. Not that I was going to have to try very hard to enjoy it. I was going to cherish every moment and never look back.

"If you're not letting me pay, then I'm not ordering!" I was one of those girls who felt uncomfortable if I didn't get to do my share of paying.

"You can get it next time."

"Until the next time comes. I know you too well, Mr. Mackinnon." I quickly realised that I was now talking to myself, because Brian was away running the bath. I lifted the phone and waited for someone to answer.

"Bonjour. Puis-je commander une bouteille de champagne et fraises s'il vous plait. Room trente-cinq. Merci, monsieur." Speaking French was hard work. Even though I wasn't not great at pronouncing the words, I learned the basics when I moved here.

"Do you know how sexy it is to hear you speak French?" It didn't matter what he said to me, because I always giggled at him. I have never laughed so much in all the time I had been here.

"Whatever floats your boat." I laughed

"Your bath awaits you, madam." I was looking forward to the bath.. Every muscle in my body is aching and the hot water will be great.

"Merci mon amour. Vous etes tres gentil." I tried my hardest to speak without bursting into laughter. His face was a picture.

"Not French! I didn't get any of that!" It was rather amusing to wind him up. I knew I was going to have more fun with the French language.

"Wow! This is lovely." I couldn't believe my eyes. The bathroom was lit with candles around a Jacuzzi bath. The dimly lit room was a prefect hangover cure. The luxurious smell of different aromas was magnificent. I felt all the cares and worries just wash away.

"You get in, babe. I'll wait for room service." I was glad to hear that, because I was desperate to soak and relax. It was perfect timing, as Brian went to open the door. I stepped into the water and I felt every muscle relax instantly. It was a fabulous moment. "You look so much more relaxed already, Lee." I was and it was weird. I just wanted him to hurry up pouring the fizz, because his body was missing beside me. I was hung-over and wished the champagne would be the hair of the dog that would make me come back to life.

"I'll be even better when you join me." As he lowered into the water, I moved to give him room. "This is exactly what I needed. How did you guess?" I was curious to know how he knew what I liked. It all couldn't be guess work.

"I just fancied a quiet day with you and this seemed like the perfect way to do so." No work. No interruptions. No worries. It was just a little bit of heaven.

"What did your mum say about us when you told her?" I couldn't refrain from asking the dreaded question. My curiosity would kill me one day.

"Surprisingly, not much. She was going to be a bit nippy, but she knows I'm the one that will cut her off and not listen. The days for me saying *yes sir, no sir, three bags full sir,* are well and truly over." It was probably the wrong moment to be talking about our past.

"Tell me if I'm being nosey… Why do I get the feeling that your mum has done something to you?" I laid with my head on his chest

and the silence made me turn to look at him. “Tell me to shut up if you like.” I could see the pain in his face and I wanted to take back my last question.

“I would never tell you to shut up, doll. I want to spend the rest of my life with you and I’m not about to hide anything from you. I thought you wouldn’t notice anything and I wouldn’t have to tell you, but you have.”

“I’m a psychologist, Brian. I’m meant to notice things. Don’t feel like you have to tell me anything, because I asked. It’s early days for us and I have no right to ask. I thought it was going to be something silly, but now I’m worried.”

“Leela. We might be early days but I know that I’m going to spend the rest of my life with you. I want you in every way possible.” I wanted to relax and I wanted him to relax with me. “Since we were kids, Mark and I were always together. We did everything together. Then when I turned eight, I was given a big party. All my school friends, neighbours, and family turned up…I thought I was the luckiest boy around. Mum always favoured Mark over me and I got used to that. But after everyone left that night I was helping with the tidying up. I was exhausted. It had been a great day. One of the best days to be truthful. Then the bombshell came. My darling mother had booked me in to boarding school. She never told my dad any of this, because I could see he was just as shocked as I was. Mark was in hysterics, because he didn’t want to go. He didn’t need to worry, because he was getting kept at home…To cut the story short, she won and I was sent to boarding school until I was sixteen. I came home on holidays or special occasions. But the older I got, the wiser I got. Everyone was walking on eggshells with mum. She got everything she wanted no matter what. She was dreading when I turned sixteen, because I was coming home. However, I sorted that out for her. I didn’t want to go home and I thought about what I wanted to do with my life. In the boarding school they helped us with all that. That’s when I decided that I wanted to go into architecture and business.” I looked up into his eyes and could see that he wasn’t angry. It took a bigger person to be like that. “I had my life made for me and I didn’t have to depend on them for any of it. Now look at me. I have everything I have ever dreamed of. Dad

never accepted what mum was like, but then he went along with her for the peaceful life. Mark went against her as well, because she didn't want him to go into the police force. I'll never have a bond with her, Lee. I don't want a bond either. I tolerate her for my dad's sake. When Mark died and she treated you like dirt, I could have hit her myself. Then when you took ill and I was cradling you in my arms, I felt some kind of force pulling me to you." I lifted my wrinkled hand and placed it on his cheek. I felt awful that I had brought it up. I felt another spell of hatred wash over me toward his mother. She didn't deserve to have kids.

"I don't want you to fall out with your family because of me. I can see why you're the way you are with your mum and I don't blame you."

"She will either come around to it or forget about us, Leela. I don't want you to be scared off when I say this, but I have never felt like this about anyone before. I am and have been for the last two years, falling head over heels in love with you." I could feel the tears well up in my eyes.

"I'm honoured, Brian. I really am. I never thought that I would fall in love again, but here you are working your way into my heart. I still hide my tears when I say Mark's name. The pain in my heart is still as strong. Though I smile and seem carefree, there's no one that misses Mark more than me. For the first time, I feel ready to move on. I feel like he has already given us his blessing by bringing us together. *It was meant to be*, so why keep fighting it?"

"I agree, honey. I can't wait to get our life started. Who knows? In ten years, we might look back and wonder why the hell it took us so long." It was crazy how things work out. I thought I was on cloud nine. Nothing was ever going to come close to the way I felt and that was because I was happy again. I just had to find a way to forget about his mum and the way she treated us. If I could do that, I would be the happiest woman alive.

***

The past twenty-four hours had been crazy. I told everyone who cared about me, that I would be single for the rest of my life. Since

bumping into Brian yesterday, we've never left each other's side. We've spent the whole day talking and getting to know one another again. I wasn't looking forward to going home alone after we had dinner.

I then had a strange rush of energy, while I fastened my shoes waiting for Brian to get ready. Just as I felt it, there was a knock on the door. I felt quite nervous, because I knew Brian wouldn't have heard it in the room. My inner devil told me to answer it. I did exactly that. I had changed overnight, because I would have never answered someone else's door.

"Oh…" The tall gentleman was shocked to see me answer the door and his expression said it all. "Is Brian there?"

"Sure, come in. I'll go get him." The moment got awkward quickly, but I was relieved when Brian came out of the room, as we reached the living quarters. "Brian. There's someone here to see you." I felt awkward, because I didn't even know the guy's name.

"Simon! What can I do for you?"

"I'm not sure, Brian." I could feel the tension and wanted to get out of it all. "I know that you've put Craig in charge, because of his expertise, but since we've come out here he's been a liability. His head is all over the place."

"I saw him this morning and he wasn't doing well. Leela checked him over. I'm back in the morning, Simon. I'll keep an eye on him. I'll also have a private word with him, because it isn't like him." Something strange was going on and I couldn't put my finger on it.

"Today was just chaos, Brian."

"Did everything get done?"

"Eventually. We just finished and it's just after seven."

"I have confirmation that our offices will be ready for Tuesday. Things should calm down then, but this company needs people with their head in the game. Thank you for letting me know, Simon. I'll take care of things tomorrow. I would do it now, but I am heading out to dinner." I felt guilty that I was taking his attention away from work. On the other hand, I was glad that he wasn't pushing me away.

"Sorry to intrude on your evening. I didn't know that you still had company." Poor Simon's face was blood red.

"Simon. This is Leela. You'll be seeing more of her around. Leela.

Simon one of my good workers."

"Nice to meet you, Simon."

"Likewise, Leela." The poor guy couldn't wait to get out of the room.

Just as he closed the door behind him, I couldn't wait to laugh. I still had that strange feeling about something, but I wasn't going to let it put a dampener on things.

"I'm making your men nervous. They can't wait to get away from me." I laughed. It actually wasn't that funny. We're all adults at the end of the day. "Have they never seen a woman before?"

"Not with me they haven't, babe. Are we ready?" I didn't expect to hear Brian say anything like that. I was just trying to be funny. I didn't expect it to come back and bite me on the arse.

"Ready? Sure." I was still a little taken aback, because I was actually realising how special I was to him. "I'm ready." I grabbed my bag and he took my hand. Tonight was going to be a funny old night. I could feel it in the pit of my stomach.

I was intrigued to find out why Mark and Brian both had issues before me and now I know. I felt like I would never be able to talk to that woman again after what I've heard. I have another feeling that it was only half of it. I hated to look down on people, because we've all done things that we're not proud of, but she has given up right to call herself a mother. I felt like a queen compared to her.

Now, I had to put everything to the back of my mind. No Mrs. Mackinnon. No work colleagues. Nothing. It was me and Brian going out for dinner and we were going to have a wonderful evening. Just the two of us.

***

Tonight had been such a wonderful evening. I enjoyed dinner and a few drinks with Brian. At 10pm we were walking along through the town hand in hand. The buzz of the nightlife and everyone having fun, rang through our ears. The warm air circulating around us just made me more aware of the happiness I felt swirling around me. The electricity soared through me at just the touch of our hands. I never wanted it to end.

Everything was perfect. I was now looking forward, hoping that we could still be doing this in the next twenty years. I knew better than anyone how quickly things could change, but I had good feelings about Brian and I.

"You're very quiet, Lee. Are you okay, sweetie?"

"I'm just taking everything in. I still have to pinch myself. This time last week I was working long hours in the paediatric ward. I didn't even think about me, not that I had any time to think about my life.

"All those dishy French doctors never even took your eye?" It was his turn to wind me up and he knew too well how to do it. His silly smirking face spoke volumes.

"No. Never, Mr. Mackinnon. Mark was my life, Brian. I've never felt like that again…until you." Why I was becoming shy, I had no idea.

"I'm honoured, Lee." We stopped dead in the middle of the street, as his free hand rested on my cheek. I was curious to find out what was different about him. Why did he make me feel so in love?

"What about you, Brian? You know why I never went with anyone after Mark. What was your excuse? Why are your colleagues so shocked that you spent the night with me? Am I just a fling and this is where you tell me you don't want to settle down?" I was throwing everything at him to unleash his thoughts and feelings. I knew I was playing with fire. It could all backfire on me, but I wanted to know everything about him no matter how bad it was.

"Leela. A fling isn't in my nature. I felt a connection with you way back and I knew that my heart and soul belonged to you. Like you, no one had ever made me feel like that." It was like we were both waiting for one another without us really knowing it.

"You do realise there's going to be so many people back home that think this is wrong on so many levels." Stating the obvious wasn't always the best thing to do, but we were facing everything at the beginning and getting it all out in the open.

"As I said, as long as your family is okay with you, that's all I care about. Our life is here and as far as I'm concerned, this is a fresh start for us both. I know that Mark and Esme will be a huge part of us, but they're giving us the strength to move on to the next stage of

our life." It all made perfect sense. We believed it and all we had to do was get everyone else to believe it. I was with him on one thing. Why care about people that don't care about us?

"Your mum. I'm going to find it hard to even tolerate her."

"She either accepts us or she doesn't. It's going to be no skin off of my nose, Lee. I have gotten this far without her and I'll get through the next chapter in my life without her as well." I loved how strong willed he was. We both needed each other's strength.

"I've got to go back for the trial Brian. I'll understand if you can't. Your business needs you right now. Throughout the last couple of years, I've had to accomplish things in order to move forward." I saw the concern in his face, as I tried to convince him that I needed to do it. "I need to close this door behind me so that we've got nothing holding us back." I might have sounded crazy, but I stood in front of him desperately waiting for him to say something.

"I'm the boss. Remember? If you're sure about doing this, then I'll be there for you. We're partners, Leela. What kind of partner would I be if I didn't support your decisions?"

"You need to be with your family for the trial and I know that. I don't want any animosity to come between us." I was worrying about things already and I wasn't even out of France yet. It only gave me a taste of what our time back in Scotland was going to be like.

"You're my family as well, Lee. You have always been my family. I'll arrange the tickets." I liked how he wasn't taking me on about his family. I was beginning to fall in love with the way he put me on some pedestal, like I was his princess.

"Open tickets. If you're needed back here, you have to promise me that you'll come back."

"Don't ask me to promise you this, Leela, because I just can't. Work will be fine for as long as I need to be away."

"I'm supposed to be off for two weeks, but I'll call in tomorrow and arrange the time off." I told my brothers that I wouldn't jump in with both feet, but that's exactly what I've done.

"Now we've got all of that sorted out, can we get back to here and now?"

"What do you have in mind, Mr. Mackinnon?" His mouth gently

touched mine and without even trying, my mouth cooperated with his. We're like yin and yang. We went together like we're meant to be together.

"I've really enjoyed this evening. Do you want to come back with me tonight?" His soft sensual voice sent tingles down my spine and I knew exactly what I wanted.

"I don't have any clothes at your hotel." I wanted to be with him, but I couldn't care less about clothes. I had no idea why I even said that.

"I didn't have any at your place last night," he replied, with a sexy smirk on his face. I couldn't argue with him. I wanted him and that could be in a trailer park if need be.

"Okay. Your hotel it is." I didn't want to go home alone, so that was the perfect excuse. When his warm lips caressed my mouth again, it washed away any doubts from my mind.

***

Walking back to Brian's hotel took little to no time. I was relieved to be going through the revolving doors, because my feet were aching.

"Bonsoir, monsieur," said the doorman.

"Bonjour." I was sure that *hello*, was the only word that Brian could speak in French.

I couldn't stop smiling. Tonight had been perfect and I was so happy with the way things had turned out for me.

"Avez-vous eu une bonne nuit?" the doorman asked.

"Oui, monsieur. Nous avons eu une bonne nuit." I knew me speaking French annoyed Brian, because he couldn't understand anything. All he could do was smile at us and be polite.

"What did he say?" We're only a couple of feet away from the doorman and I'm sure he would have heard Brian.

"He asked if we had a good night and I told him that we had a great night." Walking through the foyer, I felt like a teenager laughing and joking. I have missed feeling like this and it was crazy to think I was for giving up on ever finding true love again.

"You really need to learn French, Mr. Mackinnon."

"They talk too fast for me. I can speak it. I just struggle to understand them." He was the only one that didn't have faith in himself. I knew once he started getting the hang of it, he would be good at speaking French. He had the basics and he only had to learn to put it all together.

"You'll get used to it. The trick is to pick out the words you know and the rest will fall into place." It didn't take me too long to get the hang of it, after I got a French book of phrases.

"Good evening, boss," came a voice from behind us. I recognised the man from earlier. He was the man that wasn't feeling very well. I couldn't help but notice how tired he looked, but apart from that he was looking a lot better from this morning.

"Craig. What are you doing still ready for work?"

"I was finishing the contracts. They're all ready for you tomorrow. It will get you finished early." I was surprised at how keen he was. I didn't understand why that other guy said he wasn't pulling his weight. None of it made sense.

"Thanks, Craig. I should give you a telling off more often. I'm going home at the end of the month for the trial for my brother's murder. I'm going to need you committed. I need to know that you and Simon will get along and that you can hold things together." We all stepped into the lift and I felt like a cat stole my tongue.

"You have my word, boss. You go home and be with your family. Leela needs you more than we do." I didn't know whether to laugh or cry at Craig's comment.

"I'll Skype every day. We'll work out conference times and I'll work from Scotland until the trial is over." I didn't realise how much upheaval was going to be caused from us going back to Scotland for the trial.

"I won't let you down, Brian. You can count on me." We exited the lift. Craig went his way and we went our way, directly across to Brian's room. I saw every side of Brian that day. Even when he was like a crab to his workers, I still adored him.

"He seems like a good guy."

"He is. It just worries me, because for some reason Simon has got it in for Craig. I think it's because Simon wants his job." I knew that

something wasn't right. I got the feeling earlier.

"You don't think it could have been him that spiked his drink. Do you?" I couldn't actually believe I had said that, but it made sense.

"I don't know, Lee." We got inside the room and I couldn't take my eyes off of him. "I wouldn't like to think that I had spiteful guys working for me, but when the office is finished they'll be in different areas."

"Crazy world we live in." I flung my bag down and felt every bit of my body ache. "My feet are aching so badly." I managed to get all my words out, just before I was swept off my feet. My body was cradled in his arms. I couldn't feel more alive even if I tried. All the questions I had in my mind about Simon and Craig, were slowly disappearing. He was all I needed to focus on. "You're crazy!" I squealed, as he tickled me. I was subconscious of being in a hotel room. I didn't want to disturb other guests.

"I am crazy in love with you, Miss Park." His mouth was on mine and I felt like I was floating. That night was going to be magical, just like the night before. It's like nothing is ever too much trouble when we're together. This was after two days together. It was going to be amazing to see what weeks and months fetched us.

4 WEEKS LATER

CHAPTER 9
DEPARTURE

The last four weeks had been the most amazing weeks of my life. I had felt emotions that I never thought I could feel and it was all down to having love back in my life. I still couldn't believe I was going to give up and never have a man back in my life. It was true. If Brian hadn't come out here when he did, I would have carried on pretending I was truly happy on my own. However, I knew that I was happy and I never want to go back to just making do with life. I've had a taste of the good life and I was never going back. No matter what happened.

We've felt everything together. We have laughed, joked, cried, and made love. We got each other through to the moment that we've both been dreading and we're more than satisfied with our lives.

Three weeks ago, I decided I was going back home for the trial and I was hoping that time would be on a go slow. However, that was not the case. We knew the time was coming, but it came around really fast. I had been counting down the days. Not because I was excited about going back, but because I was hoping the days didn't grow closer so quickly.

Everything had been arranged for us going back to Scotland tomorrow. We were going to spend our last night in France, in my cottage. I couldn't wait until Brian came home from work. He said that he would be working late, because he needed to make sure everyone was ready to hold the fort on their own. I decided to take a shower at eight o' clock just to relax me.

Now, I was ready to face whatever the next couple of weeks were going to throw at me. Everything was ready to go to the airport in the morning. I was going to be at my wit's end, but a book and a glass of wine had my name on them, at the moment.

I lit my scented candles in my living room, because I loved my candles. Everything was quiet and peaceful. I was going to read until I either fell asleep with the book on my face, or my lover came home and I had a reason to be awake.

I used to fall asleep reading a book all the time. My mum would always come into my room and take it from me and made sure I was comfortable. I was her little bookworm. That's what she told me all the time. It was a weird one for me, because I tried not to think about the past. Since the trial was coming up, I had a trip down memory lane, remembering how much my mum and Mark meant to me. I managed to find love in Brian and I feel content being with him. I somehow managed to replace Mark, but I knew he would be happy for me. My mum, on the other hand, I could never replace. Not that I would want to replace her, because she was one in a million. Nothing was ever too much for her and she would have done absolutely anything for me and her boys. We were her life and she was only happy if we were happy. She brought us all up fantastically and no one could ever fault her for the way we turned out. My dad took over her role and he followed on in her footsteps to the best of his ability. My mum would have been so proud of my dad, just like we were. Not many men would have been able to carry on, after they

lost their one true love.

"Leela." I was relieved that Brian was home, because I didn't want to keep going down memory lane. Even if it was a good memory. It was nice to relive good memories. I guess that's all I had from growing up.

"In the living room." I felt my mood lift and I was ready to see his smiling face. "Hey."

"Sorry, I'm late, sweetheart. It's been a long, crazy day." He looked really done in. His tie was off and his shirt buttons were open at the top. His jacket was thrown over the chair and everything was abandoned for me.

"Don't apologise mister, I knew you were going to be late. I've been lying here with a book." His arms wrapped around me. I felt his muscular body relax around me. "I've been waiting all night for this." I felt warm and comfortable.

"Sorry, to keep you waiting, babe." He looked absolutely knackered and we hadn't even left France yet.

"Are you hungry? I can rustle you up something."

"No. I'm fine. We ordered in pizza earlier. Besides, you're not cooking at this time of night for me." I loved how he always thought about my feelings. "I'm going to take a shower and get out of these clothes. You look lovely, fresh, and all relaxed. Here I am, looking like a mess."

"You couldn't be a mess, hon. Hurry up, because I missed you." His warm mouth hungrily took my lips and I never wanted it to stop.

"I'll be back in five." I sat back and watched him. I was relieved that he was home. We could relax together before tomorrow, when everything would be hectic. The trial was going to test our love for one another. It would test anyone to the limits, even if they had been together for years. But I had to hope and pray that we could come through the next couple of weeks and come back to France. This was my life out here now and it was perfect. I could never imagine going back to Scotland, apart from holidays, special occasions, and maybe Christmas and New Year's. It's weird how life can change.

Just a few years ago, I couldn't imagine my life away from Scotland. I was a family person and I loved seeing them on a daily basis. I shocked myself when I wanted to travel. I was glad that I

took the bull by the horns and did something for me. It was the best move I ever made. My dad and brothers probably wouldn't agree, but I wouldn't expect them to understand. My thoughts were interrupted when my phone started ringing. I couldn't be bothered with anyone tonight, so I hoped that it was someone that I wanted to talk to.

"Hello?" I could hear the nerves in my voice, because normally it was bad news when people called me at that time in the evening.

"Hello, sweetheart. Did I wake you?"

"Hi, dad. No. I'm sitting with a book and a glass of wine. Is everything okay?" I was nervous.

"I'm just phoning to see what time I have to pick you up tomorrow." I sighed with relief. No bad news.

"We're going to get a taxi home."

"Don't you even think about it! It'll cost you a fortune from Glasgow. I took two weeks holiday, so I can spend some time with you guys." Just when I didn't think my dad could shock me anymore. He comes out with something like that. I was over the moon that he was okay with me and Brian.

"We're arriving in Glasgow at one o' clock tomorrow." I was going to let him do his bit, because he had gone through so much effort.

"In the afternoon?"

"Yeah, dad. You really don't have to put yourself out."

"Leela. I haven't seen you for I don't know how long and I want to pick you up. I want to see you and Brian. I want to thank him, because I can hear that spark back in your voice and you sound so much happier." His words meant so much to me.

"Okay, dad." I was happy that my dad could sense how happy I was. "I'll see you tomorrow. I love you."

"I love you too, Lee. I'm so excited to see you." I was glad my dad was looking forward to our arrival. I could even hear the excitement in his voice.

"Me too!"

"You get some rest and I'll see you and Brian tomorrow. Night, sweetheart."

"Night, dad." I placed the phone back down on the table, as

Brian's arms wrapped around my waist. I jumped, because I never even heard him approach me.

"Was that your dad making sure we're still coming?" I turned myself round to face him and stood on my tip toes to place a soft kiss on his lip. I seriously missed my multiple kisses.

"Yeah. He took two weeks off of work so he can spend some time with us. He's picking us up at the airport. He also wants to thank you for making me so happy."

"Is that so? I love how happy you've been and I'm looking forward to a happy future with you."

"I've got a bottle of wine open if you fancy a glass." I moved out of his grip and walked into the kitchen to get him a glass. I loved being a tease around him, because it drove him crazy. I put the glass down and curled up beside him on the couch. That's what I had been waiting for all night. I was relaxed and at ease in his arms.

"This is much better than work. I never thought today was going to end."

"Well we're on holiday now." I sat forward and straddled his legs, as he got cosy on the couch. "I know that we're going back for the trial, but I want us to still have time for us. I don't want to spend days not near you…not in your arms." I sounded pathetic, but I didn't care.

"I'm glad you said that, because I don't want to be apart from you either. I'm staying at your dad's with you and I'll be there through every step. Just think, when we come back here, our fresh start will begin. We can discuss our future when we come back. I've waited too long for you, Leela. I'm 31 and I don't want to be like a teenager stealing moments with you. I know we both have our own property. But what do you say we think about moving in with one another?" That was going to be a night for shocks and surprises. It all made sense. I knew exactly what he meant.

"I like the idea. The big question is going to be, which house are we going to live in?" I hated making decisions, but we were going to have to agree on something.

"We'll think about it when we're away. We can decide when we come back." I leaned in to take his mouth with mine. His hands tangled in my hair. That same electricity soared through my body, as

our bodies relaxed. The passion got out of control every time we were together. We could never get enough of each other.

That night was going to be a good one. We would be ready to leave in the morning fresh as daisies. It was going to be easier to leave, because we're both going together. I think I would have found it harder to go home alone, but everything was different now. My life was stable and I was confident. I wasn't the same weak person that came out to France and that made a huge difference. What happened when we got back to Scotland was anyone's guess.

***

A two hour flight dragged in comparison to a long haul flight. Maybe it was because I was filled with mixed emotions.

I had a wonderful night spent with Brian. We got up bright and early that morning to face the next step of our life. We were a few minutes away from landing and I could feel the butterflies in my stomach already. I knew I had no excuse to feel nervous, because my dad was over the moon for me and Brian. I knew he would make us welcome. It was the first time I had been home in nearly two years. I just didn't want to be overcome with so many feelings, that I had put to bed. I wasn't so sure if those feelings would stay locked away.

"I think you're regretting this now. Aren't you?" I laid my head back and thought about what Brian just said. He knew me better than I knew myself most of the time.

"No. Not really. I'm just really nervous about everything, because I don't want anything or anyone to come between what we've got." I sounded childish, but I was so happy with Brian. Even though we had only been together a few weeks, it seemed a lot longer.

"Leela. Nothing's going to come between us. That's a promise" His hand came up and gently caressed my face, so that I was looking into his eyes. "Tell me what I have to do in order to let you see that I want to spend the rest of my life with you?" I wasn't sure anything would take away my doubts.

"I don't know, Brian. It's just me being silly, I guess." I was so insecure when it came to going home. "We're just about to land and I feel insecure already. Now I know why I don't come home very

often."

"You have me with you in every way possible, Lee. I'm going to be by your side all of the time." His soft lips met mine and I knew that I was just being silly. The passion we shared together wasn't pretend. "Better?"

"Much." We both sat back in our seats. His hand never let mine go. The captain came over the speaker and told us that we were going to be landing. I was looking forward to seeing my dad. After hearing the excitement in his voice last night, I could see he was over the moon about me coming home, even if it was under bad circumstances. I felt sick to the pit of my stomach. I thought it was a mixture of nerves and hunger, since I didn't eat anything that morning.

I was pleased when I felt the plane land on the runway. I could breathe again. I was able to start moving from the seat. That's all I wanted, because my legs were starting to ache.

"Are you ready, babe?" I couldn't exactly turn back, but I wished I could. I hated this bit of travelling. It took forever to get out of the plane and then we had to collect our luggage. I knew why I didn't travel too much. "Are you okay, Lee?"

"Yeah. I feel sick, but it's my own fault for not eating before we left." I don't know why I was putting myself through all of it. I hadn't been so full of nerves since I left Scotland.

"You do look pale today."

"I'll be fine when I get some air." I just wanted to get out of there.

I was glad when we got into the terminal. I let Brian lead me to get our luggage. "Hopefully we're not waiting all day." I was getting fed up of listening to myself moaning. Brian must have been fed up with me as well. "I'll get us a trolley. Will you wait for our cases?" I asked.

"Sure." I was off without any more conversation I just wanted to forget about all the negative stuff and be happy like I was last night.

When I returned to Brian, I saw him standing with the three cases. At least one thing was on our side.

"They were the first ones to come out." I knew that Brian was trying to keep me going and I was grateful to have him with me. I just felt so guilty, because I knew I was moody. "Are you ready,

sweetheart?"

"Yep." His hand took mine and we started walking through to the main part of the airport.

I knew my dad would be waiting. He was always on time. As the crowds of people started separating, I saw my dad looking for us. I was over the moon when I saw him. When he spotted us, his smile was the same as mine. I ran toward him, just as my dad took to his heels. His arms wrapped around me and my head snuggled into his neck. I forgot how much I had missed him. I could have broken down in tears.

"Leela! I'm so glad to see you! You look fantastic! Something is obviously making you happy." I pulled away from my dad's arms just in time for Brian to join us. "Hi Brian. Nice to see you, son. I hope you had a good flight." My dad kept one arm round my waist, but extended one arm to shake Brian's hand.

"It wasn't too bad, Mr. Park. We were on time, for a change."

"Please, Brian. Call me Frank. You're family now." I was thrilled to hear my dad and Brian talking like they were. "I parked out front in the pick-up bay. Are you ready to go?"

"Ready as we'll ever be, dad." We all headed out of the airport and I was glad for the fresh air. It certainly made me feel much better. I felt like my lungs were now full of clean air and I could breathe easily. I could see where my dad's car was and I was glad that we didn't have far to go. I just wanted to get home.

"Leela. You get in, while me and Brian take care of the luggage." I wasn't going to argue with him. I was just happy that my two favourite guys were getting on together. I could hear them laughing and joking, as they loaded everything in the boot of the car. I couldn't stop myself from smiling, as they both joined me. "I booked us for some lunch. I thought you would be ready for something to eat when you arrived." I knew my dad would of thought about everything. I don't know why I felt shocked.

"You're well organised, dad. When did that happen?" He used to leave me to do all of the organising.

"Since you went to France. I didn't have my sidekick to keep me organised." I assumed that everyone would have gotten on without me.

"It would have done you good, I guess. How have you all gotten on with housework and washing?" That was going to be amusing. I couldn't stop smiling. I felt so happy at this moment. If only I could stay all day in the car with my dad and Brian.

"Well, I have to confess. I got a cleaner in three days a week." Now I was shocked. I never expected to hear that. I'm sure my mum would have had something to say about a cleaner.

"Are you serious?"

"Of course I am. Me and Craig were working all hours and we had no time to take care of the house. We were amazed at how much you had done for us."

"You're just full of surprises." At least they used their heads. I was amazed that they managed to get on without me. "How have you been?"

"We've all been good. Missing you like crazy. I know that Craig is looking forward to seeing you and Scott's due back up the road later tonight."

"You won't know what to do with yourself having a full house again. How are Scott and Sheree getting on? He never mentions her when we speak on the phone and I always forget to bring it up."

"They're good. I believe. Sheree is coming up with him to visit. They're both all finished with university now, so they'll be here for the full trial." That was good to know. We'll all be under one roof for the next couple of weeks and I was looking forward to catching up with everyone.

"Brian. Sorry, son. You can't get a word in edgewise."

"Not a problem, Frank. It's good to see Leela happy. She's been a nervous wreck all morning." Brian aimed to have me happy all the time and I didn't want to let him down.

"You'll be fine, sweetheart. You're much stronger this time. I know for a fact that Brian has been the best thing that has happened to you. You're so much happier."

"I'm lucky to have him, dad. Not many men would be doing half of what he has done for me."

"Don't be silly, Lee. You know I'll always be by your side." I looked round to the back seat and I knew first hand that Brian meant every word.

"Well, I don't care what you get up to in your own time, but I'm happy to have you both here." I knew exactly what my dad was getting at.

I was glad that my mum had the birds and the bees chat when we were growing up. She was always great at explaining things. We were never afraid to ask a question, no matter how silly it seemed. "Where have you booked us into dad?"

"I booked a table for two o' clock at the Web Spinner in Stirling." I was actually looking forward to it, because I still had that sickly feeling.

"You're both looking great by the way. The French air must agree with you."

"It does, dad."

"It certainly does, Frank. I can't imagine not being there now." Brian sounded confident.

"How are you getting on with the language?" I couldn't help but let out a little giggle, as I looked round at Brian.

"Leela is great! I am not so great. I'll still be learning it for the next ten years." I couldn't help but laugh. I loved it when Brian admitted defeat with the French language.

"I would be the same, son. They speak to fast for me." My dad and Brian would be great on a night out in Marseille they would end up with who knows what.

"That's what gets me. I can understand to some extent when Leela and my contacts speak it. I'm lucky most of them can speak English."

"Vous avez deux sont terribles!." I couldn't help myself.

"Yeah right, smart arse. We know that we're terrible. You don't need to rub it in." The laughter in the car was magnificent and I hoped that it could be like that the whole time we were there.

When we arrived at our destination, it was weird looking around. Everything seemed so different. France and Scotland were similar for scenery, but France was more calming. I took Brian's hand and we walked along side my dad. I was pleased my dad thought about booking us there. I used to like going there when I lived here.

"What time does Craig finish. Dad?"

"Err…I am not sure, hen. We'll soon see." I was desperate to see

my brother. I missed him so much. "After you." My dad opened the door and we walked in to be surprised by everyone we knew shouting surprise! I couldn't believe it. I looked at Brian to see if he knew anything about it, but he looked as shocked as I was. Then Craig came and hugged me. I was flung around in the air. I couldn't stop myself from giggling. I was amazed.

"I've missed you, Lee. I'm so happy to see you."

"I've missed you too." I was finally put down, when Scott came to embrace me. I had no idea that any of it was going to happen. I looked around to see where Brian was and I spotted his family also. Now I was a bit nervous, because I wasn't sure how it was going to go down, but I became side-tracked when my best friend from school, Tracey came and hugged me tight. I couldn't quite believe that there were so many people there to greet us. I thought everyone would have forgotten about us once we moved away.

"How have you been, Leela?" Tracey asked.

"I've been great. How have you been?"

"Well, I have news." I was intrigued to hear my best friend's news. It wasn't coming quick enough and I knew the pause was just to drive me crazy. "I'm engaged to Simon." She held her hand up to show me her engagement ring. I hugged her again. I was so happy for her. She deserved everything.

"Congratulations to you both! Is Simon here?"

"Yeah. He's up there with my mum and dad, but that's not all." I couldn't wait to hear what else was to come. "I'm twelve weeks pregnant!" Again, I was so happy for her. We were like teenagers again.

"I can't believe I've missed all of this. You better keep me posted on the wedding details."

"You better be back for it, because I can't get married without my Maid of Honour." I was so incredibly happy for Tracey. I was also glad she asked me to be her Maid of Honour. Today was perfect.

"I wouldn't miss it for the world."

"So, spill the beans. I heard that you and Brian are together." I linked her arm and led her to a table and sat down.

"I don't know what to say or even where to start."

"The beginning would be a start."

"We've been together a few weeks and it's been fantastic, Trace. I've never felt like this before in my life. I feel alive again. I feel fab!"

"Well, that is fab missy! I'm so happy that you've settled down again. You deserve happiness and so does Brian. You never know, it might be wedding bells and the pitter patter of little feet for you next."

"Hardly. We're just enjoying life again. Dreading the trial though." I had to bring it up. It was what I was there for and it helped to change the subject.

"That's only natural, babe. I'll be here for you as well. How are Brian's parents taking the news?"

"I've no idea. They're here, so that's a bonus, I guess." I wanted to be with Brian, but I didn't want to go over when he was with his family.

"I'll speak to you when you come up for the meal. Keep smiling honey, because you look gorgeous when you smile." I got another hug before she went back to her family. Scott and Sheree were next to come over to me.

"Hey! I was just asking my dad about you guys on the way over here. I don't know why I never guessed this."

"We just wanted to show you and Brian, that we approve of your relationship. We have missed you more than you realise." I felt so happy to be there with my loving family and friends.

"How have you guys been?"

"Well, we've got some news for you." I did a double take, because that sentence was all I had heard since I arrived.

"What now?" I interrupted. I was so pleased with everyone's news, but I was feeling a little bit nervous.

"I asked Sheree to marry me and she said yes!" Sheree held her hand up and another sparkling ring took my attention.

"Wow! Congratulations to you both. I'm so thrilled for you both. It comes in threes. Who's next?"

"Who else is getting married?" Scott seemed surprised that he wasn't the only one to share news with me.

"Tracey is and she's pregnant. I'm happy for you all. I really am."

"Come on. Let's get a seat. You must be knackered with the

travelling." I hated travelling with a passion. Only I could get jet lag on a two hour flight.

"It wasn't too bad, actually. It all went pretty quickly." I followed beside Scott and Sheree, up to the long table that was set up for us all to eat. My dad was already sitting down. I loved to see that big smile on his face. I wouldn't be able to thank him enough.

"I got you a glass of white wine, sweetheart. Is that what you still drink?"

"Dad. She lives in France. The home of wine. I'm surprised she hasn't come home an alcoholic," said Scott. As usual we were all in fits of laughter.

"I'll be back. Ladies room is shouting on me." I felt weird walking away on my own, because it was a full restaurant of people greeting us and making us feel welcome. I felt on cloud nine, but I was glad that I managed to get to the toilet without anyone else stopping me. I was feeling ecstatic and I was desperate to get back with Brian, but I was too nervous to interrupt when he was with his family. I should have been honoured that they were there to welcome us home. But when I came out of the ladies' room, I walked back and saw Brian standing inches away from the long table with a few members of his family. His face lit up when he saw me. I couldn't help but smile, until I saw the look of disapproval on his mum's face. I could have had the same look back, because I was so angry with the way she always treated Brian.

"There you are sweetheart. Are you okay?"

"Yeah, I am fine." His arm came around my waist. I wanted the ground to open up and eat me.

"Leela. I don't know if you ever met my Uncle Leroy and Aunty Davina." I managed to smile and shake my head. I had never met them, but they both came forward and took me in their arms. I was overwhelmed by it and didn't expect any of Brian's family to accept me.

"It's nice to finally meet you, Leela. You make my Godson very happy and I'm grateful to you for that." Now I could understand why they approved of me. They weren't a regular aunty and uncle, they were his Godparents as well.

"He makes me just as happy. Thank you both for coming." They

both went back to take their seats and we were left standing centimetres away from his mum and dad. I wasn't sure what was about to be said, so I went to my table without speaking to them, but Mr. Mackinnon took hold of my arm. I somehow managed to stop, before my arm became sore. I looked concerned and Brian looked alarmed as well.

"Leela. Can I speak with you for just a moment?" I wasn't sure what he was thinking and I wasn't sure if I wanted to be spoken to for a moment, but I knew for Brian's sake I needed to do it.

"Of course, but whatever you have to say, you can say it here." I wasn't going to fall for their charm. I wasn't that stupid, timid young girl that they treated me like before.

"Very well. I just wanted to tell you that I'm pleased that you and Brian have found love with one another. I wanted to welcome you to the family and let you know that there are no hard feelings on our side. We are all here for the trial and I would like it if we could be united for once." I was stunned, but I needed to snap out of it quickly.

"I appreciate that Mr. Mackinnon, but words are easily spoken. I'm not going to be made to feel awkward, because of our relationship. I'm happy about what you've said and I hope that you meant it from the bottom of your heart." I knew how quickly they could change and I was making sure they knew where they stood with me.

"I do my dear. Wherever your relationship goes with Brian, I want you to know that you have my blessing." I was gobsmacked. What came next was anyone's guess.

"I'm going to smile and play nice, but please don't ask me to accept all of this nonsense." Then Mrs. Mackinnon had to spoil it all with that tongue. "How the two of you can stand there and look so in love is beyond me." I wanted to cry or run away, but I wasn't going to give her the satisfaction.

"You can't help who you fall in love with, Mrs. Mackinnon. I don't give a flying monkey what you think. So you can crawl back into whatever hole you came out of." When I was finished, I took my place at the table. I felt the adrenalin rush through my body.

I did feel accomplished for not making any kind of scene. I said what I had to in a normal fashion. I wasn't going to stand and be

bullied by her. Not now. Not ever.

"Lee. Are you ok? What did that old cow say to you?" Craig knew as well as I did that Mrs. Mackinnon was going to do everything in her power to split me and Brian up.

"I'm fine! Just forget about it, Craig. She isn't going to ruin today." I was relieved when Brian sat beside me. His hand on my leg made me smile.

His parents sat across from us. I knew his mum was going to sit in silence and give me daggers, but I wasn't going to give her the satisfaction. I was going to smile and laugh and not give her the time of day.

"I love you, Lee." Brian's whisper in my ear, sent shivers all the way down my back. I picked up my glass, as my dad stood up and clinked his glass to get everyone's attention.

"I would like to thank you all for coming today. I'm thrilled to have my daughter and her partner Brian home. I wanted to organise this get-together, because we're all getting ready for the trial tomorrow. This was my way of letting everyone let their hair down. What better way to welcome Leela and Brian home. So, can everyone raise their glasses to Leela and Brian?" I was amazed to see everyone follow my dad's orders. Mrs. Mackinnon raised her glass, but she never uttered a word. That suited me just fine, because I was never going to accept her any more than she was going to accept me.

"Would anyone else like to say anything before we sit down to eat?" I was hoping that no one else would, because it was just going to make the witch angrier. Brian stood up with his glass in hand and I felt the butterflies float around my stomach. I looked over to my friend Tracey. I thought if I didn't take my eyes off of her smiling facc, I would be fine.

"I would like to take a few moments of your time. First of all, I would like to thank you all for coming today. Leela and I are grateful to see you here supporting us. As you all know already, Leela and I have come home to attend the trial for Mark's murderer… Over the last few weeks, Leela and I have been settled in Marseille making a life for ourselves. Fate brought us together, because Leela left here over eighteen months ago and I moved a few months later. We

bumped into one another out of the blue and instantly found a connection between us. I've spent the last few weeks having the best time of my life and that's all down to one thing." I could feel all eyes on me, but I had never moved my eyes from Tracey. "Leela." He bent down beside me and took my hand in his. I still couldn't look at him but, I knew that something was going to shock me.

"Leela. I love you more than anything on this planet and I would do anything for you." I looked into his sparkling eyes and I could feel the tears well up in my own. "Leela Park. I want to spend the rest of my life with you. I want to love and cherish you, from this day forward. Will you do me the greatest honour in front of our family and friends and be my wife?" I put my spare hand over my mouth, as the tears fell down my cheeks. I was shocked beyond belief.

"An answer would be good, sis." Everyone laughed at Craig's smart response, because I was taking too long. It brought me back into the moment.

"Yes," I whispered.

While I leaned into Brian's arms to compose myself. It was a day of surprises. I couldn't believe that he asked me today, of all days. I sat back up and wiped the tears from my face, as he placed the ring on my finger. It was perfect. I didn't know what to say.

"Everyone raise their glasses to Leela and Brian." I heard Craig toast us. I leaned back over to Brian, as he accepted me into his arms.

"I really do love you, Leela."

"I love you too, Brian! I never expected this. Not in a million years." Everyone was around the table chatting away, but we were in a world of our own. I would have done anything to have some time of our own.

"I wanted to show you how much I love you. This is the next step in our relationship. I told you that I want you for the rest of my life." His lips rested on mine and I didn't care who was watching. I was happy and floating on a new level. He was my future. For the first time in years, I could actually see how it was mapped out.

***

Being back at home was a good feeling. Everyone had gone to bed and I was sitting on the couch, waiting for Brian to come out of the shower. It felt like I had never been away. Today's shenanigans weren't expected, but I couldn't ask for more.

Tomorrow was going to start off a difficult time for us all, but I knew I had my family and Brian by my side. The quicker all of it is over with, the better it would be. After seeing Brian's mum and dad, I was a little bit more confident that our time at home would go by with few problems. However, I didn't think that Mrs. Mackinnon was too happy about Brian asking me to marry him. It's a good thing I passed caring what anyone thought. I was too happy to let anyone burst my bubble. I felt great since Brian came into my life and I never wanted him to leave. I would do anything in my power to keep our relationship as strong as possible.

"I thought you would have been sound asleep by now." The sound of Brian's voice made my body tingle. I've been waiting for hours to just have him all to myself for five minutes. I was used to the quiet life in France. Since being home among family and friends, it's been lively.

"I just wanted five minutes alone with you. I feel like today has been none stop and I've missed having you all to myself." His body leaning over me, sent the tingles further through me. He could have done anything to me and I wouldn't have protested. "Now you're just going to tease me. Aren't you?" I was surprised when his nice, fresh scented body squeezed in beside me on the couch. I could have spent the rest of my life cuddled in to this man and I wouldn't care about another thing. "I've been waiting all day for this embrace." My head snuggled onto his chest. His heartbeat always soothed me into a relaxed state.

"Today was a nice surprise. I'm sorry about the way my mum treated you. My dad wasn't amused either." It wasn't their fault the way Mrs. Mackinnon behaved.

"It isn't your fault, honey." I lifted my head up to look at him. "I would like to know what I've done to her, but I'm not going to go out of my way to be nice to her. I love you and I really wish there was none of this animosity. I can't wait to get home." I realised that Scotland wasn't home anymore. Home was where I felt comfortable.

"Are you wishing you didn't come home?" That was the second time he had asked me that question and I knew he would have me back to France as soon as possible. If that's what I wanted.

"Would you have proposed to me if we were back in France?" I was going for a different tactic and hoping that it would get me out of answering his question directly.

"Leela. I've had that ring in my pocket for over a week. Every time I went to ask you, something else came up. Then on the plane today, I asked you if I could do anything to make you realise how much I was yours. I was going to ask you then, but I bottled it."

"So you found courage today in front of all of our friends and family?"

"When I whispered in your ear *I love you* and you smiled at me, I knew that was it. Now or never. I wanted to show everyone how much I loved you and I don't care who's happy or not. I only care if you're happy, Lee."

"I am happy, Brian. Every time I look at you, I'm happy. You just keep dropping bombshells on me and you keep making me happier."

"I want to make you happy, sweetheart. I want to spend the rest of my life in your arms and I want to share everything with you." That was going to be what my life was like. I had no doubts in my head that I was madly in love with that man.

"In that case, what do you say we go up to bed? I don't mean for sleep." I wasn't shy around him. I was able to tell him what I wanted and he always gave me more.

"I thought you were never going to ask." I leaned in and took his mouth with mine. Our tongues touched and heat soared through my tingling body. I climbed over him and let him follow me. The good thing about the house was that it's massive and the rooms are great for containing any noise. I couldn't keep my hands off of him for the entire stay, so we started as we meant to go on. I found it weird, because I was always a timid lover before. I would never take the lead or tell anyone what I wanted. With Brian, I didn't need to hide myself. He made me feel like my body was a temple and I was his queen. I had never been in such a loving relationship. I got the same pleasure, as he did and sometimes more. I couldn't ask for anything else.

CHAPTER 10
START OF THE TRIAL

Of all the mornings I had to wake up feeling rotten, it had to be the day that the trial started. Brian and I spent another lovely night together, as the newly engaged couple. I was paying for the late night.

I had a quick shower, since everyone thought it was a good idea to let me sleep until 8:45am. The trial started at 10:30. Today, I was going to be off all day. I could sense it in every way possible. Drying my hair to leave it down was about as much energy as I had. But then a sudden urge to be sick, hit me and I had to run to the bathroom. I just made it in time when I wracked out my insides. It was just bile that came up. I couldn't believe I was letting the trial get to me. I had spent the last year and a half getting my confidence

back and making a life for myself, yet there I was letting it all get on top of me. Why the hell did I think it was a good idea to come back? I managed to get up and rinse my mouth out. The reflection of myself in the mirror just showed me how pale I looked. I didn't usually wear much makeup, but something was going to have to work wonders on my cheeks. Although, I had no time. My time was just about up. I had to get back to my room, which was going to be my only comfort.

"Leela! Are you okay?" Trust me to get caught being sick, by Craig of all people.

"I'm fine. Be better when today is over with." I grabbed my bag and was heading down the stairs with Craig a few feet behind me. I didn't want to stop and have a conversation about it. Everyone got sick in some way or another.

"Leela! Stop!" I listened to my brother, because I couldn't have him telling everyone that I was sick. "You being sick is not fine. What's going on?" I just wanted to get on with my day.

"Craig. Its nerves. I'm a nervous wreck. Please. Just don't make a fuss." I walked away and headed straight for the kitchen, hoping there was no one there. My lucky day it seemed, because it was empty. I poured myself a glass of water and began to drink it. I felt it bubble in my stomach, but I needed it. I needed to forget about an upset tummy, until today was over with.

"Leela." I took a deep breath and turned to put a smile on my face, so that Brian wouldn't notice me out of sorts. "Craig said you were sick. Are you okay?" I could have wrung my brother's neck. He just couldn't keep his mouth shut.

"Like I told motor mouth, I'm fine." I was pissed off and fed up with everyone treating me like a child.

"Leela. You don't look fine darling. I know what you look like and today, you look nothing like that."

"Well, I'm sorry about that Brian! What do you want me to say? I'm a nervous wreck and I'm sick of everyone fussing around me!" I took a breath and held the worktop for support. I had no idea what just happened and I never wanted to feel like that again. Something inside me had snapped and I completely felt out of control. "I am so sorry, Brian." I suddenly broke down in tears.

Before I could move, his arms were wrapped around me and my face was buried in his neck. I just snapped the head off of the person who supported me the most. The only person that loved me outside of my family. "I feel terrible and my nerves are shot. It's no excuse for me shouting at you like that." I couldn't stop the tears from falling and I felt every sob catch the back of my throat.

"Shhh, Leela. You don't need to apologise to me, darling." He pulled me away from him and lifted my chin, so he could look at me. I used the worktop to take my weight. "The nerves I can understand. We're in this together. Remember?" he responded, with the soft sincere voice that always gave me goose bumps.

"I know that and I'm grateful to you Brian. I really am. You know that it isn't normally me. I hated myself for shouting at him.

"I know. That's why I'm worried about you, Leela. I'm booking us flights home. I knew this was going to happen. I just don't know why I let you twist my arm."

"No. Don't do that." I stopped him from going any further. "I will take some medicine and put a face on for the trial."

"That's just it, doll. I don't want you to feel like you have to put a face on. You look so pale and worn out today. If you don't feel better, you'll have to see a doctor."

"It's just a bug. I'll be fine. Let's get this over with." Going home sounded great, but I was there and had to get it over with. I had to get out of the house and get day one out of the way. Then I would feel a lot better, because it was the unknown getting to me. I have never been in a court room and fear was getting on top of me.

"Are you guys okay?" I felt like ripping my brother's head off. I felt that uncontrollable urge to shout again, but I tried to keep it back.

"We would be even better if you wouldn't run about tittle tattling. I thought that we were all adults in this house." Sarcasm was the next best thing.

"Leela. I care about you."

"I'm a big girl now, Craig. I was more than capable of telling Brian that I don't feel well today. I wouldn't have needed to, because he would have noticed it." I started walking toward the door. I grabbed my car keys from the hanger.

“Leela. There’s room in my car.” I knew that my dad would have kept room for me and Brian, but I needed to be away from everyone.

“It’s fine dad. I’ll take my own car. I could kill him if I’m left with him today.”

“Time of the month, sis.” I went back to hit him, but my dad stood in my way. Brian edged around my dad to get in my way. I felt like some mad woman. Everything was getting on my nerves and I had to calm down, before I actually sent myself to the nut house.

“Stop winding her up Craig. I’m warning you.” I could hear my dad giving Craig his warning and I got into my car. It was weird being in my car again. I knew that my dad used her when I wasn’t around, but it was still strange. I missed her when I first left. But now I have another car in France and I have gotten just as attached to her.

“I’m laughing at you, but it isn’t funny… I am frightened to look at you today.” I could have laughed at Brian.

“I don’t know what’s wrong with me, Brian. I’m just going to be quiet.” His hand rested on my leg and it helped to calm me down a bit. I haven’t eaten that morning and it wasn’t doing my stomach any good either. Driving was calming me down, but the outcome of that day was going to be another story.

***

Walking up the stone stairs to the court, I saw Mark’s family standing at the top. There were reporters around, but thankfully we managed to get passed them without too much hassle. I felt like a pit-bull ready to bite someone’s head off.

“Hi, son…Leela.” I could only smile toward Mr. Mackinnon. The way I felt, he was lucky he even got that.

“What’s happening dad? Why are you out here?”

“We’re just going in. We were waiting for you guys, so we could put on a united front for Mark’s sake.”

“A pity you didn’t think about what Mark would have wanted when he died.” I couldn’t help but say it, but I was glad when no one took me on. Even Mrs. Mackinnon didn’t say anything, because she knew I was right.

"What court room are we in?" Brian's soft grip on my hand made me feel calm, as I followed alongside him.

"Room one, son." I should have been grateful that Mr. Mackinnon was there waiting for us, but I was just so fed up with the pretence from everyone. I wanted everyone to get along.

"We'll follow you in." I knew that Brian was going to try and sweet talk me into being nice. When my family followed behind the Mackinnons, I got a sense of Deja Vu. We were left behind at the funeral and that will always play on my mind. It will be something I will never forget. "Leela. Are you sure that you want to do this?" I stood there all dressed in black with a white shirt on. Where else was I going to go dressed like that? I put the nippy me back in the box and looked Brian in the eye.

"I don't want to be here, but I have to do this for Mark…for us. I'm crazy. I know, but this is going to open up a new chapter for us in the long run."

"I get why you think you need to do this for Mark. Why for us?"

"I need to do this to put that chapter out of my life. To put Mark and Esme out of my mind and store them in my heart." His arms wrapped around me and again I felt comfortable. It was a pity I couldn't spend the next week or more in Brian's arms. "We need to go in, Brian." He took my hand and squeezed it enough for me to know that he was there with me heart and soul.

I was going to be faced with the thug that shot Mark and probably even some of his family. I had to be strong and put everything out of my head.

I took my seat beside Brian. I just looked straight forward. I was going to have no distractions, and I wasn't going to get bogged down with information that I didn't need to know. I was here in person, but my soul was still back in France.

***

The first day had been a drag. I was still sitting in the court room at two o' clock in the afternoon, hoping that it got adjourned for the day. I was losing the will to live, while hearing *this one* and *that one* giving evidence. I was glad that Craig was one of the first up, because he was then able to join us. The man that shot Mark was

standing in the dock, but I just couldn't look at his smug face anymore. His family was in the other aisle with the crocodile tears going on. I couldn't cry, because I felt numb after listening to everything. I was on a totally different planet sitting there. I just wanted five minutes in a cell with the bastard who ripped my life apart.

I was angry at what happened to Mark, but I am grateful to see where my life was now. It didn't take away my pain and anger though. I couldn't imagine being stuck in that self-pity mode for the rest of my life. I just didn't know why they even had a jury. It was clear cut at the end of the day. The thug was as guilty as sin. Why he even had a lawyer fighting his case, I didn't know.

When we finished for lunch, my dad spoke with someone who said the case probably wouldn't last three days. I was hoping that was the truth, because I couldn't take it being stuck in there for weeks. It was only day one and I was falling to pieces. I imagined myself going back on a plane to France.

"Leela. It's finished for today, sweetheart." I was in a world of my own and I felt like I had been sleeping. I had that distant spaced out feeling, but I managed to stand up and take Brian's hand. The woman I thought was the thug's mother, bumped right into me as her tears continued to flow.

"I'm not invisible." If it had been anyone else I would have left it, but I had no intention of ignoring her ignorance.

"I'm sorry."

"Sorry that you bumped into me, or sorry that your son killed my fiancé?" I was angry. So angry that I could have pulled the trigger to let her see how hard it was for my family.

"For both. I know that he's guilty of shooting the policeman. I can't imagine what you're going through. I take it you're not a mother? If you were, you would understand that you would stick by your kids no matter what."

"No. I'm not a mother because your son saw to that as well. I miscarried at my fiancés funeral." I was doing myself no good standing there, reliving everything.

"I am so sorry, but when you have kids, you will realise what it's like to sit there and listen to all of this."

"Your son made it impossible to have kids..." I saw her face look at me for answers, but I wasn't going to stop. "I can't have any more kids. The big man with a gun. Don't expect me to feel sorry for you." I was the one that moved away first, because I could of hit her for being a hypocrite. I could have hit her for her son too.

"Leela! Wait!" I heard Brian coming after me, but I could only stop when I got to the front door for some air. Even then, I had to run to the bushes, because I was as sick as a pig. I felt it coming on all day and the shock and adrenaline just made it come to the surface.

"Leela!" Brian caught me as I was fishing in my bag for a mint and a tissue. "I am not taking no for an answer! You're going to see a doctor!"

"I don't need a doctor Brian! I just need an early night and plenty of tender loving care. Both of which you can give me." I wasn't going to give in and go to a doctor. They were too busy to see me with a stomach bug.

"I'm worried about you, honey. I watched you fight for your life in a coma!" Unfortunately, I couldn't remember anything about it. I could only imagine what it was like for my family to sit there day in and day out waiting for me to come around. "Let me drive us back to your dad's?" That was one thing that I could do. I took out the keys to give to him. I was glad I had someone to drive us home, because I didn't have the energy to drive. I would have ended up wrapping the car around some tree, if it was left to me.

While we started to move, I felt really light headed and grabbed Brian's arm. "What's wrong, honey?"

"I feel...dizzy."

"Have you ever felt like this before?" I tried to think, but there was only one time that I felt like that.

The next thing I knew, I felt my legs give way. Brian just caught me before I hit the ground. I was in and out of conscious and I couldn't keep myself alert.

***

"What's happening, Brian?" Everyone came rushing in toward me. I felt bombarded by everyone throwing questions at me. Leela

was my life and I felt helpless.

"I'm still waiting for the doctor to come out to tell me anything. She started to come around in the ambulance, but they didn't know what was going on. Her blood pressure was low and her heart rate was high." I just couldn't believe that we were here again. Why on earth did I let her come back here? I knew that it was going to be too much for her. I should have stood my ground and said I wasn't coming back. Maybe we wouldn't be in that position now.

"Exhaustion, maybe." I looked at Craig and I hoped that it was something stupid like that.

"Honestly Craig, Leela was happy back in France. She was like a different person. I pleaded with her not to come back. Not because I didn't want her to see you guys, but for the trial. I wish she didn't know the date, because I would have left it that way." I was blaming myself. I would never forgive myself if anything happened to her.

"You can't blame yourself, son. I heard how happy you have made Leela and I would have been the first to tell you if any of this was your fault. I'm just glad that she found love again. She can face anything if you stick by her." Hearing Frank speak to me like that made me feel honoured to be a part of their family.

"I will always stand by her, Frank. You have my word." The tears rolled down my cheek and I couldn't hide my heartache. But the minute the doors swung open and a nurse came in our direction, I stood to attention. I had never moved that quickly before in my life.

"Brian?" asked the nurse.

"Yes, that's me." My voice was shaky and I felt like I was all over the place.

"Do you want to come with me?" I looked round at Leela's family. They were all telling me to go. I followed the nurse with my heart pounding. I had no idea what I was going to be told. I was a nervous wreck. I knew how Leela must have felt. "Leela has come around. She is a bit groggy. She twisted her ankle in the fall, but she's going to be alright. I sighed in relief. The huge weight was lifted off my shoulders.

"What made her collapse then?" I was eager to find out what was going on.

"Come in and the doctor will fill you in." I was all over the place. I

just needed to see that Leela was okay. I would give my life for her.

While I walked in, I saw my vulnerable woman lying in a hospital bed hooked up to monitors. Many memories flooded through my mind of the last time when she was in a coma. But I picked up the courage and took her hand in mine. I was amazed when her eye's opened. Her smile was just perfect. Even lying in a hospital bed she managed to smile.

"Leela. I'm glad to see that you're okay. What happened, honey?" I looked to the doctor for some answers and hoped that there was nothing major going on.

"We went through Leela's case notes and we could see that an instance similar, happened nearly two years ago. Our main thing to rule out was another ectopic pregnancy."

"I can't have a baby, because of the damage..." I could see how weak and exhausted Leela was.

"There was too much damage from the last ectopic pregnancy. They said that she would never have any more children." I managed to fill in for Leela. Even Though I didn't understand where all of this was going.

"Well, you have been a miracle case Missy. They say that you had maybe a five percent chance of having another pregnancy naturally, but I performed an ultrasound when you were still unconscious. I could see the embryo growing in the right place. It's still early days. I believe four or five weeks if that. I suggest you come back in three to four weeks, so that we can see the progress of the pregnancy." Leela and I were gobsmacked.

"We don't live here anymore. We're only back for the trial for my brother's murder. How will this work?" I was glad that I thought about our situation, because Leela was still in a world of her own.

"I suggest you go home as soon as you can and get booked into your clinic. I can give you a copy of your previous history and what we found today. They'll take it from there. I know you must be shocked and worried sick, but the baby is growing in the right place and there's no other reason why you can't carry it naturally." It was a relief to hear the doctor say that. Again, I would never forgive myself if anything happened to Leela.

"When can I go home?" I knew she was stubborn.

"Let us finish with the fluids and I'll take more blood, then we'll see about letting you go home." The doctor couldn't have been any nicer.

"Thank you," I managed to say.

"Leela. The first twelve weeks in any pregnancy is crucial. I would tell anyone to take it easy and relax. I have to ask this. Do you want this baby?" I was looking at her desperately waiting to hear her answer. I squeezed her hand to let her know that I wanted her and the baby. It was our miracle and another reason to show us that we were meant to be.

"I am…shocked. I thought I was never going to have my own family. It was one thing that tore at my heart. To answer your question, of course I want the baby!" She turned to look at me. She needs to hear my thoughts out loud, because I was thrilled inside and out.

"I know that you're going to take it easy. I'll give you some vitamins to take and order plenty of rest."

"I *am* a doctor. I'll take care of myself." I could only smile.

The doctor and nurse left us. "Brian. I never expected this to happen. I'm not asking you to drop everything for us." I put my finger over her lips. I had so much I wanted to say to her.

"Leela. Just let me say this and don't interrupt me. I loved you when I asked you to marry me and I love you more than anything in this world. I'm over the moon about the baby." My hand rested on her tummy and the tears rolled down both of our faces. "I'm going to take care of you and the baby and I'm going to make sure you have peace and rest. I feel like I am on cloud nine right now. Me, you, and our own little bundle of joy. I'm going to book us flights for the weekend and you are going to take it easy. No more trial." I was waiting for her to protest, but I could see how much our child meant to her. "When we get back to your dad's, I'm going to run about for you. I don't want you to do anything strenuous." I was going to enjoy watching her bloom throughout the pregnancy. I was going to make sure both Leela and the baby were safe and well.

"Yes, Dr. Mackinnon." I was happy to see her laughing again and I had to kiss her. She was going to be my wife and mother of my child. I couldn't possibly ask for any more. I felt like the luckiest

person alive.

"Do you want to fill my dad in?"

"If you want me to, I will. Do you want me to bring them in?" I would do anything for her. It was unbelievable how much a bit of news could make you feel on top of the world.

"Tell them to come in." I was floating through the door. I was trying not to make it too obvious when I went out to get them all, but I couldn't take the smile off of my face.

"Come in you guys. Leela has something to tell you."

"What's going on?" Craig was the first to jump in, but I wasn't giving anything away. I took my place beside Leela, as I took her hand. I could see how tired she was. I couldn't wait to get her home to look after her.

"Leela. Are you okay? What did the doctor say?" Her dad was worried. I knew how he felt now.

"It isn't bad news. I don't have the energy to give you all the details, but…I'm pregnant." The silence filled the air.

"I thought you couldn't have any more," Frank said. He was as shocked as everyone else.

"The doctor just said it would have been about a five percent chance of me conceiving naturally, but they did an ultrasound and the baby is in the right place this time." Just hearing Leela say it all out loud, made me thrilled about the idea of becoming a father.

"Congratulations to you both! I'm very happy! I know you will both make great parents. Wow! Something is telling you two to be together!" We were all thinking the same thing. Frank was the first one to say it.

"*It was meant to be,* dad. They also told me to rest for the first twelve weeks. I have to go home as soon as I can."

"When?" I could hear the disappointment in Frank's voice. I knew he was looking forward to having us home for a while.

"Brian is going to get us flights for the weekend. So, we still have a few days with you guys. I'm going to have to stay away from the trial, because I can't be stressed." Every one of us sighed with relief.

"Well, I'm not going to lie. I'm disappointed, but I want you and my grandchild to be safe. I'll come out in a few weeks to see you both, if that's okay."

"You never need to ask that question, dad. I would love to have you out in France with me."

"I'm going to get home and get us all a nice meal rustled up. Brian will look after you and I'll see you when you get home." It was times like that, I could see what a great father was. My father was a joke of a man. He gave into my mum's every word. Yet, there was Frank showing his concern and listening to everyone's feelings. I hoped I could be as good a father as he was.

"Thank you, dad!" We could all see how exhausted Leela was. We were all going to do everything we could to make sure both the baby and mum were going to be okay.

"We'll go back with dad, Lee. I'm sorry for winding you up this morning," said Craig, with an aching voice. He hated himself for winding Leela up that morning.

"It's fine, Craig. I'll be home soon." I was just over the moon about the baby. It was going to be me and Lee for the rest of our lives. We were going to have a little bundle of joy to take care of, as well. I sat back beside her on the bed and kissed her hand tenderly. I loved the feel of her soft skin. The fresh scent of her moisturiser hit my senses and I couldn't stop smiling at her. "I think I'm in some kind of dream."

"I told you what I think about the baby, but I haven't asked you what you actually think." I watched her shoulders shrug, as a slight smile crept upon on her face. I knew what I hoped to hear her say, but things went quickly for us. I didn't want her to feel suffocated by it all. "I don't care what you have to say, Leela. I just want us to be honest with each other. We started off the way we were meant to go. I don't want to stop communicating."

"Brian. Don't be silly. I love you to pieces. The first time we slept together must have been when this baby was conceived. We didn't plan any of the last few weeks, but to me it was everything. I love you Brian and I want to spend the rest of my life with you. I know the first thing I told you was that I couldn't have kids and you were happy with that."

"I was happy with that, because I didn't care as long as I had you in my life."

"We're going to have a baby together, Brian! I never thought I

would have a baby. It's just another way of telling us that *it was meant to be."*

"I'm so happy to hear you say of that, because I thought that everything was happening too quickly for you."

"Everything is just right for me." I was more than happy when she sat forward and took me in her arms. Today was a funny day, but it let us all see that our love would get us through anything. We had all the main components of a happy relationship. Love, trust, happiness, and now our little bundle of joy.

***

I was never so glad to leave the hospital. Brian was amazing with everything. I was only kept in for a few hours, but already I felt it was too long. I did feel weird sitting in the passenger's seat of my own car. That had to be the first time I had experienced the car as a passenger. I could get used to being chauffeured around. I was actually looking forward to getting back to my dad's house. I knew that everyone was going to make a huge fuss over me, but that's what families were for. Come Saturday, I was going to be leaving to return home to France. It was a special time. I never experienced anything like that when I stayed at home, because I had them around every day. Now, I cherished every minute I have with them.

"Are you okay, babe?" I turned toward Brian. I was engrossed in taking in all of the changes. It was crazy how things changed.

"Yeah. I'm fine. Just being nosey."

"I'm going to have to fill my mum and dad in at some point tonight. They'll wonder where we are tomorrow if we don't turn up." He sounded as keen as I felt.

"If they were half decent at all, they would have been on the phone by now to see how you were holding up." I couldn't help but sound like a bitch. Mrs. Mackinnon and I were never going to see eye to eye. "Sorry. I'm going to blame the hormones, because I don't know what has come over me today. I've been nippy, sweetie." I was really annoyed with myself and I was hoping that the pregnancy symptom wore off.

"First of all Miss, you don't need to apologise. Second, you are

absolutely right about my parents. They should have been in contact to see how you are. Last but not least, you can nip my head off for the next 8 months if you like." I couldn't stop smiling at him. I couldn't believe how lucky I was.

"You might not be saying that in the next few months, if I'm still nipping at the least little thing."

"I think you're like that, because we're here. I quite believe that when we go back to France and settle back down with our life, you won't be a wicked witch." We both laughed. I always wondered what it would be like to be a witch. Well, now I know. "Are you ready to face everyone?" I looked at the house. It appeared in front of me, as we drove into the driveway.

"Ready as I'll ever be." I unbuckled my seatbelt and opened my door. All I had was my handbag. Brian took it off me. It wasn't going to kill me carrying a handbag, but I smiled and accepted his arm, as I hobbled into the house. My ankle was bloody sore and I had no idea how that even happened. I got inside and heard everyone laughing and joking from somewhere in the house. We entered the dining room first. Everyone was waiting patiently for us before they had dinner.

"Hello, sweetheart. How are you? Come and get a seat. Take the weight off of your ankle." I managed to keep a smile on my face, as my dad pulled a seat out for me. I got my hug and kiss on the cheek before he let me sit down. "How are you feeling?"

"I'm fine dad. My ankle is agony, but it will be right as rain in a couple of days." Brian took a seat opposite me. I just had to have Craig at the side of me. I turned to face him. He couldn't face me. "Cat got your tongue, mister?"

"Sorry, sis. I didn't want to wind you up any more." He took me in his arms. "I should just stay away from you, because I always end up causing you pain.

"Don't you dare say that!" I pulled away from him and laid my hand on his cheek. "None of this was your fault. I was just being a bitch this morning. I gave you as good as you gave me. I did wonder why I was being like that, but now I know. I'm fine Craig." He laid a soft kiss on my forehead and I turned back to face the table. My dad sat at the head of the table beside me. I had never seen him look so

happy. He had his entire family sitting around the table. He had everything he ever needed.

"What are you poisoning us with tonight, dad?" I loved hearing the laughter around the table. Craig and Scott were always the life and soul of the family. We had come through a lot and it was good to see us fighting back as a family.

"I made chilli con carne tonight. I was going to try something French for Leela and Brian, but I thought I better stick to what I know." The minute my plate was put down, I felt my stomach growling. It had dawned on me that I haven't eaten a thing.

"Even in France, we don't eat French food. You did right, dad." I'm a fussy bugger at the best of times, so I stuck with what I knew. I loved my dad's chilli and I wasn't going to stop until my plate was cleared. I looked up and saw Brian chatting away with Scott. Whatever they were talking about, they were happy and smiling at one another. "I missed your cooking, dad."

"When I come out to visit in a couple of weeks, I'll be cooking every day. I'll make sure you and the little one are eating properly."

"You mean that you'll have me the size of a house."

"It's good to see you happy, sweetheart. I am so happy for you and Brian. I suppose you will have a lot of decisions to make when you go home."

"Just a few, but for once we're making decisions for a good reason. We were going to be deciding what house we were moving into when we got back, but I think now it's pretty easy to decide." My dad and I were sitting chatting away like it was only the two of us at the table. "Brian has a house similar to this out in Marseille, with not as many rooms. It's in a good area for raising a family."

"What will you do with your little cottage?"

"I'm not sure. I'm not getting rid of it, because I love it too much. I might rent it out as a holiday home, or keep it if any of you want to come over, but don't want to stay with us. When *you* come over, you'll be staying with us. I miss you too much to let you stay in my cottage alone."

"I'm glad to hear it." My dad would always be more than just my dad. He was my best friend and I loved him to pieces. He hadn't changed, since we were kids. He was always there when we needed

him. I hoped that Brian and I can be just as good with our children.

"What are you two talking about?" I might have guessed that we would have been caught out at some point. It was Scott that clocked on to me and my dad's little chin wag.

"We're just talking in general. If I wanted you to butt in I would have thrown you a bone." Everyone burst out laughing and Craig held his hand up so I could high-five him.

"Pregnancy is going to suit you, Lee."

"Don't encourage her, Craig." I shot Brian a look and threw my napkin over at him for ganging up on me. I loved the family getting along together. I wished that we could all do that for many years to come.

"Sorry to break this great moment with you kids. Have you told your parents about the baby, Brian?" Those were the words we didn't want to hear. We were all calming down from our mad few minutes. I didn't want to interrupt my dad from speaking with Brian.

"I'm going to do it later, Frank. I don't think the news of us going home this weekend will go down too well. They'll just have to come around, because my priority is Leela and the baby." I couldn't stop myself from smiling at my fiancé. He really did love and care for me. No one could take that away from him.

"I'm honoured to call you my son-in-law, Brian. I have everything to thank you for."

"You don't need to thank me, Frank." Brian said, as my dad took my hand in his.

"You're going to take care of my little girl. God help you if this is a little girl, Brian, because then you'll have two women that steal your heart."

"So in other words, he's saying that if you have a son, it won't be the same." I was thankful that Craig broke up the serious talk.

"Don't listen to him, Brian. Having a son is just as rewarding, but a little girl is a special little angel. You'll feel it the minute she's born."

"See? I always told you two that I was daddy's princess," I chirped in, nudging Craig's arm.

"I love all of you kids with every bit of my heart and soul. I know for a fact that your mum would be so proud of you all." I loved

listening to my dad speak. He was like Brian, so sincere. You just knew that every word was the truth. “Craig. Crack open the champagne. We have a lot to celebrate today.” I rested back in my seat. Brian did the exact same, staring over at me with a sparkle in his eye. “I’m glad to see that you cleared your plate young lady.” I took my dad’s hand in mine and didn’t let it go. I felt like I was on a cloud. I was surrounded by my loved ones, while carrying my child. “I’ll cook us all breakfast in the morning, so everyone better be up bright and early. I’ll put yours in the microwave if you’re still sleeping, sweetheart.”

“She’s pregnant, not dying, dad.” I was glad that Craig said that, because everyone was going to do my head in fussing over me. “Leela? Do you want a small glass?”

“No. None for me. You can get me a glass of orange juice since you’re on your feet.”

“All the more for us then,” said my obnoxious brother.. I was so fortunate to be carrying my baby and I wasn’t going to do anything to jeopardise that. I would care for my baby, until the day he or she was ready to go out on their own. I got that protective feeling and that was the best feeling in the world. Just to think that I had a tiny little baby inside of me was overwhelming.

“You look tired, Leela,” said my dad, as he squeezed my fingers. I didn’t feel tired, but I knew that I would probably hit my pillow and be out for the count.

“I am okay, dad. I’m just glad to be home. Tonight has been another great night.”

“Let’s leave the dishes until later, so we can all go and get a soft seat in the living room.”

“You all go and get a seat. I’ll do the clearing up.” I looked round at Sheree. I felt stupid, because I hadn’t spoken to her. She was next to Craig and I had been stuck at the other side.

“Thank you, sweetheart.” My dad stood up and kissed Sheree on the cheek. Our family was going to gain another perfect member. She was quiet, but it was nice to see her coming out of her shell with us. “I’ll take your glass.” I had to smile, because my dad must have gotten fed up being pleasant to us. It wasn’t often that I heard him saying something nasty to anyone. I often wondered how he could

have worked his way up through the police force, because he was so nice.

While I stood up, Brian walked over to me, so I could take his arm. I was surprised my dad hasn't called me Hopalong Cassidy. That was his favourite thing to call us, when we were kids. My dad was a Western freak. Anyone that knew him well enough, knew he had a massive collection of videos. My mum and I were overjoyed when DVD players came out. But then he started buying the movies on D.V.D, so we couldn't win.

"How are you feeling, babe?" We were finally left on our own, as everyone headed through in front of us. I just couldn't wait to snuggle into him tonight.

"I'm feeling good." I heard a knock on the door. I didn't want anything to interrupt our family night, but I heard someone open the door. Brian and I hadn't moved and I was glad to have him to myself for a couple of minutes. He bent down and placed his lips over mine. Our mouths became one and I felt the sexual excitement rise inside of me. I managed to pull away, just as my dad put his head round the corner.

"Kids? You have a visitor." I looked back at Brian, as I tried to compose myself.

"I've wanted to do that all evening." I took his arm and we walked slowly to see who was there. I didn't know who got the bigger shock, me or Brian.

"Mum! Dad! What are you doing here?" I hoped he would have said something pleasant.

"We tried calling your mobile, but it went straight to voicemail. We were worried about Leela." I looked at Mr. Mackinnon, and I knew he was genuine. Mrs. Mackinnon never opened her mouth.

"Sorry, dad. My phone is still switched off. We got back here, because Frank made a meal for us. I totally forgot about my phone. I was going to call you in a little while. I just said that to everyone not ten minutes ago."

"Don't worry about it. I was just concerned, because I knew that Leela looked pale all morning. Are you feeling much better, my dear?" I was taken aback. I couldn't believe I was getting spoken to like that, without the she devil jumping in.

"I'm feeling much better, Mr. Mackinnon. I twisted my ankle and it's rather painful, but it will be right as rain in a few days." I looked round at Brian, because I didn't feel comfortable telling them our news. "Do you want to come through and join us? My dad has just opened a bottle of champagne." I had mellowed that night and I wasn't about to punish Mr. Mackinnon for his wife.

"That would be lovely, my dear. One glass won't harm us."

"Before we go through, I'd like to tell you a few things first." I stopped myself from moving and I clutched onto Brian's arm for support.

"Is everything okay?"

"I was going to call you, because when we were at the hospital today…" I gently squeezed his arm, as he paused. I knew he was nervous. "We found out that Leela was pregnant." Then there was silence. I just wanted someone to say something to break the ice.

"I'm…happy for you both. I never expected this kind of news, but I'm thrilled." I was even more surprised when Mr. Mackinnon came and took me in his arms. He had the same strong frame that Brian had and I felt a little bit more relaxed with his response. "Isn't this great news, honey? We're going to be grandparents!"

"What's to say she can even carry this one?" Then came exactly what I expected. Her mouth! I wanted to slap her for being so damn rude in my house, but I thought twice and stood exactly where I was.

"Leela had a scan at the hospital and the baby is growing in the right place this time. It's early days, but there is nothing to say that she will lose this baby. No one would have been told if it wasn't for what happened today. Thank you for your vote of confidence, mum." I felt hurt. Not for me, but for Brian's sake. She couldn't join him and be overjoyed. She had to find some other way to stick the knife in. "That brings us to the next piece of news. Leela needs rest and she needs to be in a stress free environment. The doctor told us to go home as soon as we can. I'm booking flights for Saturday. She won't be at anymore of the trial. It's only Monday and I think by the weekend the trial will be over with. If not, we'll be filled in daily on the progress." I was proud of Brian for being strong. He didn't crack under the pressure and he stood up tall to face his mum and dad straight on.

"I understand, son. You've got to do what's best for your fiancé and unborn child. You know, in a way this has been Mark's blessing to you both. I hope to see you both, before you leave. Please keep in touch to let us know how things go."

"Thank you, dad!" Brian stepped forward and took his dad in his arms. I was so thrilled to see that Mr. Mackinnon did what he wanted for a change and not what his wife wanted. "I was going to book us all in for a meal on Friday night, as a going away celebration. I'll phone you with the details. Do you want to go?"

"That would be nice. We would love to come. We're going to get out of your hair now and let you rest. You take things easy, Leela." I let go of Brian's arm, as he went to see his parents out. I didn't think they would have gotten a drink with us. I guess I should have been grateful that Mr. Mackinnon was so nice about it all. I dare say he would get *what for*, when he got home. I would really like to be a fly on the wall for that. It really pained me to think that Mr. Mackinnon, had a wife like her. I saw a different side of him over the last couple of days. I could see perfectly well that it's only his wife that's keeping all of the animosity going.

"Well, that went easier than expected." I managed to blurt out.

I loved to see that smile on Brian's face. I hadn't been a huge part of his family for any amount of time, but everything I had seen and heard, was clear that Mr. Mackinnon didn't want to be shut out. He wanted to be a part of his son's life and he didn't want his wife to be so horrible. He needed to speak up before he lost all contact with Brian and his grandchild.

"I was surprised to hear my mum so quiet." I let him take me in his arms. His hands resting on my waist, ignited the passion inside of me.

"Was that the calm before the storm?"

"Maybe." His lips came down onto mine and our mouths became one. I felt like I could kiss that man for as long as possible. "You

know what? I don't care as long as we have each other. You and this little one are all I'm ever going to need." Feeling his hand rest on my stomach made me all giddy inside. I loved to feel how much he wanted me and the baby. It felt wrong at the moment to be happy, but I knew that Mark would want us both to be happy.

"We better join your family before they send a search party." I rolled my eyes and let him lead me into the living room. Just hearing the general chit chat and laughter, made me feel honoured to be part of such a wonderful family. When I was growing up, I thought that everyone had a family life like mine. As I got older, I saw that I was one of the lucky ones. There are people out there that have no one. I had everything that I have ever wanted. I would make sure that my little bundle of joy had everything that he or she would ever need and that includes a loving family.

CHAPTER 11
The Long Road Ahead.

Forty-eight hours had passed since I found out that I was carrying Brian's baby. Everything was starting to sink in and I was overwhelmed by it all. It's just weird how everything had turned out for us. I was starting to get excited about going home on Saturday, but I didn't want my family to think that I didn't want to be here. I loved each and every one of them dearly, but that didn't feel like my home anymore. I was haunted by so many painful memories. I thought they would have eased away over the time I've been away, but I was wrong. France was the only place that I felt free. It's where I settled down and I was looking forward to going home and getting settled for the baby's arrival. I was more than ready to start my family with Brian. It all felt perfect. It pained me to think I thought

twice about starting a relationship with him. I shuddered every time I thought about that split moment. Even after having trouble sleeping last night, I sat there and saw clearly what my future had in store for me.

I crept out of my room earlier, because I had enough tossing and turning. When I looked at the clock it read 6:15am. It was pointless even trying to sleep. Instead of lying there and waking Brian up, I got up and went downstairs. I was looking forward to a nice cup of tea and cereal with ice cold milk. It looked like I was getting my first craving, because I hardly ever ate cereal. Even when I was a child. My mum was always up bright and early and had a hot breakfast made for us. We all liked different things in the morning and our poor mum cooked them all. I loved scrambled eggs and cheese with toast. Dad was a bacon man. He had a roll with bacon and brown sauce. Many mornings he had to change a tie or shirt, because the melted butter or brown sauce was all over him. We found that hilarious to my dad's disliking. Craig liked his toast, toasted lightly with lots of butter. Scott used to call Craig an idiot and world war three broke out. Scott liked a roll with square sausage with lashings of tomato sauce. It would have been easier if we all liked the same thing, but that just wouldn't happen for our household.

Sitting at the breakfast bar with no one around was bliss. It was weird, in a way, because the house was always busy and full of life. Me and Brian, Scott and Sheree, dad and Craig. It actually felt like a family home again. I thought that my dad and Craig would be lost when we all went back to our own lives.

"Leela? Are you okay, sweetie?" I was startled when my dad came in behind me. I was glad I was only holding a spoon or my ceral would have gone everywhere. "Sorry. I didn't mean to startle you, sweetheart." My dad massaged my shoulders to relax me.

"I never heard you come down. Are you okay?"

"Yeah. I'm fine, sweetie. I just can't sleep past six o' clock." He sat down opposite me with a cup of coffee. I was missing coffee all ready, but it was a small price to pay if my baby was healthy. "What are you doing up at this time?" I knew the concerned tone when I heard it.

"I tossed and turned all night. I don't know what's wrong with me.

I usually sleep like a log and I have to tear myself out of bed in the morning for work." It hadn't been the first time he came in before he left for work to drag me out of bed. I only had one good night since I came back and that was my first night. Even then, I blamed that good sleep on being jet lagged and all of the excitement from the welcome home party.

"You're pregnant. Your body changes in so many ways. I know that I'm not your mum, but I did stand by her when she was pregnant with you and the boys." I wasn't surprised hearing my dad tell me that. He had always been a hands on dad. He was a gem. "Your mum had a hard time sleeping when she was pregnant with you. I hope I'm not boring you by telling you about your mum. It's at times like this I really miss her. I know that she would have loved to be here telling you everything you need to know." I looked over at my dad and took his hand in mine. I was honoured to hear about my mum and the past.

"Dad. I love hearing all these stories about mum. I miss her as well. Especially, right now. You're doing a great job though." I loved to remind him how amazing he was, just to boost his confidence. "So? You were saying?" I was glad that my dad could always confide in me. I am and always will be an old-school family girl.

"Sleep…There was none of the things that are out now, but she used to prop herself up with cushions. When she had a bump, she used to have a pillow underneath the bump to stop it straining. I actually started working the nightshift, so she could get a sleep. She was getting up in the morning when I was going to bed." The huge smile on my dad's face, made me smile. "I'd put money on it." I wondered what he was talking about, as I took a spoonful of my breakfast. "I would say you're going to have a beautiful baby girl." I was surprised to hear that, because my dad wasn't a betting man. He always used to say *what is meant to be, will be*. Thinking back, that saying, *it was meant to be,* had followed me throughout my life.

"I'll take your word for it, dad." I knew that I would love a little girl.

"I'm going to miss you guys when you go home."

"I'm going to miss you too, dad, but I'll look forward to seeing

you when you come out." I was sitting there and was worried about my dad. It was like he was keeping something from me. "Are you okay, dad?" It was him and I, with no one else around.

"I'm just concerned if I come out to see you and Brian, I won't want to come home." I didn't expect to hear him say that. I was always under the expression that he loved it in Scotland.

"I thought you were happy here, dad? What's wrong?"

"I'm fine, Leela. I'm not getting any younger. The months are flying by and I'm going to be retiring soon. I want to have a good retirement. I don't want to sit here day in and day out, become a part of pensioner groups, and become addicted to daytime television. " I was smiling inside and out, because my dad wasn't going to be a pensioner. He was too young at heart for that.

"What do you want to do? Travel, bowls, dominoes?" I was confused. I had never heard him talk about retiring before. "I thought you loved this house dad?"

"Oh I do, Leela. I do. I would never get rid of this house. This will be split between you three and my grandchild when I go."

"You're not ill. Are you?" I had never heard my dad speak like that. I was really concerned.

"No sweetie. I'm fit as a fiddle. I have money in the bank, but I'm sick of crime and catching young thugs. I want to do something with the next few years I have left. I just want to come out, see you, and be around more throughout your pregnancy. I don't want to be one of those granddads that see their grandchildren at special occasions. I want to experience first steps, first teeth, and first words. That's if you won't mind."

"Mind?" I jumped in, almost biting my tongue. "Are you kidding me? I would love to have you around more. I'm going to cut out my paediatric training down, because long hours are not going to be good for me or the baby. I'm going to have lots of extra time on my hands. I haven't told Brian any of this yet, but I know he'll be thrilled." I felt like I was floating. Everything was falling into place and I was thrilled to think I would have my dad around more. I missed him so much.

"Well, keep it to yourself for now. Until I can plan things better and let Craig know what I'm doing." We had the first hurdle to

climb. I hated to think of Craig there alone.

"He's going to be lonely in this big house." I couldn't imagine what Craig would think about all of it.

"I was hoping that it would make him come out with me, but let me sort out all of that. Don't you worry yourself about it." I was thrilled at hearing what my dad wanted, but I was going to have to control my excitement. I wasn't sure if Craig would go for it, but just having that thought in my head was good enough for me.

"I'll keep it to myself, dad. I love you guys more than ever and I have loved seeing you all."

"But…," I looked back at my dad. "…I can see in your eyes that this isn't home anymore. When I picked you up at the airport I saw you long before you saw me. I could see the dread in your eyes. I hoped that it would change when we got home and you could see all of your friends and family, but it never did." I should have known that my dad would have seen right through me. "I've talked the ears off you this morning. I'm going to go for a shower and leave you to finish your breakfast in peace. Try and get some more sleep." I got a kiss on my head, as he left me sitting on yet another floating cloud. France was perfect for me. Could it be my dad's retirement getaway? Will it be where my family was meant to be as well?

***

My eye's flickered open, as I felt a warm, soft hand touch my cheek. I forgot where I was, until I registered what had happened earlier that morning. I could remember my dad going for a shower. Then I laid on the couch with a book. I obviously never got very far with the book, because I couldn't remember what I was reading. There I was, getting woken up with a soft touch and two gorgeous brown eyes looking down on me. I was smiling from ear to ear.

"Good morning, princess." Just three words from Brian, made me come alive. I felt like I had slept for hours.

"I bet I don't look much like a princess this morning."

"Leela. Without sleep or make-up, you still look like my princess. I'm not sure this prince was happy waking up on his own this morning, but because I love you and this little one more than

anything, I think I could forgive you." I pushed myself up to a sitting position with my prince charming sitting on the edge of the couch, leaning over my legs. I wanted to position myself so that I was inches away from him for my good morning kiss. I leaned in and our mouths became one, just like they had never parted. My heart began to beat faster and I could feel the heat rush to my cheeks.

"Will that help you to forgive me?" I sat back and made the space between us larger. I was grinning like a Cheshire cat.

"I forgave you the minute I saw your dad. He told me you were here. I came in to see the mother of my child so relaxed and at peace." His hand rested on my tummy and my hand covered his. I don't think I was ever going to forget moments like that. They were perfect. "You look so much better this morning, Lee."

"I feel it, considering I tossed and turned all night. I sat and ate breakfast with my dad just after six. I came in here to read a book just afterward." I looked to the floor where the closed book laid. I laughed.

"The book was that good?" I leaned forward and let him take me in his arms. I felt so calm and relaxed when I was enveloped by him. I loved him so much that it hurt.

"Have you been on Skype to your guys?"

"Check." I pulled back away from him to look over at the clock and noticed that it was 9:30am. I was fed up sleeping at odd times.

"Don't moan about sleeping until now. You obviously needed it. Besides, what do you have to do today?"

"Well, I have had a full night to think and…" I didn't know how my next revelation was going to go down.

"And?"

"I got a message from Tracey earlier. She's going to come over at lunch time for a girly afternoon. She heard about me collapsing thanks to the press and she knows about the baby."

"Cool! It will do you good to see a good friend. I'll make myself scarce."

"I actually thought you could go to the trial. I figured if I wasn't going and had Trace coming over, it would make your mum happy." I saw the look on his face. The cogs in his head started to turn, as he thought about the pros and cons.

"Are you sure, Leela? I don't want you getting worked up. It isn't good for you or the baby."

"I know! I also know that come Saturday evening, we'll be returning to France. We're going to have a couple of days together before we go back to work."

"You have been busy. Haven't you?" His sarcastic tone made me smile and feel like I had been a bossy boots.

"I'm being a cow."

"What? No. Why are you thinking that, babe?"

"I've just had too much time and thought of everything for myself. It's fine. I know you need to go back to work on Monday, so do whatever you like today."

"Leela." He put his hand over my cheek. I stopped talking and closed my eyes. I didn't want to look into his eyes. "Look at me, Lee." I paused for a couple of seconds and then did as I was told. "That's better. I'm not going back to work until a week from Monday. I've already told the guys that. They know about you and the baby and are happy to keep going with the Skype conference. You're not being a cow and don't ever call yourself that again. If you want me to go to the trial today, then I'll go for us both." My cheek leaned closer into his hand. I didn't know what I did to deserve him. "Don't tell me that I shocked you into silence?"

"I just don't know why you're with me? Why are you putting your family at jeopardy for me?" I felt like a hormonal wreck. I doubted everyone's love for me and I had no idea why.

"Do I really need to answer those questions, Leela?" A tear fell from my eye and he wiped it away with his hand. "I love you, Leela! Before this. Before everything. Now that you're my fiancé and you're carrying my child, I've never felt this kind of love for anyone before. I see what your dad meant about all of the hormonal stuff."

"You spoke with my dad about hormones?" I actually let out a laugh. "I spoke with your dad when I first got up this morning. It was just me and him for ages. We talked about everything. He told me that you were just like your mum when she was pregnant with you. She was a hormonal wreck from day one."

"Did he also tell you that he thinks I…we are having a baby girl?" I had to realise that I wasn't alone. I had become a *we* and we had

become a partnership. What happened to me, happened to him and vice versa.

"No, he didn't, but I happen to think he's right."

"You do?" I would love to know where they were getting that feeling from, because it was literally early days. I knew that older people or children were supposed to sense those things. With my dad and Brian, I had no idea.

"I better get a supply of hankies and hide all the soppy DVDs." I couldn't contain my giggle, as I wiped the rest of my tears away. "That's better." He took me back in his arms and I felt all the doubt and agitation wash away from me. I was going to make it my mission to get through the rest of the day without breaking down in tears. I was going to have a good day and enjoy the time that I had left there.

***

Coming down a large staircase with a sore ankle wasn't as easy as going up. It was with the fear of falling down them and hurting the baby that was making me feel scared.

"Why do you have to be stubborn, Leela?" There is a full house down here including your fiancé who will help you down the stairs." said Craig, sounding just like my father. He came up jumping two stairs at a time to get to me. I pulled my arm away from him. "Stop your carrying on!"

"Yes sir." I didn't know whether to laugh or cry. My brother has grown up too much. "I'm not a baby. I think I can come down some stairs on my own."

"Just do as you're told for once. There is a toilet down here or you wouldn't be getting left on your own." We got to the bottom just in time to see Brian coming out of the kitchen. He shook his head at me and smiled.

"I'll be there in a minute. Can you give me and dad here two minutes?" I didn't want anyone to think there was anything wrong.

"Of course." Brian placed a soft kiss on my head and left us on our own. I knew there was something wrong with Craig. He wasn't going to fob me off with nothing.

“What’s going on Craig? Don’t say nothing! You’re up tight and anxious. You would have never spoken to me like that before.” I saw his body relax, as he sat down on the stairs. I waited to hear his troubles.

“We’ve been here before, Lee.” I sat down on the stair just below him, just like when we were kids. Many talks were had on those stairs.

“I’m many things Craig, but I’m not a mind reader. If you want me to know what’s going through your mind, then you need to talk.”

“Everything, Lee. Everything.” I put my hands over his and turned to face him.

“Hey! You’re the strong one. You *have* been from day one and you’re not cracking on me now.” I was worried. It wasn’t him like him at all. “Tell me. Whatever it is we can get through it together as a family.”

“We’ve been here before with you Lee. I watched your world crash away from you.”

“I’m not following you, Craig.”

“I see you happy and in love with Brian. Everything is going in the right direction. Prospects, engaged, baby.” I heard the tears being held back in his voice.

“That worries you? Shouldn’t you be happy for me?”

“It isn’t that. Of course I’m happy for you, Lee. I’m thrilled for you. I really am. I just wish you were in France and away from here.”

“So you wouldn’t have to see me?”

“No! Not at all. I love seeing you, but I think this place is jinxed for you. France is your home. France is where you’re happy. Nothing will happen to you or the baby in France.”

“Craig you’re scaring me. Where are you getting this from?”

“Seeing you on those stairs struggling, I thought you were going to fall. Yesterday, when you collapsed, it was like the last time.”

“I know how that must have felt for you. Brian told me how he felt. That’s all in the past, sweetie. I’m fine. Apart from a sore ankle and morning sickness, I am perfect. Brian has even booked me into a private clinic tomorrow, just to make sure everything is okay before we fly on Saturday. Our luck has changed Craig, I can feel it.”

"When you go back to France, Leela…stay in France. Promise me? We'll visit you." I just couldn't understand where all of this was coming from. I was worried about him.

"Craig. I'm going to be fine. Just stop worrying about me and the baby. I am the happiest I have ever been. Brian is never going to let me lift a finger throughout this pregnancy." I wasn't just trying to say positive things to make my brother happy, because I knew that Brian was going to wrap me up in cotton wool.

"Leela." I never took my eyes off of him, as I lifted his head to look at me. "You're never coming back here. I'm coming to France with dad in a few weeks. Scott and Sheree have made a life away from here and you're the only one who's going to make a point to visit me and dad. You won't have to…if we're in France with you." I was gobsmacked.

"Have you been speaking to dad?" was all that I could say.

"Kind of." I stood up out of pure shock. I wanted them out in France with me forever. The last couple of days had been one surprise after another. I felt like I'm in some kind of dream. "Say something, Lee." I took him in my arms and my head rested on his chest. I could have cried with happy tears, but I didn't want to start crying again. "We love you Leela and we want a taste of this good life you keep telling us about."

"I just can't believe this."

"Sorry, guys. We need to get going if we're going to make court on time." Scott was the one that got sent to see where we were. "What's going on? Is everything okay?"

"Everything is perfect, bro." Craig said, snapping out of the doom and gloom. The devil was replaced by the angel.

"Can we go?" asked Scott.

"Yeah, go." I pushed Craig toward Scott and watched him head out the front door. I couldn't take my eyes away from my brothers who were followed by Sheree.

"Be good, sweetheart. Phone if you need us." My dad was just as bad as Brian, but I pushed him toward the door, before I broke down in tears.

My Brian walked to me and I flung my arms around him. I felt like I had been away from him for too long. I was kind of kicking myself

for telling him to go to court.

"Are you okay, Lee?" I pulled away from him and wiped my eyes. I was determined not to cry for the rest of my stay. "Lee?" Of course he was concerned, but for once there wasn't actually anything wrong. They were all happy hormonal tears.

"I'm just being silly. Do you have to go now?" I reached up and placed my lips over his. Our mouths became one and I needed to feel him with me. The tingles ran down my spine, as I leaned against the wall. His head rested against mine and I let my hands run up to unbutton his shirt buttons. "Surely you can be five minutes late." His mouth met mine again, as I still fumbled with his buttons. I was getting a dab hand at buttons, since he wore buttoned shirts most of the time.

"You know Miss Park, you certainly know how to get what you want."

"I'm just irresistible." I was swept off of my feet. I couldn't care where he took me, as long as we were going to be together. Our life together was going to be just perfect and I couldn't wait to get home to start living together like a family.

***

Watching him button his shirt back up, I wished I had never planned to have my friend over. I wanted to have that day together. Him and me, as we shared our love for one another.

"You do know that everyone is going to wonder where I am." I laughed and got up with the throw blanket wrapped around me. "Don't come over here and tease me or there will be no court and certainly no girlie day." I went up on my tip toes with no shoes on. I felt the pain in my ankle. Kissing him, was better pain relief than sitting down. "You're a tease Miss."

"A tease that you love."

"Did I tell you that?" I slapped his arm out of the playful remark. I only ended up in his arms with his tongue penetrating my mouth. "I do love you, Leela. More than anything in this world."

"Don't tell lies, Mr. Mackinnon." I moved away limping over to gather up all of my clothes and his hand caught mine.

"What do you mean, madam?"

"Don't lie. There's always going to be one thing that you love more." I could see the confusion wash over his face, as I moved his hand to my stomach. I could see the relief wash over his face. I knew with that look, that he felt like a moron.

"It's a different kind of love, doll. I'll never ever love anyone, as much as you, Leela. This little one will be showered with more love than any other child has ever seen. I have one thing to thank my mum for, she showed me how not to mess up my children's life."

"Children?" I gasped.

"Are you in one of those moods today?" I loved being able to have a laugh and a joke with Brian. We were like two peas in a pod and we just bounced off of one another.

"You better go, before someone sends out a search party." I had to get him to go or we would just end up in each other's arms all day.

"Call me if anything happens."

"Nothing is going to happen, Brian. You're as paranoid as Craig. I'm going to go and grab a bottle of wine for when Tracey comes around…" I could see his eyes widen in surprise and I couldn't help but wind him up, "…and a bottle of non-alcoholic something for me."

"I love you, Lee."

"I love you too." Our lips met again. As quickly as he was there with me, he was out in the hall grabbing my car keys and his jacket.

"See you soon."

"Bye." I felt like a little piece of me went away with him. I had never experienced anything like it before. I knew we were really meant to be and no one was going to stop us from being together.

CHAPTER 12
What Was Going To Happen Next?

I was annoyed with myself, because with everything that happened that morning, I left my phone upstairs. I thought I would have time to grab it and be back before Tracey got there. She called only five minutes ago and said she would be leaving soon.

As I got halfway back down the stairs, the doorbell rang again and again. She needed to slow down! It should of taken her about fifteen minutes to get here.

"Coming, Tracey!" I only had a sore ankle, but I was petrified of those stone stairs. Every step was taken with care trying to keep myself from falling. I finally got to the bottom and I breathed a sigh of relief that I made it in one piece. I went to open the door for my friend, but I was shocked to see who was standing in front of me. I

tried to speak, but I didn't know what to expect.

"Hi." It was the thug's mother who was at court the day I collapsed. I didn't know whether to be worried or not. I slipped my phone in my pocket without her noticing. Something told me this was going to end badly.

"You look shocked to see me." Her words rang in my ears. It was obvious that I never expected to see her.

"I am…I never expected…"

"I wanted to apologise, but noticed you haven't been in court." Now I was worried. Why would she go out of her way to come here?

"You don't need to apologise. It's fine." I went to shut the door, but she startled me by pushing it open, which made me walk backwards into the house. I knew that was nothing to do with an apology and I was petrified in my own surroundings. I hoped that Tracey would hurry up and save me.

"I wanted to come by and tell you how sorry I was about everything. You don't look so brave today." I wasn't. I had more to protect. I knew that I couldn't be arguing and bickering. I was supposed to be resting.

"I'm not feeling well. That's why I'm not at court. I'm going home to France on Saturday. You won't have to see me again."

"I heard your family congratulating your dead partner's brother. Is that right?" I managed a nod of my head without even speaking. "Kind of a funny story if you ask me. That kind of makes you a hypocrite."

"Hypocrite? How do you work that one out?" I felt my blood boiling inside of me. I was trying to stay calm until Tracey arrived. "Look. You said your piece and now I think you should go."

I went to walk past her, but she pushed me. I banged my head on the wall frame behind me. I crumbled, as my head felt like it was spinning. All I could think about was protecting my tiny little baby inside of me. I knew how much I needed rest.

"Please! Just go! I'll say I fell!" I was trying my hardest to get her out of my house.

"You get to live happily ever after, while my son rots in jail!"

"He deserves to rot in jail!" I stopped in my tracks, because I knew what she might be capable of. "He killed my fiancé! I lost my baby

and nearly died, because of the grief! You can't possibly say any of that was right!" She came flying at me and hauled me up onto my feet. I had no idea what felt worse, my head or my ankle. "Please, just go!"

"And let you lead a happy life with your dead partner's brother? Family! France! Future! You've landed on your feet. Haven't you, princess?" I saw her leg extend out and I managed to move to protect my stomach. I wasn't going to stand there and let her destroy me without a fight.

"I'm pregnant, you bitch!" I looked into her eyes and I could see that she didn't care about any of that. Then the doorbell sounded. I went to move, but I was still stuck with her in front of me. "Tracey! Help me! I took my eyes off of her to make sure all of my energy was shouting at the door. The next thing I heard was a crash and my head felt like it's going to burst open. Light was in and out and I had no idea what was going on.

***

I managed to open my eyes. I had tape over my mouth and my legs were tied together. I found it very weird that she didn't tie my hands up, but I stretched to lift my hand to my head. All I could feel was a thick sticky substance. I was panicking and felt my heart racing. I tried with all of my will to get up and move to see where she was, but I couldn't see or hear anything. I didn't hear the door either.

"Stay down, bitch! See what you made me do?"

"Is that where your son gets that saying from. *See what you made me do?* Those were his words to the police. Like mother, like son." I hoped that Tracey was still out there and she had been in contact with my dad. I don't think she would have had Brian's number yet, but she certainly had my dad's and Craig's. It was crazy what went through my head when I was thinking that someone was about to kill me. Now I knew what Craig was scared of that morning. Maybe he didn't know what was going to happen, but he certainly knew something was building up. "What do you want from me?"

"To see you suffer, like my son."

"Isn't this enough suffering? I was told any stress was going to put the baby at risk. You probably succeeded. If anything happens to my baby, I *will* suffer. Believe me. I will suffer." I was trying to plead with her mother to mother.

In a way, I understood her pain and anger.

"That was my friend at the door earlier and she would have called my dad." I felt my body getting weaker. I was feeling so cold. She caused damage to my head and I felt life slipping away from me.

I was talking to a brick wall. I used all of my psychology talking down techniques.

"Shit! The police!" I heard what she was saying, but I felt nothing. I felt like there was no ounce of energy or fight left in me. "Get up!" I felt every bit of my body ache, as she dragged me into the kitchen area. My body was flung back down to the floor like a piece of rubbish. I couldn't believe that someone could treat a human being like that. I had been sheltered from the evil in this world until our paths crossed. Was this going to be my fate?

***

"Brian! Put your foot down! We get stopped and you'll be fine." Shouted Craig.

"Craig! I couldn't give a fuck about a fine or points on my licence! I'm going as fast as I can! I'm doing sixty in a thirty zone." I knew I shouldn't have left today. I should have stayed with her when I had the chance. Court could have waited. We could have spent the day together making love and pigging out on junk food. I would never forgive myself if anything happened to her or the baby. "Did Tracey say anything else?"

"Dad said she heard Leela shouting for help. Dad told her where the spare key was, but the chain was on and the other key was in the door. After Leela shouted, she heard a smash and a thud."

"Have you guys had any bother at work from anyone?" I wanted to know what we were dealing with. I would face Goliath for Leela and our baby.

"No." Craig didn't sound too sure. I couldn't take my eyes off the road at the speed I was doing.

"Craig. What is it?"

"Did you see that thug's mum today?" I thought for a split second and I knew I had, but I saw her leave in a hurry? We pulled onto our street and there were blue lights everywhere. We couldn't get through the cordon, so I pulled over and exited the car quicker than Craig. The car was left on and the door was open. I had one thing on my mind and that was Leela. Craig knew the cops and we got under the cordon down to the house where Tracey was hysterical.

"Why are you all standing here?" Craig couldn't believe what he was seeing and neither could I, to be honest.

"We have no idea who's in there with your sister," said some big shot who thought he knew everything.

"So fucking what!" screamed Craig

"Craig. You know the drill."

"That's not the same when its family. We'll go in there. I'll die for my sister." I felt his pain, because I would have done the same thing. Then Frank and the rest of the family came and surrounded us.
"Dad! Tell them me and Brian will go in there. Tell them!"

"It isn't safe Craig. You know the drill." I couldn't believe that Frank was saying the same thing. We didn't have time for that. We needed to get to Leela.

"Fuck the drill, dad!" I took hold of Craig's arm and moved a few feet away from everyone. Just to make it look like I was trying to calm him down.

"How do we do this?" He was with me. We weren't going to stand by and let Leela die.

"We run as fast as possible. Once we are near the house, they're chicken shit and won't come near. They are waiting for armed backup. We can go round the back and see if we can see what's going on. Get a feel for what we are up against. If it's more than one, we could have a fight on our hands. If it's the mother, we break the door in. We have no idea what state Leela is in, so prepare yourself for the worst, Brian." I didn't want to hear any of that, but I supposed I was going to have to face life up straight and realise that I could have lost my one and only reason for existing.

"I'm ready."

"On my three. One…two…three! Go!" We were off like a shot.

Craig pushed an officer out of his way. I never felt adrenaline like that in my life. I had one thing on my mind and that was all I needed in order to do this. We got around the back of the house. There were patio doors that gave us a view into the kitchen. “The blinds should be drawn enough not to get us caught, but enough for us to see what we’re facing.”

I somehow managed to crawl up to the door and looked in. I jumped back in shock with tears filling my eyes.

“What is it? Brian! Damn it! What is it?”

“Leela! She’s on the ground covered in blood!” The blood made my heart race even more. We had no choice, but to get to her and quick.

“Did you see anyone else?”

“The woman only.” I felt like my heart was breaking already. I had to get to her and I had to get to her now. We got up and ran back round to the front of the house. I composed myself, while Craig beckoned to the paramedics to be on standby. Frank knew with the state I was in, that something was bad. He walked down to Craig and me.

“What is it?” Frank asked.

“Leela’s in a bad way, dad. She’s…”

“She’s what, Craig?”

“I saw her on the ground. Her head is covered in blood and there are smears of blood on different parts of the floor.” I had to be brave enough for both me and Craig.

“Who is it?”

“The mother.”

“Only the mother?” Frank’s police training was ticking through his head.

“That’s all I could see.” I couldn’t care how many are in there. We’re going in to get Leela out.

“Okay. Wait and I’ll get you right tools to get the door open.” I couldn’t believe that Frank was going against the rules to help us. He was gone in seconds and back with what looked like his boss behind him.

“Frank. If they go in there, you won’t see another day with this force,” said the top police officer.

"My daughter is more important than this force! You saved me from telling you that I'm retiring. I'm putting no other men at danger. It will be my son and son-in-law." Hearing Frank like that, made us all see how much his family meant to him.

"One of who, isn't trained."

"I'm trained enough to help my wife and child." I could see the boss throw his head back and put his hand on Frank's shoulder. He was now on board. We didn't need his permission, but it helped to have it.

"Do you need a hand?" I looked round to see a police woman standing with her full uniform on.

"I can't put your career at stake for me, partner." Hearing Craig call her partner, made me remember when Leela told me his new partner was a woman.

"We're partners. Where you go, I go." I could see the look exchanged between Craig and the officer. I was grateful for her to put her career on line for us. "Craig. I'm in."

"Good. When I say three, we just ram the door. Brian, you go in the middle if you're going with us. We'll keep you right." I took a deep breath and prepared myself. "When we get in Brian, you go for Leela. Just get her out. Give me your cuffs, chief." I was oblivious to all of it. I felt relief when the chief gave him his cuffs and we were on our way to the door. What happened when that door was open, was anyone's guess.

"On three. One…two…three." The door was battered open and I knew where I was going. I headed right to Leela and was relieved when she opened her eyes when I went to lift her.

"It's okay, sweetheart. I'm getting you out of here." I knew I could hurt her by lifting her, but I thought of that after we were out.

"She's crazy!" I heard the fear in Leela's voice and my heart broke at the thought of her going through this.

"Don't worry, darling. I have you."

"I can't, Mark. Brian…get me Brian." I wasn't sure what she was saying, but I crumbled the minute I got her outside. I felt like I was losing her for real this time. "Brian…" Her voice was weak.

"I'm here, darling. Leela. Open your eyes. I'm here, sweetie." Her eyes fluttered open. The glaze over them made me think that she

couldn't see, but her head tilted to me and her hand lifted up and it was placed on my cheek. I was relieved.

"The paramedics are here, darling. They're going to take care of you and the baby." I heard Frank do my job and reassure her. I shot him a look, because we both knew the state she was in. It was highly likely there was a problem with the baby.

"Hi Leela. My name is Marcus and this is Maria. We're going to help you. Do you know who this big strapping man is holding you?" I wanted to smile at him, but I just couldn't.

"Mark…" The tears fell down my face and I felt Frank's hand on my shoulder for support. I wasn't sure how we were going to manage if the head injury had caused serious damage.

"Are you Mark?" All I could do was shake my head.

"Marcus. Mark was Leela's dead partner," Frank said, with a grim tone.

"Sorry. How could I forget? She might have heard me tell her my name."

"She was mumbling my name and Mark's name in the house. I don't know." They all could see that I was in despair. I loved her more than anything.

"Leela. Can you open your eyes for me?" We sat and waited for her to follow Maria's orders.

"We're trying to establish what extent the head injury is. The sooner Maria has gotten her questions asked, we'll move her to hospital." I was listening to Marcus trying to stay in the loop but I didn't want to hear anything other than that she was going to be okay.

"Leela. Look over here. Can you tell me who this handsome man is comforting you?" I watched, as her eyes moved up to me. I couldn't keep the tears away. "I wish I was in his arms. He looks nice and comfortable." Maria sounded like she knew what she was doing. I didn't have any concern there.

"He is." Her hand came up and wiped my tears away. It was so soft and gentle, but I could feel how weak she was. "What are you crying for?" She never stopped amazing me.

"Leela. Do you know who this is?" Maria wasn't letting her get away with not giving proper answers.

"Of course I do."

"Who is he, sweetie?"

"Brian." I must have had the biggest smile on my face. Nothing else mattered at that second.

"What relationship is Brian to you?" I watched her shrug her shoulders and smile like she had just remembered something.

"He's my partner. Fiancé." They were looking at me to confirm all of it and all I could do was nod my head. I couldn't take my eyes off of Leela. "Stop crying! I'm fine. I'm not ready to go any where." She looked away over to the other side of her and there was nothing there that she was smiling at. But I was surprised when she took the oxygen mask off and pulled my shirt down to her. Her cold soft lips rested on my lips.

"Keep your mask on, honey. You have a head injury and we need to get you to hospital." Maria smiled as Leela tried to sit up. I was over joyed to see her enthusiasm, but I wasn't sure if it was a smart thing to do.

"Where do you think you're going, missy? I need to put this neck brace on you, because of your head. You should be on a pat slide, but if you could move like that you should be okay. Are you sore anywhere?" Maria looked surprised that we had come so far in just five minutes.

"My head. My legs."

"You can feel your legs, which is a great sign. Your dad told us that you're pregnant. Can you tell us about it?" Everything the paramedics said, sank in and reality hit her.

"She tied my legs up and threw me to the ground after she pushed me and I hit my head." We all just realised that her legs were still tied up. Marcus cut her out of her binds quickly.

"Did you get any injury to your stomach?"

"Not apart from her throwing me to the ground. I couldn't save myself. Is she alive?"

"She? Do you know what you're having?"

"No. Everyone seems to think they know though." I smiled at her response. "I can't tell you if the baby is okay. The only way to detect the heartbeat is an ultrasound. Try not to worry. You're not haemorrhaging. That's a good sign." I wanted to believe that the

paramedic was right. But going on our track record, it was highly unlikely. "Marcus is getting the trolley from the ambulance."

"Something told me not to leave you today, Lee. I'm so sorry." I managed to free one of my hands and wipe the tears away from her face. I couldn't believe how calm she was. It was like she was in a little bubble and she was content.

"I planned today, Brian. None of this is your fault."

"Leela. How are you doing?" I looked at the paramedic. Her voice had concern in it and I knew something wasn't right.

"Yeah. I'm okay. Why?" The fact that Leela was answering questions, was surely a good sign.

"Your blood pressure just dropped quite a bit. That's all. We'll soon have you at hospital." I couldn't help but panic. Her blood pressure did the same thing the first time she lost her baby. It was like Deja vu all over again, but this time Leela was actually mine to concern myself about.

"Brian. I'm going to be fine. Don't ask me how I know, but I just do." I couldn't contain my fear and worry no matter how much I tried. The whole thing was like a movie. I expected someone to say *cut*, any moment, but it was all real life.

"How long are you back home for, Leela?" I was glad the paramedic was there because I was still gobsmacked. I was struggling to share Leela's enthusiasm. Maria knew that as well.

"We got early flights book for Saturday. Will I still be able to go?"

"Let's see what happens when we get you to hospital. If it's just a sore neck and concussion, I don't see why not. The doctors will be able to tell you more."

"I feel like I've lived in hospital this week. I should move my bed there."

"Why? What happened, Leela?" I knew that Maria was just trying to keep her talking.

"I was at court, but I was feeling unwell beforehand. But… I had an argument with her and I went outside and collapsed. That's how I twisted my ankle and found out about the baby. It was the doctor's orders that made us book early flights. His orders that made me stay in the house alone today."

"Well, I'm sure the doctor will be able to discharge you when we

get you checked over."

"How is she doing, Brian?" I was glad of the distraction when Frank interrupted us. I wasn't sure what to say.

"She's…" I couldn't find the words to tell him how she was.

"I'm fine." I could feel the relief, as Frank bent down beside us. His hand took Leela's.

"What are you waiting for?" I could hear the police tone coming from Frank. I did understand what he meant because we had been like this for a while.

"Marcus is getting the trolley. We couldn't get down here, so he shouldn't be too long now. I was saying to Brian and Leela, that her blood pressure has dropped and I was a little bit concerned. Leela is responsive and she isn't complaining of any pain anywhere other than her head and neck. She should have been on a pat slide, but since she was brought out she has tried to sit up. Her legs are moving. I'm not concerned about her back. I put a neck brace on just for precaution. The oxygen is also a precaution, because she wasn't responsive. But I'm happy with everything else. I'm not giving her pain relief just yet, because of the baby. When she gets to hospital, the first thing they will do is an ultrasound and CT scan of her neck and head. I'm telling you so you don't get to the hospital and panic." Maria had been fantastic with us all.

"Thank you, Maria, I bet they miss you in the hospital." Maria was too qualified to be a paramedic.

"They're always at me to go back, but I'm happy in the field." I was listening to Frank and Maria talking away and glad that the situation was relaxed enough.

"Leela. You're going to feel a sharp prick, because I am going to hook you up to I.V. fluids. That will help your blood pressure also."

"Sorry guys. It felt like a mile away to get back to the ambulance. I was going to drive, but there was no way I was getting any closer. I called the hospital and told them to get head and neck CT organised and abdominal ultrasound to check for baby's heartbeat. It's the same doctor that was on a couple of days ago. He recognised your name, Leela." That was something I suppose. At least he knew Leela and the situation.

"I am just trying to get a vein to hook her up to fluids and we are

good to go."

"Cool. It has been your lucky day, Leela, Maria here is a fully qualified doctor and she has been out with me for a few months now." Marcus was always a good one to have in that kind of situation.

"I kind of thought she was too qualified to be out here." We all smiled at Leela's honesty. That was one thing that hadn't changed. I was still cradling her in my arms. I just wanted to get to hospital so we knew what we were facing.

"We're ready." I was relieved to hear Maria tell us that.

"I brought the pat slide with me. I don't know how you want to do this." Marcus wasn't going to start taking over. We were lucky to get two paramedics that were so great at their job.

"Leela. How are you feeling?"

"Okay."

"I am going to help you sit up straight, is that ok?" I looked at Maria with great concern. I didn't want to underestimate her, but I was concerned about Leela and the baby. Frank was standing at the trolley and I tried to relax. "Give Marcus both of your hands. I'm going to count to three and then sit you into an upright position. Tell me about any pain straight away. Okay?"

"Okay."

"One…two…three." It was all I have heard today. I would be glad if I never heard one, two, and three again. "How are you feeling, Leela?" The silence made me move so that I could see her face. I knew Leela might be able to con the paramedics, but she wouldn't be able to con me.

"Lee. Are you okay, babe?"

"Yeah. Just felt a little bit sick, but it's easing off now."

"That's part of the concussion. I'll get you a sick bowl when we get back to the ambulance." I managed to smile at Marcus, who was still holding both of Leela's hands. He wasn't going to let her go, until he knew she was stable.

"Do you think you will be able to Stand Leela?" Again I thought Maria was having a laugh, but I could see that she was being deadly serious. I know she was a doctor and I needed to trust her instinct, but I couldn't.

"I think so." I knew how stubborn Leela was and she wasn't going to show defeat at anything they asked her. I just didn't want her to push herself too far.

"Ok. Brian can you help me to get her to weight bare on her feet. Marcus is going to be in front of you and we are not going to let you fall." I was shocked when we all helped Leela onto her feet. She was either being brave or she wasn't as bad as we all initially thought. "How do you feel Leela?" I was glad Maria knew what she was doing because I felt completely helpless.

"I'm ok…My ankle is just the same."

"Do you think that you can walk, or Marcus can bring the trolley right here?"

"No it's only there, I can walk." I wasn't surprised to hear Leela say that.

"I am going to let your hands go and Maria and Brian, are going to keep you safe. God help you when she in labour Brain, because she has some grip just now." I couldn't help but laugh at Marcus. I couldn't wait to experience Leela in labour. There was a part of me that wanted to believe that the baby was going to be fine, but I had my doubts. Once we got over to the trolley I helped her mostly to get her comfortable. The back rest was made higher, and seeing her sitting up on this trolley with dry blood down her face, just made my insides cringe at what could of happened, and what still could happen. But I never let go of her hand while Maria and Marcus got everything sorted. They were so thorough with everything and I would never be able to thank them enough for everything they have done for Lee.

"Ok Leela, how are you feeling now sweetheart?" Maria, was still making sure Leela was stable. The light that she flashed in her eye's just made them sparkle more.

"I feel much better, believe it or not."

"Your blood pressure is coming back up. We will keep this oxygen going and the fluids and we're good to go."

"Leela, there is a lot of press already gathered. Now we will do everything we can to get you to the ambulance as quick as we can." I was glad that Marcus was preparing us for the pack of wolves. They were quick to get here like that.

"Frank, is there no way your men can keep them away from her. She has been through enough, and I am just getting her vital signs stable." Maria, wasn't shy that was for sure. Frank never questioned her any way. He went ahead of us, and spoke to a few police officers. They run ahead up to the cordon and done their thing. I couldn't believe how great one paramedic could be.

"How are you feeling, Lee?" I picked up the courage to finally ask the important question that I dreaded hearing her say.

"I'm fine. Honestly. I feel like I could sleep for a week though."

"If you're making progress and everything is okay, then the doctor might discharge you to your own bed tonight." Marcus was trying to make Leela more at ease and he certainly knew what to say to her. It was getting to the ambulance and away from the press, that I was more concerned about , but Leela and I would face whatever was in front of us, because that's what we do. As long as we had each other, we would get through anything.

***

It felt like we had all been sitting hours in the hospital waiting room. Maria showed us to a relative's room so we didn't have to sit in the main waiting area. At first it was just me, because I came in the ambulance with Leela. Then Frank, Craig, Scott, and Sheree joined us. There had hardly been any words spoken since we arrived, but we had the same questions on our minds. How was Leela going to be after all her tests? How was the baby? I hated leaving her when we came in, but she went right through to the treatment room. Marcus stayed with me and Maria went right through with Leela. I was relieved when Maria came back and showed me to the room. The full A&E department was busy and I don't think I would have been able to cope, sitting around everyone covered in blood. Scott brought me a cardigan from the house, which made me feel a little bit better.

The room was like ice. One word would have broken the ice and shattered us all. But I sat with my head leaning against the wall, looking up at the ceiling.

"Have you heard anything?" Maria opened the door and peeked

her head around. She had obviously been on another call and came right back to see if we knew anything.

"Heard nothing. Can't you find out what's going on?" I was glad that Frank was open enough to ask Maria. I wouldn't have had the guts to ask her to do something else for us after all of her help.

"I'll go and see what's going on." I sat forward and placed my head in my hands looking at the ground. I went from one extreme to the next. I just didn't know what to do with myself.

"What will happen to that cow that did this dad?" Scott was the first one to ask a question. He was like me. He wasn't clued up with police procedures.

"She'll join her son in prison for a long time. Attempted murder. Hostage situation. She could face a few years." I just couldn't understand what went through people's minds to do things like that. "She hasn't got any priors, so it may be seen as desperation for her son."

"Are you kidding?" I couldn't help but jump in after hearing that. Craig put his hand on my shoulder. "Less time, because she hadn't been arrested. Leela is strong willed, but there's only so much that she can take. If she loses this baby..."

"She has us all around her, Brian. As long as she has you, she'll get through anything." Frank was always positive. I wondered what it would take to make him crack.

"She shouldn't have to get through anything, Frank. None of this should have happened in the first place. I should never have left her."

"Brian. None of us should have left her. It isn't your fault, bro." Hearing Craig stick up for me, just made me feel worse. If I stayed with her that morning none of it would have happened.

"Brian. Do you want to come with me?" I looked up at Maria. I didn't know what I was going to hear. I stopped in the doorway and looked at Leela's family. Each and every one of them had a look of dread. I knew I had to go and find out what was happening, one way or another. "Don't look so worried, Brian." I wish that I had Maria's confidence. Either she knew everything was okay, or she was just doing her job and trying to reassure me.

"I'm a nervous wreck, Maria." She opened this swinging door and

I followed her in, as she held the door open for me.

I saw curtains drawn. I just knew drawn curtains meant bad news. I took a deep breath and followed her behind the curtains. Whatever was to come, was going to be okay.

"Hi Brian. How are you?" I shook the doctor's hand.

As Leela heard my name being mentioned, she opened her eyes and looked until she found where I was standing.

"I'll be better when I know what's going on, doc."

"I understand. I'm sorry that I have kept you so long." I went and took Leela's hand in mine. She looked refreshed, now that she had been cleaned up. She even had nice rosy cheeks. "Well, we've fixed the cut on Leela's head. The good news is that there's no swelling to the brain. The CT scan has come back clear from any fractures or bleeding. Her sore head is a result of concussion and the gash that she had. Leela even said that she feels much better already."

"That's such a relief," was all I could say.

"I just strapped her ankle up for some support, since it has been hurt more than once this week. It was very swollen and bruised. I know you'll make her rest when you get home. Leela told me that you were going home on Saturday. I think that will be the best thing for her. I will give her a letter to say that she can fly on Saturday." I felt like I was floating on a cloud. I thought I was going to lose her.

"I don't know what to say!"

"Maria. Put the neck brace on as a precaution." I looked down at Leela and couldn't help but kiss her. I felt so fortunate. "What I'm sure you're both dying to know is how the baby is doing." I looked at Lee and then the doctor. Maria stood beside the doctor. It felt like the good news was about to fade. "When I saw Leela after her collapse the other day, the baby was in the right place and that was the main thing. Earlier, when she arrived here I did a quick ultrasound to make sure the baby was okay. I'm overjoyed to tell you that these babies are fighters." Did he say, *babies*?

I couldn't have heard any better news right now. I watched the doctor, as he rolled Leela's top up high enough to pour jelly on her stomach. We were going to get to see the baby again and I couldn't wait.

I was actually surprised, because Leela had a pudgy little stomach.

Something I've not seen before.

"The reason I told you to go and get checked out when you got back to France, was because things change quickly in early pregnancy and it's just to keep an eye on things until you get past twelve weeks. When I scanned you today I was surprised. I looked at the screen where his pen pointed and he showed us the baby's clear heartbeat. Then he moved his pen over another little bit. Leela and I followed the doctor's pen carefully. "I didn't see it, because it was hiding behind the other one." I didn't follow what the doctor was saying, but I was looking at the screen hoping that something would jump out and tell me what I was looking at.

"Are you saying there are two heartbeats?" I looked down at Leela. I was concerned that there was something wrong if the baby had two heartbeats. I just wasn't following what I was seeing.

"I am Leela. They are little fighters and they're meant to be here." Why were they talking plural? He mentioned babies earlier, but it didn't register.

"Brian. Do you understand what the doctor is saying?" I was glad that Maria could see that I was confused. I couldn't understand what I was seeing. I managed to shake my head and look down at Leela' smiling face. I was definitely missing something.

"Brian." I looked down at Leela and managed to take my eyes off the screen for a moment. "There are two heartbeats, because there are two babies. We're having twins!" Twins. Was that some kind of joke? I managed a smile, as I looked back at the screen where the doctor pointed out the two heartbeats again.

"Twins. Two." I was letting it all sink in. Maria congratulated Leela and I, then exited the room. The doctor cleared all of the gel away, as I watched the big smile on his face.

"I'll go and get all your letters sorted. We'll keep an eye on you for a couple of hours. We'll get you moved out of here to a room of your own and then your family can come and see you. Brian. You're fine as you are. I'll leave the curtains drawn."

"Thank you, doctor. I don't know how to thank you." I leaned over and shook his hand. I just couldn't believe that we had gone through what we did and we still came out the other end smiling.

When my thoughts cleared, we were on our own and I leaned over

Leela. I put my hand on her cheek and tried to relax. I have never seen her look so exhausted before. She wasn't going to lift another finger for the next several months.

"Leela. I feel like the luckiest person alive! You have gone through all of this and I feel guilty for being happy." It was so weird.

"Don't feel guilty, honey. I have gone through this and I'm happy as well." I placed my free hand over her tummy and looked at it as if the babies were going to talk to me. "It's crazy. Isn't it?"

"Crazy. I can't believe that we are going to have twins." Even saying it out loud didn't make it sound less crazy.

"You jinxed us by saying children this morning."

"Yeah." We were both laughing. Then Leela held her head with her hand. I hated to see her in pain. I was going to cope with her giving birth to not one, but two babies. "No laughing for the next few days." Just saying that made us both giggle. "I better go and fill the rest of the family in on everything. They're going crazy with worry."

"No! Don't leave me! We can fill them in when I get moved. Just don't leave me Brian!" I heard the terror in her voice. I was glad that we were going home on Saturday. Maybe then she would be able to relax in the comfort of her own home.

"Leela. I'm never going to leave your side. Just don't worry about anything, sweetheart. No one is ever going to hurt you again." She sat slightly forward and took me in her arms. I felt like I was so lucky to be there getting all of that good news. We were never going to feel settled, while we were still in Scotland. Fear was a terrible thing and it wasn't going to be put to the back of our minds, while we were still there. The countdown to going back to France had begun.

CHAPTER 13
Our Final Farewell

"AARRRGGGHHH." I woke up with Brian lying over the top of me, breaking me out of the terrible nightmare I was having.

"Leela! You're okay, sweetheart. You're at home." His bare skin touching me, made me realise that I was okay. I thought that coming home tonight was going to be the best thing for me. For the first time in my life, I didn't feel safe in my childhood home anymore.

"I'm sorry." I was more relieved to know that I was there with Brian and no one else.

"For what?" he asked softly.

"Waking you."

"Don't be silly, doll. You've been through so much today. It's to be expected. I will never let anything hurt you again." I knew he meant everything he was saying. I didn't want to push him away.

I suddenly felt in the pit of my stomach that I was going to be sick. I managed to stumble out of bed and limp my way to the bathroom. I was glad that it was vacant. The whole house was silent. I was surprised I didn't wake everyone up, screaming like a banshee. However, I made the toilet in time and I felt like I was bringing my insides out. Only trouble was, I didn't eat anything to bring up. The minute I felt Brian wrap my housecoat round my shoulders, his hand rubbed my back. I wanted to tell him to go, but I didn't want to be there on my own.

"What can I do to help you, Lee?" All I managed to do was shake my head, because I felt like I couldn't speak. I managed to get up, flush the toilet, and take myself to the sink to wash my mouth out. I hated being sick. It was one of the worst things ever. Staring at myself in the mirror, I was glad I looked better than I felt. I was happier when Brian came up behind me. He was going to be with me through thick and thin and by the look of things, the pregnancy was going to take its toll on me. "Feel better?"

"A bit." I managed a smile, as his hands met in the middle at my stomach. I knew in just a short time, he wasn't going to be able to do that.

"It looks like these two are going to give mummy a hard time," he said, proudly.

"And you, If you get up every time with me." I didn't mean to sound nasty, but turning toward his frame was more comfortable. My head rested on his chest, as his heartbeat soothed me back down.

"When are you going to accept that we're in this together, missy?"

"Maybe when you take me back to bed and never let me out of your arms." His hand lifted my face up to him and his lips parted mine. I would never give him a kiss with me just being sick, but it felt nice to have that intimacy back. He took my hand and led me back into our room. I knew it was still early in the morning, because it was pitch black throughout the house. It was hard to believe it was the same house where all hell broke loose. While my aching body was laid back into bed, his arms wrapped around me. "I love you, Brian."

"I love you to, Lee. I thought I was never going to be able to do this again." I lifted my head up to meet his. Although the room was

dark, I could feel his gaze on me. My hand ran across his cheek. He managed to kiss it softly.

"If I tell you something, will you promise not to think I'm going crazy?" His silence worried me.

"Leela. I nearly lost you three times. I think crazy follows us, but that's why I love you. You're going to be my wife and mother of my babies. I don't want us to have secrets."

"When I was knocked out today, I felt like I was losing my battle. I was cold and felt every inch of my body die. When you got to me, I saw…Mark."

"That was why you were talking to him." I didn't believe that it was going to be so easy.

"I wasn't ready to leave you. I'll never ever be ready to leave you. I love you with every ounce of my soul and I want us to get married." I lifted up to be up closer to him, but winced with the aches in my body. "Don't tell me I stunned you to silence."

"I don't know what to say, Lee."

"Tell me that you want the same and we'll draw a line under today and move on with our life from now on."

"Of course, I want the same. I felt second best to Mark before…" I leaned over and turned on my lamp. I couldn't believe that I was hearing that.

"Are you being serious?" I didn't know if I felt angry or upset.

"I love you Leela and you know that I'll go to the end of the earth for you and our future, but to hear you say that you wanted me over Mark, just shocked me."

"Brian. I agreed to marry you. I have fallen head over heels in love with you. I'm carrying not one, but two of your babies. What more can I offer you?"

"Nothing Lee. You've done it all. I want us to go back to Marseille and get married before our beautiful twins come along. I want to do it all properly. I love you." I heard enough. I pulled his mouth down to me and our tongues touched together. I felt like it had been so long since we were like that. Back home, we would sleep together more, but here something always cropped up. "Lee. We can't." I looked directly into his eyes. He wanted it just as much as I did. "You need rest."

"I need you." His mouth leaned in and kissed my neck. My body relaxed instantly. My hands rubbed along his chest, as he stopped and looked at me.

"Are you sure about this?" he asked.

"I never had this much bother to get you to sleep with me before."

"You haven't been pregnant with twins before."

"I was this morning. So, what's the real problem, Brian?"

"I don't want to hurt you…or them."

"The only way you're going to hurt me, is by pushing me away. This has been the first time today that I haven't felt sick or bloated. In a few weeks, you're not going to want me, because I'll be a fat whale."

"Stop. I want you now. I will want you when you are a whale. I want to make love to you every time I lay eyes on you." I felt his body leaning over me and I could feel his package on my leg. I knew that he wanted me, as much as I did him. I needed to reassure him that I was fine. His hands slipped up my vest top. "If I'm hurting you at any time just tell me and we'll stop."

"Shhh." He was so soft and gentle with me, like I was a flower that was going to break. He lifted my top over my head. I was surprised at how he managed it. His soft lips caressed my breasts. He then moved and kissed every inch of my stomach, until he took my bottom half off. Before I knew it we were both completely naked and every spot that he touched was completely electrifying. I hadn't wanted him as much, as I wanted him then. His hand reached down into my soft spot and I was ready. I needed it. Our mouths were as one and our breathing was all over the place, until I felt him slowly enter me inch by inch. Every piece of me that he touched set me wild. The slow thrusting made my body climax almost instantly, as he continued to treat me like that fragile flower. I felt like I was going to explode with him thrusting inside of me. His moans with mine, made me feel his desire to be with me. As the final thrust made our bodies climax together, I was breathless and on fire. Our bodies laid together. It was just our legs that were tangled together, as he moved any weight off of my stomach. I felt my heart pounding, but the gentlest kisses on my neck made me giggle.

"No laughing. It hurts your head."

"Surprisingly, my head isn't sore at the moment. You know what that means, Mr. Mackinnon?"

"What?" His head lifted up and leaned on his arm, as his twinkling eyes looked directly into mine.

"Every time my head hurts, you have to make love to me."

"Is that so? I'm glad you find yourself funny, missy. I will be glad to help your head though."

"I'm glad to hear it. Do you know what I want now?"

"What?" His voice was sounding shaky, because he was terrified to know what I wanted. I couldn't help but laugh again.

"Don't sound so terrified. I was only going to say I want to cuddle into you so I can sleep peacefully."

"That, I can do. I better get all the cuddles in before these two put a big wedge between us." I slapped his arm in a playful protest. I rested my head onto his chest and I felt really sleepy. "Try and get some sleep babe. You've been up and down all night." I couldn't speak. I was so relaxed that I didn't want to move until it was time to get up.

***

I managed to get off the bed and make myself decent, without waking Leela. It was only nine in the morning, but I was going to leave her sleep for a while. She had such a disturbed night and needed all the rest she could get. I couldn't believe that I gave in and made love to her. She drove a hard bargain, but it did settle her down and she had a couple of hours of undisturbed sleep.

Once I was out of the room, I heard someone banging downstairs. It dawned on me that the door was only made secure for the night. I hoped that none of it disturbed Leela. I ignored the work men and went into the kitchen where Frank and Craig were sitting and drinking coffee.

"Good morning, son. How's Leela?"

"I crawled out of the room to let her sleep. She was up and down all night, but the last three maybe four hours she slept."

"I heard her screaming a couple of times," explained Frank. I thought no one heard her, but Frank obviously knew that I would

have taken care of her. I was honoured that he let me take care of his girl.

"I heard her being sick, but I didn't get up, because I heard you follow her. You must be shattered, Brian," said Craig, who looked just as tired as I was.

"It's a small price to pay to have her here with us."

"You're right, son. I was going to cancel the gathering today. What do you think?" I was surprised to hear Frank asking me. I didn't know what to say.

"I don't know, Frank. I think it will do Leela good. She isn't planning on coming back to Scotland, so it would be a good thing for her to see everyone she's closest to under the same roof."

"You know me too well, Mr. Mackinnon." We were all shocked to see Leela coming into the kitchen. I expected her to sleep for a while. But I opened my arms to her, as she leaned in and kissed me.

"How are you feeling?"

"I need a coffee and I'm hungry, so that's a good start." I couldn't stop smiling at her, as I pulled a seat out for her. She looked over at the floor and froze. I felt her body stiffen in my arms.

"Leela, darling? Are you ok?" We could all hear Frank's fear, as I touched her cheek to try to snap her out of her trance.

"I need to go and get a shower." I looked at Craig and Frank. None of us said a word. I quickly caught up with her in the hall where she was watching the men replacing the door.

"Leela? Are you okay, babe?" I could feel her shaking underneath her robe. "Leela?"

"I need to get out of here, Brian."

"Okay. Where do you want to go?"

"I can't stay here, Brian. I can't." I took her trembling body into my arms. I hated to see her like that.

"You don't have to stay here. I can book us into a hotel for tonight. Listen to me, Lee. I'm going to run you a bath. I'll come back and get you a coffee and something to eat. We can pack our things and after our goodbye gathering, we can go to the hotel. Okay?"

"Okay, but I feel pathetic."

"You're not pathetic, Leela."

"Hey, sis. You're not pathetic." I was pleased when Craig came

out into the hall. "Go and do everything Brian said. Dad's going to make you both coffee and breakfast and I'll bring it up to your room."

"Thanks, Craig." I kept Leela in my arms and headed toward the stairs. She didn't acknowledge Craig and that wasn't like her. Her ankle was a lot better, because she was quicker on her feet. I took her right back into our room and sat her down on the bed. "What do you say we have a couple of hours curled up in here? There are no bad reminders in here and Craig is going to bring us breakfast."

I was thrilled to see her relax again, as she moved back up the bed. I threw the cover back over her and relaxed slightly. I sat on top of the covers beside her. Her head relaxed perfectly on my chest just like always. Tomorrow wasn't coming quick enough. I would breathe a sigh a relief when the plane started to take off, because a week here felt like an eternity.

***

I came back from having a shower and I couldn't believe how beautiful Leela was looking. She did her hair all down to one side, so I couldn't see the gash in her head. Her make-up was naturally done and she was dressed with jeans and a lovely red top off of her shoulder. I didn't want to make a big deal of it, but she was stunningly beautiful.

"I didn't pack any of your clothes in the wardrobe, because I wasn't sure what you wanted to put on."

"I'm going the same way you are, babe."

"Red top and jeans would suit you." I walked up to her and wrapped my arms around her. I loved to feel her in my arms. I was going to love seeing her stomach bloom, as our babies grew inside her.

"You are so beautiful, Lee. Now I know what a pregnancy glow means."

"Is that a compliment?"

"Always. I've never seen you do your hair like this before."

"It hides that horrible cut. I'm lucky I have dark hair." She didn't feel good about herself and it was going to be my mission to make

her feel good.

"It's gorgeous just like it is. It's just a shame that you're all ready for dinner. I could quite easily take those clothes off of you." I stroked her bare shoulder where the top was hinging off and I placed soft gentle kisses all the way up her neck. I had the same urge that she must have had in the night. It was so powerful.

"Are you trying to seduce me, mister?"

"Am I succeeding?"

"You will always succeed if you try hard enough." I loved to hear her playful tone. I knew we had plenty of time to spend together, before we had to go to our farewell gathering. I placed my hand underneath her top and I could feel her body relax. I knew she wasn't going to resist me. She turned around and placed her hands around my neck, as our mouths became one. I hated the idea of a quickie, but we needed this. I pulled the top over her head to leave a red lace strapless bra shouting at me to be removed. I only had a towel wrapped around my waist. Which she cheekily pulled it off and let it drop to the ground. I was surprised how easy it was to undress her without any effort. I laid her slowly and softly down onto the bed. Without any hesitation, I entered her softly. Just hearing her cries of pleasure, made me satisfied. I entered her with every thrust and became more lost in our passion. The power grew inside of me, until I couldn't contain it anymore. Our bodies laid on the edge of the bed wrapped around one another. I was so in love with this woman that it hurt. I lifted from her and placed soft kisses on her stomach, as she sat up and placed a tender kiss on my mouth.

"I hope, in twenty years we can still be so in love."

"I promise that I'll love you forever, even when I take my last breath." Our mouths became one again, as she took my towel and wrapped it around her. She left me standing in oblivion. I couldn't believe the love I had for one person, could be so powerful.

***

Half an hour later, we were both fully clothed. Leela was just as breath-taking, as she was the first time I saw her when I entered the room after my shower. I was going to find it hard keeping my hands

off of her, while we were out with our friends and family. Again, I had that urge in the pit of my stomach, but I knew if we carried on we were never going to make it for a lovely meal.

"I already feel fat just putting these jeans on." I sat on the bed and wrapped my hands around her waist, as she sat on my knee.

"Will you stop thinking that you're going to be anything but beautiful? I'm going to love seeing you bloom, as our two gorgeous little babies grow inside you."

"You just know all the right things to say." She stood up and lifted her hand bag. That was my sign to tell me she was ready.

I was glad to see her so eager to go out. We were the only ones left in the house, because everyone was going to meet us at the restaurant. I felt like I was taking ages to catch up with Leela, but tying my shoes had to be done. We had enough of hospitals for the week.

I stood up and took the stairs nearly two and three at a time. As I got down stairs, I heard Lee in the living room. I hoped she didn't go back into the kitchen.

"Are you ready, babe?" I didn't mean to startle her, but I knew what it was going to be like the longer we stayed in that house

"Sorry. I thought you would have heard me coming in."

"It's okay. Don't apologise. Can we just get out of here?"

"Sure." She quickly came and took my hand. Before we knew it, we were outside at the car. The minute we got outside, I saw her relax. I was worried that she was never going to be able to come back home. But then, time was a healer and we would get through anything, as long as we had each other.

***

Pulling into the Abercrombie car park, Brian turned off the ignition and we sat for a moment. He wanted to make sure that I was going to be okay to do this. I knew I would be, because I wasn't in that house.

"Are you ready to face everyone?"

"The quicker we do this, the quicker we can get back to the hotel. It's our last day of this torture." He shared my enthusiasm.

"I just wish we stayed in France, Lee."

"That makes two of us, but we can't turn the clocks back. We're going to go in and make the most of our last day here. If this trip has taught me anything, it's that I need you. I never loved another soul as much as I've loved you and we can face anything as a couple." I couldn't help but smile, as I got out of the car. Brian met me at the back of the car and my hand took his. I was determined to face today head on.

We entered the lounge door. It wasn't a great big area, but it was filled with our nearest and dearest. Even Brian's parents made an effort to show up. Then it dawned on me, they knew nothing about yesterday. Brian wanted to fill them in on me and the twins, unless they had already been told.

"Leela." Tracey embraced me. That was the first time she had seen me since the ordeal. "Are you okay? I've been going out of my mind."

"Yeah. I'm perfect Trace. I have you to thank for sounding the alarm."

"No, you don't! You're really okay though?" I felt for Tracey. I could see her colour starting to come back in her cheeks. She was relieved to see me up and walking around.

"I have a sore head, but apart from that I'm doing well."

"And the baby? Your dad said it was your news to tell." I couldn't help but smile. I thought my dad would let us fill everyone in.

"I'm fine and so is the baby, but…."

"But what? Stop teasing me, Lee." Trace was just like my family, but she wasn't contacted last night. I felt kind of bad.

"There isn't just one baby. We're having twins." I was tossed back in her arms. I winced, as my neck ached and she pulled away from quickly.

"Leela. I'm sorry I forgot about your neck."

"I'm good Trace. I'm just a bit achy."

"Well, I'll leave you to mingle with everyone, I'll see you soon. Take it easy today. Sit down and let everyone come to you." I actually thought that was a good idea. I looked around for Brian and saw that he was talking with his family. Then I spotted my dad already sitting at the table, so I did what Tracey told me to do. I went

and placed myself down where my dad was. I was actually glad to get a comfy seat.

"Hi, sweetie. How are you feeling now?"

"I'm okay, dad. I just can't get comfortable in the house. I hope you understand why I have to go to a hotel tonight. I feel like I'm letting you and mum down, but I can't help how I feel."

"Of course I understand, hen. Don't ever speak like that again. Me and your mum are proud of you. Your mum would have been the first one out of the house if she was still here." I bowed my head slightly, as I felt a little bit more at ease. "I'll come and pick you both up at noon. We're all going to take you to the airport."

"That would be nice dad. What about you and Craig? What's happening with you two?"

"I handed my notice in at work. I'm coming out to Marseille in a couple of weeks. I haven't really had a chance to talk to Craig about it, but I'll let you know when I know anything."

"Good." I looked up to see Craig placing a drink in front of me. I should have known that he would have gotten me a fresh orange and lemonade. It was one of my favourite drinks when I was out. Especially since I couldn't have a glass of wine. "Thank you, Craig."

"You okay, sis?"

"I'm fine. I wish everyone would stop asking me."

"It will be the last time I ask." His cheeky smile and his hands held up to signify he was surrendering, made me smile at him. "You look lovely. You look different today."

"I wish everyone would stop saying that to me as well." I laughed.

"Sorry. I'm going to stop talking." Today was going to be perfect. I knew I should have gotten up and spoke to a few people, but I was happy sitting there. I knew other people wouldn't know how to approach me and I liked to sit back and watch everyone laughing and talking together. It was a change to be in a happy environment and I was glad.

***

I was separated from Brian most of the afternoon, because Scott sat beside me and dad was at the other side of me. Craig was

opposite me and Brian ended up in the middle of the table. I kept feeling his eyes looking up to me. I could only smile and look like I was enjoying being among my family. However, I had enough. I needed to get up to go to the little girl's room. I had sat too long without moving and my body started to ache.

"Are you okay, sweetheart?" My dad knew I was sore, but he didn't make it obvious.

"Yeah. I'm fine dad. Just going to the toilet."

"Do you want another drink when you come back?"

"No thanks, dad. I'm getting sick of drinking for the sake of it." I made my way from the table and I didn't look over at anyone. I knew where the toilet was and that's where I was going.

The minute I got into the toilet, Brian's mum was washing her hands. "Hi," was all I could say, before entering the cubicle. I hoped that when I came out she would have been gone, because I didn't want any confrontation today. I've had my fair share of it that week. I would be glad to be back in France where it's happy and relaxed.

Who was I kidding? When I came out she was leaning against the sinks. I managed a smile, before I placed my bag down to wash my hands. I felt nervous around her.

"Leela. I'm glad we're getting this chance to talk." I dried my hands and looked over at her to elaborate. "I heard what happened to you yesterday and Brian told me about the baby being…babies. I know we've never seen eye to eye and it was all of my fault, but I want to be a part of your life. I'm happy that you've made both of my son's happy. I've never seen Brian so happy before and that's all thanks to you."

"Why now, Mrs. Mackinnon?" I didn't know what made her change her mind about me.

"Have you ever heard the saying *you never know what you've got, until it's too late*?" I managed a nod in her direction, but I wasn't letting her sweet talk me with phrases. "Yesterday, when Brian and Craig rushed out of court with the rest of your family behind them, I panicked. When I heard what happened and no one knew if you were okay, I realised we could have lost you and the baby. *Babies.* Please Leela. Accept my apology. I know that you and Brian are going back to France tomorrow and I couldn't bear it if you went back hating

me."

"I've never hated you, Mrs. Mackinnon. I have disliked the way you treated me. However, for Brian's sake, I will accept your apology."

"I don't know what to say, Leela. I know I don't deserve this, but I can promise you that I will never cause you or Brian any more problems."

"That's nice to know." I smiled and pulled the door open, while waiting for her to exit first. "I hope that you and Mr. Mackinnon will be able to visit us in France sometime."

"I would like that very much, Leela." She stopped me before I went to get my seat. I felt all eyes on us. "I do hope that you have a speedy recovery and these two don't cause you too many problems." I was gobsmacked when she took me in her arms. I didn't know what to say or do, apart from walk back to my seat. I noticed there was an empty seat next to Brian, so I sat down and joined him.

I sat down slowly, because my back and neck were starting to ache. I hoped he wouldn't notice too much.

"Is everything okay, Lee?"

"Yeah, it is honey. I missed you sitting here."

"Snap! It looks like I had competition to see who was sitting beside you first." His hand rested on my leg. I loved any kind of physical contact from him. "Do I even want to know what just happened between you and my mum?"

"Nothing bad. She apologised and I accepted."

"Really?" He sounded shocked. I could only laugh.

"Really." He leaned in to me and placed a soft kiss on my lips. I wondered what I had done to deserve that, but I wasn't going to complain. Everyone started to move into groups or stand around the lounge bar. I was glad to be there with my husband to be.

"You look sore, sweetheart. Are you okay?"

"A little bit, but I'm sure you'll fix me later." His cheeky smile told me all that I needed to know.

"We can make our exit whenever you want."

"Good. I take it everyone has been filled in about the twins. Your mum said she was happy for us."

"The people that need to know…You know what we forgot to do

today?" I shook my head, because I couldn't think.

"Your appointment at the clinic. It wasn't until my dad asked how you got on, that I realised."

"I completely forgot. I dare say they wouldn't have told us any more than we heard yesterday."

"We can go on Monday when we're back home and get you booked into the clinic."

"Is this what it's going to be like for the next eight months?"

"Me fussing and making sure you don't overdo it. Pretty much."

For the first time since yesterday I felt normal again. I have enjoyed the afternoon very much. It's been really good to see everyone again. The worst part was knowing that I was probably not going to see them all for a long time. It was going to be calls, texts, and Facebook. It's a good thing that we've got many good ways of keeping in touch. Never in a million years did I expect to come home and be on the countdown to leave again. This place used to be my home. I used to work in this pub when I was studying at university. Normally I would have loved to go through to the bar and see if there was anyone that I knew, but I was looking forward to getting away to our hotel for the night. It's probably going to be the best night of this entire break here. Here's hoping.

***

When my dad pulled up outside the Golden Lion Hotel in Stirling, I looked up at the huge golden lion hanging over the entrance. It hadn't changed, as far as I could remember.

"Well, as much as it pains me to see you here, I do understand, Lee. Just have a nice relaxing night and I'll pick you up tomorrow." I hated to hear my dad feeling down, but there wasn't anything I could do about it. "Don't forget that I always love you. If you need anything before tomorrow, just phone me."

"Thanks dad. I love you too." I rested in my dad's arms. I always felt safe in his hugs. Just a pity I couldn't feel safe in his house anymore. "I think these bags will do us for tonight. We'll leave the rest in the car for tomorrow."

"Okay. Have a nice night." I hated walking away from my dad, but

I knew we would just go back and forth like that all night if I didn't.

Brian had the bags. He placed a protective arm around the base of my back and his warm hand made me feel relaxed. I was looking forward to a night on our own. I guess we should make the most of it, because in the next few months we were going to have another two little bundles depending on our love and attention.

***

I felt like a totally different person, as I opened my eyes. I quickly looked to the opposite side of the bed and it was empty. Just then, Brian came from the bathroom all nice and fresh with just a towel wrapped around his waist. I felt like I had the biggest smile on my face, as he laid on the bed beside me. The silk sheets on my naked skin, made me come alive instantly.

"Good morning, babe. You look so much better today after a good night's sleep."

"I'm just glad that I had no nightmares. I would have terrified the guests."

"It was good to wake up this morning after a good sleep and see you so relaxed." His cheesy grin made me remember our night of love and passion.

"A good sleep. Did we actually sleep?" I loved being the playful tease and it was nice to have it back that morning. I pulled the towel that he had wrapped around his neck and placed my lips over his. Again our mouths became one. "What time is it?"

"Just after nine. What do you have in mind?" Again my mouth took his and within seconds, his hunky frame was on top of me with only the sheets separating us. His hands pushed the sheets down and his kisses lingered down to my breasts. Every touch made my body feel electric. His gentle hand rubbed across my tummy and came back up to eye level with me. "Why do you have to be so beautiful?" I couldn't help but giggle, as his thumb ran across my lips.

"You won't be saying that in a few months, when I can't see my toes" His kisses up my neck and across onto my lips, told me to just shut up.

"You will always beautiful, my love."

"I'll remind you of that in a year's time." I cheekily pulled his towel off of him completely and felt his package on my tummy. I was never going to get fed up of making love to that man, because every time the passion got more powerful.

He slowly entered inside of me and our bodies cried out together, as we instantly became one again. The slow feeling of him thrusting inside of me, made me climax. His soft kisses trailing down my neck made me want more. The feel of his soft tender lips caressing my breasts, made my body arch. That time my climax rushed through the core of my body. He quickly climaxed right after me. His shuddering body leaned softly over me, making sure he never laid any weight on my tummy. His kind and considerate way of thinking just made me love him ten times more.

I've never felt as good, as Brian made me feel. I hoped that he got the same enjoyment as I did. Which I don't doubt for one second. However, now that was over with, we were going to have to get ready and wait for my dad to take us to the Airport. I couldn't wait to depart from Glasgow Airport.

CHAPTER 14
Home Sweet Home

It was hard to believe that we were in the taxi on our way back to my cottage. My body felt exhausted. When I looked at the time, it was nearly six in the evening. I had already sent Pierre a message to tell him I was home and I would fill him in next week. I was just looking forward to getting back to normality and plan our future as a family.

The taxi pulled up outside. I wasn't going to argue who was paying for the taxi. I climbed out of the car and just stood looking in front of me and then at my cottage. I left Brian and the driver to get the luggage out. It wasn't like he was going to let me lift anything, so there was no point trying.

"Bonjour, Leela! C'est agréable de vous avoir chez nous. J'ai vous ai raté." Just hearing my neighbour Mrs. Smithe talk in French to me, made me smile.

"Bonjour, Mme Smith. Il est bon d'etre la maison." As quickly, as she stopped to see me, she was away again. It was good to be back.

I then felt Brian's arms wrap around me from behind and rest in the middle on my tummy. I could feel a little bump low down in my tummy. Definitely not enough for anyone to notice apart from me and Brian, but it was there.

"This is what I've missed." Resting my head back on his shoulder, I had a funny feeling I knew what he was going to say. "I love to see how happy you are now. This is the Leela that I never want to lose." I turned to face him and placed my hand on his cheek. "I never thought I would say this, but this is our home now."

"You're never going to lose me Brian. You're stuck with us forever and we're home for good. Marseille is home."

"Does that mean you're going to move in with me?"

"You're very clever when you want to be, Mr. Mackinnon. I can't see this little cottage raising two babies. Can you? It will do for family when they come to visit. Just give me a few days to settle back in and I'll be all yours." I placed a soft kiss on his lips and I felt like I couldn't stop smiling.

"Does this mean that you still want to marry me, as soon as possible?" enquired Brian.

"Of course. If you still want us." That was the easiest question that I answered all week.

"Now let me think about that one." We both couldn't stop smiling right. It was a really good feeling to be there. "Just you try stopping me, being a part of you and our babies' lives. I will never stop loving you, Lee."

"I don't exactly want to walk down an isle like a big fat beached whale."

"Big fat beached whale or not, you will be as gorgeous as ever. Just please don't say that you want to go home to get married."

"This *is* home, Brian. I never want to go back to Scotland. I will marry you here or nowhere." Again his mouth placed a passionate kiss on mine. He lifted me off of my feet to carry me over the threshold. "Is this in case you can't carry me when we get married?" We both laughed, as he placed me over the threshold and went back for the luggage. I sat down on my couch and took my whole

surroundings in. I never felt as happy in my whole life.

3 MONTHS LATER

CHAPTER 15
I do

A quick three months had passed and already my bump was quite big. I felt uncomfortable thinking about what I was going to be like at 40 weeks.

Today was the day that I was marrying Brian. All of our nearest and dearest were there to see us get married. I didn't want to have the babies first and then get married. I wanted to do it properly and now was the time. I spent the first night away from Brian since we started our relationship and it was the longest night ever. I came home to my own cottage surrounded by my family and Tracey as my bridesmaid. She was five months pregnant, but I felt like I was bigger than her. Having twins certainly had its downsides. All morning, I spent getting ready. Even though I felt like a whale, I also felt like a princess. I have been pampered. Hair, nails, and make-up

were all done. Sheree helped me get into my dress. Since we were in sunny France, I have gone for a simple elegant wedding dress. It made me look stunning, as I stood there looking at my glowing figure. Even Sheree was crying when she saw me.

"Don't you start crying! I'm 4 months pregnant and very hormonal. Do you want to start me off?" We both started laughing.

"I'm sorry, Leela. I've seen you go through so much and I'm so happy to see you like this." She took me in her arms.

"Finally, we're having something to celebrate. So what do you say we start this new chapter off with a bang?" We straightened up and looked at our reflections in the mirror. It was now or never.

"Let's go, Lee." I was pleased that she was with me on this. I wanted to get today started. The quicker I became Mrs. Leela McKinnon, the better it would be for us all.

Now was the time to leave the comfort of my room and head through to my family. The only one who was gone already was Craig, because he was Brian's best man. I loved the fact that Brian and Craig had a bond, because I loved them both dearly. My dad and Scott were giving me away, because I wanted them both to walk me down the aisle. Our wedding was taking part on the beach and it was a glorious day. When I went to see it all set up earlier, it was gorgeous. All it needed was me to move my backside and get there. They all heard my heels clip clop on the tiles and were standing to see me walking through. Sheree and Tracey were in gorgeous baby pink dresses, while my dad and Scott where in lovely suits with pink ties.

"Leela! You're lucky I love you, because these pink ties are a first and a last for me." We were all laughing at Scott, as he protested, but they all looked gorgeous.

"Sweetheart, you look stunning. I can't believe this day has come. You know that your mum would have loved to be here. I found these when I was clearing through some things. Your mum wore these on our wedding day." He handed me the box and I opened it to see beautiful pearl earrings. I didn't know what to say, but it wasn't going to take much to make me cry.

"They're lovely dad. I don't know what to say."

"Don't cry!" Shouted Tracey. While Sheree took the box from me

to exchange the earrings. I dreamt of this day when I was growing up. Tracey and I used to talk about weddings all the time, when we were in our teens. Never did I think it would me standing there first.

"Your carriage awaits." I never booked the transport, so it was going to be a lovely surprise to see what I was arriving in. I took a hold of Sheree's arm, because I hated wearing heels and I was kind of wobbly.

The minute I got outside, there were people standing. Some I knew and some were strangers. Once passed all of the well-wishers, I saw two gorgeous horse drawn carriages. Pure white horses with pink bows. I was speechless, as Sheree wiped away my tears.

"They are lovely. Aren't they?" I couldn't answer my dad. I just walked over and took my place in the open carriage. The beach was only five minutes away and I couldn't wait to see my groom. Beside me, were my dad and Scott, while the second carriage held Sheree and Tracey. I felt blown away and it was only the beginning. I had the rest of the day to go. The only problem I faced was to hold it together.

***

Pulling up at the beach I could see everyone waiting for us. The whole area was lovely. It was perfect. That cove was used for weddings and now I know why.

I saw everyone waiting for us. The music was soft and made the hairs on my neck stand up. I just wanted to make it to Brian without falling.

"Are you ready, Lee?" I looked up at my dad and his arm was extended for me to take. I couldn't stop smiling.

"We'll see you when you're Mrs. Mackinnon." I watched Tracey and Sheree walk off in front of us. It was me in the middle of Scott and my dad. I could feel my heels sink into the sand. I was glad when I got onto the red carpet.

"No doing the runaway bride on us, Lee." I giggled at Scott. I looked at him and lifted my foot to show him my heels. There was no chance of that happening.

"In these and with this." I motioned to my stomach, as we made

our way to the end of the aisle.

Both Brian and Craig turn around. I thought I was going to look straight ahead and never look down.

"You two better not let me fall." I was glad that I could amuse them with my silly words. Meanwhile, our wedding song, *A Thousand Years,* started playing. I felt both Scott and my dad grip onto my arms. They were never going to let me fall and that was all I could hope for. I just hated having everyone's eyes on me. I would be glad when this bit was over.

Then just as we reached the end of the aisle, I got a kiss off Scott and my dad before I was left to stand with Brian. I was glad when he took my hand. I was hiding in to the side of him as my security blanket. I was so nervous I didn't think I was ever going to say my vows. I was just looking forward to our future. If I kept that in my mind, everything else would fall into place.

***

"You may kiss the bride." I felt Brian's warm lips part mine, as our tongues touched. I never wanted this moment to end, but I pulled away before I passed out due to lack of air. We turned around, as everyone cheered.

We walked back down the aisle hand in hand. It was hard to believe that we were now husband and wife. It was crazy. We stood at the end of the aisle to get photos done and we felt like royalty. We walked over to where the waitresses were balancing trays of champaign. There were two glasses of orange juice just for me and Tracey. We were the only two that couldn't drink alcohol. I didn't miss the wine though. I have been having too much fun with my husband.

"Lee! You look absolutely gorgeous." I don't know why I felt my cheeks flush, because Brian knew me inside and out. "Have I got you blushing, Mrs. Mackinnon?"

"Just shut up and kiss me." He bent down and placed his lips over mine. Photos were still getting snapped away and I couldn't care. Everyone was giving us some space at the moment and I was so happy at that.

I clutched my stomach, as I got a strong kick or an elbow in the top of my stomach. “Ouch.”

“What is it, Lee?” Poor Brian was a nervous wreck.

I took his hand and placed it where one of the babies was kicking. He hadn’t felt them before, because they wouldn’t move for him. His face was priceless.

“That was the most perfect wedding gift that I could have ever received.” Just at that moment, everyone came and congratulated us.

We got hundreds of different photos done with all different people. I felt like I didn’t need to smile anymore, because it was permanently stuck on my face. Most of our guests had entered the hotel on the beach in time for the meal. I took a hold of Brian’s arm, because I had to take my shoes off. My feet were aching.

“Better?”

“Much. I lasted longer than I expected. It didn’t help that these two toe rags have moved and kicked all afternoon.” When I looked around, I noticed that our entire wedding party had made it into the hotel. Brian and I were standing on the beach and the sun was starting to set. “I take the shoes off and they stop. Would you believe that?” I was glad that he thought I was funny. Everyone seemed to find me amusing today.

“They’re just trying to tell you that you weren’t comfortable with those shoes on.”

“Is this daddy sticking up for his monsters, already?”

“I wish I could take the pain away from you. I hate seeing you uncomfortable.” He took the shoes off me in one hand, took my hand in the other, and started heading over to the hotel.

“It’s all worth it just to have them both in our lives,” I said.

He stopped dead and our bodies faced one another. His hand traced the outline of my face and the shivers ran down my spine. “You do know that you’re going to have to help me out of this dress later.”

“I will do anything you want me to, Lee. I don’t want to get you crying, but I need to tell you this. You’re a remarkable person, Lee. I have never come across another soul like you and I adore you for being my wife and mother to my children. I know we said that we’re not going to give one another gifts today, but I have something for you. I know that we’ve been living in my place, but we’ve never

been as happy there."

"It will take time, honey." I placed my hand over his.

"What would you say if we didn't have to give it time?" I was feeling confused. All I managed to do was smile and shrug my shoulders. "I don't know if I have been silly or not, but I have bought us a cottage. A rather big cottage actually." I now knew what he was saying to me and I knew what cottage he was talking about. At the end of my street where my cottage was, there was a large cottage that overlooked the beach. I turned around and looked at the cottage. "How did you guess, Lee?"

"I told you how great it would be overlooking the beach and feeding the twins. The morning walks along the beach. Dinner on the patio." I looked back at him and wanted to hug the life out of him. I wasn't sure that I would have gotten close to him with my ever expanding bump in the way.

"I want us to be happy, Lee. I know how much you loved living on this side. Your cottage was just too small, but this is perfect."

"*You're perfect*, Brian. I love you." Our wedding day was perfect and it wasn't even halfway through. Everything was crazy. Our life had transformed for the better. I seriously couldn't believe that we were going to give up on love because of what happened to Mark. That had taught me one thing for sure. What is meant to be, will be. If it's meant to happen it will.

All along, Brian and I were destined to be together.

5 MONTHS LATER

CHAPTER 16
41 weeks and counting

I had been so uncomfortable lately and the babies were not for making an appearance. My twins were meant to be early, but oh no! The luck I have, I'm one week past my due date. I'm so big that I felt like I was a waddling penguin.

Brian had been working from home for the last couple of days, because we're all on tender hooks waiting for the arrival of our babies. I had spent the last 8 weeks on maternity leave and have loved getting our new cottage all decked out the way I like it. Our nursery was finished and my cottage was sparkling clean. I went into the nesting instinct weeks ago. I was hoping that the smell of all the cleaning stuff would have made them come quicker.

Not my babies.

I was getting agitated and pissed off at everything. I hated the waiting game. My dad and Craig had been here in France for five

weeks and they're living in my cottage just a few doors up from me. My dad retired and is living out here for the time being. Craig handed in his notice with his job back home and he's enjoying the good life out here. We were all happy apart from me.

I was walking from one end of the beach to the other and walking up and down the stairs all the time, just to get this pregnancy over with. Pierre told me to have plenty of hot sex with Brian. We've done that in every position possible. Still nothing. I was getting ready to pull them out one by one myself. Their eviction notice was served when I turned 30 plus weeks.

I had a huge craving for croissants. Every day my dad brings me fresh ones in from the bakery. I even have both my dad and Brian hooked on them. It was going to take me years to lose the baby weight.

"Morning, Lee. How are you today, sweetie?" I somehow managed to get up off the couch and greet my dad before putting the kettle on.

"I'm still fat and exhausted. Patiently waiting for these two gremlins to leave my body and let me breathe again." I have become so honest since becoming heavily pregnant. Everyone was frightened to ask me any questions.

"So you won't want croissants if you're fat?"

"You value your life too much, not to bring me my snack. I'll put the kettle on. Go and tell Brian to join us. He's in the study." I have also lost count how much tea I drank lately. I was drinking it like it's going out of fashion.

Lifting the cups from the shelf, I felt a couple of sharp twinges. I wasn't going to get excited, because I had sharp twinges before and nothing happened. The sudden striking pain made me drop the milk jug. It smashed to the ground. *Oh shit!* I yelled out for Brian. I gripped hold of the worktop for support, because the pain was gripping me so hard.

"Shit, Lee! Are you okay?" Brian raced to my side and slipped on the milk. Luckily he managed to save himself from falling. Then he managed to guide me through to the living room. He was relatively calm considering I was yelling and in labour. "What do we do, Lee?"

"I don't know, Brian! I'm not a fucking magician!" Then, I starting

breathing through the contraction. The pain eased enough to make me realise what I had just said. “I’m sorry Brian, I didn’t mean…”

“Don’t apologise, Lee. You can say what you like today. I think you have the perfect excuse.” I was glad that he understood, but I didn’t want to turn into a monster. I have watched too many films and I could feel myself turning already.

“Another one is coming! Make it stop! Make it stop!” My dad came back from where ever the hell he had been and was shocked to see me in the state I was in.

“Leela! Look at me!” I managed to look up at my dad, while I was leaning on the back of the couch. “Take slow deep breaths. In and out. Slowly.”

“I can’t do this now! Just take them out!”

“You need to calm down, sweetheart. It isn’t good for you or the babies,” said my dad.

“This pregnancy isn’t good for me! Damn it!” The pain was getting stronger and I wasn’t coping. I thought I was well prepared, but I didn’t have a clue what to do.

“There’s no time to follow the rules. I’ll go and get the car. Brian! Just keep talking to her and help her breathe. Don’t listen to anything she says to you. She doesn’t mean it.”

“Just hurry up, dad, before the babies are born here!”

“Leela, baby! Look at me! Give me your hands!” I tried to do as he asked, because I knew he was trying to help me. Brian was going to have to just ignore me screaming and shouting, because I never expected any of this. “That’s it. Now breathe slowly. Remember your birthing classes. In and out. Slowly.” I was looking him square in the eyes and followed his breathing.

“Another one is coming, Brian! I can’t do this! It’s too painful! Just make it stop! Please!” I felt the tears and sweat running down my face and I knew I wasn’t going to be able to do this.

“Your dad has the car. Your bags are still in the boot and we’re going to get you to the hospital. Just keep breathing and take slow steps.” I wished for that day for so long and now that it’s here, I can’t cope. “You’re doing great, Lee.”

“Stop lying to me, Brian! I’m a mess!”

“You’re about to give birth to twins, Lee! I would like to think that

you're a mess! Now just keep breathing and you'll get to meet your two pests soon."

"I don't think there's time, Brian! I need to push!" I was panicking more than ever. I didn't want to give birth to my babies on the floor or in the car.

"It is okay, babe. We're five minutes away from the hospital. Keep breathing." I was glad when I got outside. The cool air from the sea was nice. "You're doing great, Lee. You just need to get into the car." I loved this man to the moon and back and I hated the way I was treating him.

"I can't sit down Brian! I'm too sore! Another one is coming! Damn it!" My dad came round to help me, but I was losing patience with them both.

"Leela. You need to get in the car, babe. It's the only way you're going to get to hospital, because you're not in any state to walk."

"I can't sit down! Damn it!"

"What's going on?" We were all glad to see Craig, because if anyone was going to make me see sense, it would be him.

"You need to get in the car. The twins are on their way and not far away by the looks of things. I just timed your contractions and they are three minutes apart." Even my dad was pissing me off.

"Leela! Sit in the car! Unless you want to give birth to your babies here in front of the world." Frank and I looked at Craig like he had a death wish.

"Get in the fucking car? You get in the fucking car! I can't sit down, Craig! Please! Make it stop!" My energy was slowly running out by the minute.

"Well, lie down then!" I looked at Craig like he was a genius, because I never thought of that.

"Leela. I'll go in at the other side and I will help you lie down." I sat down on the back seat of the car and all of a sudden my water broke. Maybe now the pain would ease, so I was hoping.

I was in the car and Brian was rubbing my back and holding my hand. My dad was driving like a maniac and Craig was leaning around holding my other hand. It was like something out of the funny film. I would never forget that day in my life.

"I need to push, Brian! I need to push!"

"Look! We're just about at the hospital. Your dad will drop us off at the front door and Craig and I will wheel you in."

"I can't sit down! I need to walk!" I knew the babies were on the way. I could feel all the pressure and the pain. "I can't do this! Just make it stop!"

"You can sweetheart, because you're the bravest person I have ever met. If I could take it away from you, Lee I would, baby. You're doing great."

"Let's go!" I was glad when I heard Craig say that I was getting out. It had been the longest drive of my life. I was opening the door, as my dad pulled up. Craig helped me out, while Brian ran around to help. I started walking, while clutching both of their hands. I was surprised their hands were not broken by now.

"Doctor! We need help!" Craig pulled the first doctor he saw, who took me right through to a room. "I'll stay here and sign her in. I'll follow you when dad comes. You can do this, Lee. I love you." I heard Craig, but both Brian and I were following the doctor into a room.

"I need to push! I need to push!"

"What's her name?"

"My name's Leela! Just listen to me and get these babies out of me!" I was in agony. I had never felt a pain like that in my life.

"Dr. Mario is Leela's gynaecologist." I watched the nurse run away to do whatever it was, while Brian rubbed my back as I was leaning over the bed.

"Okay, Leela. I need to get your clothes off so we can see what's going on."

"I'm having twins! That's what's going on!"

"Brian. I'll leave these gowns here. Can you help her get into them and onto the bed? I'll be back in a few minutes." Brian never said a word, but helped me take of my clothes in record time. The gowns were passion killers, but I managed to get up onto the bed and clutch Brian's hand. The poor man was wiping the hair out of my face and getting the last word out of my mouth.

"Hi, Leela. My name is Kate. I'm going to help you." English was all good. I don't think I knew any French right now.

"Another one is coming! Make it stop!"

"Leela. Dr. Mario is coming, but in the meantime breathe on this when the contractions are here." I took the tube and did what she said. I had no idea what it was meant to do, but anything was worth a try.

"Help me, Brian! Please!"

"Darling. I would if I could. Breathe on this and squeeze my hand. You're doing fab!"

"Hi, Leela." I was never so glad to see the doctor. "I'm going to need to examine you to see how many centimetres dilated you are. Okay?"

"Just do whatever it takes! Another contraction…is…coming!" I was gripping Brian's hand with everything I had.

"Breathe through it, Leela. You can do it. I'll examine you when it's over with." The doctor's voice was irritating me and I just wanted to get them out. The French accent trying to communicate in English, was just pissing me off. "Okay. This could be uncomfortable, but I'll be as quick as I can." The silence was good, but I knew that I could feel another contraction coming just as quickly as the last one finished. "Leela. You're fully dilated and I can feel baby number one's head. Your right. You need to push. So, when this contraction comes, I want you to push down as hard as you can." Finally, I was getting to push. I needed to push for ages and now it was coming. I was trying to keep calm, as I tried to push the baby out, but it wasn't happening.

"You're doing great, babe! Keep pushing!" said Brian.

"Fantastic, Leela. On the next contraction, your baby's head will be out. It will then be one more big push and it will be one down. Now push!"

"I love you, Lee! You're doing great, babe."

"I can't do it anymore! I'm too tired, Brian!"

"One more push, Leela and you will meet your first baby. Now, push! Harder!" I was going to push my fist in her mouth if she didn't stop barking orders. "Fabulous, Leela! You have a beautiful baby boy." Boy? I couldn't take my eyes off of him when they placed him on my chest.

"You did it, Lee! I'm so proud of you, honey! He's gorgeous, just like you!" I heard Brian full of pride with tears running down his

face. The nurse wrapped him up and handed him to Brian. I saw him wipe his tears, as he held his son for the first time. I knew that he instantly fell in love with his son like I did. “He’s perfect, Lee.”

“No! Not again!” I was exhausted and had to do it all over again. The pain felt stronger and I had no idea how I was going to cope without Brian’s hand.

“You can do it, sweetheart!” I looked at Brian holding his son with one hand and placing his other hand back in mine. He must have read my mind.

“Okay, Leela. On this contraction, I want you to push again. Now, push! Push!” I loved them easing off, but I felt the pressure again and I knew baby two was coming. “Well done, Leela! One more big push and the head will be out!”

“I can’t! I’m too tired!”

“You can, babe! You’ve done it once and you can do it again!”

“Leela! Push! Push! Push! Fabulous! Your baby’s head is out! On the next contraction, one big push and your baby will be out and this will be over with. Ready? Now, push! Leela! Push!” I was going to hear that word in my sleep. I needed to get this over. “Fabulous, Leela! You have a beautiful baby girl!” Girl? I couldn’t believe it.

The baby was placed on my chest and I cried with the relief. It was over. They were beautiful and they were mine. I felt ridiculous sobbing, but I was so overwhelmed by it all.

“Well done, sweetheart! I knew you could do it! They are both gorgeous, just like there mum!” I couldn’t stop crying. I managed to kiss Brian, as he leaned down to look at his daughter. Forty-one weeks and I had my babies here with me. I was exhausted, but it was well worth the wait. I couldn’t take my eyes off of both babies lying on my chest. Whatever was going on around me didn’t matter. I was so in love with my two little angels.

***

One hour had passed, since I gave birth to two beautiful babies. I had been freshened up and took a shower. I was cradling one baby and Brian was cradling the other. Our baby girl weighed 5lb 1oz and our little boy weighed 5lb 5oz. They were both beautiful. I couldn’t

stop staring at them, because they were so tiny.

"I found some family members outside. Can I let them in?" I forgot all about my dad and Craig.

"Yes, please." I had been side-tracked with all the excitement. I didn't think about anything other than our babies. "It's unbelievable to think that they grew inside me and now they're here."

"You did a fantastic job, Lee. I can't tell you how much I love the three of you."

"Brian. I love you all. I am just glad it's all over with. That was crazy." I laughed just thinking about it, when in came my dad and Craig. I didn't even know if they knew I had the babies, but they looked relieved when they could see both Brian and I holding them.

"I can't believe it, sweetheart! Congratulations to you both! They are adorable!" Even my dad had tears in his eyes. It was just one big emotional roller coaster and it was worth everything.

"Say hello to your granddaughter and grandson," I said, proudly.

"One of each? How wonderful. Do they have names yet?" My dad was like a child on a big adventure. He was on cloud nine.

"This is Sienna and the little man is Mark." I saw Craig's face, as he came over to look at Sienna first. I couldn't get enough of them both. They stole my heart.

"I am so proud of you, Leela," gushed Craig.

"I'm proud of myself. I have no idea how I managed that. Get the nurse to take a picture of us all." We all had family pictures done in the hospital bed. Brian sat on the bed beside me with Mark in his arms. Craig was beside me cooing over his niece and my dad stood beside Brian. We were one big happy family and nothing was ever going to spoil that. Looking down at my babies, I would go through the last three years all over again. The pain and heartache from Mark's death, only made me the strong and determined person I was today. Marrying Brian was the courage that I needed to rebuild my life here in Marseille. I certainly did that.

Me, Brian, Sienna, and Mark were going to live our life to the max and never look back again. We had everything to look forward to and today just proved that.

THE END

It Was Meant To Be

Leela Park was a happy twenty-eight year old. She thought she had everything going for her, until a bombshell came crashing down on her life.

Leela was happily engaged to her partner Mark. He was a police constable at Strathclyde Police Force. When he went to work one day, he never expected it to be his last day on earth.

Leela had a hard time coming to terms with Mark's death, because she recently found out that she was pregnant with his baby. More tragic obstacles in her way of grieving and she ends up in hospital fighting for her life.

Happier events unfold when Leela decides to take time off work to go travelling for the year. She never expected to travel, let alone end up in France. She was glad she did. Touring around France, made her settle down in Marseille. What was in store for her there? What was going to happen when she bumped into an old face? Was everything going to go crashing down around her, or was it meant to be?

Music List

Please see below for a list of music that inspired my writing of this book. I hope it can give you some insight to every emotion I felt while writing.

1 – Ben Haenow – Something I Need
2 – Emeli Sande – Clown
3 – Emeli Sande – Heaven
4 – Christina Perri – A Thousand Years
5 – Christina Perri – Jar Of Hearts
6 – Sia – My Love
7 – Ellie Goulding – Explosions
8 – Sam Bailey – Sky Scraper
9 – Demi Lovato – Let It Go
10 - Demi Lovato – Sky Scrapper
11 – Katie Perry – Firework
12 – Bruno Mars –Just the Way You Are
13 – Sam Smith – Stay With Me
14 – Sam Smith – Like I can
15 – Savage Garden – Truly Madly Deeply

Other Books By K.M Lowe

The Beautiful Life Trilogy

The Smile (part 1)

The Smile – New Beginnings (Part 2)

The Smile – Forever After (Part 3)

All My Love

K.M Lowe

40404059R00154

Made in the USA
Charleston, SC
02 April 2015

Printed in Great Britain
by Amazon

79912818R00099